"Fare Thee V

By Ian S. Varty

Dedication
In memory of WO2 SSM George Hickinson 10
February 1956 – 19 December 2012, WO1 Steve
'Scrapper' Carter MBE 20 November 1957 – 9 October
2015 and all members of the Regiment and others, who
have passed away in conflicts, illness or in tragic
circumstances.
"Quis Separabit" and "Fare Thee Well"

Contents

Prologue
Chapter 1 – Northern Ireland
Chapter 2 – The Streets of Portadown
Chapter 3 – Northern Ireland Final Days
Chapter 4 – Handover and Return to Germany
Chapter 5 – Return to Camp and Guided Weapons
Chapter 6 – Hohne GW Conversion & Qualifying
Chapter 7 – Squadron Boxing
Chapter 8 – Engagement
Chapter 9 – GW Exercise
Chapter 10 – Leadership Cadre Introduction
Chapter 11 – Fieldcraft
Chapter 12 – Orienteering & Close Target Recce
Chapter 13 – Final Exercise
Chapter 14 – Parachute Training & Pass off
Chapter 15 – Recce Troop
Chapter 16 – The Plains of Alberta
Chapter 17 – The Long March & River Crossing
Chapter 18 – Vehicle Handover and R&R
Chapter 19 – Consequences & R&R
Chapter 20 – Long Range Reconnaissance Patrol
Chapter 21 – Cyprus
Chapter 22 – Incidents
Chapter 23 – Relaxation & R&R
Chapter 24 – Back to UN Duties
Chapter 25 – Return to Tanks
Chapter 26 – Qualifying for Command
Chapter 27 – Perfumed Garden
Chapter 28 – Lionheart FTX
Chapter 29 – Canada Medicine Man 7
Chapter 30 – Site Guards
Chapter 31 – Troop Trip

Chapter 32 – "Fare Thee Well"
About the Author
Other books by the Author
Acknowledgements

Prologue

Richard picked up his empty wine glass and bottle, then got up from his chair. He made his way into the kitchen, placed the bottle under the sink and put the glass in the dishwasher. Standing there a short while, he stared out of the window, contemplating the memories he had just recalled. They were always more vivid when alcohol was involved. A broad grin spread across his face, as he thought of the many drunken nights he had experienced, while serving. His thoughts were interrupted by Birgit, who had entered the kitchen.

'What you smiling at?' she said, chuckling, delighted at finding her husband in a more pleasant mood.

'Just thinking of the times me and the lads shared, over a beer or five,' he answered, laughing at his own attempt at humour.

Birgit preferred it when he was in this frame of mind. She had watched him the whole evening, as he had rummaged through the photograph album, on his lap. Over the past year, he had become more and more frustrated with his job. He had transitioned from military life into Civvy Street, surprisingly easily. He had, initially, worked at a secondary school, in the suburbs of Durham. He had remained there for two years, before realising there was no prospect of advancement and so, had looked elsewhere.

The environment of the National Health Service had been an alien one, but one he had found exciting. Over the next seven years, Birgit noticed that Richard had become more and more disillusioned with his career, often returning home in a foul mood and venting his frustrations on family members. The comradeship he had shared over the 23 years he had served was now, sadly, lacking. Richard took every opportunity to keep in touch with his former colleagues, attending as many reunions as he could.

After clearing everything away and turning off the lights, the pair climbed the stairs, to their bedroom. Being a creature of habit, Richard placed his clothes in the same position every night. This came from the training received in his former life, where everything was done in a precise way, in order that things would not be forgotten or mislaid. Setting the alarm next to his bed, Richard threw back the quilt, picked up a book and turned on to his right side. With the bedside light on, he opened the book, to the place he had marked, the previous evening. Birgit climbed into bed beside him, turned off her light and, facing his back, put her left arm around him. They performed this ritual every night, until Richard dozed off and Birgit would stretch over and turn off his light. Richard could not fall asleep without reading. The reason, he maintained, from somewhere in his subconscious, was when he had experienced a traumatic childhood event.

The year was 1963. His mother had taken the infant Richard to join his father, who had been posted to Munster, in West Germany. For the first three months, they had spent their introduction to military life in a caravan, situated in the camp, due to the lack of availability of married quarters (MQ's) in the garrison. Tommy, his father, was a young Trooper and did not have the required number of points to qualify for one of the few remaining flats. The Commanding Officer (CO) had arranged for the hire of caravans for those families who, in the same situation as Richard's parents, needed accommodation. Although Richard could not remember that first winter, he had heard countless times since, how bitterly cold it had been. These reminders were normally after Tommy's tours, on a Friday night, after his father's consumption of a great deal of brandy and Coke.

Richard had also been told many times, of an occasion when he had refused to eat his dinner. His father held the child's head and planted Richard's face, firmly, in the mixture of mashed potatoes, carrots and gravy. Richard was sure that this was one of the reasons he was not that fond of carrots, to the present day.

The winter had just ended. His parents were informed that married quarters had become available, a flat located about two kilometres from camp, on one of the military estates. Although usually surrounded by the civilian population, these were almost like a 'mini England'. They came kitted out with all that was needed for a young family starting out, furniture, crockery, linen and white goods. All items were checked during the 'marching in' process, where the occupant and estate warden would check the general hygiene and serviceability of the quarters. Any damages found were clearly marked on the 'handover/ takeover' sheet. Once everything was checked, the incoming occupant confirmed the inventory was correct and signed, acknowledging it must be handed back in the same condition.

Richard was almost one year old by this time. Although he could walk a little, he preferred to crawl.

It was spring time and the family had now settled into their new accommodation. Like a good housewife, Richard's mother, Tina, decided to do a bit of spring cleaning. Not always an easy task, with a young child crawling about the place, she began by removing everything from the fridge and unplugged it, to defrost the ice compartment. Moving into the living room, she began taking down the curtains and removing the covers that protected the cushions underneath. The covers and curtains were of such a bright design, it seemed like they had been created by someone on a mind tripping drug. Having removed the covers and curtains, Tina left the living room and entered the bedroom. Richard crawled after her, eager to find out what she was doing next. By the time he had reached the bedroom, his mother was exiting, with an

*armful of curtains. She looked down, smiling at him.
Bending at the waist, she scooped her child up in her free
arm and made her way back to the kitchen. Putting him
down on the hard, tiled floor, she began loading the
washing machine. After all the items were placed in the
machine, she poured fabric softener and washing powder
in the compartments. The sound of Richard banging his
plastic cup on the floor attracted her attention. Taking the
cup from him, she filled it with diluted orange juice and
returned it to him. He took it, eagerly and began sucking on
the spout. Tina reached up to one of the cupboards and
withdrew a Farley's Rusk, which Richard took, gratefully.*

*Her first task finished, she left the young Richard to his
biscuit and drink, and went into the bathroom. Richard did
not notice her leave, so engrossed was he with his snack. In
no time at all, he had finished his drink and biscuit, so
decided to explore a little further. Noticing the fridge door
wide open, he crawled across the cold, tiled floor and
decided to climb into it. Once inside, he sat on the bottom
of it, looking around. The freezer compartment had, by this
time, defrosted and the water began seeping through
Richard's nappy. He was happy enough, though, in his new
found den.*

*His mother returned to the kitchen, to collect some
more cleaning materials. Walking into the kitchen, she
decided that the fridge had probably defrosted. Without
looking inside, she closed the door, with a sweep of her
arm. Picking out a can of scouring powder, she made her
way back to the bathroom.*

*The new found den went black. Richard stared around,
wondering what had just happened. In his child's mind, he
thought that this must be a game his mother was playing
with him. He chuckled to himself, happy enough just to sit
there. He imagined it was a game of hide and seek. It was
not until the minutes passed, and his mother did not return,
that he decided he would crawl out and find her. Placing*

7

his hand in front of him, it came into contact with the fridge door. However, pushing the door, he found it did not give. Panic started to form in his mind, as he continued to attempt an escape. As the time went by, he began to get more and more frightened.

Tina, once again, returned to the kitchen, having completed cleaning the bathroom. She found it empty, with no sign of Richard. Doing a complete 360 degree turn, she walked into the living room, checking behind the furniture. There was still no sign of Richard. Her heart rate began to rise rapidly, as she quickly moved along the corridor, to check the two bedrooms. She found Tommy in the second one, tidying out one of the cupboards.

'Have you seen Richard?' she asked him, anxiously.

Tommy could see the panic in her eyes and knew at once that something was wrong.

'No, I thought he was with you,' he said, trying to sound calm.

Realising that her son was nowhere to be found, Tina's mind began to race. 'Where could he be?' she thought to herself. The only place she had not checked was the balcony. Rushing down the corridor, she flew into the living room. The door to the balcony was wide open. Tina began to feel physically sick. She discovered the balcony empty. The thought that Richard may have crawled in between the metal bars filled her with dread. Steeling herself to look over, Tina approached, gingerly, with tiny footsteps. Peering down at the grass, three floors below, she was relieved to see only a couple of older children, playing below. Tommy had joined her by this time. He had also started to feel panic, but tried not to show it.

'He might have crawled out the door. I'll take a look,' he tried to assure her, placing a comforting hand on her shoulder.

With that, he rushed through the living room, towards the front door of the flat, which he found closed. Throwing

*it open, he rushed down the stairs, to begin his search. Tina
was beside herself at this point, wandering aimlessly
around the rooms. By the time Tommy returned, ten
minutes later, he found her in a flood of tears.*

*In a consoling tone, he asked her, 'Where did you see
him last?'*

*'In the kitchen,' she replied, sobbing between every
word.*

*Tommy turned around and went into the kitchen, with
Tina following closely behind. They found that the room
was still, with no sign at all of Richard.*

*'He has to be somewhere!' Tommy exclaimed, his voice
now starting to sound angry.*

*As the couple stared at each other, each one looking for
some kind of inspiration, they heard a muffled whining.*

'Waah! Waah!' came the distorted sound.

*Tommy and Tina, now filled with anxiety, began to
search around for a clue as to where the sound was coming
from. As they neared the end of the kitchen, the sound grew
louder and ever more frantic. Listening intently at the door
of the fridge, Tommy smiled and threw open the door.
Richard blinked his eyes, trying to adjust to the light. He
clambered out of his temporary prison and crawled
towards his mother, who immediately picked him up. The
relief was evident on her face, as she smothered him with
affection.*

*'You stupid, little bugger, why did you go in there?' she
chastised him, but the anguish had now left both her and
Tommy.*

As the memory started to fade, Richard felt the weight
of Birgit, as she leaned over him and switched off the
bedside light. He drifted into a deep sleep and returned to
the streets of Northern Ireland, in his dreams.

Chapter 1 - Northern Ireland

The blackness and mist started to clear. Richard was looking up into the face of Ron, who was smiling down on him. He could feel something warm and sticky by his eyebrow. Investigating with his hand, he put his fingers in front of his eyes. Slowly focusing on his hand, he could see that the fingers were covered in what was obviously blood. When he had been hit, he had instinctively felt for the talisman that Birgit's father had given him, prior to their deployment. The missile, a rock, lay next to him, traces of blood on the rough shape. The stone had caught him at the corner of the eye. Splitting the eyebrow, the blood had seeped into his eye. The shock had knocked him out, accounting for the blackness he had experienced. The young kids who had thrown the missile were standing outside the school gates, giggling among themselves. Assaulting the Brit soldiers was a rite of passage for some of the youth of Northern Ireland.

'Your first war wound, mate,' Ron joked, patting Richard on the back, and assisted him to his feet.

'Was I out for long?' Richard asked.

'Just a couple of minutes, you'll be all right in a moment,' Ron replied.

Richard swayed for a moment, as Ron helped him to his feet, after he had fallen out the back of the Land Rover. The four man team or 'brick' commander, Martin, gave him a quick once over, to ensure he was okay to carry on the mobile patrol. Richard confirmed to him he was and the team mounted back up inside the Land Rover. Ron and Richard assumed their alert positions, with their weapons pointing out the rear of the vehicle. Martin checked the map, for the location of the Ulster Defence Regiment (UDR) barracks, where they would be staying for the next week. Satisfied that he knew the route they were going to take, he informed Hesh, the team second in command (2ic) and driver, to make best speed. Hesh's vehicle lurched forward with Richard's Land Rover following on behind, at a safe distance.

This was always the policy adopted, in case of an Improvised Explosive Device (IED) being detonated. In no time at all, and without further incident, they were entering the gates of the UDR barracks, which were thrown open by the armed sentry manning them. With a wave of his hand, Martin acknowledged his thanks. He stopped the Land Rover by the sentry and wound down his window.

'We're here for the next week, mate, where do we park our vehicles?' he asked, politely.

The sentry nodded his head and said that they had been expected. He gave Martin directions to where they should park the vehicles. They were to be staying in two wooden porta cabins, just next to the vehicle park. There would be a briefing at 19:00 that evening, for the next day's tasking's. Martin thanked him and the two Land Rovers sped off, in the direction of the vehicle park. Screeching to a halt, the crews disembarked from their vehicles. The brick commanders called their teams over to the unloading bay, where they went through the procedure of making sure their weapons were clear. Once each commander was happy, they instructed the troops to collect their sleeping bags and other equipment and make their way to the accommodation. Looking to the far side of the vehicle park, Richard spotted their 'five star' accommodation, two run-down, dilapidated porta cabins, grey in colour and not at all inviting. 'At least we will be dry,' mused Richard, as he entered one of the basic wooden structures. Throwing his sleeping bag and Bergen (rucksack) on the bed, he began to make himself at home. Ron and the rest of the team did the same and settled in, for an hour. Martin left the room, to find out what time the evening meal would be. It wasn't long before he returned, informing them that they could grab something to eat there and then.

The two teams made their way to the cookhouse, which was situated on the other side of the vehicle park. It was very quiet, with only a handful of people seated, tucking into the evening meal. Richard and the rest of the blokes loaded up their plates and sat down at one of the many available tables. The food was surprisingly good and they chatted among themselves. Meal times were always a highlight of every soldier's life, and the debate on the quality of what was served to them was a top subject of conversation. Tonight, the verdict was that this was better than the food they been given back in Germany. Martin pointed out the fact that the chefs here were not cooking for the larger numbers that the ones back in Germany had. Everyone nodded their agreement, as this was a part time unit the cookhouse was never as busy as the ones supporting regular troops.

After the evening meal, the eight patrol members crashed out on their beds and caught a quick hour's sleep. It was not long before Martin was rousing them, in time for them to get ready for the 19:00 briefing. Richard swung his legs off the bed and put on his boots. As there were to be no patrols, as far as he knew, that evening, he left his body armour on the end of his bed. Once everyone was ready, they exited the porta cabins and crossed the tarmac square towards the main HQ building, where Martin had established the briefing was to be held.

On their arrival, they were met by a Captain of the Ulster Defence Regiment. He introduced himself as Captain Bird, the unit's Intelligence Officer. A number of chairs had been arranged, around a map on the wall, which showed a detailed layout of Portadown. Bird began by going through any incidents that had happened over the past couple of days. These included an IED explosion on one of the roads which connected the town with the main motorway to Belfast, in the north. He went through a list of known local Provisional Irish Republican Army (PIRA) members. To accompany this, he had a montage of photographs, with the names of the individuals underneath. Copies of these were handed out to the team members and they were asked to commit them to memory. The men in question were all members of 'Active Service Units' (ASU's) in the area. Sightings of any of these men, while on patrol, were to be noted and reported at once. The briefing went on for the next 45 minutes. The following day was to be spent patrolling Portadown itself. This was mostly a familiarisation exercise, to get the troops used to the general area. They were to begin at 07:00, so with the briefing finished, the teams returned to the porta cabins, to get their heads down.

Entering the accommodation, Richard took his wash bag and towel from his Bergen and wandered off, to find the showers. Finding the ablutions block, he quickly undressed, placing his clothes on the hooks and bench provided and stepped into the shower. As the water hit his body, he gasped a quick intake of breath, as the water was freezing cold, causing him to cry out in surprise.

'What the fuck?' he exclaimed.

'I take it the showers are cold, then?' came a voice, from behind him. It was Ron, who had followed him over, not two minutes after Richard had left.

'Too right, they're cold, mate, I hope it's not like this for the next week!' was Richard's irate reply.

The pair of them made short work of their hygiene routine and dressed quickly. Returning to the porta cabin, they informed Martin that the showers were freezing. He made a note that he would speak to the camp Quartermaster (QM), at the earliest opportunity.

There were a number of factors that contributed to good morale, one was food and another was home comforts. A happy soldier performs better than an unhappy one, although some just liked to whinge for the sake of it. It was a well-known saying, that a soldier was never happy unless he was complaining. However, knowing that this was a reasonable request, Martin told Richard that he would get it sorted as soon as he could. Satisfied with Martin's response, Richard unzipped his sleeping bag, referred to as a 'maggot', took his Walkman and headphones out of his Bergen and climbed into the bag. As he listened to Stevie Wonder telling him that *"I Just Called to Say I Love You"*, he drifted off to sleep.

Richard did not know how long he had been asleep, when he was woken by a reverberating boom, followed by the sound of breaking glass. He sat bolt upright in his green maggot. Smoke drifted through the newly broken window of the porta cabin. There was confusion among the men, who were hastily donning their body armour, boots and helmets. Richard called to mind the training they had just gone through, in the facility in Sennelager, known as 'Tin City'. Although he had never experienced this before, he knew, instinctively, they had been subjected to a mortar attack. Just as this thought entered his mind, a siren wailed, confirming his fears. The initial action, or IA drill for this event, was to find some form of overhead cover.

'Mortar attack!' he called out, at the top of his voice and flung himself under the bed.

Ron copied his example, followed by the rest of the team. They waited with bated breath, for the sound of further explosions. None came and the all clear was sounded some five minutes later. The sound of vehicles' engines revving and tyres screeching heralded the sound of the 'Quick Reaction Force' (QRF), crashing out of the camp. It was their remit to find and secure the mortar base plate firing point. If possible, they were to apprehend any person, thought to be connected to mounting the attack. Both teams made their way from the accommodation to the loading bay and placed their magazines on their weapons. The two brick commanders sprinted off, to see if the teams would be required to help. As Richard turned from the loading bay, he noticed a crater in the centre of the vehicle park, from which a plume of smoke bellowed. This was obviously where the mortar round had landed. There was debris littered around the area. Gauging from the size of the crater, he thought to himself, they would have not have survived, if the device had hit their accommodation.

As Richard mulled over this conclusion, Martin and the other brick commander returned and informed them that the firing point had been located by the QRF. It was a flatbed lorry, with a tube mounted on the rear. From this, the improvised mortar round, in this case, a long gas cylinder, had been lobbed over the perimeter fence. The culprits had set the tube on a timer and were well away by the time the QRF had located the firing point. They were to learn quickly that their adversaries were well skilled in the art of terrorism. It started to hit home this was not a training exercise or a game. They had come within 100 metres of serious injury, even death. With this sobering thought, and the all clear given, the troops trudged back to the loading bay, to clear their weapons. It was 03:30 and they would be getting up again in about two hours' time. 'If this is how the week is going to continue, God help us,' Richard thought.

Chapter 2 - The Streets of Portadown

It was 06:00 and the two teams had already showered, shaved and dressed. They had eaten a hearty breakfast, not knowing the next time they would have a chance to eat. Martin and the other brick commander had returned to the Operations Room (Ops), to ascertain if there had been any incidents overnight or, indeed, anything that they needed to be aware of, in the area of patrols for the day. They were informed that it had been quiet. Nothing had been flagged that they needed to be aware of. After confirming the call signs and radio frequencies they were to use, the two commanders returned to their troops.

Gathering them round, they laid out a map on the bonnet of one of the Land Rovers. For the next twenty minutes, they ran through the tasks for the day, asking, at the end, if anyone had any questions. Everyone seemed satisfied with what was required of them. They dressed over to the loading bay and charged their weapons. Each person checked his mate's equipment, to ensure it was secure. This was standard operating procedure (SOP), to minimise the risk of a team member losing something. It had been known for PIRA to booby trap a piece of lost equipment and place it in a prominent position. When someone from the security forces picked it up, it would detonate a device, designed to either maim or kill.

Mounting up in the vehicles, Richard and Ron took up their alert positions, with the weapons covering opposite sides of the vehicle. Martin carried out a radio check with both the Ops room, call sign zero, and the other team commander. Once he was happy, he signalled for the other Land Rover to set off. They approached the front gates, where the barrier had already been lifted, for their departure. Turning left out of the camp, they joined the main road, which would take them into the centre of the town.

The traffic on the roads was building steadily, as the early morning commuters made their way to work. They did not give the two Land Rovers a second glance, the sight of military vehicles and armed soldiers had become the norm over the past twenty years. The troops scanned vehicle registrations, and took mental note of the occupants. They were hoping to spot any members of the local ASU's, men they had been briefed on, the night before.

For the next two hours, the patrol wound its way through the streets of Portadown, familiarising themselves with key areas. Places where incidents had occurred in the past, from shootings, kneecappings to IED explosions. Although terrorists did not seem to strike twice in the same place, it was always a good idea to see the kind of places where they carried out these acts. Richard was on a heightened sense of alert, after the incident the previous day. His eyebrow still throbbed from where the rock had struck him. This was highlighted as they passed a school, where the kids were already gathering outside the gates.

It was 08:45 and the school day was about to start. This time, instead of being greeted with a wave of stones, the young school kids, ranging from around nine to sixteen, waved at them. Richard smiled to himself and contemplated, what a fucked up country this was. He had never been very big on religion, and this difference in attitude from the Catholic and Protestant populations affirmed this. He could not understand how religion could divide a country so much, causing some of its more fervent supporters to commit acts of terror. However when he

17

thought about it, religion was one of the biggest causes of war and conflict throughout the globe. This had been going on for hundreds of years. He was shaken from his thoughts by Martin, who informed them that they were moving to the local police station for a quick brew, before heading out again on their next task.

The Land Rovers entered the fortified police station, with its heavy armoured gates and Rocket Propelled Grenade (RPG) wire, surrounding its watchtowers, overlooking the entrance. They were waved through by a member of the Royal Ulster Constabulary (RUC), dressed in his dark green uniform, body armour and MP5 machine pistol, slung across his chest. Not a normal sight on the streets of mainland UK, but in the 'Province', it was, unfortunately, a necessity. He bid them a good morning, and directed them to an area where they could park up. The vehicles did so, the troops dismounting and automatically making their way to the unloading bay. The weapons checked by the team leaders, they slung them over their shoulders and entered the building in search of a canteen. Asking a passing female officer where they could grab a brew, they were shown to a room filled with officers, who had, it seemed, just swapped over shifts. They were busily chatting with the off-going relief, enquiring about any incidents which had occurred during the night. The troops were largely ignored, so grabbed themselves a brew and found a couple of tables to sit at.

The main reason that troops were stationed in Northern Ireland, was to support the RUC in policing the Province. The troops themselves were only there for a period of four to six months. Once their tour was complete, they could return to their families and forget the Troubles. This was not the case for the people of Northern Ireland, who lived through it every day. This, at times, caused resentment among the security forces they were there to support. The majority of the time, their presence was welcomed by the members of the RUC and a good rapport was struck up. They were a fountain of knowledge about the local terrorists, on both sides of the fence. Although the Provisionals (PIRA), were more often in the public eye than their Loyalist counterparts, offences were committed from both factions; this could range to punishment beatings, organised crime and, of course, attacks on the security forces. The RUC were made up mostly of members of the Protestant community, so it was understandable that there was suspicion in the Catholic communities, as to their impartiality.

Their brews were finished. Martin and the other brick commander quickly ran over the next patrol task. It was to be a foot patrol in the town centre, They were not aware of any incidents which would cause them any concern. It was to be a low key patrol, with no RUC presence; a good time to get a feel of the place. The troops cleared away their cups and exited the canteen by the door they had earlier entered. Going through the loading drills as normal, Richard realised that this was to be his first foot patrol in a built up area.

He quickly went through the drills in his mind, which they had practised in 'Tin City' prior to their departure. Hopefully, there would be no need to employ the 'actions on' contact drills, which they had been practising relentlessly over the last four months, prior to deployment. Lining up by the gate, one behind the other, they waited for the policeman manning the gate, to open it for them. Checking everyone was ready, Martin nodded to the member of the RUC that he should open the gate. With a grind of metal on metal, the gate was flung open. The first member of the patrol, Ron, sprinted out from the compound and took up a position on the junction across the road. He covered an area to his left, pointing his weapon down the street. As soon as he had adopted the kneeling position, the second member of the team burst out from the cover of the gates. He, too, took up a stance, pointing his weapon down the opposite side of the road. This continued until the full eight man patrol had exited the confines of the police station.

As soon as they were all in position, without a signal, they rose from their kneeling positions and began to patrol, in the direction of the town centre. One team was on one side of the road, with the other directly opposite, but slightly staggered, on the other. After approximately ten minutes, they had settled into a steady pace. Each team member was assessing their new environment, taking in the people and geographical landmarks. The atmosphere seemed friendly enough and some of the population actually bid them a good morning. Richard returned the greeting with a broad smile. Winning the hearts and minds of the local populace was an important part of the war on terror. This was a predominately Protestant or 'Loyalist' area, so this friendly attitude was to be expected. Reaching a junction, Martin indicated to Fred, who was the brick commander of the other team, that they were taking a change in direction. They turned left at the crossing and began to patrol through the side streets of the town.

They had reached about 100 metres down the first street, when Richard observed one of the patrol, 'Fencer' a jovial guy from the West Country, talking with a local lad. The boy's age was around ten years old, and he had a skateboard at his feet. Richard and the lads had heard stories during their time in training for the Province, that kids who became too friendly with the security forces were given punishments by the Provisional Irish Republican Army. These could be having their heads shaved, beatings or far worse. As they were in a Protestant area, this kid was probably quite safe. After a few moments of chatting, and to Richard's surprise, Fencer bent down and picked up the skateboard from the young lad. Placing his left foot on it, he began to push himself along the street, until he built up speed. After building up enough velocity, he positioned his right foot on the board, as if riding a surfboard. With his rifle pointing across his body in the alert position, he hurtled down the street, much to the enjoyment of the watching troops. It wasn't long before Martin decided that enough was enough and called over to Fencer:

'Right, you clown! Give the lad his skateboard back, we have a job to do here!'

A groan went up from the rest of the teams, who had been enjoying the spectacle. Fencer nodded his head in recognition of Martin's order. He bent down, picked up the young boy's toy and placed it under his arm. Trudging back up the street, he offered it back, expressing his thanks, as he did so. The lad took the board gratefully, jumped on it, sped off down the road and disappeared out of sight. The event had broken up the morning and, smiling, the two teams carried on the task of patrolling the streets.

A couple of hours had passed, and the troops began to make their way back on to the main high street of the town. Martin sent a message over the air to Fred, with a previously arranged code word, meaning that they were going to stop for lunch. He directed Richard to make his way towards a fish shop they had passed earlier in the day. Arriving outside the shop, he ordered Richard and Hesh to take up positions on either side of it. They did as they were commanded and faced in opposite directions down the high street. Once Martin was satisfied that the other team had positioned itself on the other side of the road, both he and Ron unloaded their weapons. Each of them checked that the other did not have any rounds chambered. Letting their working parts slide forward, they pressed the trigger, in the drill known as 'easing springs'.

As they entered the bustling fish shop, they were greeted with wide eyed amazement and looks of fear from the occupants. People started to leave the shop in a disorderly fashion. Martin wondered what the problem was.

It hadn't occurred to him that the sight of soldiers with weapons in a chip shop might cause some concern.

'Is it a bomb scare?' the proprietor asked, nervously.

The penny had dropped. Martin smiled and said, 'No mate, we just want eight portions of fish and chips.'

He could sense the wave of relief that had lifted from not only the shop owner, but the rest of the customers who had not already fled the premises. Richard and Hesh had wondered why there had been a mad exodus from the establishment, not long after the other two had entered. Looking in their direction, Martin simply gave them the thumbs up, and a big grin spread across his face.

Ten minutes later, the two teams were tucking into their lunch from the newspaper wrapping, in a car park, behind the main street. They thought it not very professional to grab food in full view of the general public. They laughed as Martin relayed the story of what had happened on entering the chippy. Little episodes like this lightened up the sometimes mundane tasks they were given, during not only this tour of Northern Ireland, but also subsequent ones.

Over the next week, the troops carried out various tasks including mobile patrols, foot patrols, 30 minute standby, which was like a day off. They would be fully kitted up and were required to react when called upon. In truth, they spent most of the time watching pornographic videos or comedy shows. The rest of the time was spent either eating, sleeping or trying to amuse themselves in any way they could. Some would exercise in the gym but would always have their equipment close to hand, so they could 'crash out', if required. Keeping the peace on the streets of the Province was not always as exciting as they had first anticipated.

On their final day before returning to the Maze Prison, they were tasked with carrying out mobile patrols in the Portadown area. It was drawing close to Christmas, and

Richard realised that it was, in fact, Christmas Eve. This would not the last time he would spend time away over this period or miss 'special occasions'. Most of the lads took it in their stride, as it was all part of the job. It was married personnel, with young kids, who were most affected.

The divorce rate in the Armed Forces was proportionally higher than that of couples in Civvy Street. This was understandable, as wives were left for long periods of time, on their own, to bring up children. On the soldiers' return, it took some time for them to adjust back into family life, and this caused a great deal of friction in many households.

The day passed without any great incident, apart from their final mobile patrol in the town centre. It was around 17:00 and night had already fallen. The two Land Rovers criss-crossed the town, varying their routes as they went. At a particular crossroads, the traffic lights had turned to red. The vehicles halted, waiting patiently to continue with the patrol. Richard and Hesh scanned the streets, from the rear of the vehicle. Stumbling towards them, came the dishevelled figure of an old man. From this gait, it seemed he had spent most of the day in the public house he had just left. He seemed drawn to the vehicle, like a bee to honey. Reaching them, he started to engage Richard in conversation. Due to the amount of alcohol he had consumed and the broadness of his accent, Richard was finding it difficult to understand him. He seemed friendly enough, and was not being aggressive, in any way. He began to pat Richard on the shoulder, wishing him what Richard understood to be a Merry Christmas. Both Ron, who was driving, and Martin in the front, were oblivious to what was going on behind them. The lights turned to red and amber. Ron engaged first gear and, on green, he let out the clutch and the vehicle began to move forward. The drunken reveller fell forward, grabbing Richard's webbing straps, to steady himself. The vehicle continued to pull forward, dragging the elderly reveller with it.

'Stop! Stop! Stop!' exclaimed Hesh, in a concerted attempt at catching the driver's attention.

Martin looked over his shoulder, and seeing the situation, gave the order for Ron to brake. The sudden halting of the Land Rover caused the pedestrian to fall flat on his face. Hesh and Richard jumped from the vehicle and helped the man regain his footing. He had blood streaming from his nose and a few scratches on his face. Luckily, the amount of booze in his system had dulled any initial pain from the fall.

'You okay, mate?' Richard asked, wiping the blood from the old man's upper lip, while inspecting the other cuts.

The man mumbled some unintelligible reply, but seemed not seriously injured. After clearing the rest of the blood away, Hesh and Richard escorted the drunk to the side of the road. They bid him farewell and a Merry Christmas and returned to the vehicle. They laughed and joked about the incident, as they continued on the last part of the patrol. Martin came up on the radio and informed the Ulster Defence Regiment (UDR) that the patrol was complete and that they were moving back to the HMP Maze. This was acknowledged by the Operations Room and the two Land Rovers started to make their way from the town. On the outskirts, Martin spotted an off licence and decided they would get a couple of cans, for the journey home. Letting the commander of the other vehicle know his intention, they parked outside and Martin entered, with a member of the other team. In the space of five minutes, they were mounting back up again, each with a four pack of beer, in their arms. Once the patrol had reached the M1 Motorway, they headed North, in the direction of the Maze prison. The vehicle was filled with the sound of cans being opened and the spark of cigarette lighters, as the troops drank and smoked on the short journey back. Although this behaviour was against the rules, what harm could one can of beer do, thought Richard?

Chapter 3 – Northern Ireland Final Days

Richard was rudely awakened by Martin, shaking his shoulder. He had slept through from 22:00, when they had returned to the Maze. The week's patrolling and lack of sleep had seriously caught up with him. Dragging his head off the pillow, he glanced at his watch. It was 07:30. He wondered why Martin had disturbed him, as it was supposed to be the team's day off.

'What's the score, Martin?' he asked, through puffy eyes, still unable to focus correctly.

'We've been summoned to the debrief room in fifteen minutes. Get your arse into gear and get dressed!' he replied, unpleasantly.

Richard threw back the blankets and swung his feet over the bed. As the bare skin of his feet came into contact with the cold lino floor, he shivered. Other members of the two patrols were also stirring and donning their uniforms. The two brick commanders were rushing around, hastening them along. Once everyone was dressed, they moved together, towards the operations room. There, they were met by a stern looking Squadron Leader and Squadron Sergeant Major (SSM). They were ordered to take a seat; Richard knew by the tone of the SSM's voice that this wasn't going to be a pleasant debrief. As soon as everyone had settled down and the noise had subsided, the Officer Commanding B Squadron (OC) stepped forward.

He eyed everyone in the room with a steely glare, shaking his head as he did so.

'I received a call from the RUC in Portadown this morning.' He paused, waiting for this news to sink in, before continuing. 'Apparently a patrol of two vehicles entered an off licence on the edge of the town last night. This establishment is well known in the area as having sympathetic links with the local 'Provos'. The owner of the shop took the registrations of the vehicles from which soldiers had purchased cans of beer from him, around 21:00 last night. Imagine, if you will, my outrage and embarrassment, when it was brought to my attention that those vehicles belonged to members of this Squadron!'

Again, he paused for dramatic effect. 'To say that I am angry and disappointed is an understatement. I will not even ask if it was you, as the facts speak for themselves,' he said, in a sorrowful manner. 'Your patrol commanders know full well the rules regarding alcohol while on duty. I will be speaking to them separately.' With that, he nodded to the SSM.

The SSM brought the room up to attention and waited for the OC to leave. He left the troops standing, eyeing each one with a look of loathing. To tarnish the good name of the Squadron was a crime, unforgiveable in his eyes. It would not be long before the story got back to other Squadrons in the Regiment and their name would be shit. For the next five minutes, the SSM hurled a tirade of abuse at the now sheepish looking group. They knew that they had fucked up, but worse, they had been caught.

The SSM informed them that they were no longer on a day off and that they were to report to the briefing room in an hour's time, for further tasking. With that, he screamed at them to get the fuck out of his sight. The eight, less their commanders, who had been asked to stay behind with the SSM, beat a hasty retreat to the accommodation. On their way, they passed two individuals dressed in jeans, t-shirts and bomber jackets. Their hair was almost shoulder length and Richard took them to be civilian contractors. It wasn't until they had passed, that Richard heard a voice call his name.

'Hunter, you not speaking then?'

Richard turned round and looked at one of the blokes, who was smiling at him. It took him at least 30 seconds before the penny dropped. There was something familiar about this guy, the voice rang a distant bell. Richard's mind went back to the Squadron bar in Germany, when he had first joined the Regiment. The Squadron barman, Kevin, had been one of the first people he had met. Kevin had disappeared about two years ago and Richard assumed that he had been posted. Recognising his old mate, Richard returned the grin and extended his hand to Kevin.

'Bloody hell, mate, how you doing?' he asked, genuinely surprised to see him.

'I'm doing well, mate, bit more laid back in my present posting,' was the cryptic reply. Kevin then turned to his companion, who had been observing the exchange, with a pleasant grin. 'This is Larry, he is working with me at the moment. He's also on 'posting' from the Regiment.'

Richard took Larry's extended hand and was not surprised at the firmness of the grip. He had a steely stare and an air of confidence.

Richard didn't know it yet, but Larry was to become his boss in the not too distant future. Pleasantries exchanged, the two long haired 'hippies' stated that they had to get going.

Richard wished them all the best and turned to leave. It wasn't until back at the accommodation the realisation hit home. Richard thought back to all Kevin's runs in the mornings and evenings, the hours spent in the gym. Very rarely seen without a Bergen on his back and pounding the range road that ran behind their camp in Germany, Kevin had been on his selection course for the Special Air Service (SAS). From his looks and attire, it appeared that Kevin must have achieved his ambition.

Richard mused on the subject, entertaining the romantic idea that maybe one day, it would be something he may want to attempt. However, before he could think any more on the notion, he was interrupted by the pissed-off voice of

Martin, who had, no doubt, been torn a new arsehole by the SSM.

Martin clattered about the billet room and threw open his door, almost taking it off its hinges. He turned round before going in and called out.

'Get your patrol kit ready! Be in the briefing room in twenty minutes!'

With that, he slammed his door shut. The troops did as they were told and busied themselves with their equipment. It then dawned on Richard that it was Christmas Day. 'Happy fucking Christmas,' he murmured to himself.

The patrol brief lasted around 30 minutes. They were given various tasks for that morning. As they left the briefing room, it began to rain, just to add a little more misery to the situation. They trudged towards the loading bay, where they went through the normal loading drills and communications checks. Once Martin was satisfied, they mounted up in their Land Rovers and sped off towards the gates. The guard at 'Tally Lodge', which was the main entrance to HMP Maze, threw open the gate to allow them to depart. Turning left out of the gates on to the main road, the patrols began their first task of the morning, a sweep of the roads which converged on the prison.

When they had reached approximately 800 metres from the prison, they came across their first culvert. It was necessary to check them on a daily basis, to see if they had any Improvised Explosive Devices hidden in them. It was a favourite tactic of the IRA to detonate the IED, as a member of the prison force was on his or her way to work.

The drill for clearing them was to dismount, approximately 100 metres before a culvert, a structure that allows water to flow under a road, railroad or similar obstruction from one side to the other side. One member of the patrol was designated to go forward and do a 'close recce' of the area. He would approach the culvert from either the left or right side and peer in to ensure there were no obstructions which could contain a device. Once this was done, he gave the all clear. Everyone would mount back up and the procedure was repeated at every culvert they came to. After checking around six or seven, it became quite tiresome.

It was not unheard of for patrols to check the culvert by simply driving over them. If there was no explosion, it was deemed to be clear.

This was a cavalier and unprofessional attitude and one not adopted by Richard's patrol that day. The ear bending both team leaders had received from the SSM had obviously struck a chord. For the next three hours, they travelled the approach roads, checking every culvert they came across, in the correct manner.

After the run was complete, they moved to their next tasking, to check vehicles entering or leaving from the visitors' gate at the Maze.

It was Christmas Day, so they were going to be busy, Richard thought. Over the next couple of hours, they checked numerous cars, vans and other vehicles. They saw nothing out of the ordinary, although they received the expected abuse from the families and friends of the inmates. This was, by now, like water off a duck's back to the Troops and they simply smiled back, as they knew this infuriated the abusers.

The rain was starting to fall more heavily and Martin was about to call it a day. From around a bend in the road, came a white transit van. As it drew close to the Vehicle Checkpoint (VCP), Richard could see the worried look on the face of the driver, who was accompanied by a woman and three children. As Richard approached the vehicle, he gave the usual sign for the driver to wind down his window. The driver complied and had to shout over the noise of the kids, to make himself heard.

'Good afternoon, is there a problem?' he asked, nervously.

'No, just a routine check,' Richard replied, in a friendly manner. 'Are you visiting someone today?'

'Yes, my uncle. We are running a bit late, visiting time finishes in an hour. Can you just let us through? It's Christmas Day, after all.'

The tone of his voice and the way he was behaving rang alarm bells. Something wasn't quite right. Richard asked for the driver's driving licence, so he could run a Personal Check (P Check). Getting the information from the driver, he passed it on to Martin, who sent it over the radio. While Richard waited for the report to come back, he chatted with the driver, where he had come from, how long had the journey taken and how often did he visit. It took only two minutes for Martin to say that the 'P Check' had come back clear. However, something didn't sit right with Richard, so he asked the driver, in passing.

'What you got in the back of the van, mate?'

The driver's eyes widened slightly. He replied in a nervous voice, 'Just some bags of rubbish we are taking to the tip, later.'

'Do you mind stepping out of the vehicle and opening up, so we can take a look, please, sir?' Richard asked, politely.

The driver was now starting to get irate. His wife started to hurl obscenities at the troops. But, he did as he was asked and made his way to the rear of the van. Pausing for a moment, he looked at the bunch of keys in his hand, selecting the one he needed. With a creak of metal on metal, the rusty door was flung open. The stench emitted from inside was horrendous and Richard turned his head away. He called out to Ron to do a quick rummage through the bags, making the excuse that he needed to ask the driver a few more questions. From the smell, he knew what the bags contained and didn't fancy the job himself. As Richard tried to engage the driver in conversation, Ron

31

began to rummage through the first bag. Out the corner of his eye, he saw Ron hold up something white.

'For fuck sake!' he proclaimed, as he drew Richard's attention to the soiled nappy he was holding aloft.

The driver smirked and said that the bags were full of them. Not deterred, Richard asked Ron to continue to rummage through all the bags, thoroughly. As expected, after emptying the first bag of its 'shitty' contents, Ron turned to Richard and said,

'Got a video recorder in a box, here. I wonder what else is stashed away?' he mumbled, to himself. By the time he had emptied the eight bags, there were eight video recorders, brand new in boxes.

The shifty looking driver knew the game was up, but protested that he had never seen the items before. As this was a civil matter, Martin decided to call the Royal Ulster Constabulary in, to deal with it. For good measure, and because the wife was becoming more offensive, he made the driver stand outside in the rain, until they arrived, some 30 minutes later. The RUC went to town on the couple, who had, by now, become compliant, afraid of the consequences.

Martin was given the okay for the patrol to leave, as the RUC would take it from there. The Troops mounted up and roared off, in the direction of the front gates. Within twenty minutes, they had parked up, unloaded, debriefed and were lying on their beds.

'Well, that was a Christmas Day I won't forget in a long time,' thought Richard. Indeed, nor would Ron, who had spent the first half hour back washing his gloves, trying to remove the smell of baby shit.

Chapter 4 – Handover and Return to Germany

The final weeks flew by and were interspersed with tower sentry duties, Tally Lodge and the odd patrol. The troops were looking forward to the handover, which was to start the following week. Martin had already begun his preparations for the upcoming handover, by initiating equipment checks. On a particular morning, the team had every piece of their equipment laid out on their beds; as Martin called out each item, they held it up for inspection. The teams were used to this activity, as they performed a similar routine with their tank equipment and tools, on a regular basis. These were known as 'Complete Equipment Schedule' (CES) checks. The team commanders did periodic checks, after patrols, to see if anyone had lost anything on the streets. This was normal operating procedure and any lost, damaged or deficient equipment was to be reported, through the chain of command.

The reason for these constant checks was that various terrorist organisations would, at times, use lost equipment as a means of causing injury. Booby trapped equipment would be left in a prominent place on the streets, deliberately to be found. Although soldiers were taught never to pick up 'foreign' items, the typical soldier was like a magpie, drawn to nice, new, shiny objects. This tactic, by the terrorists, had caused a significant number of serious injuries and deaths, to unsuspecting troops.

The CES checks lasted around an hour and the final check was to ensure that each soldier had his allotted ammunition for his rifles and other weapons.

After packing all his equipment away in his locker and Bergen, Richard sat on his bed and began to unload the 7.62mm rounds from his four magazines. Laying them out in rows of ten, he breathed a sigh of relief, as he emptied the last magazine and confirmed that he had all 80 rounds. When Martin had checked everyone, they charged their magazines again. Just as Richard placed the last round in his final magazine, a siren sounded with an unfamiliar wail. He looked across at Ron, who had a quizzical look on his face. Both knew that they had heard this sound before, in one of the briefings they had received, at the beginning of the tour. While they racked their brains for what it denoted, they were put out of their misery by the SSM, who had thrown open the accommodation door.

'Op Todber, grab your kit and get fell in outside!' with that, he moved on to the next block, where he could be heard, shouting the same order.

Operation Todber was the name given to an attempted breakout of a prisoner, from the 'H' Blocks. The Squadron hastily assembled, outside the cookhouse, where a number of 'snatch' Land Rovers were waiting. As Richard ran out the door of the accommodation, he bumped into one of the other members of the Troop. A magazine flew from his left hand pouch. He had not had time to check they were secure. It bounced down the steps. Richard bent down, to retrieve it quickly and place it back in its home. Ensuring the pouch was now secure, he followed the rest of the Troop, to a position opposite the cookhouse doors.

The sound of the 'war dogs', which were also located in the prison grounds, barking in excitement, added further tension to the already fuelled situation. Their handlers were fighting to hold them back, as they snarled at the assembling bodies. No one knew, at this point, if the alarm was for real or just another drill. When the troops were assembled in their various teams, the SSM took a roll call. Within five minutes, the roll call complete, the SSM handed over to the Squadron Second in Command (2ic).

'Right, guys, this, as you know from the alarm, is Op Todber. On this , it is just a drill, but you will carry out the exercise as if it was for real!'

With this, he began to call the Troop Leaders together, after dispatching the war dogs and their handlers, to predesignated positions. The Troop Leaders were briefed quickly and nodded their heads, confirming they understood their various tasks. They turned about and strode back, to the individual Troops and briefed them accordingly.

Richard's Troop had been allocated a section of the wall, from where a possible escape could be made. They mounted the snatch Land Rovers and were conveyed to the area they were to cover. The 'Federal Riot Gun' (FRG) or baton gun man from each team dressed forward, to around ten metres from the wall. The mechanism of the FRG was broken and a baton round placed in the chamber. They left the weapons 'broke', until they were given the order to be ready.

The remainder of the Troop were positioned approximately ten metres behind them, covering the top of the wall and the entrance/ exit gate, with their rifles. The remainder of the Squadron were either performing this same routine on other walls or backing up sentries, in the towers.

One Troop was held back in reserve, in case they were needed, to be deployed to an area that required further numbers. Although it was just an exercise, the wailing of the sirens, the searchlights dancing through the early evening sky and the urgency of the commands being sent from the radio all added to the confusion, realism and excitement.

Within the space of ten minutes the Squadron Quarter Master Sergeant (SQMS) turned up in his Land Rover, tyres screeching. He jumped from the vehicle and called out to two of the team commanders, who turned immediately and went to the rear of his vehicle. They quickly unloaded a number of Perspex riot shields, which were distributed throughout the Troop. No sooner had the

Troop formed a baseline, with the FRG men interspersed along it, when the siren gave the signal for them to stand down. To confirm this, the senior team commander called out:

'Endex! Endex! Endex! Stand down, guys!'

The announcement was met with a mixture of groans and sarcastic comments. The soldiers with the riot shields made their way to the SQMS Land Rover and began to hand them back, to the waiting storeman. Content that he had gathered them all back in, he gave the nod to the SQMS, who mounted back up and then sped away. The teams got back into the waiting vehicles and were taken back to the assembly area, outside the cookhouse. There, they were met by the OC, who seemed genuinely pleased with the things had gone.

'Well done to everyone, on your reaction times and deployment. If this had been genuine, I can safely say that we would have contained any breakout. I called the exercise to test whether we were all still on our toes, toward the end of our tour. We have just one week left to push, before we begin our handover to the Artillery, who will begin arriving, with their advance party, tomorrow. Keep switched on and I would like to take this opportunity to thank you for all your efforts, over the last four months. SSM please carry on!'

With this parting remark, he saluted the SSM, who returned the salute. Once the men were given the order to fall out, they wandered off, to their accommodation.

The following days passed slowly. It was Richard's Troop's week to man the towers, surrounding the prison. Each two hour 'stag' or period of time sitting in the towers, observing the 'H' Blocks and the approaches to the prison, seemed to drag. The reading material, both pornographic and literary, which had been hidden away in various hiding places, had become familiar and redundant. These would, however, be left in position for the incoming unit, to while

36

away the hours of tedium, during their tour. It was Richard's final stag and he waited, eagerly, for his relief, who would be one of the gunners, now taking over the duties of guarding the facility.

The whine of the snatch Land Rover's engine drew Richard's attention, and its headlights drew closer to his tower. With a squeal of brakes, it halted, at the bottom of the structure. It wasn't long before he could hear the sound of someone climbing the steel ladders, up to his position. He opened the trapdoor, to enable his relief and the posting NCO, to gain access. Squeezing through the small gap, fully laden with his webbing and weapon, the Artilleryman offered a greeting to Richard. He was closely followed by the NCO, who asked Richard to give his replacement a full brief. This he had done a hundred times before and, so, did not have to refer to the script, written down for the purpose of handovers.

Completing his briefing, Richard asked his relief if he had any questions, to which he answered that he was happy.

Richard almost broke his neck, descending the ladders, as quickly as he could. Unloading in the small pit, outside the tower, he jumped into the back of the Land Rover. It was full of his own Troop apart from one gunner, who was to take the final position in the last tower.

Shortly afterwards, the Land Rover was pulling up outside the accommodation, the guys filed in and began to take off their equipment. They would be handing everything into the SQMS in two hours' time. Richard sniffed his body armour, which had encased him every moment on patrol or guard duty. It was stained and smelled of stale sweat. He turned his head away in disgust.

These returned items would all go through the Army cleaning system, before being issued out, again, to other units. The last thing Richard did, after accounting for all of his equipment, was to check his ammunition. Martin was waiting, in his room, for everyone to confirm that they had all their rounds. Richard emptied his magazine onto his bed and began to count. As he neared the end, he could not believe his eyes. One was missing!

Starting from the beginning, he began to count them again, ending up at the same number 79. Four magazines of twenty rounds should have meant 80 rounds. His heart sank. What was he going to do about this? He racked his brains, back to the last time he had counted them. It came to him! It had been the week before, prior to the 'Op Todber' exercise. Richard remembered he had dropped his magazine, from its pouch, when leaving the block. One of his rounds must have become dislodged and bounced out. Taking a deep breath, he approached Martin's door, to tell him the bad news. Knocking on the door, Richard waited, nervously, for Martin to acknowledge his presence.

'What can I do for you?' Martin said, matter of factly.

Plucking up courage, Richard came straight out with it:

'I'm a round diffy (deficient),' he stammered. He waited for the outburst, which he was expecting from Martin, but to his surprise, it never came.

·Instead, a broad smile spread across Martin's face, 'I wondered which of you fuckwits this belonged to,' as he stood and removed a 7.62 round from his combat trouser pocket. 'Someone handed this in last week, just after the Op Todber exercise. I thought I would wait and see if it was any of my retards.' He said the words jokingly and handed over the round to Richard, ending with 'that's a pint you owe me. Now, fuck off and get your kit ready to hand into the SQMS, we are due to leave at 13:00.'

Richard breathed a sigh of relief, turned around and returned to his bed space. The rest of the Troop were busy packing away their clothing, in their kit bags and suitcases. It wasn't long before they were all lined up, outside the SQMS stores. They were the last Troop to hand in their kit, so the process had been refined. It took only a short space of time before they were all assembling, with the rest of the Squadron, outside the cookhouse.

Their flight out of the Province was due to leave at 18:30, from Aldergrove Airport. They would form the main party, leaving only a handful of people behind, to tie up the final part of the handover.

As the SSM called their names, they were directed to a series of 4 tonne Bedford trucks, sitting, with their engines running. They climbed aboard, past the two Artillery blokes who sat at the rear, their rifles pointing out the back. They were obviously riding shotgun, for the journey up to the airport. Richard settled down and got himself as comfortable as he could. He closed his eyes and his mind wandered off, as he recalled what had happened over the past few months.

Chapter 5 – Return to Camp and Guided Weapons

The uneventful journey from the Maze prison to Aldergrove took just over an hour. It wasn't long before the VC 10 aircraft touched down at RAF Gutersloh in Germany. The soldiers disembarked and transited through the arrivals, straight on to waiting buses, which would transport them back to their barracks. There was no need to collect their luggage at this point, as a 'baggage party' had already been nominated, or 'dicked', to do this. Baggage parties were normally made up of individuals who had remained in Germany and had not been on operational tour. A lot of these were labelled sick, lame and lazy, so Richard and the rest of the Squadron didn't give them a second thought.

The journey down the A2 Autobahn, toward the town where they were garrisoned, gave Richard time to reflect on the last four months. He had managed to survive his first operational tour, albeit with a slight scar, which would remain for the rest of his life. He began to think of Birgit, looking forward to seeing her, after such a break. They had grown closer during the months prior to his deployment to Northern Ireland. They had even spoken of possibly getting engaged, on his return. That was for the future though, all Richard wanted to do was to climb into a warm, comfortable bed.

Richard had fallen into a deep sleep, his arms wrapped round the waist of Birgit. The night was still, save the intermittent hoot of an owl, coming from the back garden of Birgit's family home. His slumber was not a peaceful one, he tossed and turned for most of the night. Perspiration from his brow ran down his face, like rivers in miniature. The sounds of the teenage kids outside the school in Northern Ireland created a cacophony inside his head.

Richard was reliving that first patrol, four months earlier. As the missile struck him, in his dream, he woke with a scream. He stared around the darkened room. His eyes focusing in the gloom, he saw the shape of someone on the floor, advancing, slowly, toward him on their knees.

'It's okay,' came a soft, gentle voice, 'you've just had a bad dream.' Birgit was beside him, wiping the sweat away from his brow, trying to calm him down.

As she stroked his face, waiting for him to recognise what was going on, he stared back at her, gathering his thoughts, before he spoke.

'What happened?' he asked, startled.

'You had a nightmare,' she replied, knowing that it must have come from his experiences 'over the water'. She continued to soothe his brow. She explained that, somehow, during his dream, he had physically thrown her, from the bed, across the room. This frightened Richard and all he could do was to apologise. Climbing into bed, she snuggled up to him. He adopted the foetal position. Birgit ran her fingers down his back. It wasn't long, with the rhythmic stroking action, before he, once again, fell into a deep sleep.

The first day back at work, after the Northern Ireland leave, was a busy one. While they were away, they had learned that the Regiment was forming a 'Guided Weapons' (GW) Troop. 30 had been selected to man this Troop and among them was Richard. They were to be equipped with nine AFV438 tracked vehicles, two Ferret Scout Cars (FSC), two 4 tonne Bedford trucks and a Land Rover. The AFV438 itself was derived from the chassis of the AFV430 series. In fact it was a converted AFV432 which was in use by the infantry as the main Armoured Personnel Carrier (APC) of the British Army. It had two firing bins, and could carry fourteen missiles, which could be reloaded from inside the vehicle. Instead of using the mounted guidance system a control unit could be deployed

and the missiles aimed and fired from up to 100 metres
away, allowing the vehicle to remain completely hidden
from the enemy; the Swingfire missile was capable of
making a ninety-degree turn immediately after firing.
(Wikipedia)

The newly formed Troop gathered on the Tank Park,
next to hangars that housed the new vehicles. They paraded
under their new Troop Sergeant Major (TSM), Stu Pearson.
It was a tradition in the Regiment for Staff Sergeants in
Troops to be given the title of TSM. They formed up in
their three ranks, as for a normal 'first parade' and awaited
the arrival of their Troop Leader. Richard had read the list
of names, prior to the formation of the Troop. The name of
the Troop Leader rang a bell. It was Captain Ian McKelvie,
the very same person who had torn him a new arsehole in
his father's office, when he had first joined the Regiment,
some four years ago. He had been 'A' Squadron Sergeant
Major at that time (SSM), but had since then served his
time as Regimental Sergeant Major (RSM), before being
commissioned as a Captain, directly after that. This was to
be his first command and Richard was not looking forward
to it.

Richard was later to find out McKelvie was a firm man
but fair. As he strode toward the Troop, the TSM called
them to attention. He waited until Captain McKelvie was
about three paces from him and took a short pace forward
with his left foot, driving his right into the tarmac, saluting
smartly, at the same time.

'Guided Weapons Troop on parade and awaiting your
inspection, Sir!' he announced, formally.

'Stand them at ease, please, TSM,' the Troop Leader
commanded. With that, the TSM saluted, turned about and
gave the order for the guys to stand at ease.

Once everyone had settled down, the Troop Leader
addressed the Troop. He introduced himself to those who
did not know him. This was not really necessary, merely a

formality, as he was renowned throughout the Regiment. Those selected to form the Troop had all served at least three years, so there was little doubt who their new Troop Leader was. He went on to explain which crews were to man each vehicle.

Guided Weapons worked in four sections, with two AFV438s in each section. Each of the vehicles had a three man crew and he read out the names of those manning each vehicle. Richard waited pensively for his name to be called out. At last, he learned he was to drive the TSM, in his Ferret Scout Car. As his name was read out, Stu nodded in his direction, a smile crossing his lips.

The Ferret was produced between 1952 and 1971 by the UK Company, Daimler. It was widely adopted by regiments in the British Army as well as Commonwealth countries throughout the period. (Wikipedia)

Richard was unfamiliar with this vehicle, having never driven it before. He called to mind stories his father had told him about the time when he had served in Aden in the 1960s. He had numerous photographs of his father either standing next to, or mounted on, one of these vehicles. Here he was, some twenty years later, operating on the same vehicle.

Stu was a Qualified Testing Officer (QTO). These QTOs were the equivalent of a UK driving examiner and Richard knew that his driving skills, or lack of them, would be under scrutiny. The briefing finished, the Troop Leader asked the TSM to fall out the men. This he did, reminding them that an Officer was on parade, which told them they needed to salute, before marching off the three regulatory paces. Gathering inside the hangar, the new crews were exploring their vehicles and getting to know one another. Stu called Richard over to the Ferret, where he was walking round it, giving it a quick inspection.

'Have you ever driven one of these?' he asked Richard, as he presented himself, in front of the vehicle.

'Never, TSM,' he admitted, shaking his head at the same time.

'You can call me Stu, when there are no Officers about, you know,' he said, smiling. Stu was laying down the normal ground rules. For the next hour, he took Richard over the engine and the components, inside the vehicle. The space within was quite limited and the first thing that struck Richard was the position of the steering wheel. It was quite large and set at an angle, tilted down, slightly. This was to ease driving whilst closed down, with hatches shut. The armament of the vehicle was a .30 calibre Browning Machine Gun (MG). This, of course, was not fitted, as all weapons were stored in the armoury, unless drawn out, either for cleaning, exercise or the ranges. The gearbox was a pre-select one. The gear had to be engaged, then the clutch was depressed twice, to allow the gear to be selected. Stu explained that if this was done wrongly, sometimes the clutch would fly back, causing the driver's knee to jerk up violently. This would happen to Richard on more than one occasion, over the coming months.

By dinner time, the Troop had finished familiarising themselves with their vehicles and retired to their rooms, to wash in preparation for their midday meal. When Richard entered his room, his new roommate, Isaac Brown, turned round, offering his hand in greeting. Richard took the offered hand and introduced himself. The pleasantries over with, the pair of them gathered their mugs and set off for the cookhouse. The place was a hive of activity, with people queueing at the hotplates, waiting to be served. The pair joined on the end of the queue, after collecting trays and plates from the end of the pass. Loading up their plates, they picked out a table to sit at. After five minutes, they were joined by another member of the Troop. His name was Will Stevens, who had been a member of the Berlin Armoured Squadron, along with Richard. Although they had been in different Troops then, they knew each other quite well. Will was from Lancashire, not a popular place for those serving in a Yorkshire Regiment. His manner was pleasant and he was easy to get along with. The three of them chatted about how the day had gone and about the new personalities they had met, that morning. They were all of the same opinion; the Troop, as a whole, was full of good lads. Over the coming months, the three of them were to become good friends. Will would end up being best man at Richard's wedding. He was going out with Birgit's best friend at the time, so they would regularly spend evenings together, in the local town the girls came from.

Lunchtime over with, the Troop gathered again, in the new hangars, which had been purpose built for them. They spent the rest of the week going over the sighting equipment, which controlled the guided missiles. This was in preparation for a trip to Hohne to an Artillery Gunnery Training Establishment, where they would be converted to their new role. In the Troop were a couple of men, who had operated this equipment in the past. They had completed a form of 'pre course' training. At the end of the following week, the Troop moved to Hohne to begin their conversion training.

Chapter 6 – Hohne GW Conversion and Qualifying

The vehicles rolled off the railway flats at Bergen Hohne. It had been an easier task loading these up, than it had been with the Chieftain Main Battle Tanks (MBTs). As the members of GW were all seasoned soldiers, they had unloaded and were lined up, in the space of an hour. Once everyone was ready, the vehicles set off, under the direction of the local Military Police (MPs). One of their Land Rovers was at the head of the convoy, for the fifteen minute drive into Hohne camp. There, they released the vehicles, to move to the hangars they had been allocated, in the Artillery barracks. Parking up the vehicles, the crews did their final 'halt parades', to ensure they did not have any leaks, and so, were ready to use, the next day. The TSM and Troop Leader were happy that all was in order and knocked the blokes off for the evening. They were ordered to report to the Gunnery Wing at 08:30 the next morning.

The first part of the evening was spent taking over their temporary accommodation and settling in. Richard put away his kit in his locker and headed off for a shower. With nothing planned for the evening, they had decided to spend the time in the NAAFI bar. This was a normal practice, while troops were away on training courses. It was an opportunity seized by the 'pads', or married personnel, to let their hair down. The blokes met up in the bar around 19:00, apart from the senior NCOs and Troop Leader, who chose to use the Officers', the Warrant Officers' and Sergeants' Mess.

This was a different arrangement from normal annual firing camps in 'Sabre' Squadrons. There, the tank Squadrons would be provided with their own bar by the Squadron SQMS. It was a way of generating money for

Squadron funds, which was not say that all the money went there. A good SQMS would always make a little for himself and his staff. As GW did not have the luxury of having the SQMS with them on this occasion, they would have to entertain themselves for the duration.

They were joined, later in the evening, by a couple of Gurkha soldiers, who were also there on a course. These soldiers from Nepal, small in stature, had served the British Army since 1815. They had a fearsome reputation and were greatly respected. Although they could not speak much English, they joined in the conversation, as best they could. They did not drink as a rule but enjoyed the evening, nonetheless. As the bar was starting to clear, one of the lads suggested they take a trip into Bergen, to carry on their evening. Richard was in two minds but, with a little persuasion, he relented. Downing their remaining drinks, four of them, including two of the Gurkhas, headed off to the main guardroom, to call a taxi.

Richard, along with Isaac, Will and a bloke called Guy Richardson, jumped in the first taxi. They assumed that the Gurkhas would follow on and find them. Guy was a big unit, who hailed from Huddersfield. He stood out from the crowd because of the large scar that ran across his face. He had acquired this 'badge of honour' in a bar in the town where Richard had first joined the Regiment. A local Turkish man had thrust a glass in his face during a bar brawl. Guy was a humorous bloke, always on the lookout for women to chat up. The taxi pulled up outside the night club they had been told was the place to go. Before he knew it, Richard was on his own, as the other three exited the taxi, leaving him to pay the fare. Digging down into his pocket, he withdrew a twenty Deutsche Mark (DM) note and paid the driver. He received five DM in change and stuffed it into his pocket. He made his way into the establishment and found the other three, already at the bar, ordering the drinks.

'I'll get this round, seeing as you covered the taxi fare,' Guy said, grinning.

'I'll get the taxi back,' Isaac chipped in.

Richard knew that this not going to happen, as it was common for groups to split up, during the evening. Accepting the half litre glasses of beer, the four found an empty table. It was not long before they were joined by the two Gurkhas, dressed in blazers and ties. They stood out like sore thumbs, among the scantily clad young ladies and denim wearing off duty soldiers.

The bar was obviously popular with the local units, as nearly every customer was a squaddie. The locals did not appreciate it when soldiers took over the town bars and stole their women. It was not uncommon for owners to ban soldiers from using their establishments. On more than one occasion, soldiers had been refused entry to a pub or bar. That wasn't the case on this evening, as the staff were only too pleased to take their money. The local girls were quite taken with a man in uniform, as the bar had about 60 percent female clientele.

Guy was like a dog with two dicks, as he scanned the dance floor like a Cylon, the predatory robots from the TV series Battlestar Galactica. Finding a 'target' who took his fancy, he strode over to her and, before long, was engaged in deep conversation. It was not long before Isaac decided to make a play for her friend, who was standing awkwardly, nearby.

Richard and Will ignored the lovebirds, concentrating on their beers, which were going down too quickly. Richard knew he would not feel well in the morning. The next day, in a classroom, was not going to be fun, he thought.

The two Gurkhas were chatting between themselves at this point. Their gaze was drawn to the girls Guy and Isaac were chatting up. Hours flew by. The next time Richard glanced at his watch, it was 02:30. Leaning over to Will, he suggested it would be best if they left now. Will nodded in agreement and the pair began to search for Isaac and Guy. After a fruitless period, they decided the others must have gone off with the two girls. They exited the club and jumped into one of the taxis, lined up outside. As Richard had paid for the taxi on the way there, Will offered to reciprocate and paid the driver, when they arrived back at camp. It was winter and the two soldiers braced themselves against the cold wind that faced them, as they trudged from the guardroom. Climbing into bed, it took about half an hour before Richard warmed up enough to fall asleep.

It was 06:30 and Richard woke at the sound of people getting up. He had only had three and half hours' sleep and had a mouth like 'Ghandi's flip flop'. Sleepily, he grabbed his towel and wash kit and headed off to the ablutions. A quick shower, shave and a clean of the teeth, and he was feeling a little more human. As he left the washrooms and carried on down the corridor, he bumped into Guy and Isaac, who, from the looks of them, were just returning from their night out. Richard noticed that Isaac was holding his crotch and seemed to be in pain.

'Good night was it, fellas?' he asked them.

'Fuckin' scary, mate, those two birds wouldn't let us leave. We had to escape through a window in the cellar.' Guy seemed genuinely disturbed by the experience. Isaac just kept quiet and went on his way.

Everyone had made it to breakfast. They were now congregating in the lecture room of the training block, for their course briefing. The Instructors read through the course agenda and timetable. It all seemed pretty laid back and Richard thought that he would enjoy this course. The Troop broke for cups of coffee and fags, before making their way down to the hangars. They were accompanied by two of the Instructors, who would mentor them through the course. The course itself was only going to last a couple of days, ending with the Troop firing their missiles on the range, to qualify.

The first thing covered, once reaching the hangars, was how a missile was made up. It had a length of just over a metre and a diameter of seventeen cm. It weighed in at 27 kg, which included the seven kg High Explosive Anti-Tank (HEAT) warhead. Its minimum range was 150 m up to 4000 m, at a velocity of 185 metres per second. The guidance system was via manual command to line of sight (MCLOS). Or, to put it simply, the operator guided the weapon manually, via a toggle switch. The missile itself came equipped with a magnesium flare, which ignited upon launch. This enabled the operator to visually track the missile and make adjustments to its flight. The movement of the weapon was achieved by Thrust Vectored Control (TVC), and could penetrate up to 800 mm of armour. This little package came in at the bargain price of £7,500. So, every time a missile was fired, the cost was equivalent to launching a BMW 7 series down the range.

After 80 minutes of instruction, the crews were fell out for a coffee and smoke break. Isaac was still nursing his groin and didn't seem at all well. Feeling a little sorry for him, Richard ambled over to see what the problem was.

'You okay, buddy?' he asked his worried looking roommate.

His eyes welling up, Isaac forced a reply, 'Not really, pal, take a look at this!' With that, he gingerly opened the front of his coveralls. Reaching down into his boxer shorts, he withdrew his manhood. Catching sight of it, Richard recoiled in horror. The head was enlarged and bleeding, slightly. The cock looked like a small blood orange and obviously was causing a lot of discomfort.

'How the fuck did you manage that?' cried Richard, incredulously.

'Shagged that bird up the arse, last night. I fell asleep and my foreskin got stuck behind my bellend. It must have

50

cut off the circulation. Now, it's so swollen, I can't get it forward again!'

Trying not to laugh, Richard looked round and spotted a tub of Swarfega, used to clean oil from dirty hands.

'Why don't you use that to see if you can get your foreskin forward?' Richard pointed with his finger at the tin, in the corner of the hangar. Isaac was so desperate, by this stage, that he made a bee-line for the tin. Without hesitation, he prised off the lid, took a handful of the green slime and applied it to his throbbing tool. As soon as the substance touched his bleeding shaft, he almost hit the roof of the hangar. What the two had not taken into account was that the hand cleaner was largely alcohol based. This was not an ideal solution to be apply to raw skin.

It seemed like Isaac's eyes were going to pop out of his head, as he scurried around the hanger, with his todger in his hand. One of the quick thinking commanders grabbed a jerry can of water, from a vehicle, and started to pour it over Isaac's genitals. A wave of relief swept over him, as the throbbing began to ease. Stu wandered over and took a look at the situation. After his initial assessment, and between fits of laughter, he ordered Isaac to go to the medical centre, to get it sorted out. Sheepishly, Isaac put away his 'old fella' and headed off, out of the hangar.

The rest of the day was spent going through the vehicle equipment, both internal and external. They practised setting up the separated sight, which allowed the vehicle to remain hidden, either behind a hill or off to the side. The weapon could be controlled from this sight and controlled by way of a cable, connected to the vehicle. They also went through dummy runs, loading the launches and selecting the missiles. Satisfied that the crews had become proficient enough in the drills, the Instructors called it a day and dismissed them, to their accommodation.

The men left the hangar and chatted among themselves, as they headed back to the block. The topic of conversation was mostly about Isaac and his recent injury. It was a topic of great merriment, and more than one said they had never before seen anything so horrific. This, however, did not prevent them from taking the piss out of Isaac, as was the army way. They could not wait to do it to his face. Entering the room, however, he was nowhere to be found.

As they sorted out their own personal admin, some read their pamphlets, on the lessons they had gone through that day. Richard found this was the best way of learning, taking only 30 minutes, or so, to review the lessons. Happy that he had retained everything, he decided to take a shower, before the evening meal. Before he could leave the room, Stu appeared, at the doorway. He had a sardonic smile on his face and announced that Isaac had been taken to hospital, as he couldn't be sorted at the medical centre. He was to have an emergency circumcision and this caused the room to break into fits of laughter.

'He is going to live up to his nickname, then,' exclaimed one of the commanders, who had served with Isaac before.

Richard had always thought that Isaac was his mate's real name. He had to ask how he had come by the nickname. The commander revealed that Isaac had met a girl before joining the army. Her entire family was Jewish and very devout. 'Isaac' had omitted to tell her that he was a Gentile, called Simon. He had been very clever at covering up this fact, until one day, at the synagogue with her family, his secret was exposed. The Rabbi gave the Torah, the Jewish equivalent of the first five books of the Old Testament, to his girlfriend's father, to read a passage. As 'Isaac' had become accepted by her family, he was passed the book, respectfully, by the girl's father. Accepting it, and knowing that he would not be able to read the scripture, he shrugged his shoulders, and looked, mystified, at the expectant parent.

'Read it, my son,' urged his girlfriend's father.

Hearing 'Isaac's' admission that he could not read it, as he was not Jewish, caused the assembled congregation to gasp in disbelief. He was ordered out of the synagogue and never saw the girl again.

Of course, after he blurted out the story, in the Squadron bar after joining the Regiment, he was dubbed 'Isaac'. When given nicknames, real names become forgotten and so Simon henceforth became Isaac.

Someone else in the Troop recounted another story about Isaac, who had been a Chieftain driver, at the time, in D Squadron. The Squadron were travelling by 'Antar', large flatbed Tank Transporter vehicles, manned mostly by Polish drivers. They were given the nickname Mojos, although Richard had no idea what this stood for. On this particular occasion, Isaac had been travelling in the cab of the Antar with a Polish driver. He had consumed a couple of bottles of beer, all that he had. With almost three hours to go until they reached their destination, he decided he would retrieve another container of beer, called a 'yellow handbag' by the lads, from the driver's cab. The vehicle was travelling on the Autobahn, at a steady rate. Isaac left the cab and climbed back. Opening the padlock on the turret, he climbed inside and grabbed the beer. Back outside, he placed the carton on top of the turret. Locking the padlock, he stood up and collided with the bridge they were passing under. He was thrown straight on to the back decks and knocked unconscious. That escapade resulted in Isaac spending a number of weeks in hospital. He had been very lucky to escape serious injury or worse. The story would become legendary.

The course almost ended, the Troopers were mounted on their vehicles, at 04:00, on the Friday morning. They were to travel the short distance to the range, where they would carry out their conversion firing, to qualify as Swingfire Guided Weapon operators.

Richard was excited and nervous at the same time, knowing that he would be required to hit a target, up to 4000 metres away, with two of his three allocated missiles to qualify. As the cost of each missile had been explained to them, it would be a considerable waste of money and time, if he were to cock it up. He was not the only one pondering this, even the more experienced men, who had been in GW before, knew the unpredictable nature of the weapon system.

As they pulled on to the firing point, the TSM and Troop Leader lined the vehicles up. They dismounted and were given a range safety brief by the Artillery Instructors, who would be running the day. The safety brief completed, they were given the order of firing. Richard was to fire midway through the day. The first crews were told to mount up and sped off to their vehicles, to prepare themselves.

Richard was offered binoculars, which Stu had been using, to survey the range. He scanned from left to right. The range staff had placed a number of 'hard targets' in various places across the range. These 'hard targets' were tanks, Armoured personnel carriers (APCs) and the like, taken out of service. They were easier to observe when hit by the missiles, unlike some of the screen targets normally used for tank firing.

30 minutes had passed since the first crews had mounted their vehicles. The flag on the tower had been changed to red, denoting the range was live and that firing could commence. Suddenly, one of the vehicle commanders appeared in his hatch and exchanged his green flag for a red one. This indicated to the watching Troops that he had been given the order to go to action. Richard was going through the loading drills in his mind, imagining what was going on, inside the vehicle. The two launch bins would have been loaded with two missiles. On receipt of the fire order, the loader would throw up one of the launch

bins and select the bin by pushing a lever across. Once he had confirmed this to the commander, who would at this point be in the operator's seat, he would fire the missile.

All of a sudden, a deep orange and yellow glow appeared at the rear of the launch tube, which had been elevated, from inside. Then, the sound of the rocket motor could be heard, as it started its initialisation phase. Leaving the tube at its optimum launch angle, the controller or operator waited until it appeared in his circular reticule. From here, he 'gathered' the missile. Using his joystick thumb controller, he guided the missile, with delicate inputs. These were received through the wire, trailing behind the missile. The directional changes were achieved by thrusting jets, built into the missile. The weapon snaked across the range, hugging the features as it went. It seemed an age, until a bright flash erupted, in the distance. The missile had scored a direct hit on the hulk of a tank, at its extreme range of 4000 metres. A great cheer went up from the on-looking Troop. Richard felt a sense of relief. This had given him confidence for when his turn came.

The firing continued for the rest of the morning, with all the crews passing with their allotted missiles. Some did slightly better than others, achieving their pass with only two missiles, while others needed the full three. It was coming close to Richard's turn and, just as he was preparing to make his way to one of the vehicles, a shout came up from the tower. Richard did not hear exactly what it was, but, looking down range, it soon became apparent. A missile had left the launcher. Instead of following the flight path to target, it had turned back on itself. There was confusion as bodies ran this way and that, looking for some form of cover. The NAAFI wagon which had turned up on the range to serve tea and sandwiches, hastily shut its doors, started its engine and fled from the firing point.

There was a safety feature built into the missiles which meant they could be detonated remotely. This was done by one of the range staff conducting the firing, much to the relief of the panic-stricken onlookers. With the danger averted, Richard was given the go ahead to mount up. He had gone from being confident to somewhat apprehensive, in the space of a minute. As he climbed into the vehicle, he was joined by one of the experienced guys who had been in GW before. He would be loading for him and immediately put Richard at ease. They waited for the tower to give them the order to go to action, which was forthcoming after two minutes. They were given a target to engage and Richard gave the order to select the missile. The launcher bin was thrown up and confirmed as loaded. Richard took a deep breath, and yelled out:

'Firing now!'

The sound of the motor starting up was muffled inside the vehicle, but grew increasingly louder, as it launched from the tube. Staring through his sight, Richard waited for it to appear in the circular reticle. As it came into view, he depressed the switch to take command, or 'gather' the weapon. As the rocket motor entered its boost phase, he fought to keep it under control, on its way to the target. Suddenly, it disappeared from view and Richard thought it had gone into the ground. He instinctively gave an up demand on the joystick, as he took his head away from the sight.

'It's there! It's there!' came the cry from the driver, who was observing, through his periscope.

Placing his face back into the sight, Richard could indeed see the tell-tale 'flare' from the rear of the missile. Guiding it once again, it seemed like an age before the target lit up, in a flash of light. Richard had never felt so relieved, in all his life.

'Target!' he exclaimed into his microphone, while pressing the Pressel and informing the tower.

'Target stop!' the confirmation came back.

Richard turned to the loader, who was grinning at him and patting him on the back. It was not over yet, he needed to hit another target to qualify. This time, it was at a shorter range and the flight went without a hitch. In the space of twenty seconds, he had 'gathered' the weapon and flew it successfully on to the target.

After being given the order to dismount, the crew made their way back to the tower for debriefing. Reaching the bottom of the tower, one of the Artillery Instructors was waiting for them. He asked them how they thought it had gone. Richard explained that he thought he had lost the first one. Apparently, the Instructors knew nothing of this and said that the flight of the missile had looked perfect, from the tower. They thought that Richard had used the contours and features of the ground to guide the missile to target. They had thought it quite impressive, until he admitted he had lost sight of it. It made no difference, as a hit was a hit, no matter how it was achieved. He had qualified.

The afternoon was spent getting the remainder of the crews through their conversion. Once this had been done, a few were selected to fire from the separated sight, some 30 metres in front of the vehicle, off on an angle. This was highly impressive, as the missiles were guided from the sight, by a lone operator, in a trench. They only had time to fire six missiles and all were direct hits. By the end of the day, everyone in the Troop had passed and the Troop Leader congratulated them all on their efforts. The crews mounted up, their morale soaring as they drove their vehicles back to the railway siding, for the journey back to camp.

Chapter 7 – Squadron Boxing

Richard had been back in camp for six weeks and the tank park routine of servicing the vehicles, in preparation for exercise, was underway. This was to take a secondary role at the moment, as he had been chosen to represent the Squadron in the upcoming boxing competition. Although a yearly event, Richard had never volunteered, until now. His father, Tommy, had boxed for a local club in the North East of England and had always promoted the sport to his son. His father had left the Regiment the year before, so was no longer there to give him guidance.

It was 06:00 on a Monday morning and the newly formed Squadron boxing team paraded, outside the gym. There, they were met by Rob Newlands, or 'Gunny', as he was known. He was a short man, with a walrus moustache and not an inch of fat on him. His features proved that he had been engaged in quite a few contact sports. Although his face was angular and slightly handsome, the flattened nose gave away the truth to his past. Richard recalled his father telling him that he had never met a good boxer with a broken nose. Tommy's nose was still sharp and not spread across his face, which made Richard smile at his father's compliment to himself. He was to find that this little man, in front of them, was a formidable opponent, even for his advancing years.

'Right, guys, we are going to do a little warm up, before we start any training. We will begin with a steady six mile run. So, if you would like to fall in, in three ranks, and face that way,' he indicated, with his hand, the direction he wished them to turn. Once they were in position, he set them off in a steady jog, setting the pace himself. It took only half a mile for the group to get into a steady rhythm. Richard didn't like running per se but knew it was all part of the conditioning. The next four miles were done at a leisurely pace, until they could see the entrance to the camp, in the distance. Suddenly, Gunny halted the squad of potential boxers, letting them get their breath back, as he went on to explain what he wanted next.

'Right, what we are going to do, now, is a form of training called Fartlek. I want you to pair up. Starting from this lamp post,' he pointed to the side of the road, 'you will jog, in pairs, to the next one. From there, sprint to the next. You will repeat the drill, at every lamp post, until we reach the camp gates,' he grinned at the group, as they looked into the distance. It was a good half to three quarters of a mile to the entrance to the camp. Richard was already suffering, from the five miles they had just covered, and was not looking forward to this exercise.

The lads paired up and Gunny set them off at ten second intervals. The first two or three lamp posts were fairly easy going but, by the time they had reached the end, to a man, everyone's lungs were searing with pain. As the first pair reached the final lamp post, they were told to jog on the spot, until the last pair had finished. The squad, now back together, set off again, through the gates and headed towards the gym.

Reaching their destination, they were fallen out and directed to go inside. Entering the gym, they were met by various instruments of torture, laid out on the gymnasium floor. The scene took Richard back to his time in training and the many 'beasting' sessions he had been made to endure. A figure, dressed in tight-fitting, blue bottoms and a white vest with red trim, strode from the office, at the end of the hall. On his chest was a red badge with a crown and two crossed swords. This was the insignia of the 'Physical Training Corps', whose job it was to see that Regiments attained the fitness required for the British Army. He was a giant of a man, shaped like a wedge, with a small waist and broad shoulders. His arms were the shape of ordinary men's calf muscles. His biceps rippled and flexed, as he moved his arms. He had just been posted to the Regiment, so was an unknown quantity.

Introducing himself, he went on to explain the various exercises they be performing over the next 40 minutes. Satisfying himself that everyone was up to speed with the programme, he split them up, dispersing the equipment. Richard was paired with another guy around the same size. They had been given the medicine balls to use, as their first drill. They had to stand back to back and pass the medicine ball around their bodies to the other person, five times in one direction, then repeat, in the other. As the whistle blew, they were to change exercise stations, in a clockwise direction. The torture went on for half an hour, until, at last, the Physical Training Instructor (PTI) blew a long blast on his whistle. Just as they had been taught in training, the last ten minutes of the session was dedicated to warming down.

The first training session over, the team made its way to their accommodation. They showered, then faced a late breakfast, which had been laid on for them, one of the perks of participating in Regimental sports. As they scoffed the hot fare, they smiled, in the collective knowledge that they were being allowed time off from the tank park.

The rest of the morning was spent on the vehicles, preparing them for exercises. Richard worked with Stu, modifying the Ferret, to make life a little more bearable. It was a small vehicle, with limited storage space. Stu had called in a favour from one of the Royal Electrical & Mechanical Engineers (REME) welders. Stu had designed a basket which would cover the entire rear of the vehicle. It stood a foot high from the engine decks, allowing access to gauge levels that needed to be checked, such as engine oil level. The basket, itself, was big enough to contain all their personal equipment, as well as extra rations. It was covered with a tarpaulin, to ensure it would remain dry in the shitty weather that always came with being on exercise.

Stu, being a Signal Instructor, was particularly obsessed with making sure all the communications equipment was in full working order. This was one of the reasons that Richard had been chosen to drive the vehicle. As he was now a Control Signaller, he was fully qualified to perform this role.

The days passed and the boxing tournament was getting closer. Training had been increased and they were completing between four and five hours every day, improving fitness and skill. The morning runs got longer and faster. The gym sessions got more intense. The Instructor had also thrown in at least six rounds of sparring in every session, which took the form of three rounds of two minutes, then some work with light weights, followed by another three rounds. Gunny would, at times, spar with the boxers and one day completed nine rounds, before calling it a day. 'Not bad,' thought Richard, 'for a man in his mid-thirties.' He had sparred with Gunny the previous day and hadn't come close to putting a glove on him. By the end of the three rounds, Richard was worn out and could hardly lift his arms. Gunny praised him on his footwork, stance and general movement and stated that with a little more conditioning and training, Richard might prove to be a very good boxer. The words rang in Richard's ears, as his head hit the pillow that evening and he fell into a deep sleep, tired but contented.

The sun broke through the window in Richard's room. It was 04:30 and he was wide awake. Looking across, he saw Isaac, his quilt moving up and down in time with his breathing. He was obviously fast asleep, so Richard tried hard not to disturb him, as he crept out of the room. With his towel over his shoulder and washbag in hand, he walked into the ablutions.

As expected, he had the place to himself. He started the shower running, before undressing and placed his clothes on the bench. Stepping into the shower cubicle, the water cascaded over him, making him tingle. As he applied the shampoo to his hair, he began to think about how things might go that evening. He had trained hard over the last four weeks. Now, the day had arrived and the competition was only fourteen hours away.

As he cleansed his body, he became more awake with each motion of his hands. It was not fear that gripped him, but a heightened sense of excitement at the challenge to come. All he could do was to do his best. He remembered the old adage, 'It's not the winning, it's the taking part that counts'. 'What a load of bollocks,' he thought. Most soldiers were of a competitive nature, so his opponent that evening would be fighting to win and not just 'taking part'.

Richard turned the shower off and stepped out of the cubicle. Drying himself off, he returned to the room and opened the door, gently, so as not to disturb Isaac. Peeking round the door, he confirmed that Isaac was still fast asleep. He looked so innocent, not the colossal deviant that he was. A couple of weeks ago, the pair had been watching porn, on the sofa, which they had acquired from one of the married corporals. Richard was engrossed in the action that was going on before him. Out the corner of his eye, he caught a movement, and turned to investigate the cause. Isaac had his dick in one hand and a thin knitting needle in the other. He was poking the needle down the centre of his Jap's eye.

'What the fuck are you doing?' Richard exclaimed in total shock.

'Giving me pipe a bit of a clean,' Isaac replied, as if it was the most natural thing in the world to be doing. He had been with many prostitutes, indeed anyone who would let him bed them. The inevitable consequence was that he had contracted every sexually transmitted disease known to man. At this particular moment in time, gonorrhoea was 'flavour of the month'.

'Put it away, you dirty bastard,' Richard retorted, as he turned his eyes away, in disgust.

Isaac did as he was asked, shrugging, genuinely unaware that he was doing anything wrong. This was not the same person sleeping so peacefully in bed right now, Richard thought to himself.

He wandered over to the table in the corner, which was set up with a kettle, mugs and brew kit. He flicked the switch on the kettle, added a spoonful of coffee and sugar to a mug, then sat on his bed, waiting for the kettle to boil. The birds had begun to sing outside. It was a gorgeous morning, with bright, blue skies. Richard was not looking forward to the little jog, with his team mates, this morning. Gunny had said they would just do a couple of miles, then some light weights to finish off. Richard knew that it would entail some other form of pain thrown in, for good measure.

He was disturbed from his thoughts by the sound of the kettle switching itself off. As Richard rose to fill his mug, Isaac stirred, opened his eyes, then went back to sleep. He wouldn't be getting up for at least a couple more hours, Richard thought.

The training session was easier than Richard had imagined, consisting of a couple of miles jogging, a small cardio session and ending with light weights. He showered, straight afterwards, then consumed a full breakfast, with the rest of the squad. All the talk was about the competition that evening. They had been informed two days ago who they were going to fight. Richard's opponent was an ex Parachute Regiment bloke, who had transferred to the Regiment, four years earlier. He was a quiet, unassuming guy, not the normal characteristics of a Para. After digging into his past, Richard had learned that he had boxed before, whilst in the Paras. That knowledge dented Richard's confidence about the outcome of the bout. All he could do was carry out what he had been taught by Gunny, over the past weeks.

The remainder of the day was spent watching TV, reading and sleeping. The entire team had been given the time off work, to relax. This was a reward for the hard work they had put in over the last month and a bit. The question was, would all the early mornings, countless miles, hours of beasting and numerous sparring rounds, be enough to see each of them victorious? Realistically, he knew in his heart of hearts, that some of the team would come second best, that evening.

Looking across, at the clock above the TV, he saw that it was almost time for him to make his way down to the gym. Gunny had asked that they all meet at the same time, regardless of when they were fighting. He wanted to give them a last minute pep talk and ensure that no one had picked up any injuries, after the light training session that morning. Richard pulled on his Squadron tracksuit and trainers and headed off, out of the block.

When he arrived, the gym was already a hive of activity. The finishing touches were being made to the ring, the ropes were being tightened and the bunting arranged around the edge. Two men, in grey trousers and blazers, were examining the ring. These, Richard assumed, were the referees, called in from outside Units, to officiate.

Boxers from other Squadrons had also turned up for the weigh in. Gunny called the team together and got them to strip down to their shorts or underpants, ready for the scales. Richard was fighting in the lightweight division, so needed to be under 63.5 kg. He waited, nervously, for his turn to step on the highly calibrated machine. When he was called forward, he took a deep breath and stepped on to the scales. It seemed an eternity until the PTI carrying out the weigh in finished adjusting the scales. When he announced exactly 63 kg, a wave of relief rushed over Richard. He had made the weigh in 500 grams under the maximum weight. Gunny patted him on the back, as he stepped off the scales.

The processing of all the boxers lasted around an hour. They were then called together by the officials, who explained what was expected of the fighters, that evening. This completed, the men were dismissed to the dressing rooms, to prepare themselves. The first bout was to be a light flyweight contest, the first of six fights before Richard was due on. With nothing to do, he began to think about the fight. Then came the butterflies. At least Birgit would not be there to witness it, he mused. It was tradition that partners or wives were not allowed to attend these events. The tradition seemed out-dated, as females were allowed to watch civilian fights, both amateur and professional.

The noise of the crowd, starting to fill the seats in the gymnasium, grew louder, as the first fighters readied themselves, to do battle. Richard took a quick look through the door, at the Squadrons in their No 2 dress uniforms and the Officers and Senior Non Commissioned Officers, in their Mess dress.

He identified Stu and Ian McKelvie, who had situated themselves as close to the ring as they could. The rest of the Troop was seated not far from them and Isaac caught his eye, giving him a thumbs up. He smiled back, nervously, and acknowledged the gesture with a wave of his hand. The Regimental Sergeant Major (RSM), dressed in his full Mess dress, climbed into the ring. He took the microphone offered by the referee. In his most official voice, he welcomed the seated soldiers. He went on to explain the etiquette for the evening and how it would run. Once he had finished, he called the names of the first two fighters and the Squadrons they were representing.

A great cheer went up from the crowd, as the two slightly built young men made their way towards the ring. They were accompanied, on their journey, by the theme 'Eye of the Tiger', from the film Rocky. Richard thought this was corny, glad he did not have any say in the matter. The introductions over and rules explained by the referee, the bell sounded and the two fighters got down to it. Richard turned away, not wanting to witness the fight and tried to focus on what he needed to do.

The fights continued, some lasting less than the three rounds allotted. Headquarter Squadron were doing okay and had won two out of their three fights. Gunny called Richard over and started to wrap his hands, in bandages, before lacing up his gloves. Richard's fight was next and he spent the last couple of minutes warming up. Before long, the two fighters from the last bout entered the dressing room. The RSM gave a brief pause, for the noise to die down, before announcing Richard and his opponent, Martin Brown of A Squadron. He put his hands on Gunny's shoulders and was led from the dressing room, towards the ring. Having climbed into the ring, he walked to the centre and the waiting referee. Once Martin had joined him and the rules explained, the pair touched gloves and returned to their respective corners. The bell sounded for the first round and the boxers advanced, to face each other.

Richard's heart was racing with adrenalin, coursing through his body. For someone who had boxed before, Martin's guard did not seem adequate. Richard shot out two lightning quick left jabs and his adversary's head jolted backwards. Stepping to the side, to avoid the return that did not come, he followed it up with a further two jabs and a blow to the stomach. There was still no reply from his opponent. For the next two minutes, he danced round Martin, letting fly with a flurry of punches, from various angles. This was too easy, he thought to himself, having only been hit around three times in the full three minutes. The bell sounded for the end of the round and the fighters were directed to their corners.

Richard sat down on the stool which had been placed there for him. He was immediately dowsed with water and given a bottle to drink from. This he did and spat out most of the liquid into the bucket, next to the stool.

'Fuckin' outstanding, that, mate, you got this won. Just straight lefts and back off, don't do anything stupid,' came the words of advice from Gunny.

The bell sounded for round two and the fighters took up their positions, in the centre of the ring. For the next three minutes, Richard carried out the same routine as he had in the previous round. Martin's face had become puffy and he was bleeding from his nose. Although his chest was searing with pain, Richard's legs were still fresh. The sound of the bell for the end of the round was welcomed by both fighters. Richard took in huge gulps of air and tried to steady his breathing. Only another round, and it would all be over. Gunny gave him exactly the same pep talk as before, which was that he should just jab and move, and the victory would be his.

Approaching the centre of the ring after the bell, the fighters touched gloves, taking up their stances. Richard threw a powerful combination of punches into Martin's face. His opponent was looking almost spent. In the distance, Richard heard a cry go up.

'Good lad, Hunter! You've got this in the bag!'

Richard knew the voice and recognised that it belonged to his Troop Leader, Ian. Turning to his right, he raised his arm, in acknowledgement. That was the last thing he remembered, as the canvas came up to meet him. Hearing the referee's count, Richard heard the number four. By the time he struggled to his feet, the count was at seven. He rubbed his gloves on his vest, to show that he was okay to continue. Looking at the referee, he was disappointed to see him waving his arms, to indicate to the crowd that the fight was over. In the referee's opinion, Richard had not recovered from the stray haymaker, which had connected with his chin, while he was acknowledging the adulation of the crowd. Still a little dazed and not believing what had just happened, he walked across to his corner, where Gunny stood, open mouthed.

'You fuckin' prat!' were the words of 'sympathy' Richard received, from his trainer, who unlaced his gloves for him and told him to join the referee. Back in the centre of the ring, the official declared Martin the winner and raised his arm. The boxers embraced and congratulated each other on a good fight.

The rest of the night was over an hour later. The highlight of the evening had been a bout between two men, one from B Squadron, one from HQ. Although they were both in the heavyweight division, there was a notable difference in size between them. The HQ fighter hailed from York and was an Assistant PTI. His arms were massive and he had a chest to match. His opponent, who came from Halifax, was a more typical, wiry Yorkshireman. Everyone in the hall expected it to be a bloodbath and to be over in the first round. Although Richard had not seen the fight, it was one that would last in the memory of all that witnessed it, for the rest of their lives. The pair of protagonists had gone toe to toe, for the full nine minutes. At one point, the B Squadron man, Tim Greenfield, suffered an assault of blows from the much larger HQ guy. Just as the crowd thought he was going to go down, Greenfield rallied and continued the fight. The result was a unanimous decision. The smaller man had won the contest. This was greeted by a standing ovation for both boxers, by the whole Regiment.

The after party, which was held in one of the Squadron bars, lasted way on into the early hours. Richard spent a lot of the evening in conversation with Martin, who he had fought and lost to. Richard knew he had to take a lot of abuse. If he hadn't been 'showboating', he would almost certainly have won. He did not need them to tell him that. His aching jaw was a constant reminder.

Chapter 8 – Engagement

Richard's jaw ached for around a week after the boxing competition. Now, some four months later, Birgit told him that she didn't want him to box again, as it was a mug's game. He could end up either punch drunk or seriously damaged. He submitted to her will and swore he would not box again. During the last few weeks, Richard had completed a demolitions course and the Troop had completed their first Troop exercise.

On the way back to barracks, after that exercise, they drove past Her Royal Highness (HRH) the Duchess of Kent, who took the salute. The Duchess was visiting the Regiment, as a highlight of the celebration of their tercentenary or 300 years anniversary of their founding. This was an important time for the Regiment and former members had made the journey over, from the UK, to take part in the festivities. Richard considered this the ideal time to become engaged to Birgit, as he knew his parents, brother and sister would be attending the parade that weekend.

He had arranged a few days off, prior to the parade on the Saturday. This was to celebrate his engagement, and so that his family could meet Birgit's family. His family arrived on Wednesday morning, after a long bus journey, from the north east of England. Richard's brother, Melvin, had brought his best friend, 'Knocker', along. Barbara, his sister, had her boyfriend, Steve, in tow. As soon as the introductions had been made, Melvin and Knocker wanted to know where the nearest pub was. Melvin had told his friend about the pubs in Germany and Knocker couldn't wait to sample them for himself. Once they had freshened up, Birgit, Richard, Melvin and Knocker headed out to a local pub.

The smell of the hops, mixed in with the smoke from cigarettes, hit Richard's nostrils, as soon as they walked through the door. Birgit greeted the young girl behind the bar and ordered a round of beers. While she did this, Richard found a table in the corner of the bar, which was small but cosy. There were only a couple of locals in at that time of day, sitting at the bar. They turned to see who was speaking English. Although Birgit's home town was near a British Garrison, soldiers did not normally frequent bars in this little German town. This was probably a good thing, Richard thought, as any drunken exploits or trouble would spoil the hard- earned reputation of the British Army. Some, but not all, squaddies would go on a night out, purely to let off steam. This, almost invariably, ended in a fight with locals or, among themselves. As the three young men settled down, they were joined bit later, by Birgit, with a tray of beers.

'What took ya?' Knocker asked.

'A good German beer takes time to pour but you will discover that it is worth the wait,' Birgit replied. With that, she placed a beer mat in front of each of them and dished out the drinks. Taking a big gulp, Knocker's eyes widened, in astonishment.

'Fucking hell, that's good!' he beamed, in genuine surprise.

They sat and chatted, taking draughts of beer, as they talked. Birgit called over to the barmaid, who, in no time at all, appeared with another tray of shot glasses, each filled with a clear liquid. This, Birgit explained to Melvin and Knocker was called *Wacholder*, a gin flavoured schnapps. The other three drunk it many times before, but it was new to Knocker, who was told he had to down it in one. They clinked their glasses together and emptied them in a single swallow.

'That is strong shit!' Knocker screamed, as he licked his lips. 'We getting another round? How do you order four beers and four more of those things?' he asked Birgit. Speaking the words slowly, she got him to repeat the phrase back, before he headed off, to the bar. Knocker returned, moments later, with a puzzled look on his face.

'Think I've ordered them. The Doris behind the bar said some shit in German and pointed at the table,' he spoke, loudly. He was a very outgoing character and had caught the attention of the locals at the bar. The German people were mostly quite reserved and it was alien to them to see people to act like this.

In no time at all, they received their second round of drinks. As the barmaid placed them down, she put a mark on each beer mat, with her pen. Richard guessed that Knocker did not know what this was all about.

'You don't pay for your drinks until you leave. Each mark means a beer or a schnapps. When you've finished, they count the marks and you pay the bill. Knocker thought this was great and ordered another round. They stayed in the pub for another two hours, before returning home, where Melvin and Knocker hit the sack, for some much needed sleep.

The following morning, the whole family had breakfast together. It was a typical German one, consisting of fresh bread rolls, preserves, cold meats and cheese. This was a cultural awakening for Knocker, who had never before left the small town in the North East where he had been born and raised. Breakfast over, they were interrupted by the sound of the doorbell. Birgit's father got up to answer it. He returned and said something to Birgit and Richard. They translated that the truck had arrived with the Marquee for the evening's *Polterabend*, the German equivalent of a Hen or Stag party. However, here, it was attended by both sexes.

Everyone filed outside, to help with the unloading of the Marquee, which came complete with a wooden floor. By this time, they had been joined by some of Birgit's brother's friends and a couple of her cousins. It took the party around two hours to complete the erection of the Marquee, which was topped off with the setting up of a proper bar, with beer pumps and glass washing facilities. The Brits had never seen anything like it. During the putting together of the Marquee, Richard and a couple of other guys nipped away, to collect barrels of beer, from a drinks' wholesaler, at the end of the street. Once the first barrel was installed in the bar, everyone was poured a glass to toast Birgit and Richard. A second drink followed as a 'well done' in completing the preparations so quickly.

A skip arrived, half an hour later, and was dropped off on the drive, next to the house. Richard told his parents and family, that it was for the broken glass or pottery. They had no idea what he was on about, so he told them the reason for the skip. Friends would turn up to be greeted by the pair and given a drink as a welcome. The guests would bring with them glass bottles and smash them on the driveway, when empty. Some more kind-hearted guests would throw the redundant bottles in the skip. This was where the name Polterabend, came from; the German verb *poltern* (making a lot of noise) and this was much like the tradition at Greek weddings of smashing plates. All the glass would then have to be cleared up by the newly engaged couple.

The revelry went on, until early morning. Almost all the barrels of beer were empty, as were the bottles of wine and spirits that Richard and Birgit had collected over the past six months. The clear up operation took longer to perform than the erection of the Marquee, which, probably, had something to do with the fragility of the party goers, who were nursing hangovers.

Over the weekend, the Regiment paraded in front of HRH the Duchess of Kent, and was presented a new standard on the occasion of its 300 year anniversary. No one knew at the time, but only seven years later, the Regiment would be consigned to history.

The party after the ceremony lasted the whole weekend.
By the end of it, Richard was worn out and not looking
forward to leaving for exercise, the following week.

Chapter 9 – GW Exercise

Monday morning saw the Troop welcome their new Troop Leader. Ian McKelvie had been given the job of Quartermaster Technical and had been replaced by a face familiar to Richard. He was another 'Mac', and his face and name struck a chord. His mind returned to the Maze Prison in Northern Ireland, one year earlier. He remembered meeting a then long-haired Kevin Webster, who introduced him, briefly, to the similar looking man he was with. Now, he stood before them, introducing himself, in a broad Northern Irish accent, as Larry McKinley. Richard wondered why he was back in the Regiment, away from his life of undercover operations, in the Province. The reason behind it would emerge later, but in the meantime, he would be running the Troop. He had a relaxed air about him and was immediately accepted by the men. Some of the more experienced members had served with him before and knew his background. One was Stu, who had been good friends with Larry, for many years.

Richard had been taken off the Ferret and had been given a place, as a second controller, on one of the AFV438 Swingfire vehicles. His new crew consisted of a Corporal, called Paul and a driver, named Roger Warden. Paul was a big man, but quiet with it, nothing seemed to bother him. Roger, on the other hand, was full of the joys of spring and always laughing. He had served as Richard's father's Clerk, when Tommy was A Squadron SSM. He came from Settle in Yorkshire, but had married a girl from Middlesbrough. His long, thick, black moustache gave him the appearance of Freddie Mercury, from the band Queen. Roger took advantage of this, at fancy dress parties, donning a bright, yellow leotard and wig. The three, immediately, got on like a house on fire and Richard was looking forward to the upcoming exercise.

The long train journey behind them, the vehicles were unloaded from the railway flats, at the now all too familiar *Reinsehlen Camp*. As soon as the chains, chocks and wedges had been returned, the vehicles lined up, ready to move onto the area. The Troop Leader gave the order to set off and the Troop transited around the camp. towards the wash-down area. Passing the wash-down on their left, they headed under the viaduct and began the ascent onto the area.

Before long they were heading east over the tank bridge, towards finger and strip wood. These features were the culminating sight of nearly every exercise on the Soltau Luneburger Training area. Continuing east, passed Strip and Finger Wood, they swung south, in the direction of Bivouac 4, or 'Bivvy 4', as it was known to all. This was the first area in which Richard had stayed, on his first exercise in the Regiment.

The ride there had been really smooth; Roger was obviously a very good driver. Although Richard felt a little motion sickness, it was not as bad as when he had been a gunner, on a Chieftain tank. Pulling into the hide, under the direction of Stu, the TSM, they immediately went into their hide drills. Crews were busy, covering their tracks into the wood and starting to put up their camouflage nets (cam nets). Richard recalled his last visit there, when he had been accused of sleeping on duty and being terrified of the legendary 'drop bears'. Richard had learned that it was all a wind up, that drop bears didn't exist. It was a joke played on all newcomers to a Squadron or Troop. Had it really been nearly five years since then, he mused. He looked around the hide and observed how slick the drills were from the Troop. No one needed to be told what to do, they were all seasoned professionals.

The hide drills complete, the guys were called together, for a brief by Larry. He set out what he expected to cover, over the coming week. It was the same format as every year, low level Troop tactics and drills. This would culminate in a Regimental exercise at the end, to put everything into practice. The usual questions and answers were dispensed with, everyone was fallen out, to chill for the evening. Of course, they would need to maintain a radio watch and have a ground sentry posted, but that was normal.

The first thing Richard did was to retrieve a shovel, from one of the stowage bins. He grabbed a roll of toilet paper from inside the vehicle and trudged off, into the now failing light. He had some perverted gratification about taking a shit outdoors. Maybe it was the freedom of his arse being exposed to the elements that gave him a kick. Whatever the reason, he began to search for a tree he could utilise. He had developed a preference for finding a fallen down tree and using it as a seat. This was much easier than squatting, trying to hold his coveralls away from the falling faeces. This was especially useful at night, when the crapper couldn't see what he was doing. As luck would have it, he found a tree that had recently blown down. It was at the perfect height for him, he dropped his coveralls and adopted the necessary position. Sitting there, waiting to evacuate his bowels, he listened to the sounds of the nocturnal woodland creatures, which had begun to emerge, for the evening. The last time he had been in this location, he had had a run in with a wild boar mother, defending her piglets. So, for the next five minutes, while he waited for nature to take its course, he constantly peered into the darkness, for any enraged wildlife. His business completed, he cleaned himself up, not an easy task in the darkness and made his way back, to the vehicle.

Paul informed him that Stu had been round, with the stag list. All the commanders and operators/2nd Controllers were to provide the radio stags. The drivers, of whom there were twelve, including the attached REME section, would be carrying out a roving sentry duty. Richard found that as

76

a soldier progressed in his career, he was afforded certain perks. One of these was to be assigned radio watch, rather than a sentry stag in a trench or wandering round the hide. It was not much of an issue in the summer, but in the winter that could be a godsend. He would spend his allotted hour reading one of the books he had brought with him and drinking brews. Roger had opened a crate of beer, from one of the orange containers they had stowed in the vehicle. As Richard put away the shovel, he was asked if he wanted one.

'Does a bear shit in the woods?' he replied, using the familiar phrase, which meant of course he fucking did. For the next couple of hours, the three of them chewed the fat, recalling past exercises and re-telling funny anecdotes from times gone by. This was a usual pastime. Richard wondered if somewhere, someone was recalling a story involving him and the many jokes that had been played on him in the past. He knew, in his heart, that, at some point in his career, he would be doing exactly the same thing, to another unsuspecting new member of the Squadron. The stories told and the night drawing in, the three decided to turn in for the night. As it was summer the temperature was still quite warm, so Richard lay on top of his sleeping bag. Due to the beers he had consumed, it was only a matter of minutes until he fell into a deep sleep.

It seemed like his eyes had been closed for only a short while, when he felt his shoulder being shaken, by a hand, in the morning light. The all too familiar words, 'You're on stag, mate,' caused him to glance at his watch, confirming it was 04:55, five minutes before his radio watch began. He hastily put on his boots, not bothering to lace them up. Trying not to disturb Paul and Roger, who had already completed their shifts, he opened the side of the tent and climbed inside the rear of the vehicle. Checking the folder next to the two Clansman VRC 353 radios, he confirmed the correct frequencies were set and started them up. Once he ensured everything was in order, he carried out a radio check with Battlegroup HQ, call sign 'zero'. When HQ replied, he settled down, to read his book. As this was the last radio watch of the night, Richard would not get a chance to go back to bed, as the rest of the Troop would be getting up in an hour's time. The last ground sentry would be going round, lighting the cookers, which had been placed next to each vehicle. Before he knew it, the door to the vehicle opened and he was bid good morning by Paul, who was rubbing his eyes, in an attempt to wake himself up.

'You made a brew?' he asked Richard.

'Not yet, mate, but I heard the ground stag light the cooker, around ten minutes ago, so the water should be boiled. I have put the brew stuff in the cups, just needs the water pouring in.'

'You fuckin' slacker,' Paul remarked, humorously, turning to fill up the mugs.

By this time, Roger had emerged from the tent and had the frying pan on the go. He had taken out the sausages from their tin, which had been sitting in boiling water. He pushed them out of their container and split them up, into the frying pan. The sound of sizzling and the smell from the cookers filled the wood. In the space of fifteen minutes, breakfast was served and the three of them were tucking in. The 'dixie', or water container, had been filled again and was starting to boil. They would use this water for a wash and to do the washing up. Breakfast finished, the washing up was done and the crew shaved and cleaned themselves. They began to take down the cam nets, in preparation for the training day ahead. Other vehicles were doing the same and by 07:30 the Troop mounted and was ready to move out.

Communications checks were given by Larry. As soon as he was happy, he gave the order for the Troop to move to the areas they had been given, the previous evening.

They were to work as sections, two vehicles working together. He had asked that they spend the morning, using their on board training simulators, to practise engaging targets, at various distances. As there were tanks on the area from two of the Regiment's Squadrons, they would target these as enemy vehicles.

Richard's tank moved smoothly, over the undulating terrain, driven expertly by Roger. The area they would be working in was only a short distance away, so Richard did not have time to feel motion sick. Being driven, rather than driving was something Richard could put up with. He had only driven a Chieftain tank once. He was so bad, that his commander at the time, swapped him over, halfway through the exercise. He had not fared much better, when he had driven Stu in the Ferret Scout Car, on the last trip to Soltau. He had managed to get them stuck in a muddy track, almost tipping the top heavy vehicle over. Stu had managed to jump from the commander's station, as the vehicle reached an angle of 45 degrees. Fortunately, it stopped at that point, but they had to get REME out, to pull the Ferret back to level ground. Although it was fun to drive on the roads and on flat terrain, the Ferret was notorious for injuring inexperienced drivers. The steering wheels were not to be grasped in the manner of a private car. If the wheels encountered a rut, they were prone to cause the steering wheel to turn violently. Any driver unlucky enough to have his hands placed in the wrong position on the steering wheel would have his thumbs jarred or, even worse, dislocated. So, to be chauffeured around the training area was a delight.

Before long, the two vehicle section had taken up their firing positions, just below the crest of a hill. The Battlegroup Commander would site the vehicles, forward of the main force. Due to their extended firing range, they were able to take out high priority targets, which was their primary role. They, like their counterparts in

Reconnaissance Troop (Recce), were highly trained in vehicle recognition. The ability to knock out command vehicles was a great tactical advantage, causing confusion within the enemy's ranks. These types of vehicle were usually identified by several characteristics, including having more than the usual two antennae. They not only took out these types of vehicle but also heavy armour. It was a waste of the fourteen missiles they carried to engage a target which could be destroyed by lower calibre, less expensive armaments.

As soon as they were in position, Paul took up his seat, behind the sight of the Swingfire system. He scanned the ground in front of them, until he identified a small force of Chieftain Tanks, advancing across the open ground. Giving the order to Richard to select the missile, he began to ready himself to engage, using the on board simulator. Richard went through the drills of loading a missile, took hold of the launch bin and threw it up, into the launch position.

'Loaded!' he screamed out to Paul, who immediately pressed the firing button. Even though there was no missile to launch, the simulator emitted a green flare, in the optical sight. As soon as it came into Paul's peripheral vision, he 'gathered' the weapon, by pressing a button. He had already put a range into the simulator, which would give the flight time. Using the toggle switch, he expertly guided the green dot towards his target and after around fifteen seconds, the simulator confirmed that he had hit it. The other vehicle crews were carrying out the same drills, across the frontage of their given area. This continued all morning, until the Troop Leader was satisfied and pulled the Troop back to the hide, for a debrief.

'That seemed to go well,' he confirmed to them, in his deep Northern Irish accent. 'Grab yourselves a brew and something to eat. We will continue in an hour's time, going through separated sight drills and engagements.'

With those parting words, the crews returned to their vehicles, to brew up and grab themselves a quick sandwich. Roger immediately started the engine and Richard switched on the 'Boiling Vessel' (BV). This was the crew's kettle and was continuously in use so, in no time at all, the water was hot enough for them to make a brew. Paul had already made the sandwiches from the contents of a tin of bacon grill he had taken from one of the stowage bins. They spent the next hour chatting about previous exercises and funny incidents that had happened. Paul called to mind an exercise, when he was in a tank Squadron.

Ken Davison, another commander in the Troop, was commanding a Chieftain, on a prairie in Canada. He had been sitting in the cupola, studying his map, when, suddenly, he was disturbed by a tap on his helmet. Looking up, he saw a face and the red collar patches of the British Army Training Unit Suffield (BATUS) Commander. Noticing the name tape, above Ken's left breast pocket, the BATUS Commander asked.

'Well, Corporal Davison, do you know where you are?' The Officer was met by a quizzical look. Ken was renowned for having a dry sense of humour. After studying his map for a moment, he replied, matter-of-factly.

'Canada!' Ken answered, a wry smile breaking across his face. The BATUS Commander's face turned crimson. He dismounted the vehicle and returned to his Land Rover, parked next to the tank. With its engine roaring, it sped off, into the distance. Ken shrugged and carried on with the exercise. It was not until later, he was called before the Commanding Officer and received the biggest bollocking of his life. Richard and Roger fell about, in fits of laughter, knowing that was the sort of thing Ken would do. He was always coming out with some sarcastic or dry comment.

The break over, the crews mounted up and made their way to the same area where they had been operating that morning. This time, instead of crawling to the crest, they remained in the 'dead ground', behind the hill. Dismounting, the crews removed the separated sight from the rear bin of the vehicle. This was accompanied by a tripod base, on which the sight would rest, giving it the ability to be turned in 'azimuth' *(a horizontal angle measured clockwise from a north base line or meridian.)*. Moving over the crest of the hill, Roger began to dig a trench, deep enough for a man to sit in. He was soon helped by Paul and Richard, who had carried the sight and base to the location, on the forward slope of the hill. It took the three of them around 45 minutes to dig the trench and mount the sight.

They ran the control armoured black cable over the crest and plugged it into the rear of the vehicle. This enabled the sight to connect to the vehicle firing control system. Once everything was ready, Paul asked Richard to man the sight. Both he and Roger returned to the vehicle and ran out some thin cable called 'D10' and a remote handset, so that Richard had communications with the vehicle. When they had checked that 'comms' were working, Richard began to scan the area, to his front. It wasn't long before three tanks came rumbling out the wood line, about 3000 metres ahead. He immediately gave the order for Paul to select a missile.

There followed the unmistakeable sound of the clunk, as the launcher bin was locked into its upright position. The word 'Loaded!' rang in Richard's ears. He selected a target to track, going through the drills, as if engaging for real. However, the separated sight did not have the simulation capabilities as the one mounted to the vehicle had. He imagined himself gathering the missile and flying it to target. After around twenty seconds, he reported to Paul that he had destroyed the target and that Paul should select the alternative missile. This Paul did, reporting once again that it was loaded. Richard tracked the second vehicle, as before, and, counting slowly, allowed a little less time, as the vehicles had closed the range. For the second time, he reported back that the target had been destroyed.

The crews were then ordered to pack up their equipment and move to another location. For the rest of the day, they dismounted the site, dug a trench and went through drills, as practised before. It was tiring, as the site itself was not light and digging was harder each time, as their energy levels began to deplete.

As the sun went down, the Troop were ordered back to the hide. As they were only semi-tactical, they enjoyed a few beers together and the inevitable stories were banded about.

One of the more recent ones was from the last exercise. One of the launchers had pulled into a firing position. The crew had gone to action. At this particular time the Battlegroup Commander had been observing the drills, approximately 200 metres away. As the launch bin was thrown up, the flap that opened at the rear, opened up. This revealed the DayGlo orange container, stowed inside. As this was a training exercise and there were no live missiles loaded, it could mean only one thing. The alien container was nothing less than a 'yellow handbag', the squaddies' term for a crate of Herforder beer. As the exercise was supposed to have been dry at that point, the commander was summoned to the CO and given a 'gypsy's warning'. The stories continued late into the night, with the fire growing ever larger. The beer in the crates dwindled, until, one by one, wearied souls drifted off to bed and another 'smoker' was over.

The following week was taken up with yet more Troop drills, until the start of the final exercise. Guided Weapons had been tasked to take up a position, forward of the Battlegroup and engage any enemy to their fronts. With the aid of Recce Troop to report enemy makeup and strengths to Battlegroup Command. The Troop Leader had already done a map appreciation of the area the CO had chosen. He sent Stu off in the Ferret to do a recce, to ascertain if it was suitable.

Stu reported back that the area was good and commanded an excellent field of view. The Troop waited for 'H' hour and at the allotted time, pulled out of the woods. It took them around an hour to reach the position they had been given. They parked at the rear of the wood, on the eastern side, so as not to be observed by the enemy, who would be advancing from the west. The Commanders dismounted and made their way, on foot, to the edge of the wood. Here, they would choose a position for their vehicles and assess where they would position their separated sights. This would allow them to keep their vehicles back in the woods, avoiding detection, from any reconnaissance force sent forward to probe.

Paul's recce complete, he returned half an hour later, as light was starting to break. Signalling to Roger to follow him, he retraced his steps into the woods and halted the vehicle, some 75 metres back from the treeline. Instinctively, once in position, Roger cut his engine. Richard flew open the door at the rear of the vehicle, grabbed a shovel and made his way forward, to the edge of the wood, where he joined Paul. Whispering to Roger and Paul, Richard indicated where the site trench was to be dug. Taking their shovels, the three began the laborious task of digging the trench. The ground was quite soft and the digging was quite easy. They had, over the past week, honed their skills in excavation and had took a pride in their labours. It had become a competition, within the Troop, as to who could build the best site.

For the next three hours, the crew dug down around six feet. As they were going to be there for some considerable time, they tried to make it as comfortable as possible. They shaped a seat at the rear of the trench, so that when they were on 'stag', their feet would not have to touch the earth, preventing the cold seeping into their boots. After placing the separated sight, with the head slightly protruding above ground, they covered the top, with a poncho. Disguising the top with foliage, they stepped to the front of the wood line, to admire their work. Satisfied with a job well done, Paul drew up a rota, for manning the trench. Roger took the first hour. Paul and Richard returned to the vehicle, to make a late breakfast. When it was ready, Richard returned to the trench, climbing down from the rear, armed with a mug of tea and a plate full of breakfast, which he handed it to Roger, who received it, gratefully.

The rest of the day was spent taking turns in the trench, observing the ground, to their front. It was a laborious job and they had to concentrate, to prevent their minds wandering.

Richard heard a noise behind him. He looked at his watch, confirming it was not yet time to change stag. He was joined by Larry, the Troop Leader, who greeted him, in his usual friendly manner. Larry was going round the Troops, making sure they were okay. He was vastly experienced in this sort of work, having carried out many covert operations in Northern Ireland. He knew what it was like to be sitting in a bush or ditch for hours, sometimes days, on end. Thus, he could relate to the job his Troops were now undertaking. As he left to check on the rest of the Troop, Richard was reminded of the type of Leader Larry was.

One morning, on first parade, one of the blokes was found to be absent. Larry asked if anyone knew where the missing man was. A couple of the guys said they had seen him leave a bar the previous evening, with a German girl.

'If you see him, tell him to pop to my house, for a chat,' he informed the assembled Troops.

The men confirmed they would. Two days passed without any sign of the missing Trooper. Then, on the third day, Richard and a couple of others, in a bar, came across the absconder. Asking why he had gone missing, he told them he had woken up, next to the girl, the following morning. He had looked at the clock and had seen that it was 09:30 and he was already late for first parade. His mind, still in an alcohol induced state, did not allow him to think things through. He decided he would continue his drinking session for as long as he could. He would face the consequences when his money ran out and he would have to return.

Richard related to him what Larry had said and convinced him to go back. Larry had not posted him 'Absent without Leave' (AWOL), as he should have done. Hearing this, the embarrassed Trooper went to Larry's married quarter. He was met at the door by Larry's wife, who brought him through to Larry, sitting in the living room. After learning what had happened, Larry asked that he be back on parade, first thing in the morning. If he did not show up, then he would be posted as AWOL. Not believing his luck, the guy did as he was told, turned up the next day and nothing more was said or done. This elevated the respect Larry already had from the guys. They would do anything for him.

Richard was again disturbed by a noise, this time it was Paul, relieving him. After reporting that his arcs of observation were quiet, he handed over and set off back, to get his head down.

The day dragged on until last light, the crews each taking their turns, in the trenches. A replen had been arranged for that night. However, due to the location of the vehicles, the SQMS had to park at the rear of the wood. This meant that the Troop needed to carry all fuel, water and rations from there, some 500 metres into the woods. This took several trips and, by the end of it, they were all dripping in sweat. The hide drills and observations continued through the night. It was not until the sun rose the following morning, that one of the call signs broke radio silence to say they had vehicle movement, to their front. It was a reconnaissance screen, probing forward, trying to detect any enemy positions. The Troop had been given express orders not to engage any recce. They complied with this, thus ensuring the recce passed them and, not observing any vehicles, reported back to the main force that they were safe to advance. Richard, who was manning the trench, was now at a high state of alertness. Slowly scanning his sight, he saw the turrets of four main battle tanks rising, just above a crest, 3000 metres in front of their position. Hitting the presell switch, which rested on the centre of his chest, he gave the call.

'Contact tanks…wait out!'

The air became alive with other crews reporting the same or other vehicles, in relation their own positions. Over the next two hours, a constant barrage of contact reports and situation reports were sent back to Battlegroup HQ.

After Guided Weapons had depleted most of their fictitious ammunition, that they were withdrawn from the engagement.. The remainder of the Battlegroup, after having formed a quick attack plan, launched a deliberate attack. The outcome was that the enemy advance was stopped and the Battlegroup was victorious. Although this was always the ending to this type of scenario, it was commented on later by the Commanding Officer that a lot of the success was down to the good work of GW Troop. This gave a great deal of satisfaction to all involved and Richard wore a huge grin, on the journey back to camp. This was to be his final exercise, as he had been chosen to go to Recce Troop after GW was disbanded, later that year. After such a successful two years for the Troop, he simply didn't understand who had made the decision to do away with it, or why.

Chapter 10 – Leadership Cadre
Introduction

Before joining Recce Troop, Richard had been told that he was to complete a Junior Non Commissioned Officer (JNCO) leadership cadre. This was a course, run to identify who, of the aspiring troopers, actually had the abilities to move up the promotion ladder. The aim of the cadre was to develop leadership, command and management, in all conditions: to enable the young, future NCOs to be role models for their subordinates and contribute to a team ethos and overall operational effectiveness. In the British Army, leadership is visionary. The cadre was set up to enable the young soldiers to project their personalities and character. The position of command and authority was one facet of the British Army which was taken very seriously.

Richard was aware that anyone may be appointed into a position of authority but that person would not be regarded as a leader until accepted as such by his subordinates. Management is a multi-level skill, which can include the control of resources, both human and material, to achieve a common goal. Successful military leaders are those who understand not only themselves and their organisation but also the environment in which they are operating.

The final factor was understanding the people they were appointed to lead. There is no prescribed style of leader in the Army. They take many forms from the autocratic, to the democratic. They would lead by example and, hopefully, persuasion, dependant on the given situation.

All this went through Richard's head, as he assembled, with the other candidates, on the drill square, on a bitterly cold winter morning. He had been taught these principles during his time in training, at the 'Junior Leaders Regiment' in Bovington, Dorset. Now, five years on, the same principles would be reinforced.

There were sixteen of them, all wearing barrack dress; dark green trousers, khaki shirt and tie, with a green, woollen pullover, the dress they had been told to parade in. In front of them stood an Officer, wearing full service dress, with blue forage cap. The cap was adorned with a badge and, in the bright winter's sun, the star of St Patrick glinted. The Officer was accompanied by a Sergeant, on his left and four Junior Non Commissioned Officers, all full Corporals (Full Screws), on his right. The Sergeant carried a pace stick and reminded Richard of his Drill Sergeant, in training. However, this individual was not as tall, probably reaching five feet six. He was, nonetheless, immaculate and intimidating. The Officer took a pace forward to address the waiting soldiers.

'For those of you who don't know me, I am Captain Hamlin. I will be your Cadre Officer, for the duration of this course. To my left is Sergeant Green, who will be your drill instructor. We also have four Corporals, who will be your syndicate leaders.'

He then went on to introduce each one individually. Over the next ten minutes, he outlined the course and the principles of leadership and what was expected of the candidates. Richard had seen the Officer before, although he had never served with him and knew that he came from an aristocratic background, a Count, or something along those lines. This was not unusual in Cavalry Regiments, which had their fair share of 'Blue Bloods'. There was an arrogance about him. He seemed to sneer at each and every one of them. It seemed to Richard that Hamlin thought that ordinary soldiers were beneath him. This was just a façade. By the end of the course, Richard would develop a great respect for the man.

The introductions concluded, Captain Hamlin handed over to Sergeant Green, who called the course up to attention. He had them fall out, informing them there was an officer on parade, indicating they should salute. He then instructed them to make their way, under the direction of the JNCOs, to the barrack block, where they would be staying for the duration. An accommodation block, or part of it, had been set aside for this purpose. The blokes followed the JNCOs, and were divided up into two rooms, of eight men. They had brought with them all of their military clothing and equipment, the night before and deposited it, early that morning, in the hallway. They were given the rest of the morning to put it all away in the lockers, provided for them.

The rooms were a bustle of activity, as clothing was folded, hung and put away. As Richard looked about the room, he saw a few familiar faces. He spotted Ron, from his team in Northern Ireland, Spike from his Control Signaller Course and Rob, with whom he had served in Command Troop.

Strangely, for a Yorkshire Regiment, there were two Geordies, one from B Squadron, the other from A Squadron. Kieron, the B Squadron individual, came from Durham and was well-set. He was wearing a chevron, which meant he had already been promoted. Richard knew that Kieron had to complete the course before being paid for his promotion.

The other guy was from the outskirts of Newcastle and was a little reserved. He would prove to be the complete opposite to Kieron, who was loud and brash. His name was Trev. He was a bit of an athlete, renowned for winning long distance races at the annual Regimental athletic meetings. This was no surprise, as he had run, semi-professionally, for his local team in the North East, before he joined the Army. He would have no problem at all with the fitness side of the course, Richard mused.

Both rooms were split into four man syndicates, each assigned a JNCO. Richard's syndicate consisted of Rob, from Command Troop, Trev, the athlete and Spike, from the Control Signaller course. Their JNCO called Steve

London, an ardent Leeds United fan, who came from that city. The first question he asked them was what football teams they supported. Hearing that Richard was also a Leeds fan, he smiled.

'Looks like you're going to pass then, lad,' he said, grinning at the rest of the syndicate.

Steve handed each of them a programme of events for the coming week, then dismissed them, for lunch. They were to parade outside in lightweight trousers, boots, combat high and red PT vest. With that, he left them to their own devices.

Richard looked around the group and felt they had a strong syndicate. He knew they would be easy to get along with. They all seemed genuinely pleased to be working with one another, for the next two weeks. Even though Rob was married, he was required to live in the accommodation, for the duration of the course. Rob was always smartly turned out and it would emerge that he and Richard would ultimately be competing for the accolade of best student, a prize that immediate promotion to Lance Corporal, once the course ended. The four headed off to the cookhouse together, for a quick lunch.

Their food consumed and a little time spent finishing off tidying their lockers, the candidates dressed in their PT gear, as ordered before lunch. They filed outside, where the syndicate leaders and a PTI were waiting for them. As soon as they had formed up in three ranks, the PTI turned them, to the right.

'Listen in. By the left, double march!' he called out.

There had been no indication as to how far they were going, but Richard expected this to be short and fast. It was just like being in training all over again, he thought. The PTI and one of the JNCOs led the squad, from the front. The pace was quite sedate and as Richard had recently completed training for the boxing competition, he was feeling it quite easy going. They trudged through the gates and headed right, alongside the main road. The pace hadn't changed since they left camp. They had been going for around twenty minutes, when they headed over a bridge, spanning the main road. In the distance, all they could see was farmland and woods. Running along country lanes, they headed past a farmhouse and, again, turned right, into a field. There was a muddy track along the side of the field, which ascended into a wood, on top of a hill, in the distance. Some of the candidates looked at each other and, without saying a word, read each other's minds. This was going to be a killer; not something they were expecting on the first day. They did not know it, but they were being assessed from the moment the course had started. Any sign of weakness or complaining would be noted.

As they began to wind their way through the wood, towards the top of the hill, the path began to get muddier. The gradient increased and the candidates were finding it difficult to keep their footing. The lactic acid was starting to build up in their quadriceps, due to the effort needed. Constantly, they were being bawled at by the JNCOs and the PTI, to dig in and keep up the pace, which had now slowed to a crawl, as the troops fought their way up the hill. They reached the top in dribs and drabs; those first up were ordered to continue jogging, on the spot. Once the complete cadre had made it, they set off again, without a rest.

By this time, they had completed about five miles and had been running for around an hour. They continued along the brow of the hill, before slowly descending the other side. The strain had been relaxed on the 'quads', only to be put on other muscle groups, as they made their way, to the bottom.

The whole course were still together, apart from two, who had fallen about 50 metres behind. They waited for them to catch up, jogging on the spot. Together again, they turned right and Richard could tell from the direction of the sun that they were heading further away from camp.

However, after 300 metres, the PTI changed direction, to Richard's relief. The PTI was playing mind games, to see what his charges were made of. There had been some grumbling among the ranks and these individuals were warned that, if they had enough breath to talk, then they could pick up the pace. With that, the PTI and lead JNCO started to stretch their legs, calling for the troops behind them to keep up.

For the final three miles back to camp, they kept the same pace. By the time they jogged on to the square, the guys were blowing out their arses. Just when they thought it was over, they were ordered to pair up and dress off, at the end of the square. The PTI positioned himself 100 metres in front of them. He asked that the first man hoist his partner onto his shoulders, in the 'fireman's lift' position. On his command, they were to carry their partner to where he stood. They were then to swap over and make their way back to the start.

Once this exercise was complete, the guys were warmed down for ten minutes, with a combination of stretching exercises. As they were fallen out, the JNCOs told them to grab a shower and be in the lecture theatre in 40 minutes. The course fell wearily out, slowly making their way, to the accommodation. Conversation among them was practically non-existent. Richard noticed that Trev, the Geordie athlete, hadn't broken sweat. Richard, however, felt that he himself was going to die and was dreading the next two weeks.

Showered and a little refreshed, the cadre assembled in the Regimental lecture theatre. Here, Captain Hamlin stood behind the lectern, awaiting their arrival. He delayed speaking, until they had taken their seats and settled down.

'Okay, gents, what I am going to cover for the next hour are the principles of leadership and command. However, before I commence, I want each of you to get up and give a five minute lecture about yourself.'

He paused, while he waited for his words to sink in, before selecting a name at random, from the list on his lectern. 'Trooper Parsons, you can go first,' he pointed in Ron's direction, with his Officer's cane.

Ron's head dropped. He rose from his seat and slowly walked towards the lectern. Turning round to face the cadre, his face had turned bright crimson. This seemed strange to Richard, as Ron had not been shy, when they had served in Northern Ireland together. One by one, each name was called and they delivered a little talk about themselves. Richard did not find it daunting at all, having done numerous lessons and lectures at the Junior Leaders' Regiment (JLR), Bovington.

Once everyone had taken their turn, Captain Hamlin returned to the lectern and thanked them, for their varied efforts. The men who had performed better than the others seemed to be those who had attended JLR. For the next hour, as he had promised, Hamlin went through the principles of what constituted a good leader. Richard, having heard these before, drummed into him in training, fought hard to keep his concentration. Knowing that he was being watched by the JNCOs, he tried to look interested and attentive. As the lecture drew to a close, Captain Hamlin sought confirmation that his lecture had sunk home. He did this by a series of quick fire questions, thrown at random students. Richard had learned the way not to be chosen, was to stare the questioner, directly in the eye. Those who avoided Hamlin's gaze would, inevitably, be chosen. It was a game of psychology and one that some of them had learned, by attending various courses, during their careers. Having satisfied himself that they were all up to speed, the course officer handed them back, to the JNCOs. The day of exercise and learning drew to a close.

They were marched back to the accommodation, where they broke for the evening meal, then spent the rest of the night, pressing their uniforms, cleaning the ablutions and sorting out their lockers, for the room inspection, the following morning.

Richard woke at 06:00, fifteen minutes before his alarm was due to go off. He shivered, as he threw back the blankets and swung his feet over the edge of the bed. He rubbed his eyes, wiping the sleep away and sat for a moment. Although this whole course was like being in training again, they did not have anyone coming round, waking them up or making sure they were on time for their next lesson. They were 'big boys' now and, as a potential JNCO, they were expected to have self-discipline.

As he looked about the room, others were also stirring. Richard took his wash bag and towel from his locker and left the room, in search of the ablutions. Ron was already standing at one of the basins, shaving. He greeted Richard, as he selected the space next to him. He placed the plug in its receptor and started running the hot water. Today's first lesson was to be drill, so Richard ensured that he shaved perfectly. Inspections were just as rigorous as the drill itself. He quickly finished his morning routine and returned to the room. By now, the light was on and everyone was up, either heading to the washrooms or dressing, for breakfast. As Richard placed his bag back in the locker and hung his towel neatly over its rail, he felt his muscles ache from the eight mile run they had completed, the previous day. He was not the only one feeling its effects. Some of the guys were hobbling about and this was only day two.

With breakfast finished, the troops started to put on their barrack dress. Once they were ready, in turn, they checked each other. Happy that everything was in order, they then made sure the room was in good order, for the inspection. They had drawn up a rota for the 'block jobs', the previous night. All knew what was required, so tasks were done, automatically, unlike training, where they were not spoon fed everything by instructors. This was all part of being in a position of responsibility.

95

The tip tapping of ammunition boots on the lino floor heralded the arrival of Sergeant Green. He entered the room, dressed as he had been the previous day, complete with pace stick. Corporal London and the other JNCO, who had been allocated the other syndicate in the room, stood behind him.

'Room, room, 'shun!' the second Corporal bawled.

The room, as one, raised their right legs and slammed them on to the floor, resulting in a resounding thump. The Cadre Sergeant nodded his head, in recognition of a drill movement, well carried out. He began his inspection of the room, starting with Ron's bed space, closest to the door. Firstly, he inspected Ron's dress, making slight adjustments, here and there, before inspecting the locker. In turn, he transited the room, stopping at each bed space. There was no yelling or throwing around of clothing and equipment, only friendly advice on how things could be improved for the next inspection. He did, however, expect any points raised to be rectified. Richard admired the small man, as he imparted his words of wisdom, in a way the candidates respected. There was no manual to tell how to be a good leader, nor was there any one way of achieving that. Respect had to be earned from the men under a command.

His inspection of the room complete, Sergeant Green handed over to the two room JNCOs and moved on to the second room. They acknowledged with a nod and, once he had left, congratulated the men on a successful outcome on their first room inspection. They were, however, expecting a marked improvement the next day. It didn't matter if the room and locker layouts seemed perfect, there was always something that could be improved on. The cadre was to teach them attention to detail, teamwork and a respect for others.

The course paraded on the square, five minutes before the lesson was due to begin. The demeanour of Sergeant

Green had changed. This was his world and, with the pace stick wedged firmly under his right armpit, he marched briskly on to the parade square, halting directly in front of the cadre.

'Right, gents, not a bad start to the day. We will now have our first drill lesson. As always, before carrying out any physical exercise, we must ensure we are fully warmed up. Squad, squad 'shun!' he screamed. 'Turn to the left in threes.'

The course forced their bodies round 90 degrees and drove their right feet on to the tarmac. 'Listen in to my timing. By the left, quick march!' The speed of his words made them indecipherable. The troops, however, knew, instinctively, to step off with the left foot and march as quickly as possible. When they had reached the far end of the square, the drill instructor turned them about and repeated the motion, to the other side. This went on for a full ten minutes. Breathing heavily, their limbs aching, he halted them in the spot from where they had started.

'Right, cadre, what we are going to go through, in the next hour, is simple foot drill. There will be a slight difference though.' The cadre assumed this would involve something unpleasant and, for some, this would prove to be true. 'As future JNCOs, you may be expected to move soldiers under your command in a smart, soldier-like fashion. The way we do this is by the use of drill. Your voice is the most important tool you possess, so take care of it. I find a glass or two of port normally does the trick.' The humour caused a titter to break out among the ranks. 'In each session, I will pick one or two of you to take the lesson. Today, Trooper Hunter will be taking the first part of the lesson.' Hearing this, Richard gulped and the whole course grinned, as they looked at him.

'Come out here and face your squad,' Sergeant Green pointed to a position, just to his left, with his pace stick. Richard did as he was requested and took his place, next to the Drill Sergeant, facing the troops. 'Right, I want you to bring them up to attention, turn them to the left and march them to the end of the square. Once there, you will turn them about and halt them, in the position they are in now. Do you have any questions?' he asked, looking directly into Richard's eyes. Richard shook his head, confirming that he did not and turned to face the squad. 'In your own time, carry on,' Green instructed. Taking a deep lungful of air, Richard issued his first command of the course.

'Squad, squad 'shun!' The cadre reacted just as Richard wanted. They stood motionless, awaiting the next command. 'Move to the left in threes. Left turn. By the right, quick march!' The last part of command was screamed out, taking the guys by surprise. The shock of the delivery had the desired effect and they stepped off, in unison. The drill instructor whispered words of encouragement in Richard's ear, telling Richard he had made a good start and to keep it up. As the squad neared the end of the square, Sergeant Green informed him that, to turn them around, Richard must anticipate. His voice needed to carry the distance. The command should be given just as the men's left feet passed their right. They would then take a further check pace, then carry out the drill movement. Richard watched the blur of feet and gave his next command, when he thought it was the right moment.

'The squad will retire, about.....' and, as the left feet passed the right, 'turn!' he bellowed, at the top of his voice. He didn't know if it was luck or good judgement, but the squad executed the movement, perfectly. For the next ten minutes, Richard was in charge and drilled the cadre up and down the square. Halted them back in their original place, Sergeant Green asked the cadre how they thought it had gone. Richard was gratified to hear that, to a man, the whole course agreed he had done an outstanding job. This was confirmed by the drill instructor, who directed Richard back, to his place in the squad. Green then chose another victim, who immediately broke ranks and joined him, at the front.

The whole process was repeated for the next 50 minutes, until they were halted, for the final time. Sergeant Green congratulated them all on a good morning's work. Some had performed better than others. However, as he explained, they were here to learn and improve. As they departed the square, for their next lesson, which was to be fieldcraft, Ron turned to Richard.

'Fuckin' drill pig,' he joked and, with that, the whole course were in fits of laughter. Richard blushed visibly and hung his head. He didn't want to stand out, at this stage, but had secretly enjoyed his success in the lesson.

Chapter 11 – Fieldcraft

They had been given half an hour to get into their combats, Combat Equipment Fighting Order (CEFO). This consisted of a set of '58 pattern webbing, comprising belt, ammo pouches, water bottle pouch and kidney pouches. To complete the ensemble, they donned their helmets, topped by a camouflage cover. Still perspiring from the drill lesson, they gathered outside, to mount the truck provided to take them to the nearby training area. Before they could do this, they needed to draw their weapons from the armoury. Lining up outside the armoury door, they gave their weapon numbers to the arms storeman.

The course had been issued with the Self Loading Rifle (SLR), which was 7.62mm calibre. It had come into service in the British Army in 1954 and was the main weapon carried by all infantry units, throughout the 1980s. The candidates also signed for a Blank Firing Attachment (BFA). This was to be attached to the muzzle of the weapon and, as its name suggested, was used with blank rounds. It was bright yellow in colour and stood out like a bulldog's bollocks, in dense foliage. Their weapons collected, the guys headed back to the square and mounted the truck.

The journey was a short one, taking only half an hour. On arrival, they debussed and gathered round the waiting instructors. The morning was going to comprise the composition and responsibilities of an infantry section. Then, they would proceed to section battle drills, finishing off with patrolling. They had all been through similar lessons, during their time in Northern Ireland and they reckoned this would be a refresher course. A Corporal, from a nearby infantry Regiment, would be taking them for fieldcraft, during their course. He was from the valleys of South Wales and almost sang, as he talked.

'Good morning, guys. I'm Corporal Roy Evans of the Royal Regiment of Wales and I will be taking you through your fieldcraft training, on this course.' Having introduced himself, he then continued. 'I will be covering the composition and responsibilities of an infantry section. Then, we will move on to section battle drills, ending with patrolling skills. Do we have any questions before I start?' He looked around the eager faces in front of him. He was happy that everyone was 'good to go', so continued.

'The standard light infantry section consists of eight personnel.' He began, in his dulcet tones, then went on to explain its breakdown and responsibilities. 'The section commander has responsibility for the overall effectiveness of the section. He plans for operations and patrols, prepares orders and conducts briefings. He positions himself centrally in any attack, driving the section forward.'

Corporal Evans then explained the role of the second in command or 2ic, who was the section commander's deputy. He administers to the welfare needs of the section. He is also responsible for checking their physical and administrative needs, before and after operations, such as seeing they have enough water, ammunition and rations and that their welfare needs are met. During operations, he is responsible for controlling the fire support elements and driving the section forward, from the rear.

Also in the section was the 'runner', always in close proximity to the section commander and usually supplied with a radio on a manpack frame. His function was distribute any messages to the section commander and pass the same on, from him to the section. He also gave fire and support to the section commander.

The next member of the team was the 'gunner', who usually carried the heavy weapon of the section. On this course, it would be a 'General Purpose Machine Gun' (GPMG). He would be the first man into the attack, laying down covering fire on the objective, under the direction of the 2ic. The section was completed by two 'fire teams', named Charlie and Delta, each consisting of two men. These were the 'bread and butter' of the section and would use fire and manoeuvre onto the objective.

The infantry instructor went on to emphasise that it takes time to develop trust among section members. Much practice must be put into all round defence, attacks, administration and welfare, to ensure that the section operates effectively. This effectiveness could only be achieved through prolonged exercises. In every well taught lesson, the instructor should sum up, then confirm his guidance had been taken in, usually by a series of questions to the 'pupils'. Evans rapidly picked people at random, asking each a question. Not one of the candidates faltered, then he moved on, to the next phase.

Section battle drills were the responsibility of the commander and his 2ic. While the section commander prepared his orders, the 2ic would prepare the section. He would go through the procedures already outlined by the instructor.

'Section quick attack orders are necessary for the following situations,' he continued, 'to capture a small enemy location, including observation posts (OPs), sentry or machine gun posts and trenches. Standard Operating Procedures (SOPs) needed to be adhered to, for any quick attack. They followed a similar pattern. The section commander should consider what protection, ammunition, personal cam, radios and webbing was needed. He should consider the reaction to enemy fire. Depending on the given situation, they could choose to return fire, take cover, regroup or fight through.

The enemy could be located by shape, shine or movement and, once located they would either supress it, thereby preventing it from moving, or take the position. For this the patrol leader would have to formulate his orders. This would highlight how they would take the position.

Once the location had been taken, they would reorganise, count casualties, check water and count and redistribute ammunition, then await further orders.

The instructor went on to explain that locating the enemy was to be done by patrolling. The aims of patrolling were to obtain information, to destroy or disrupt enemy forces or to dominate a defensive position. The type of patrolling was dependent on the situation or mission and could take the form of a recce patrol, standing, fighting or standby. The recce patrol was used for gathering information, such as collecting topographical information, locating the enemy, using a Close Target Recce (CTR), while, at times, they may be required to gain information on obstacles such as minefields.

A standing patrol was used in harbour areas, where a platoon or company was static, and would patrol the local vicinity, ensuring it was secure from attack.

The fighting patrol was more aggressive. It was used to find and destroy the enemy, disrupt enemy activity or work parties; to distract the enemy as part of a deception plan or setting up ambushes.

The standby patrol gave assistance to other patrols, after a contact. If required, they would take over the mission of another patrol after a contact, allowing it to reorganise. The spacing of patrol members was five metres at night and ten to twenty metres during the day.

To clarify the principles of a good patrol, the Infantryman explained the essentials of good patrolling skills. Communication was a key part of this, ensuring that all members covered opposite arcs of fire. This was to be done either when moving or static. The first man, the 2ic, would cover the front, the second man left, the third, right and so on. The last man, the tail end Charlie, would face the rear. Spacing and battle discipline needed to be maintained. The patrol should be carried out tactically, in silence and in cover. The section should never patrol in open ground and should always utilise local cover, when in the open. The order of the patrol would be; the 2ic as lead scout, the runner, Charlie fire team, Section Commander, Delta fire team, the gunner at the rear.

His experience imparted, the instructor asked if there were any questions and received a negative response. Moving on, he then broke the sixteen into two sections of eight. He asked the Cadre Corporals to list the men in each syndicate. The syndicates formed a half section, each with four men. This done, he then gave appointment to each section, designating each man his duties.

Richard was placed in a section commanded by a bloke called Blackey from C Squadron. Richard was appointed as 2ic, with Ron as his gunner. The rest of the fire teams and runner were made up by the remainder. After they had carried out their patrol prep and the section commander had briefed them on their mission, they went out on patrol. They were given the task of carrying out a reconnaissance patrol, in a given area.

Leaving what they were told was their harbour area, Richard led them in a westerly direction. Even though they had been told not to cross open ground, the initial 500 metres was just that. Richard picked a route where natural features gave as much protection as possible. He used the dead ground where possible, obscuring the patrol from any enemy who may have been observing. From time to time, he checked behind to make sure that the runner was at the required distance. He indicated with his hand when he intended to change direction. The gunner passed this down the line, so that communication was maintained in silence. After an hour patrolling, the section entered a wooded area, with a single track running through it. This was a perfect point for an ambush, Richard thought to himself and he became more alert. The rest of the section, seeing Richard slowing his pace slightly, did the same, to maintain their distance.

About 600 metres into the wood, the sound of automatic fire erupted, to their right. They instinctively went to ground and the section commander began to assess the situation. Richard began to crawl towards the rear of the patrol, to join the gunner, as it would be his job to direct the fire on to the enemy position, once the commander had formulated his quick attack orders. As they had not been fully briefed on a quick attack plan, it took a little time to formulate this.

All this time, the Directing Staff (DS) were screaming at them, asking what they were going to do. Blackey began to flap a little and thought that he had better do something quickly. He shouted out to the section, the direction and location of the firing post that had engaged them. He directed Richard and the GPMG man to give covering fire, on his order to move. Meanwhile, he and the radio man were making sure they were still central in the formation. As soon as he was happy that all were in position, facing the right direction and had identified the enemy position, he gave Charlie fire team the command to advance and report when firm.

At the same time, Richard gave the order for the GPMG gunner to open up, with supressing fire, on the enemy location. Once Charlie fire team had gone firm and reported, Delta fire time were given the order to move. They threw themselves forward and went to ground, around 30 metres in front of Blackey. He waited until they started to engage, ten, with the runner, ran forward and halted, in line with both fire teams. They repeated this, until they had fought through the position. At that point the DS called an end to the exercise.

They made their way back to the hide area, where they were told to relax, for a moment. Once the other section had returned, Corporal Evans debriefed them. All in all, he was genuinely happy with their first attempt. He could tell that they had recently deployed in Northern Ireland, as some of their drills were quite slick. The candidates smiled with pride, until they were told that it wasn't perfect and that there was room for improvement. This caused shoulders to slump, but the men were soon heartened, when Jones reminded them, they were there to improve.

'Even some infantry sections don't get it right all the time. Like I said in my first lesson, these drills take practice. The more you do it, the more familiar you will get with how you all work. Now, if no one has any questions, section commanders and 2ics, make sure your guys have all your equipment and fuck off, out of my sight,' he laughed.

The course took his comment in the light hearted way it was meant. They began gathering their equipment and checking nothing had been left behind. On the way back, in the truck, there was much back slapping and congratulations for those who had been appointed section commanders and 2ics. They all knew that, over the course, they would each fulfil a different role. Richard thought to himself at least he had got one of the command jobs out of the way, even though it was only 2ic. He closed his eyes and tried to sleep on the short journey back to camp.

Chapter 12 – Orienteering and Close Target Recce

The first week passed, with countless drills and PT lessons, interspersed with lectures on fieldcraft and leadership. The candidates were given an assortment of command tasks to complete, each man taking it in turns to lead. Richard was doing well and began to enjoy the course. The next morning's activity took the form of an orienteering competition. The troops assembled in the classroom, wearing tracksuit and trainers, given a brief on the course and handed out sheets by the DS. They were split into pairs and would run the course together. The course consisted of ten checkpoints, each with the answer to a question on the sheets. Richard was teamed up with Rob from Command Troop. It had been rumoured that the pair of them were in the running for top student. Rob, like Richard, had taken naturally to leadership and had completed his section commander and 2ic tasks in the fieldcraft lessons. Richard was yet to have his turn as section commander, but, with only a week left until the end of the course, that wouldn't be long.

Once the briefing was complete, the pairs were given 30 minutes to study the maps they had been given, in order to form a strategy. Map appreciation was a fundamental skill for an NCO and was transferrable from foot patrols to their normal job of commanding armoured vehicles. Rob and Richard studied the map together and agreed on the route they would take and that, by tackling the furthest checkpoints first, they would conserve energy. Looking at the map, these checkpoints were at high locations and, with fresh legs, the task would be made a little easier.

It wasn't long before the 30 minutes were up and the first pair set off. The pairs set off at five minute intervals and, after a quarter of an hour, Rob and Richard were jogging out the gates. Rob was a better runner than Richard, but ran at the slower man's pace. It was a team effort and both members needed to come back together. With Rob map reading for the first half of the course, Richard put his head down and ran in the direction Rob indicated.

After half an hour, they passed a couple of groups going in the opposite direction. They had decided to take the nearest checkpoints first. Suddenly, a plan sprang to mind and Richard asked the first group they met which checkpoints they had reached and if they had the required answers. Although it was a competition, they readily supplied the information. Richard and Rob promised if they passed them on the course, they would give any information they had collected. In agreement, the pairs set off again in search of the next answer to the clue on their sheets. Rob and Richard had crossed off the two checkpoints they had been given by the others and, in due time, reached the first of their own. Looking around the feature, it wasn't long before they saw the marker which held the clue. An hour had passed and they had already had answers for half of the questions on the sheet. They had only been to three checkpoints, but had been given some of the answers by other pairs. Of course, they had reciprocated and everyone was happy. It was a game and everyone was in the same boat, teamwork was essential, so they did not view it as cheating.

After all, if this had been a recce, different patrols would share the information they had been sent out to gain. With only two hours to complete the course, the pair started to make their way back. The final clues were easy to find and were only a short distance from camp. As they jogged into camp, they had completed the course in just under an hour and a half. They were the first ones back and, after being congratulated by the DS, they handed in their answer sheets. Five minutes later, Trev the athlete was crossing the finishing line, with his partner. He looked in disbelief, to see Rob and Richard already drinking a brew and laughing.

'How the fuck did you two finish so quickly?' he asked, still regaining his breath.

'Because we can read a map, ya Geordie numpty,' Rob replied, grinning at the disbelieving and now suspicious lad from Gateshead. Shaking his head, the guy from A Squadron grabbed himself a brew, after handing in the pair's answer sheet to the DS. As the last group completed the course, they were told to relax, while the instructors checked all the answer papers.

Everyone had completed the course in the time given. Some had not managed to collect all the answers, but that was to be expected. After a short period of deliberation, it was announced that Rob and Richard had won the competition. A round of applause broke out, the pair were quite popular and had given some of their answers to other groups, too.

As the troops broke away to shower and get ready for the next lesson, they noticed Trev speaking to the DS. They could tell by his body language that he was not happy. Rob and Richard just chuckled to themselves. It came to light afterwards, that the instructors had told Trev that it was not just a physical challenge, but one of intelligence. If Rob and Richard had got answers from other people, then they had used their heads. Not happy, Trev stormed off. Not being one to hold a grudge, he later congratulated the pair, when they confirmed his suspicions. He agreed that it was all part of the game and only pride had prevented him from doing the same.

The rest of the day was taken up with drill and the men on the course had become quite adept at taking the squad and giving clear and concise orders. They were working well as a team and Sergeant Green was happy with their progress. All of the candidates had taken at least one lesson, either foot drill, arms drill or a combination of both.

That day's lesson would only last an hour, as the course were to assemble in the lecture room, directly after the evening meal. They were to take part in a 36 hour exercise, which would be a Close Target Reconnaissance (CTR) task. As soon as the drill lesson was over, the troops disappeared, to collect the webbing, weapons and other equipment needed for the activity.

The evening meal consumed, the course assembled in the lecture room and awaited the arrival of the course officer, Captain Hamlin. The guys were dressed in full combats, webbing, Bergens, with enough rations and equipment to last them 36 hours. They had all applied camouflage cream on their faces and extremities. The first phase of the exercise would be in darkness and, as it was mid-winter, they had dressed appropriately for the conditions. There was a buzz of excitement in the room, as Captain Hamlin entered and took his place, behind the lectern. He was also dressed in full combats but, instead of combat boots, was wearing his cavalry officer's boots. He looked down at his notes briefly and smiled to himself. Behind him was a map of the local area, with map pins stuck into various locations. From each pin, a piece of string was stretched to the edge of the map. At the end of each piece of string, was a card explaining what the pin represented.

'Good evening, gentlemen,' the course officer began. 'The exercise for this evening and the next 36 hours is named 'Operation Herman' and will be a CTR task. You will be dropped off at different locations and will work in your syndicates. You are members of 26 Special Air Service Group and, in your four man teams, will carry out a passive CTR of the following location.

'At the following grid square,' he pointed to the map as he spoke, 'is a television mast and communication complex. Your mission will be to gather as much intelligence about the installation as possible. The information we are after is; how many personnel are stationed there, the methods of entry, patrol and security rotas; any weakness in security or obvious blind spots, which could be used to gain access. One thing I must say is that if you are caught, we will deny knowledge of you.'

He emphasised this point by raising his voice slightly and became more serious. The troops looked at each other with apprehension. The scenario given was creditable and believable but surely this couldn't be true. This was a training exercise and not part of a real selection process for the famed 'Special Air Service' (SAS).

'Each team will meet with an undercover operative at appointed locations,' he indicated four points on the map, with his pointer. 'To prove the identity of the operative, you will each receive a challenge and reply code word. Only on receipt of the correct code word will your operative give you the further information you require, to complete your mission. I must also add that there will be a hunter force in the area, so you must avoid any contact with them or local civilians. He made it sound so realistic that the teams were eager to get underway.

The briefing over, the course climbed aboard the 4 Tonne Bedford truck, waiting with its engine running, outside the block. They sat in their syndicates of four for the trip to their various drop off locations. The mood was one of anticipation and excitement, it all seemed so real, even though they knew it wasn't. The warning that if they were reported to the German Civil Police (GCP), they would be disowned had added extra tension to the situation.

Trev had been given the job of patrol leader, with Ron as his 2ic. This was an easy one, Richard thought to himself and was disturbed by the sound of the brakes of the vehicle. Sergeant Green appeared at the tailgate and whispered their syndicate's number, instructing them to dismount. They had only been travelling for about twenty minutes. When

Sergeant Green confirmed their location with Trev, he climbed back into the truck and it moved away.

The four team members immediately went to ground in all round defence, even though for this particular exercise, they were unarmed. It was thought that was not a good idea, just in case they were caught carrying out their reconnaissance. Trev examined the map and confirmed with Ron where they were to meet their 'agent'. Once they were happy with the direction they were to take, they moved out of cover. The track they were going to take was firm, but because of dense foliage, it was pitch black.

Ron led the patrol as lead scout, with Spike second, then Trev, with Richard bringing up the rear. They spaced themselves the standard five metres apart, as for night patrols and began the slow ascent. The feature they were climbing was the highest point in the local area. On top was a well-known landmark, a statue known to all soldiers as 'Herman the German'. The character commemorated was Arminius, who had succeeded in defeating the Roman army, in the battle of the Teutoburg Forest in 9 AD. Beyond this feature was their final destination, a tower on a neighbouring hill. On this hill, they needed to meet their agent, at a grid reference about half way up. This arrangement was obviously to make the exercise a little more difficult.

They continued their ascent for the next hour, with Trev checking their progress, on the map. Ron was counting his paces, so he knew, roughly, when to expect any junctions or features they could use to confirm their destination. Trev whispered to Spike that their final position should be coming up shortly and to pass this on to Ron. This he did and Ron, as a result, slowed his pace.

Suddenly, he raised his hand in a signal for the patrol to halt. He had spotted something, in the darkness. He called Trev forward to let him know. In the darkness, they saw the glow of a cigarette. They assumed this was their contact, who else would be wandering round the woods, at that time of night? Making themselves appear as small as possible, they began to crawl forward, halting about twenty metres from the now distinct silhouette of a figure. Ron slid forward, whispered the challenge and received the correct response. The team approached the figure, to find it was their JNCO, Steve London.

'You okay, boys?' he greeted them, not expecting a reply. 'You made good time. I've another task for you. I want you to find the type of security system that is fitted to the gates of the installation. Do you have any questions and do you know what direction you are heading?' London asked and waited for an answer. They told him they understood and knew where they were going. So, with a wave, he bid them farewell.

Ron turned 45 degrees and headed in the direction Trev had given him, prior to meeting with the agent. There was a break in the trees and the team could see a series of red lights, rising vertically, from the opposite hill. As it was at night, they couldn't tell how far away they were. They had, however, studied the map, and knew the lights were around five kilometres, as the crow flies. This meant it would probably take them around two hours to get there, factoring in the terrain they needed to negotiate. They started to descend and, in fifteen minutes, they reached the bottom of the hill they needed to climb next.

The track which they chose consisted of a series of hairpins, snaking their way up the feature. They put their heads down and slowly trudged onwards, stopping every 500 metres or so, to check the map. With only one main track, it wasn't going to be hard to find their way.

As expected, after two hours, they could see bright lights, flooding an area, approximately 300 metres, in front of them. They moved off the track and started to move through the dense wood, which surrounded the installation. As the woods grew thinner, the outline of the Television

Station came into view. Cover was sparse from the edge of the wood-line to the fence surrounding the mast and the outlying buildings. They lined up, in an extended line, facing the installation. Trev lifted the binoculars from around his neck. As he scanned the complex, he made observations to Richard, who was jotting them down in his notebook. They took note of any changes of security staff over the next hour, how alert they seemed to be and whether they varied their patrol routes. They counted the number of floodlights and any areas of darkness, which could be used to approach the installation, unseen. Just as they completed their initial recce, a vehicle's headlights were seen, approaching the main gate. The car was dark in colour, with writing emblazoned on the side. Due to the darkness, it was difficult to read the words.

No one disembarked, a window was lowered and an arm reached out to place something in a post, which rose from the ground. The gates then began to swing open, of their own accord. A figure appeared, approximately fifteen metres inside the compound. The vehicle stopped, once again. The darkly dressed figure leaned inside the open window then, after a short time, leaned back and waved the vehicle on. Was this a change of shift, Richard thought, writing the time in his sheets.

Once the activity had died down, Trev decided they would proceed with their secondary task, given to them by Steve London; to find what type of access the installation had. Richard had picked the short straw; he was given the job of moving forward and trying to establish the entry system. He crawled, slowly, across the open ground, using as much cover as he could find. The first twenty metres were easy, as they were not covered by illumination from the floodlights. As he neared the entrance to the complex, he became aware that he could be spotted, so moved more slowly. It took him a good fifteen minutes, before he reached the post outside the gate. Checking that no one was outside the guard house, just inside the gate, he prepared to inspect the method of entry. Rising cautiously, he observed that there were two methods of gaining entry. One was by a keypad, the other by inserting a card into a slot, situated just below the keypad.

Satisfied with his recce, Richard began the slow movement, back to his team, in the treeline. Just as he made it back, the barking of a dog could be heard, from inside the compound. Had they been discovered? To their relief, the barking appeared to come from the far side of the installation. It was possible that another team, approaching from that direction, had alerted the canine. Deciding they had gathered enough information, they quietly slipped back, into the safety of the woods and began their retreat down the slope.

As they reached the bottom of the hill, they came to the conclusion that it would be first light in an hour or so. Not wishing to move during daylight hours, they suitable cover and made themselves as comfortable as they could. The temperature had fallen below zero and the frost had already formed on the foliage. Having no sleeping bags with them, they took out their ponchos and wrapped themselves up. One man was set as sentry, to be relieved hourly.

The weak winter sun rose into the valley, where they were laid up. Richard could not stop his body from shaking, as he took his turn, on stag. Vehicles started to move along the road just 200 metres from where they lay. Richard stared through the binoculars, checking that none were military. Captain Hamlin had said that a hunter force may be out, looking for them. It was tedious, but kept his mind from the numbing cold, which had seeped into his body. He kept glancing at his watch, until his shift was over and he woke Ron, who was on next. It had been sixteen hours since they last ate and Richard felt his stomach rumble. They knew that, in their current situation, it would be unwise to heat up the rations they had brought. There was, however, a beauty to British Army rations, or 'Compo' as they were colloquially known. They could be eaten straight from the can, as they had already been processed.

The other two were now awake and a tin of sausages and beans was opened. Passing it around, they took a couple of spoonfuls each, leaving enough for Ron when he came off stag. They then passed out some oatmeal biscuits, which they covered in jam and processed cheese. 'If a civilian saw this they would probably puke,' remarked Richard. Yet, when they had not eaten for so long, this delicacy was as attractive as a curry at closing time. The team's hunger satisfied for the moment, they checked that their camouflage, of laying up point (LUP), was up to standard. Satisfied, they covered themselves with their ponchos and tried to catch some sleep.

They were woken by Trev, shaking them. 'Land Rover has stopped, just off the road. Looks like it's a hunter force. Start to pack away your gear, we need to move.' he whispered.

The team rolled up their ponchos and prepared to move. It was mid-afternoon and it would be another five hours until they were due at the RV point, to be picked up. Scrambling through the undergrowth, keeping as low as possible, they retreated, into the woods. Once they were safely concealed, Trev took out the binoculars and scanned the area where the Land Rover had stopped. A party of four, dressed in combats, were studying a map on the bonnet of the vehicle. A brief conversation among them ensued, then, with a nod of the head, they left one man with the vehicle, the other three heading in the direction of the woods.

'Looks like we're on the run, for the next five hours,' Trev revealed, as he lowered the binoculars and placed them back in his rucksack. The group turned in the direction of the hill and began to run.

For the next few hours, they moved from hiding place to hiding place. They were met at every location with the presence of more and more troops, on the ground. Darkness was starting to fall, a welcome sight for the now very tired, young men. They only needed to trek another two kilometres to the pick-up point. Having only eaten briefly that morning, their energy levels were starting to drop, as was the temperature. They shivered, as they waited, in a ditch, around 100 metres from the car park, in the woods. At last, and to their relief, the unmistakeable sound of a Bedford engine was heard and headlights illuminated the area. They waited for it to halt and for the engine to be turned off. An eerie silence filled the air, as the four friends made their way, cautiously, to the edge of the car park. Satisfied that it was safe to do so, they stood up and walked to the waiting DS, who was standing, having a brew.

'Well done, guys, grab yourselves a drink and get on the back of the truck. For you, the war is over.' Sergeant Green smiled, as he pointed to the tea urn, which had been placed behind the truck. The friends gratefully filled their mugs and loaded them with copious amounts of sugar. The warm liquid drifted down Richard's throat and rejuvenated his spirit. It wasn't until they made their way to the truck, that they saw it was already half full. They learned that two of the teams had been captured, earlier that afternoon. Richard's team was the first to make it back, without being discovered. A sense of achievement was felt by the whole team. After another 30 minutes, the final patrol entered the car park, grabbed a brew and the course headed off, back to camp. It had been a difficult exercise and one Richard wouldn't forget, for a long time. Little did he know, but there were more tasking times ahead.

Chapter 13 – Final Exercise

The CTR task debrief lasted over an hour. Each team's patrol leader stood and shared the information each had gathered, on the installation. Some of the teams had gained a little more intelligence than others. Richard's patrol had made the best sketch map of the area, however, another had more detailed information. While praiseworthy, it nonetheless pointed out that they had spent to long 'on task' at the complex. This had compromised that team's position and they had been reported by a member of the security staff. Obviously, if this had been for real, then it would have had serious consequences. Another team had been captured by the hunter force, whilst digging into their currywurst and chips, by the side of a road. Although the instructors laughed about it, Captain Hamlin was far from impressed.

After a day's rest, the course prepared for the final exercise, after which they would pass off. As the exercise would last a little over 48 hours, all uniforms for the parade had been cleaned and pressed. They would only have time to make finishing touches, after they returned. That day, Richard was told that he would lead one of the sections, on the final exercise. He knew that this was coming, so had mentally prepared himself. He had excelled in most of the lessons given and the rumour was that the accolade of best student was still between him and Rob. He spent the day preparing his webbing and Bergen. He made sure he had everything on the kit list, which they had been given.

It was a trait of the Instructors to check equipment, prior to an exercise. If anyone was found to have an item missing, this normally meant a punishment of some form or another, for the room. Once he was happy with his preparations, Richard looked over his notes on battle drills. He ensured he had the section on battle drills and quick attack orders firmly fixed in his mind. He had a tactical aide memoire to jog his memory, but it looked more professional if it could be done without referring to the book.

The course collected their equipment and drew their weapons from the armoury. The briefing was to be held, as usual, in the lecture room, in Regimental Headquarters (RHQ). The troops settled down in their seats and waited for Captain Hamlin to begin. Firstly, he congratulated them all on getting this far. Although a few had picked up minor injuries, they were all present for the final exercise.

'The scenario remains the same from your CTR briefing. You are two patrols from 26 Special Air Service. The exercise will take the form of a fighting patrol.' he began. 'You will start from camp and make your way, on foot, in your two sections, to these two locations.' He pointed to the red pins, stuck in the map, on the board. 'The distance is around twenty kilometres and, once there, you will move into a 'Laying Up Position' (LUP). This will be for the night and will be tactical. He then went on to go through the Situation, enemy and friendly forces, communications and the rest of a full set of formal orders. 'At first light, you are to make your way to this feature here,' he pointed, 'where you will be met by some of the DS.' He indicated a blue feature on the map, which could only represent water. 'The DS will brief you on the next phase of the exercise from there. Does anyone have any questions?' He looked around the room, acknowledging one raised hand. 'Yes, Trooper Groves?' he enquired.

'When does the exercise finish, Sir?' he asked, bashfully.

Grinning like a Cheshire cat, Captain Hamlin simply replied, 'When it's over. So, if there are no other stupid questions, get your shit together and be prepared to move in half an hour. The briefing over, and with a scraping of chairs, the candidates gathered, in their sections. The section commanders were checking their maps, while the 2ics were checking the administration of the guys. Ron who was Richard's 2ic, was busy handing out twenty rounds of blank 7.62mm ammunition, to each man in the section. Once he had done that, he ensured that the radio operator had communication with control, call sign 'Zero'. Their own call sign was Tango 10 and the other section Tango 20. Twenty minutes after preparations had been completed, they gathered outside and waited for the order to move out. When the order came, Richard lined the section up, in the right patrol order and they set off, out of camp.

The first twelve kilometres were on main roads and as they were patrolling tactically, they drew attention from the local German population. Some of the guys simply waved at people in passing and carried on. The pace set was a brisk one and Richard could feel it in his shins. He called forward, for Ron to slow the pace slightly, as this was not a race. They wouldn't arrive till well after dark, anyway, so there was no need to rush. As they progressed, buildings started to become fewer and fewer and, before they knew it, they were heading cross country. It was still almost another six kilometres to their laying up point and the cold, winter wind picked up. It was a relief when they entered a wooded area of thick pines, which gave them respite from the cutting wind. As they neared the area where they were to 'harbour' for the evening, Ron stopped and raised his hand. Richard moved forward to see if there was a problem.

'As we discussed on our preparation, do you want me and one other to go forward and make sure the hide is safe?' Ron reminded him.

'Yes, please, mate. We will go firm here. Make sure you do a complete sweep of the area,' he smiled, showing his appreciation for Ron's prompt. They had learned to work well as a team, over the past two weeks and it showed. Richard passed the message back, down the line. The six remaining blokes from the section took up all round defence, while Ron and Trev went forward, to recce the harbour area. Richard could feel the cold creeping into his body, after the twenty kilometre 'tab'. The section had dressed appropriately for the exercise, but with the temperature well below zero, there was little they could do to combat the cold. Time dragged on, as they awaited the return of Trev and Ron. Out of the darkness, two figures approached. As they got closer, Richard recognised Ron's figure.

'All clear, mate,' he signalled to Richard. The section stood as one and made its way into the harbour area. No orders were needed, as each man took a position around the LUP, providing mutual support. As soon as they were in position, they waited for a period of time, watching and listening for anything alien. Happy that it was all in order, Richard began to draw up a rota for sentry duty. He chose the point of a likely approach to the hide and placed the GPMG there. Each one in the section, in turn, would man the position, for an hour at a time. This would take them to first light, when they would be moving out to the water feature Captain Hamlin had shown them.

Simon, a bloke from Recce Troop, took first stag. He was a typical 'chirpy Cockney', hailing from the East End of London. All through the course, he never had a bad word to say about anyone, simply getting on and doing the job. Richard had grown to like him and, after the course was over, they would be serving together, in the same Troop. He gave Simon a quick brief and, once satisfied, he retired the short distance, back to the hide. He had explained to Simon and the rest of the section, that if they were to come under attack during the night, they should make for the emergency RV, which he had briefed them on, before entering the hide. This was a safe area, out of contact, where they could reorganise and plan their next move.

Taking out his poncho, he placed it on the ground, as some form of protection from the cold surface. It was not long before the hide area was full of the sound of snoring, as they caught some sleep.

The night gave way, slowly, into first light, as Richard looked over the sights of the GPMG. He had taken last stag and decided it was time to wake the rest of the section. The expected attack had never come, but Richard had tossed and turned, expecting it. He was not the only one, none had managed to grab more than a couple of hours sleep, due to the intense cold. Quietly packing away their equipment, they prepared to move, out to the next location.

The sun was breaking over the horizon and, though it was not warm, it gave them a psychological boost. Ron confirmed with Richard the direction in which they were to head and took up his place, as lead scout. He was given the nod by Richard to begin their four kilometre patrol to the lake on the map. The mood was sombre, as they trudged towards their destination. Their minds were set on what was coming next and the speed they had set warmed up their bodies. That pace was brisk and it wasn't long until the lake was before them. Mist was rolling across the still, almost stagnant feature and a Land Rover, with two of the DS stood, waiting their arrival. The other section were already there, standing chatting. On this occasion, the two DS were Steve London and Sergeant Green, who instructed them to place down their Bergens and gather round for a briefing. This they did, thankful for ridding themselves of the burden.

'Okay, guys, this is the scenario,' Sergeant Green began. 'You have come across this feature and there is no way round it, as a minefield stretches on either side of it. You are to get your sections, men and equipment across it. There are a few things to help you, in the vicinity,' he indicated some planks and plastic containers. 'It is not a

122

race, simply a test of your teamwork.' With that, he instructed them to begin devising a plan.

Knowing that to swim across the lake, with the layers of clothing they had on, would be too difficult, Richard made the decision for them to strip down, to their boxer shorts. They took out the black, plastic bags they had earlier placed in their Bergens, to keep their kit dry. The bags, with their clothing inside, could be used as flotation devices. Before they stripped, they began to assemble a floating platform, with the items placed around the area. There were pieces of rope, planks and large blue containers, which they strapped together in a makeshift manner.

There was no time limit, but the teams were racing against each other. Everything in the military ended up in a competition, due to the nature of the British soldier. It had only taken around 45 minutes, to construct their rafts and, after confirming they floated, the men began to strip. Getting as much air as possible in the black plastic bags, they placed their clothing inside. The Bergens and weapons were put on to the rafts and the sections slowly entered the water. The weaker swimmers were detailed to hold on to the rafts, to give them more buoyancy, while the rest of the teams used their plastic bags to help keep them afloat. The water was so cold, it immediately numbed the senses. Richard had never felt so cold in all his life, as he pushed out, toward the opposite bank. Halfway across, he started to panic and had to dig into his mental reserves, to continue. He wondered if anyone else was feeling the same. Looking round at the faces of the section, he knew he was not alone. The desire to avoid letting down their mates spurred them all on. Something scraped against Richard's feet. To his amazement and relief, he could feel the ground beneath them. There were still around fifteen metres to go, but the water was shallower, on this side of the lake. It wasn't long before they were dragging the rafts onto dry land.

They were met by Steve and Sergeant Green, who had made their way round to the other side of the lake in the Land Rover. They ordered a change, into dry clothing. Of course, the soaked squad didn't need to be told twice, some had already started. They were also surprised to find a tea urn had been set up. Gratefully, mugs were filled with steaming, hot brew and loaded with large helpings of sugar. Richard thought the hot, sweet tea was like nectar of the gods, as it trickled down his throat. He began to warm from the inside out. Like many of the other candidates, he had taken a pack of cigarettes from his Bergen and was busy puffing away.

The DS let them relax for a little while, before informing them they were in a safe, secure area, advising them to get something to eat. They were given 30 minutes to take out their hexamine stoves and prepare breakfast. The sections busied themselves lighting the stoves, placing mess tins containing a little water on them, adding a 'boil in the bag' breakfast meal. It took only fifteen minutes for the water to boil. The troops ripped open the bags and consumed the contents, in the knowledge they had no idea when they would get to eat.

Breakfast finished and the stoves cooled, the course put away their rubbish and cooking equipment in their Bergens. This done, Sergeant Green called them to gather round.

'Your next task is to form two fighting patrols and make your way to two separate locations, here and here,' he pointed to the map. He gave them a grid reference for each and explained that intelligence had reported it was possible troops were occupying these positions. The sections were to assess the enemy defences and numbers. If feasible, they were to put in a quick attack on both. Once any attack was over, they were to reorganise, at the starting point, a small wooded area, 500 metres east of both objectives. There, they were to wait for further orders, from control. The section commanders nodded their heads in compliance. The brief over, the 2ics quickly ensured that everyone had filled their water bottles and that they had comms with Zero; reporting in to their respective section commanders that they were good to go. Richard made his map appreciation and decided on the route they would take. He passed this on to Ron and the rest of the section. They then took up their positions and patrolled out of the area.

The ground they were to cover was off the beaten track and, although firm, was undulating and pretty hard going. As they were moving tactically, it would take them around four hours to reach their objective. At points along the route, Richard stopped and made the sign for an emergency RV, in case they came under fire en route and needed a rallying point. Their destination was some 25 kilometres away and, at around halfway, Richard noticed that some of the section were starting to feel the pace of the last 24 hours. He passed a message to Ron that they should stop for a water break and a ten minute rest. This news was received with pleasure by the troops, who took cover and removed their Bergens. Trev removed his boots and discovered a huge blister, on his right foot.

'That looks nasty,' Ron said to him, with concern. 'I've got a needle and some Tinc Benz, it's good for blisters. Do you want me to pop it for you?' He waited for Trev to nod his head and look away. Taking a needle from the pack attached to his webbing, he popped the blister and gently squeezed out the fluid. With the blister deflated, he applied the Tinc Benz to the sore. Drying it off, he applied some Tinc Benz surgical tape, to prevent infection and to stop it rubbing. 'That should see you good for another 20 clicks,' he laughed, as Trev grimaced his thanks.

With everyone rested, the section heaved their Bergens on to their backs and fell in line, once again, resuming the patrol. After another two hours of 'tabbing', Ron held up his hand, in a signal for the patrol to stop. He motioned for them to get down, then pointed to Richard and placed his hand on his head, meaning 'on me'. This was a sign for Richard to join him. Crawling on his stomach, Richard joined Ron, at the edge of the wood. Reaching him, a burst of automatic fire erupted from a small copse, some 300 metres ahead of them.

'Contact machine gun position, wait out!' he screamed back to his radio operator, who relayed the message to Zero. Training his binoculars on the position, he confirmed that it was manned by two soldiers, dug in with a GPMG. He checked there were no other forces embedded within the small copse. Mentally, Richard had already formulated his quick attack orders. He motioned for Ron to follow him, back to cover and re-join the section. Once there, he gave a more detailed contact report to Zero.

'Zero, this is T10, contact grid 454676. Enemy machine gun post on edge of copse, we have come under automatic fire, am preparing to assault, wait out!' He completed his report and released the pressel switch.

Gathering the section together, he began to give his formal orders. 'We are at grid 453673. To our front is open ground, with a small copse 300 metres plus. We have an enemy machine gun post at gird 454676, dug in at edge of the copse.' He paused, waiting for the detail to sink in, then continued. 'Friendly forces, we have a patrol from Tango 20 to our north flank. Our mission is to destroy the machine gun post and go firm, 100 metres plus of the objective.'

In good military fashion, he repeated the mission and carried on. 'The forming up point will be the edge of this wood line. Ron, you will give fire support with Simon on the GPMG, on the right flank. Charlie fire team left, with Delta fire team right, myself and runner in the centre. H hour will be in five minutes. Before the final assault, Ron, if you can lob a grenade into the position, that would be grand. Are there any questions?'

The lads shook their heads and Richard smiled. 'Let's get it done, then.' He turned to get into position. The section did likewise, with the GPMG, under the direction of Ron, on the right flank. As the time ticked towards H hour, Richard gave the fire order to the GPMG, to open up. With a belch of flame, Simon squeezed off five or six blank rounds at a time, in the direction of the enemy. Charlie fire team got to their feet and sprinted twenty metres in front of them, threw themselves down and opened fire.

Once in position, Delta fire team did the same, quickly followed by Richard and the radio operator, once they reported firm. Last to move were Ron and Simon, with the GPMG. They continued the motion, until they were around 30 metres from the enemy position. Then, Ron threw a thunder flash into the vicinity of the enemy GPMG. After a few seconds, the thunder flash exploded and the section, apart from Ron and Simon, continued to pour fire into the position, then assaulted the trench. Not halting, they fought through, as they had been taught and reorganised 100 metres past it.

As soon as they were firm, Richard sent two men back, to check for casualties or take prisoners. They quickly reported that both enemy had been 'killed' and that they had not received any casualties themselves. Richard quickly got on the radio and sent a detailed contact report of what had happened. Just as he did, they heard automatic fire, coming from a position north of theirs. They reckoned this must be the other section, assaulting their given objective. After twenty minutes, the gun fire settled down. The section commander of Tango 20 also sent his full contact report, confirming they, too, had taken their objective. Both call signs were ordered to remain in position and await further taskings.

Richard's section immediately went into their administration after reorg. Ron, as 2ic, was busy seeing that everyone had enough ammunition and water left. He reported the ammo state to Richard, who then consolidated his situation report, to send back to Zero. They were down to around five rounds per man and had almost run out of water. They had enough rations to last twelve hours, but didn't know how long this phase was going to last.

After sending his report to Zero, Richard was surprised to hear that they were to prepare a helicopter landing site (HLS) in the clearing, 200 metres north of their position. He wondered if they were going to be visited by the Commanding Officer, checking how the course was going. Richard immediately tasked one of his blokes to go and prepare the site, Tango 20 also sent one person to help achieve this. Just over half an hour passed, when the troops were informed over the air that they would be extracted from their current location by helicopter.

The aircraft would be approaching from the east and they were to mark the HLS with blue smoke, in five minutes. As soon as this instruction had been received, from a distance, came the unmistakable sound of the Merlin engines of a Puma helicopter. As it came into view, Richard gave the order for the HLS to 'pop' the smoke grenades they were carrying. The sections readied themselves, for the incoming transport. There were two aircraft, one for each section and, in no time, they were touching down at the HLS. The aircraft were only on the ground a short time before the pilots gave the thumbs up for the sections to board. Crouching low from the downdraft of the rotor blades, the troops climbed aboard. Settling down, there was an excited buzz within the aircraft. 'Thank fuck it's all over,' Richard thought to himself. Little did he know there was one major hurdle to clear.

Chapter 14 – Parachute Training and Pass Off

The grins on the faces of the weary course members soon faded, when one of them remarked they were going in the wrong direction for camp. This remark caused everyone to look out of the windows and, seeing the position of the sun, and noting the time of day, this appeared to be correct. Ron asked the pilot where they were going and got back the simple reply, 'Bad Lippspringe', from the man, who to fight to disguise the pleasure on his face.

Richard had been to this place a couple of years before and had completed a two week, free fall parachute course. He knew there was nothing else there, apart from a neighbouring golf course. Assuming golf skills had not been made part of a leadership course, it could only mean one thing. Richard chuckled to himself, before announcing to the rest of the section:

'Looks like they're going to throw us out of a perfectly serviceable aircraft.' A look of fear took over the faces of some. They had thought the course was all over but, for some, the most difficult part was still to come. Inside the Puma, there was deathly silence, for the remaining ten minutes of the flight. The Pumas began to hover and slowly descend, until the bounce of wheels on the ground signified they had landed. The rotors continued to turn and the pilot gave the signal for them to disembark. One of the section pulled open the door and they jumped out, again keeping low, to avoid the rotors. Gathering at a safe distance, both sections watched, as the aircraft wound up the speed of the rotors and lifted off, in the direction from which they had come.

Turning round, they saw Captain Hamlin and the instructors, waiting for them. They appeared to have a serious look about them and the troops wondered if they had fucked up the last task. Instead of a issuing a bollocking, Captain Hamlin asked them, in a quiet manner, to gather round. They picked up their Bergens, assembling in a semi-circle around the officer and the instructors.

'First of all, gents, I would like to congratulate you, not only for the last 36 hours, but also for the effort you have put in over the duration of the course. Welcome to the parachute centre at Bad Lippspringe, for your final task.'

He waited for the enormity of the statement to sink in. The look of terror on some of the candidates' faces was apparent and was not unexpected. They shuffled nervously, from foot to foot. 'If you would follow me, I will take you to meet your instructors.' With that, he turned and headed for a hangar. The troops and their JNCOs followed on behind, the mood was solemn. Entering the hangar, they were faced with two athletic looking types, dressed in blue overall jump suits. The realisation hit them that this was not a joke and that they were really going to be thrown out of an aircraft, attached to a flimsy piece of silk.

'Good afternoon, I'm Staff Sergeant Todd and this is Corporal Newlands. We are both instructors here at the British Army Parachute Centre. It is our remit, over the next 24 hours, to bring you to a standard that will enable you to complete a static line parachute jump.'

The look of terror on the faces of the students was one Todd had seen many times before. He, therefore, went on to try to put their fears at rest. 'I know that some of you will be harbouring feelings of trepidation, even fear. I can assure you if you listen to what we teach you, this exercise will be a walk in the park.' He delivered the words with confidence, which allayed some of the fears. Some, understandably, still had looks of dread on their faces.

For their first demonstration, the two instructors went through the process of packing a parachute, one of which had already been laid out on the hangar floor. Methodically, and talking as they did so, Todd and Newlands went through the stages of packing away the massive dome-like material into the small backpack, which would house it. The whole demonstration took less than twenty minutes.

The men were then split into twos and provided with a chute each. They practiced folding the silk canopies into the small receptacles. Some of the students gave up, after numerous attempts. After an hour, they were pleased to be told to stand at ease. The instructors took great delight in seeing the wide, beaming grins as they told their students they would not be packing their own parachutes, for the jump. Richard knew this would be the case, as he had not done this until the second week of his course, a couple of years previously.

For the next lesson, they were taken through techniques on how to fall properly. In the skydiving world, this was known as the parachute landing fall (PLF). A parachute landing fall is a safety technique which allows a parachutist to land safely, without injury. The technique is performed by paratroopers and novice recreational parachutists, when using round parachutes, deployed by static line. A series of boxes, at varying heights, had been set up, at one end of the hangar. The students were invited to climb on to a box each and, once there, the instructors continued with the lesson.

'While landing under a parachute canopy, the feet strike the ground first and, immediately, the jumper throws himself sideways, to distribute the landing shock sequentially, along five points of body contact with the ground,' Sergeant Todd explained. Then, he demonstrated the technique itself, beginning with landing on the balls of the feet; the side of the calf to the thigh; the side of the hips or buttocks and ending on the back. This dissipated the inertia of the landing, through these different parts of the body.

'During a parachute landing fall, the jumper's legs should be slightly bent at the knee, the chin tucked in and the parachute risers grasped, in an arm-bar, protecting the face and throat, with elbows tucked in, to the sides, to prevent injury. Alternatively, the hands can be linked, behind the neck, with elbows tucked in close.' He demonstrated the movements, as he continued:

'The direction the jumper is coming in determines which way he will fall, left front, left side and left rear or right front, right side and right rear.'

Sergeant Todd's demonstration and explanation finished, he invited the students to jump from the boxes. As they neared the ground, he called out the direction for them to fall. Between the two instructors, any bad drills carried out along the line were corrected. The drills continued for about an hour, until they were content the students had got it right. The instructors were happy with their progress and fell them out, for the night.

They were shown to their accommodation, where bedding had been provided for them. After settling themselves in, the course then went for the evening meal. Some of the blokes were genuinely excited about the next day, while others were silent during the meal, not saying a word. 'There will be some sleepless nights tonight for some,' Richard thought, to himself.

The evening meal over, the students were invited to use the bar, however, were told that they were not to kick the arse out of things. They gathered together, for the next few hours, more for mutual support than anything else. They drank a couple of beers and chatted over what might happen the next day. Even though Richard had completed around 25 jumps on his last visit to the parachute centre, he was starting to feel apprehensive. Some of the guys even swore they wouldn't get into the plane the next day. By the end of the evening, the mood was a little lighter and the alcohol subdued students made their way to bed.

It was 06:30 and people were already milling around the room. Some wanted to get on with it, some, having experienced a restless night, were not so keen. The washrooms were strangely quiet, with none of the usual banter. They washed in silence and returned to the room, to dress, in readiness for the day. They had been told the previous evening that they would be practising exiting the aircraft, plus emergency drills. The word 'emergency' was enough to cause disconcertion among the troops. Richard tried to use his previous experience to put their minds at rest. He had been told this drill was very rarely put into practice. On his previous course consisting of twelve students, none had needed to use it. This did little to reassure them and the clock ticked closer to jump time.

The course assembled, once again, in the hangar. The two instructors were already waiting for them, with eager looks on their faces. They waited for the class to settle down, before Sergeant Todd addressed them.

'Okay, gents, I hope you all slept well last night,' he smirked as he spoke and, without pausing, continued. 'This morning, we will cover how to enter and exit the aircraft, how to adopt a stable position and, finally, how to deal with an emergency. Hopefully, we should be finished by 11:30, when we will take an early lunch and the first 'stick' boards at 12:15. The weather forecast is clear, with light winds, so it should be a piece of piss!' Todd beamed at his charges. The instructors had seen many frightened faces in the past and understood how these young soldiers felt. However, they still took a little pleasure in the students' uneasiness.

For the first fifteen minutes, they went through how each stick, of eight men, would line up and be given a number. They would enter the aircraft, strictly in that order. Each would be given a piece of paper, to be handed to the jump master, on their entry. When they reached 1500 feet, they would be asked to turn on their emergency deployment device, a gadget attached to their reserve chute, which would pop, if they were to pass out and reach terminal velocity. Then, Todd went on to explain that when their number was called, they would shuffle to the door, place their hands on either side of the doorframe and look back, over their shoulders, at the jump master.

When he tapped them on the shoulder, they were to push themselves out and away from the aircraft. Once clear, they needed to adopt the correct body position, to enable a safe deployment of their chutes. The first thing they needed to check was that their parachutes had deployed correctly, fully deflated and with no twisted lines. Secondly, they had to take hold of the 'risers', the two broad straps attaching the lines to the chute.

On the drill, they were to shout 'check canopy'. Once they were happy, they were to check that it was safe to manoeuvre, then begin their descent, to the airfield. They would be guided by a radio and earpiece, which they would be issued.

'In the event of checking your parachute and it not being deployed properly, you will initiate the emergency drill.' He then explained how this was to be carried out. 'Make sure that you pull the release on your emergency chute, then throw it forward. The reason for this is that you need 'clean air' and not have it collapse, due to a partially opened main chute. This could cause your secondary to collapse as well, so bear that in mind.' He looked at the open mouths of some students, who looked horrified. 'This procedure is very rarely used, if your chute is packed properly and you make a clean, stable exit from the aircraft.'

With that, he asked the course to line up, in two rows of eight. He waited until they did as instructed and proceeded to walk along each line, handing a piece of paper to every man, at the same time giving them a number. This done, he then called them forward, to a wooden replica of a Cessna aircraft, located in a corner of the hangar. They practised boarding the aircraft as well as their exit drills. As each man launched himself, he counted, 'One thousand, ... two thousand, ... three thousand. Check canopy!' and simulated checking their chutes and taking control of the risers.

As one group carried out exit drills, the other eight man stick were taken under the control of Corporal Newlands. He took them to another part of the hangar, where a series of what looked like scaffolding pipes were arranged. Each station had a harness next to it, which they were told to put on. The harnesses had clips attached, with a reserve chute at the front. The Corporal gave a demonstration of how to attach themselves to the scaffold, then went through the complete emergency drill. After answering questions, he invited them to strap themselves on to the equipment. They practised the drills, until they were swapped with the other group. The morning flew past and before long, with the training now complete, the students were fallen out for something to eat. They were told to arrive back at 12:15 to collect their parachutes and jump equipment.

It was noticeable at the midday meal that not everyone was eating. The nervousness in the group was starting to rub off on Richard and doubts began to enter his mind. 'What if my chute doesn't deploy properly, or even worse, not at all?' he thought, to himself. It was too late for these thoughts now. They had been taught the drills and just needed to get on with it. By the end of the day, the jumps would all be over.

Gathering back at the hangar, a table had been set out, with jump suits, parachutes and harnesses. The students were handed one set each and told to get dressed. In a slow, methodical manner, they prepared themselves, checking every last detail, not just once, but numerous times. They had been spared the task of packing their own chutes.

Richard didn't know if this was a good or bad thing. As soon as they were dressed, the instructors went round and double checked the security of the harnesses, ensuring that everything was in order.

They detailed them to assemble outside, where the Cessna was waiting, its engine running. Simon, the happy-go-lucky Cockney, was a different man, his face was ashen and he looked as though he was about to be sick. The man most affected was Rob, from Command Troop. He had sworn that he wasn't even going to board the plane, yet, there he was, making his way to the flight line. His plan had been to place himself as last man in the stick. This, however, backfired, as the instructors numbered them off. Although last man in the back row, the instructors began from the end of the line, allocating him the number 1.

'I think you got this wrong, Staff, I should be number 8.' he tried to argue.

'Can't you fucking read? That says '1' and that's your number. Now, shut the fuck up and prepare to board' snapped the instructor.

The first stick, including Rob, was ordered to board. With his head hung low, he led his fellow students toward the plane, waiting ominously, 50 metres away. Reaching the door, he handed over his paper to the jump master and tentatively climbed in. The jump master counted them all in, then gave a thumbs up to the instructors, on the ground.

On the ground, Richard's stick watched, in anticipation, as the Cessna's engine noise increased, as it taxied off, to the end of the runway. Gathering speed, it lifted off from the tarmac, into the clear, winter sky. Slowly turning, it began its climb, above the airfield. Before long, it was at the height required for the jump.

Richard wondered if the others, like him, were expecting Rob to bottle it and refuse to jump. They spotted a figure exit the plane, then another and another, until all eight bodies were in the air. The first three chutes opened in a text book manner, but the fourth didn't look right. The chute had deployed, although apparently not fully. The figure sped past the first three. The onlookers could see that the lines were twisted. The figure, who they realised was Cockney Simon, was kicking his feet, frantically, in an attempt to untangle his lines. Richard felt physically sick, as Simon continued to descend, at high speed. It was with a collective sigh of relief that, at around 1000 feet, the chute deployed fully. The men on the ground looked at each other in dread, knowing they were going to be next.

It only took another ten minutes, for the whole stick to navigate their way to the landing zone. They watched as each one readied themselves for the landing and safely reach 'terra firma'. The aircraft had already landed and was making its way back to the waiting students. The first stick had already gathered their chutes and were walking over towards them, with shit eating grins on their faces.

'That was fuckin' ace!' Rob exclaimed, as he approached them. 'I want to go again!' he laughed. His fellow students knew that he didn't really mean it, it was just adrenalin talking. Their thoughts were interrupted by Sergeant Todd, ordering them to climb aboard the plane. They made a last minute check of their equipment and started the dreaded walk, towards the aircraft. With what they had just witnessed, they were shitting themselves. Surely what had happened to Simon couldn't happen again? Or could it?

The men safely aboard, once again, the jump master gave the thumbs up and the aircraft taxied off. Slowly climbing above the countryside, Richard looked out, as the building they trained in got smaller and smaller. At 1500 feet, the jump master gave the signal for them to turn on their Automatic Deployment devices. They then sat, for the next fifteen minutes, waiting for the Cessna to reach its target altitude. This attained, the door was flung open and the jump master called for number '1' to get in the doorframe. Trev reluctantly shuffled his way to the yawning gap, placed his hands on each side of the door and looked, over his shoulder, at the jump master. Feeling a tap on his shoulder, he pushed himself away and made a perfect exit. Richard, at number '4', went through the anguish of waiting for the next two to jump. Then, before he knew it, he was looking into the face of the jump master, who smiled and simply said 'Go!'

Richard pushed away and, immediately, adopted a stable swept position. The sound of the wind in his ears was familiar. With a snap and crack and, with a distinct pressure on his shoulders and groin, he felt the parachute deploy. Looking up, he was thankful to see a fully developed canopy. He took hold of the risers and awaited instructions from the ground. The air was so still, the view serene and beautiful. Suddenly, his radio erupted in his ear.

'Number 4, pull left toggle.' Richard complied and, banking to the left, he continued his descent.

After a series of right and left turns, descending further each time, he could see the distinct cross, which marked the target landing area. He could see the windsock, at the end of the airfield and knew he would need to make his last turn shortly, so that he came into the wind. The ground was starting to rush up to meet him, so he adopted the PLF position. As the ground drew ever closer, he pulled down both risers, to 'flare' the parachute and landed gently, with a roll to his right. He quickly got to his feet, ran round the parachute and began to gather it in. Of all his jumps, he felt this had been one of the best.

The course gathered in the lecture room and each was given a photograph of his exit from the aircraft, taken by a camera fixed to the wing, and a certificate for his one day parachute course. The atmosphere in the room was buzzing. All the talk was of Simon's disco dancing antics on his way to earth. Everyone, to a man, was thankful that they had completed the jump. Only one thing remained. That was the pass off parade, the next day.

The course had rose early that morning and put on their number 2 service dress and forage caps. Each man checked his buddy, to make sure he hadn't forgotten anything. The course instructors had them to fall in, outside. Once there, the course officer, Captain Hamlin, addressed them.

'Gentlemen, may I, on behalf of all the instructors, thank you for all your efforts, during the past two weeks. You have entered into the spirit of the course and will make fine JNCOs. We hope the lessons you have learned will stand you in good stead, during your careers. There is only one thing left for me to do, which is to announce the award of best student of the course.'

The students looked around at each other, but most eyes were on Rob and Richard. 'The best student award goes to …' he paused for dramatic effect, 'Trooper, now Lance Corporal, Jones!' Rob slammed his foot in and marched out to receive the chevron which Captain Hamlin held in his hand. With a handshake and brief exchange of words, Rob saluted and turned about. His last job was to march the Course on to the parade square. It came to light later that Captain Hamlin had wanted to give the accolade to Richard, but Rob just pipped him on turnout. This was immaterial to Richard, who had just enjoyed doing the course. It would be another year before Richard would attain his first stripe, due to his occasional lack of self-discipline.

Chapter 15 – Recce Troop

The leadership cadre was now but a memory, as Richard prepared the Scorpion (CVRT) reconnaissance vehicle, for their next exercise. The vehicle was manufactured by Alvis and was introduced into the British Army in 1973. It held the Guinness World Record for the fastest production light tank, at 51.1 mph. It was armed with a low velocity 76mm L23A1 gun, which fired high explosive, smoke, and canister rounds. It could carry a mixture of rounds, up to 42 in total. It was also fitted with a 7.62mm co-axial machine gun and smoke grenade dischargers, placed left and right of the turret. With its Jaguar 4.2 litre engine, it could accelerate from 0 – 30 mph in 16 seconds. To top it all, a rare luxury, it was fitted with a built-in shithouse, located directly under the commander's seat. The crew didn't even have to leave the vehicle for a crap!

Richard had been working as part of his new three man crew for two months. The driver was Reg Graves and the commander, Brummy Carter, a Sergeant and the Troop TSM. He hailed, originally, from the Black Country, in the West Midlands. He had taken a shine to Richard, who was his operator/gunner, in the short time they had been together; so much so that he would drive Richard all the way home to Birgit's place after work. Brummy liked a beer and, before dropping Richard off, would sink a few in a local pub with him. He would then drive back the twenty kilometres to camp, picking him up the next morning.

This had gone on for two months and Richard was very appreciative. He still didn't have a car, although Birgit did, an old Volkswagen Passat, with which she sometimes picked him up. They were planning to buy a new one, after they married, later that year.

The Troop had undergone a conversion course to the new vehicle and were therefore practised in its use. This proficiency was going to be tested, on exercise, the following week, and on the plains of Canada, three months on. Reg had been a mechanic, prior to joining the army, loving nothing more than being in vehicle decks. His love of all things mechanical was surpassed only by his love of all things alcoholic, and he was frequently half-cut at work. He had been given the nickname Gramps since, for a Trooper, he was quite old, having joined the Regiment some two years earlier, at the age of 28. Although at times he turned up worse for wear through drink, he always did his job and was never late. More importantly, the vehicle was always on the road and very rarely broke down. This was all Brummy required of them, do your job and you could get away with murder. He was one for hard work and hard play and would give them as many opportunities as he could for time off the tank park.

The previous month he had organised an adventure training week, away in southern Germany. The event was at an American Forces base, by Lake Chimsee, which began with an evening in the base bar. British soldiers were a novelty at the base and drew quite a lot of attention. Although only twenty in number, they immediately took over the bar. Within a couple of hours, they emptied the establishment's stock of Budweiser and had to send out for more. As the party mood heightened, some of the guys were up on the dance floor, cutting some moves. The local population had never witnessed blokes dancing together, doing the 'squaddie two step'. As quickly as the beer was going down, it was passing through Richard and, on one of his many trips to the bog, he noticed a machine on the wall.

'What's this?' he enquired, to a huge African American.

'It's an alcohol meter, we use it to see if you're safe to drive. Take a straw from the side and place it in that hole, there,' he pointed, with a massive index finger. 'Then, blow till you hear the beep and the reading registers, on the screen.' Taking a straw and placing it in the orifice provided, Richard began to blow. The digital reading increased rapidly, until the sound, which told Richard to stop blowing.

'Jesus Christ, man! You should be fucking dead!' was the surprised exclamation from the giant, black guy. Richard simply smiled at him, turned and entered the toilets, leaving the bemused American soldier, in his wake.

The rest of the week was taken up, mostly, by long hikes in the Bavarian countryside, always ending up with a session on the beer, in a local hostelry. Brummy, who was keen on biathlons, disciplines consisting of cross-country skiing and shooting, was familiar with the area. He took them to the small town of Rupholding, which nestled in the valley of the local mountain range. He knew the proprietor of a nearby restaurant and, one evening, wangled them a free meal there. The meal was on the house but the owner was compensated by the Troops bar bill. The boss of the place must have been rubbing his hands when they left, Richard thought.

The only thing that soured the trip was the fact that someone nicked the American flag, from the flagpole, on the evening before they were due to leave. A couple of days after their return, the Troop Leader, Captain Fishburn, was called into the Commanding Officer's office. The CO had received a letter from the Commandant of the American base, referring strongly to the flag incident. The Troop Leader received the bollocking of his life, which, on his return, he duly passed on to the members of the Troop.

That was all behind them now, as Richard looked across at Brummy, who was staring through his binoculars, at the edge of a wood. It was 07:00, on a warm, summer morning, on the second day of the exercise. The exercise was not on Soltau training area, but, was a large one, held

142

in the German countryside. It was more realistic than normal. There were umpires, who followed the troops and decided if anyone had been knocked out, during an engagement. It was Recce Troop's job to be the eyes and ears of the Battlegroup Commander.

They were tasked with gaining information on key features, terrain and enemy forces. As specialist troops, they sometimes were involved in marking or clearing minefields or route denial, by use of explosives. Richard, who had spent a short time in the Royal Engineers (RE) before transferring, was quite adept at this function. He had given lectures on mine warfare, on request from Brummy. He had also, along with a few others, attended an Assault Pioneers course at an RE camp in Hameln. It had covered subjects such as mines, explosives and the use of boats. Little did Richard know, he would meet one of the instructors from the course, later in life, and they were to become good friends. Although he came from a rough part of Glasgow, he held the same ideals and values as Richard.

Brummy, deciding that the village to their front seemed to be clear, gave Reg the order to advance. The familiar sound of the gear being engaged was heard and the Scorpion, along with the other vehicle in the section, crept forward. They made their way, slowly, towards the village, stopping just outside it.

Checking again through his binoculars, Brummy asked the second vehicle to push on, past him and take a cautious look in the village. As the vehicle passed them, on the other side of the road, Richard raised his hand, in acknowledgement. He would have loved to have been commanding but it wouldn't be long, before he would get his chance. It took only a short time for their second vehicle to confirm that the village was clear. The section then sped off, along the road, towards their next task. As they moved along, at around 30 mph, they were alerted by a banging sound. The cause was the track, bouncing and hitting the top of the suspension. The vehicle lurched to the right and, at the same time, the left hand track snaked out, in front of them and ended in a ditch, at the side of the road. Reg fought to keep the vehicle on the road and, after releasing his foot off the accelerator, the Scorpion eventually ground to a halt.

'When was the last time you tightened those fuckin' tracks?' growled Brummy, at Reg.

'Yesterday morning,' came the defensive reply, from the red faced Trooper.

'Bollocks! You couldn't have, that's the first time I have seen a vehicle throw a track, while travelling on a road. I could understand it, if we were moving cross-country!' Brummy screamed, at the embarrassed driver.

For the next hour, they struggled, dismantling the track into sections, so they could extract it, from the ditch. They then needed to join the pieces together again, before dragging the track back on to the vehicle. Once they had finished, Reg turned to Brummy and asked:

'Can we have a beer? I'm spitting feathers here.'

A broad grin spread across Brummy's face, the anger gone and the incident forgotten.

'Rich, get the beers out, marra,' he indicated with his thumb, in the direction of the turret. Richard returned with three open bottles of beer and handed them out to the crew. They gulped them, while wiping the sweat away from their brows. It was only 09:30 in the morning, but this was normal for this crew. Thirsts quenched, the crew mounted back up and carried on with their task. Just before arriving at the next village, they were met, by one of the exercise umpires. He motioned for them to stop and climbed up the front of the vehicle, placing his hand on Brummy's shoulder.

'You have been subject to an artillery bombardment and you have been taken out,' he informed Brummy and asked him to get out of the vehicle. He led him to the Land

144

Rover, parked at the side of the road and gestured for him to get in. Richard's heart sank, as he realised he had just been promoted to vehicle commander. He immediately got on the air and let the other section vehicle know what had happened. Between them, they decided to move back into the cover of a nearby wood, to formulate their next move.

As they positioned their vehicles at the edge of the wood, Richard made his way over to the other vehicle commander, to enquire what he wanted to do next. They decided that they would go ahead with their original task of probing the nearby village. Looking through their binoculars, they spotted what looked like two radio masts. It was possible this was a command location and they decided they would take a closer look. Before they could decide who would approach from which direction, their attention was drawn to Reg, who was walking towards them, with a crate of beer in his arms. He was accompanied by Paul Robson, the gunner operator of the other vehicle, who was carrying a similar container.

'Where did you get that?' Smudge, the new section commander, asked.

'From that shed, behind us,' Reg smiled, as he indicated, over his shoulder, with his thumb. It came to light that they had parked next to the premises of a local German football club. The shed they were referring to, was their sports club, where they stowed drinks, for after match parties. Smudge shrugged, taking one of the beers, offered by Paul.

'Would be a shame to refuse free drink,' he chuckled, as he removed the top with his teeth.

For the next half hour, they sipped on their beers, listening to what was going on, over the air. Things were quiet, so they came to the conclusion the war could wait a little longer for them. After the five consumed the two crates, Smudge gave the order for them to mount up. He would approach the village from the west, while Richard was to take his vehicle in, from the east. With engines revving, they pulled out of the woods and turned, in opposite directions. Making their way, slowly and under low revs, Richard crawled towards the eastern edge of the village, stopping around 200 metres short.

He picked up the binoculars and scanned the village, for any sign of military movement. While scanning the rooftops, he saw, clearly, the two masts they had spotted from the edge of the wood, now more clearly defined. One was slightly higher than the other and both had 'pineapples' atop. Richard, from his time in Command Troop, recognised these as Antennae Matching Units. This confirmed their suspicions, that this was probably some type of command set up. He guessed these were 8 and 12 metre masts, used for communication to forward battlegroup forces. To try and assess the numbers, he asked Reg to pull forward, to the edge of the village. Keeping the engine in a low gear and revs, they inched forward, up the main street. Suddenly, from the side of the road, they were met by a guy wearing a beret, with a cap badge indicating he was part of their Regiment. Richard eyed him suspiciously, as he had never seen this character before.

'There's a large concentration of vehicles in the farm complex, to the rear of the village. If you follow me, I can lead you there,' he said, excitedly.

Wouldn't have got an Oscar for that one, Richard smirked, to himself. 'Aye, okay mate, just a minute,' he replied, while whispering to Reg to select reverse and get them the fuck out of there. With a clunk, Reg engaged reverse gear and, with high revs and under the direction of Richard, steered backwards, out of the village.

As they cleared the built up area, he slammed the vehicle into first gear and they headed back to the safety of the woods. Arriving there, it came as no surprise that they were alone. They hadn't heard from Smudge's vehicle, since they left some 40 minutes earlier. Richard came to the conclusion that they had no doubt been captured or umpired out, having made a radio check with no reply. He immediately got on the air and reported back to control that they had come across a possible enemy communications complex. After finishing his report to Zero, he began to formulate a 'fire mission' order. This was the first time he had done it, since completing his Control Signallers' course, a couple of years earlier.

'Hello, Golf 10, this is Tango 22, fire mission over,' he took a deep breath, waiting for a reply.

'Golf 10, fire mission send over,' came the answer.

'Tango 22, fire mission grid 768679, direction 1600 mils, communication complex at edge of village, neutralise in two minutes.' Richard completed the fire mission request and waited for it to be confirmed. There was a short pause, before G10 repeated back the request, ending with' wait out'. Two minutes passed, when the silence was broken once again.

'Tango 22, this is Golf 10, shot two zero over,' indicating that the rounds would be landing in twenty seconds. Richard, instinctively, raised the binoculars, to observe the fall of shot. They had been told even though no live rounds were being fired, for obvious reasons, artillery fire would be simulated by smoke, from the artillery umpires. After twenty seconds, Richard could see the tell-tale sign of an orange smoke grenade, around 200 metres minus of the target.

'Golf 10, this is Tango 22, add 200 on target fire for effect,' he said, confidently. This was repeated by the artillery and he was given the flight time, once again. After another twenty seconds, a pall of orange smoke rose up, from the centre of the area where the masts were located. Richard smiled to himself, this was his first fire mission and it had been successful. Little did he know that he would be doing it for real, in about three weeks' time, on the plains of Alberta.

147

The short week's exercise was behind them, as they boarded the aircraft, for the long flight to Calgary Airport. This was a regular trip made by most combat troops every year. There were seven exercises, run every year at the British Army Training Units Suffield (BATUS). They were designated Medicine Man (Med Man) 1 through to 7 and, luckily, they were taking part in Med Man 5, which was a summer exercise. Although they would not have Canadian cold weather to contend with, he remembered, from earlier visits, mosquitos were a constant nuisance. The previous exercise in Germany had gone well and, now, they were going to put it into practice, in a live firing environment. The training was as close to real combat that they could experience.

The aircraft landed in Keflavik Airport, in Iceland, to refuel and the troops were given the order to disembark. This was a normal stopover and, although it was 01:00 am, they knew that the bar would be open. The crowd rushed through the airport, all attempting to be first at the bar. Normally, it would be closed at this time of the morning but, as they approached, they saw the smiling face of a young Icelandic woman, waiting to greet them. The staff were used to this and opened the bar specially for military flights.

For the next hour, the lads threw as much alcohol down their throats as was physically possible. They were all too soon given the disappointing news that they were to board the aircraft, once again. They savoured the last dregs of their beers, then returned to their seats. Making himself as comfortable as possible, on this cramped aircraft, Richard drifted off to sleep. He dreamt about the previous week and his marriage to Birgit.

It had begun early, with a family breakfast, which included his brother, sister and her partner, his parents and Knocker, his brother's friend. Shortly after breakfast was finished the Sekt, German sparkling wine, was opened

148

and they proposed a toast to the future Mr and Mrs Hunter. This was a double celebration, as it was Richard's father's birthday, the following day. The toast complete, the doorbell interrupted the celebrations. Birgit left the room, to answer it. She returned with Will and three others from the Regiment, who included Ron and Rob, from his leadership cadre. The other member was Peter Newstead, whose daughters were acting as bridesmaids. All four friends were dressed in 'Blues', complete with chainmail on their shoulders and white cross belts.

They clinked as they entered the room, their spurs catching the tiled floor. Will was to be Richard's best man and the other three were ushers. Weddings were different in Germany, where the ceremony was only legally binding in a Registration Office. So, for this reason, Richard was dressed in civilian clothing. He would have time to change afterwards, before the church ceremony. They drank another glass of Sekt, before Birgit, Richard and the immediate family left for the Rathaus, or Town Hall.

The wedding ceremony was very official and serious, making the couple contemplate the contract they were entering into. It was similar to those held in England, but done with the efficiency for which Germans were renowned. The paperwork was filled in and signed by the couple and their witnesses, then they paraded outside, for the obligatory photoshoot.

When they returned to the house, Richard quickly got dressed into his Blues and joined Will outside, for a cigarette. The other three friends were already at the church, awaiting the arrival of the first guests. Will and Richard joined them ten minutes later and took their place, in the front row. As they walked in, Richard noticed everyone turn round, at the clink of spurs, as they marched down the aisle. There were so many friends and family already seated and, although this was nice, it did not stop

Richard feeling nervous. As he took his place next to Will, he bowed his head, in silent contemplation.

'You look like a condemned man,' Will broke his train of thought with the remark, trying to make light of the situation.

'I feel like it, mate,' was all Richard could reply. His thoughts were disturbed, by the sound of the church organ, sounding out the wedding march. The congregation stood to receive the bride, who was accompanied by her father, as they walked, slowly, to the front of the church. It was unusual in Germany for the bride's father to give her away, but all had agreed it would be a nice touch.

The ceremony itself was a blur and, after exchanging rings, the couple departed the church, as a married couple. Once again, a photoshoot took over, lasting around twenty minutes. Thinking that it was all over and time to party, Richard started to make his way, to the car which was to convey them to the reception. He was halted by Birgit, who grabbed his arm, stopping him in his tracks.

'We can't go yet,' she said, smiling. 'We have to cut that first,' she pointed over, to a wooden trestle, which had a log placed on it. To the side and leaning against it, was a double handed saw. Richard knew what was coming. The log itself must have been nearly two feet in diameter and he quickly deduced this was going to be hard work. With the wedding guests looking on, Birgit and Richard took their places on either side of the trestle. They picked up the saw and placed it on the centre of the log. With a forward and backward motion, pushing and pulling, they began the process of cutting through it. This was accompanied by the sound of clapping, from the onlookers. The first few inches went quite easily but, after a while, as they began to tire, it got more difficult. Sweat was beginning to run into Richard's eyes, due to the tight fitting, thick uniform and the midday sun. The guests continued to give their encouragement, and to the couple's great relief, the log

split into two parts. Richard slumped forward, exhausted. The idea behind the tradition was to promote the idea of working together as a couple, which he thought to be a lovely way of emphasising the point. The years ahead would be full of give and take and compromises.

For the rest of the day, the wedding party ate, drank, danced and made merry at a hunting lodge hired for the occasion. Birgit's father had paid for the whole reception, a fact the couple were not aware, of at the time. The money they had saved towards the wedding could now put to good use, furnishing their brand new married quarter.

The sound of the Captain's voice on the intercom announced their descent to Calgary International Airport. They had been travelling for thirteen hours, including the bus journey to the airport in Germany. As the engines were cut, the Troops lined up in the aisles, waiting, eagerly, to stretch their legs, before the next leg by bus to BATUS. With no luggage to collect, they made their way through airport arrivals, to the coaches, waiting for them outside. The temperature was already in the mid-twenties centigrade and it was only 06:30. The journey to 'Crowfoot Camp' took just under two hours to complete.

Disembarking the coach, the troops were directed to the bar, where a briefing by the local Military Police (RMP) was given. Although they had jurisdiction for the camp, the soldiers came under the law of the local civilian police authorities. The briefing was given for every Battlegroup and, although many had heard it before, the RMP gave no apologies for repeating it. The legal age for drinking was very different from the law of the UK. It also differed from Province to Province, so the troops needed to be made aware of the facts. Also, the consent for sexual relations differed and the RMP highlighted an example of a soldier, who had been imprisoned for 'statutory rape', for having had sex with a seventeen years old. Some of the younger members of the Battlegroup looked at each other, nervously. They wondered if they were supposed to ask for ID, before jumping into bed with a local girl. The briefing lasted approximately 40 minutes, after which the troops were fallen out and told they were to parade on the tank park at 08:30 the next morning.

The crowd dispersed to their accommodation allocated to the different Squadrons, Companies, Batteries and all other support arms that made up the Battlegroup. Richard knew from experience if he was to go to bed now, he would wake in the early hours. His body was telling him it was 02:00 in the morning and he needed to go to sleep. To counteract this, some of the troop decided to get a taxi into town and have a few beers. Quickly getting showered and changing into 'civvies', half a dozen met at the camp gates for their ride into Medicine Hat, the nearest town, a 35 minute taxi ride away. It was only 10:30 local time and the bars didn't open until 11:00. Their timing would be perfect, Richard thought, as the taxi pulled up and the friends climbed aboard. The vehicle made its way, at a steady 55 mph, towards the Metropolis that was 'The Hat'. During the journey, they passed a train, which seemed to go on forever. This was normal in Canada, as goods trains carried their cargo the breadth of this vast country, from East to West. The landscape was just one huge prairie plain; no trees and fields as far as the eye could see.

Pulling up outside the first pub, O'Reilly's, one of the lads paid the taxi driver and they entered. They spent the next hour relaxing and sinking a few Guinnesses, before deciding to find a bit more exotic entertainment. It was now midday and, just over the road, Cheetahs would be commencing its first floorshow of the day. The bar was well known to members of the Battlegroup, past and present. The buddies crossed the road, carefully, keeping an eye out for police cars. It was not unheard of for members of the British military to be hit with on the spot fines for jaywalking, in the town. The crossing safely negotiated, they entered the dimly lit bar, choosing a table just by the circular stage. The stage was adorned with a tall pole in the centre.

A pretty waitress approached and explained that the bar offered a deal on beer. Rather than ordering pints, they could opt for pitchers of beer, containing four measures but being charged for three. The boys beamed at each other and said they would go for pitchers. The girl smiled and asked how many pitchers they wanted among the six. Again, as one, the troops smiled, Richard advising her that they would have one pitcher each.

On her return, she placed six pitchers and six glasses in front of them. Richard gave her a bundle of notes and told her to keep the change. She smiled and thanked him, wishing them a good-day.

The sound of the compere introducing the first act of the day stopped all conversation. Out of a door to the right of the bar, stepped a gorgeous looking female. The beauty of these girls never ceased to amaze Richard. He had often wondered why they would get involved in such a career, but knew the answer, having chatted to a couple of them, on previous visits. The work was well paid and a lot of the girls were single mothers, trying to make ends meet. Others just loved the lifestyle and got off giving enjoyment to the customers. For the next two hours, the pals sat in silence, watching the girls gyrate, in front of them, on the stage.

The crowd would throw money at them in appreciation. Richard recalled a time when one of the members of the Battlegroup had been ejected for heating up coins with his lighter and throwing them at the delicate area covered by one of the dancer's G-strings. After this incident, the club positioned a bouncer close to the stage, so that he could quickly intervene, if anything untoward should happen again.

As it was early in the day, the crowd was quite sedate and appreciative of the show. Some of the friends were beginning to show signs of tiredness and, as the jet lag was hitting them, they decided to make their way back to camp, to get their heads down, until the following day.

Chapter 16 – The Plains of Alberta

The Troop woke at around 06:30, fully refreshed and, after a hearty breakfast, made their way to the tank park. There followed a quick roll call, to ensure no one was missing, then they began the process of taking over the vehicles and equipment, from the previous Battlegroup. For the past week, the Troops coming off worked day and night, to try and fix their vehicles, to a standard that could be used by the new Battlegroup. This was a time honoured tradition, as well as a matter of pride.

The results were always hotly contested, the incoming guys were never satisfied with the state of what they were handed. Numerous arguments would ensue and some of the Troop Leaders, under guidance of the Troop Sergeants, would totally refuse to take them over. The outgoing men knew that a time would come when the new Troops would be forced to take what was left, so they continued to play the game. This was to their detriment, as the longer it took, the less time they would have on 'Rest and Recuperation' (R&R).

The Recce Troop that were handing over seemed a nice bunch of lads and bent over backwards, to ensure the handover went as smoothly as possible. By the end of the day, Brummy was happy and the Troop Leader signed his life away. It had been a long day and, after the evening meal, Richard crashed out on his bed, for a couple of hours. Despite Jon Bon Jovi blasting in his ears, he drifted away into a deep sleep.

'Richard, you coming to the bar?' came Reg's voice blaring in his ear, as he was unceremoniously awakened from his dreams.

'Aye, why not? Let me have a shower first,' he replied, rubbing his eyes, trying to gather his thoughts.

Picking up his towel and washbag, from inside his locker, he slipped into flip flops and he shuffled off, to the showers. Looking at his watch, he saw it was 7pm and made a mental note to phone Birgit, the next day. They were seven hours behind Germany, so he calculated that he should ring around 2pm, to catch her, before she went to work. Taking off his watch, he removed the towel from around his waist and stepped into the shower.

The water, cascading from his head, down his body, washed away any remnants of sleep that remained. He quickly massaged the shower gel into his body, wiping away the grime of the tank park. It took him five minutes to make himself feel more human again and he made his way back to the room. A few of the Troop were already dressed and making their way out the door, saying they would see him in the bar. Richard acknowledged with a wave of the hand. He opened his locker, grabbed a pair of boxer shorts and put them on. With a squirt of deodorant under his arms, he put on a pair of jeans and a t-shirt. He ran a brush through his hair, which didn't take long, as he had visited the barber the week before and had most of it removed. Richard knew from past experience, that the prairie, at this time of year, could be unbearably warm and thought it expedient to make things as comfortable as possible. Happy that he had everything squared away, he placed the padlock on his locker and left the accommodation hut.

The sound of the jukebox blasted out, as he entered the bar, which was already full of members of the Battlegroup. Richard surveyed the room, looking for members of his troop and caught sight of Reg, who nodded over. Richard walked to the table, to join him. At least half the troop had taken a table as close to the bar as possible. The group comprised three of the section commanders and two blokes from Golcar, near Huddersfield, Hendo and Tommo. The latter two were straight talking Yorkshiremen and Richard enjoyed their company. Simon and Paul Robson were also

there, deep in conversation but turned and smiled, as
Richard joined them. The table was covered in cans of
Labatt's Blue, a local Canadian beer, popular with the
troops. Asking if anyone wanted another, Richard turned,
to go to the bar. He came back a short while later, armed
with a six pack. The friends spent the evening drinking and
talking about the upcoming exercise. The topic was
secondary only to what was planned for R&R, the highlight
of the trip, every year. Richard had big plans to fly to
Hawaii, with Isaac, his old roommate. Little did he know
that events would conspire to put a stop to this proposed
trip. Although Isaac was not a member of Recce, he was
the RSM's driver and, as a member of HQ Squadron, their
paths crossed from time to time. They had planned to visit
Hawaii after a drunken night in the Squadron bar, back in
Germany.

The beer kept flowing and the crowd in the bar was
getting more and more rowdy. The infantry element of the
Battlegroup was made up of A and B Company of the 1st
Battalion, the Royal Anglians, known as The Vikings. They
kicked off the Regimental songs, goading other troops to
'Sing, sing or show us your ring.' This invited other arms
to reply in song or bare their arses in defeat. Every
Regiment, Troop or Squadron had their very own
songsmith, a person who would lead singing and, in Recce
Troop, Hendo was the man. Being a proud Yorkshireman,
he got to his feet and began a rendition of On Ilkla Moor
Baht 'at.

Hendo was immediately joined by the rest of the
Regiment, present in the bar and, even though they were
outnumbered by the other support arms, their voices filled
the hall. This vocal competition went on, to and fro, as
members of all Regiments gave forth renditions, good and
bad. It was all good natured banter but could at times, with
the amount of alcohol consumed, sometimes turn ugly. This
evening was friendly enough, and the Troops made their

way back, to their own accommodation huts, after the bar had been closed, by the duty NCO.

The rest of the week was spent working on the tank park and preparing for the exercise. The heat on the park was searing and numerous breaks were required. Breaks were normally spent in the base Canex, fondly known as the *'Gag and puke'*. The troop consumed massive hamburgers and gallons of coke or cream soda, served in 'buckets'. It was the perfect hangover cure, greatly needed after a night in the bar or down The Hat. They would visit at least two or three times a day, as it was quicker than taking the long walk back to their own cookhouse in Camp Crowfoot.

The week passed quickly and, before they knew it, they gathered on the dust bowl, where they had parked the vehicles, the previous day. They also received their allocation of ammunition for the next few days, including 76mm rounds, comprising illumination, high explosive, smoke and canister rounds. The illumination rounds were used for night firing and would light up an area, for around 30 seconds. This was achieved by setting a time fuse on the round and, with a varied time setting, an illumination plan to cover a vast area for up to two minutes or more could be achieved. This was an invaluable tool for vehicles to be able to engage targets, if they did not have night fighting sights fitted. The canister rounds consisted of a thin walled, cylindrical body, filled with steel pellets, which spread out after leaving the gun muzzle. They were highly lethal at a range of up to 100 metres and were perfect, when used at soft targets, usually infantry, caught in the open.

Brummy, Reg and Richard gathered round the vehicle and made their final stowage checks, before doing a first parade on their transport, checking oil levels were correct and that no leaks had occurred during the night. Richard climbed inside and turned on the radios, checking the frequency for that morning. He turned the dials, before performing a power tune of the antennae. He placed his headset on and awaited the morning radio check, which would be coming from the Troop Leader, prior to moving, from the dust bowl.

'Hello all stations, this is Golf 21, radio check, over,' came the distinctive voice of Captain Fishburn.

Each call sign acknowledged, one by one, until all were confirmed as listening on the Troop frequency. There was a period of waiting, until the Troop Leader had been given the okay, to move on to the area, from Exercise Control. With a belch of smoke, the vehicles lurched forward, one behind the other. As they left the dust bowl, they entered one of the main transit routes, known as 'Rattlesnake Road'.

The training facility covered an area of 2,690 square kilometres (1,040 square miles), bordering an area south of the Saskatchewan River. It was originally designed for testing chemical weapons, after the Second World War. In 1967, it was renamed the Defence Research Establishment Suffield (DRES) and was used by the Canadian Army until 1971. From August 1971, it was agreed that the British Army could use it for Tank, Infantry and Artillery live firing exercises. These 'MEDICINE MAN' exercises, which could be up to 30 days duration, were split into two phases; Live Fire and Tactical Effects Simulation (TESEX), the latter with a live enemy. The TESEX system identified when vehicles have been fired at and damaged or destroyed and also informed soldiers when they are being fired at and, if hit, what injuries they have sustained.

Recce Troop had been given area to move to, just north of a place called Wells Junction. On the way, they passed the Exercise Control building, known as 'Brutus', set high on an area of ground dominating the training area. The building was imposing, with an array of radio masts, enabling the staff to monitor radio traffic, over the whole area. This was primarily used as a precautionary measure, as a number of safety vehicles were always present, when live firing was taking place. These vehicles were locally known as 'Red Tops', from their distinctive red painted areas. They would work very closely with all troops on the ground, calling a cease to firing, if there was any element of danger.

It took the Troop around 45 minutes to arrive at Wells Junction, where the Battlegroup Command vehicles had already formed their distinctive crucifix formation. Recce Troop took up positions of all round defence, around the complex. Once in place, the Troop Leader headed off, into the complex, for a briefing by the Battlegroup Commander, who was also the Regimental Commanding Officer. The rest of the troop took the opportunity to brew up, gathering round their vehicles, waiting for Captain Fishburn's return. They were not yet tactical, as the exercise had not officially started. On the Troop Leader's return, all vehicle commanders were called together and he outlined the CO's plans, for the next 48 hours. The briefing only lasted ten minutes; Brummy returned and quickly let the lads know what was happening.

'We are to move to a forward position, here,' he indicated an area on the map. 'The Troop will align itself north to south, along this ridge line. From there, we will probe forward, approximately four to five kilometres in front of the lead vehicles, comprising elements from our B Squadron and A Company of the Vikings. If we encounter any enemy positions, we are to report back to Zero and, once they have formulated a plan, one section will mark the Forming Up Point. The remainder of the Troop will disperse to the flanks, to give flank protection. We are to move out in ten minutes. Do you have any questions?' he asked, in a no nonsense manner. Satisfied they knew what was required, he asked them to mount up and prepare to move out. The minutes ticked by and, at 10:00 on the dot, the Scorpions set off, on the axis line they had been given.

Using the dead ground on the rolling prairie, Reg expertly steered the vehicle, a bound at a time, needing only rough directions from Brummy.

The morning was spent slowly advancing, from west to east, until, in the early afternoon haze, Brummy spotted three forward facing targets, in the shape of tanks, as well as a number of figure 11 targets, which represented infantry. He immediately checked his map and noted down the grid reference.

'Hello, Golf 21, this is Golf 22, sighting tanks and dug in infantry, wait out!' he said, raising the pitch of his voice, as he spoke.

As he was formulating his sighting report (Sitrep), another of the Troop came up on the air, confirming he, too, had come into contact. Brummy scanned the ground, from left to right, to ensure there were no other targets, to their front. He came to the conclusion that the other call sign must have encountered the same targets. Giving his full Sitrep to the Troop Leader and confirming he was observing, they sat, waiting for his direction as what they would do.

After a minute or two, the other section vehicle which had come into contact, confirmed it was indeed the same target. The information was relayed back to Battlegroup Command. Richard knew, from his time in Command Troop, that the CO would now be preparing his orders, to send to the Squadron, Company Commanders and any other support arms, which would be required. It took only fifteen minutes for the information to be passed down, then the process of decoding began. As suspected, Recce were to deploy two cars to mark the FUP, in the dead ground, two kilometres to their front.

Brummy's section had been chosen for this task, while the remainder began their move to the flanks. Brummy called to his 22 Alpha call sign, for them to begin the move into the FUP. Both vehicles slowly backed off the ridge,

161

meandering their way, out of sight of the enemy, into the dead ground. They lined up 400 - 500 metres apart, facing east and waited for the tanks and infantry to join them. The rumble of heavy armour and the whine of the Armoured Personnel Carriers could be heard above the 4.2 litre Jaguar engine of the Scorpion. They were joined by a Squadron of tanks and half a Company of Infantry. They placed themselves just below the ridge, between Richard's vehicle and the other Scorpion marking the FUP and pointed their barrels, in the direction of the enemy. Behind them, was a number of Red Tops, which would follow the vehicles into the attack, ensuring, in theory, that everything was safe.

Brummy glanced at his watch, ready for the artillery barrage to begin, which would continue until the assaulting troops attempted to take the position. At the appointed time, the distant sound of artillery was heard and, as they observed to their front, after 30 seconds elapsed, explosions erupted, around the vehicle and infantry targets. The barrage lasted a mere two minutes, but was impressive nonetheless. Before it ended, one troop of tanks, acting as close support, began to make its way forward, towards the position, with the infantry following on, close behind.

The remaining tanks placed themselves on the ridge line, to lay down fire on the position, providing an overwatch, for the advancing friendly forces. As they approached 400 metres from the objective, the artillery ceased and vehicles closed with the position, until they were 100 metres short. The door of the APCs were thrown open, the infantry dismounted and went to ground. The sound of automatic fire, from the coaxially mounted general purpose machine guns, rang across the valley. The infantry platoons leapfrogged each other, as they fought their way into position. Once there, they fought through and past it, organising themselves in all round defence. At the same time, the close support troop of tanks rolled through the position and past the infantry, defending any attack that may come from their front. Meantime, the remainder of the Squadron moved forward, to join the close support Troop, scanning the ground ahead. The empty APCs moved forward and collected the infantry on the ground. Once this was complete, Recce were given the order to continue the advance.

For the remainder of the day, the Battlegroup probed forward, until given the order to move to individual hide locations. It had been a good start to the day, from Recce's perspective. A highlight was a fire mission called in by a young Army Air Corps officer, attached to Recce. As they advanced, as a forward recce screen, they came across a series of hard targets. The officer instantly called a fire mission on the position. Brummy, Richard and Greg observed the action, from a ridge line. As they waited for the rounds to fall, on or near the target, they were amazed to see them land some two kilometres north of the position. Checking the gird reference on his map, Brummy burst into fits of laughter. Richard asked what was so funny and Brummy pointed to the spot on the map the young, inexperienced officer had given. Sure enough, it was way off where the targets were actually located. Richard thought to himself that the young man must have been cringing in his turret, as the rounds fell. The tale of his mistake would be told many times within the troop and would serve as a lesson to be learned by all. The safety vehicles did not called a stop to the mission, as no vehicles were in the vicinity of the fall of shot.

The evening was spent with the usual tasks of providing ground and radio sentries. Richard drew a radio stag at 05:00 in the morning. As he crawled out of his sleeping bag, after being woken by the off going ground sentry, he shivered. Although it was the middle of summer, there was a definite chill in the air. He quickly dressed, as quietly as he could, taking care not to disturb Brummy or Reg. He opened the tent flap and made his way, to the front of the vehicle. Climbing up the front, he opened one of the two hatches on the turret and clambered in. Rubbing the sleep from his eyes, he picked up his radio folder, containing all the reports and frequencies. Scanning the pages, he found the frequencies for the day and placed them on both the VRC 353 radios, one on the BG net, the other for the Troop. As no one else was listening on the Troop net, he needed to monitor BG, for any incoming orders.

They had been told the previous evening that they were on 30 minutes' notice to move. Once he was happy that all was in order, he retrieved a book he had placed beside his seat. He read a few pages of the novel, based on the life of a German soldier during the Second World War. The author was Sven Hassel, who had been a particular favourite of Richard's father. After a few pages, his attention was drawn to the sky. A shooting star flashed over him, as he peered upwards, out of the hatch.

Deciding to do a bit of star gazing, he climbed out of the hatch, still with the headsets attached and lay prone, on top of the vehicle. With no artificial lights for many miles around, the night sky was glorious. It was a star gazer's heaven, with no light pollution, the expanse of the universe was displayed in its full splendour. He spent the next half hour in awe of the beautiful sight of the Northern Lights or Aurora Borealis. This spectacle, visible in both winter and summer months, had always fascinated Richard. He glanced at his watch, to see how long he had left on his stag. He smiled when he realised he only had ten minutes left on duty, then climbed back inside and waited until his shift would be finished, so he could close down the radios. As he reached over to close down the sets, he was startled by the sound of radio traffic, in his ears.

'Hello, Golf 20, this is Zero, orders, over.' Recognising the Troop's call sign, he quickly opened his folder and withdrew a pen, from his top pocket.

'Golf 20, send, over,' he replied, confirming he was ready for the incoming message.

There ensued a series of encoded serials, each of them contained on one of the reports within his folder. The meaning of the message only became apparent after Richard decoded it, by the use of Battle Code (BATCO), contained on sheets and changed daily. A 'key setting' would be given and, on the right hand side of the page, cipher alphabets, comprising 26 horizontal lines of scrambled alphabet with the letters printed in pairs, would be consulted. Plain text numbers 0 to 9 and two symbols were printed at the top, with the 0 repeated. Richard had become skilled at decoding these messages rapidly. Once he had received confirmation from Zero that the message was complete, he gave the reply to 'wait out', while his eyes ran through the message. The initial message gave him the report he should be using. His heartbeat began to rise, as he trawled through the encrypted letters. It took him over ten minutes to translate and read it through, to make sure it all made sense.

'Zero, this is Golf 20, reference your last roger, wait out!' he responded, excitement in his voice. Throwing off the headsets, he jumped from the vehicle and woke Brummy and Reg.

'There's been a helicopter landing on a plateau. Two Mi8 HIP aircraft have set down there and dropped off troops. We've been tasked to go and check it out,' he ended, breathlessly.

'Okay, marra, wake the rest of the Troop, I'll go and see the Troop Leader and brief him. Have you got the details?' Brummy asked. Handing over the folder, Richard told him that everything was in there. Smiling at the efficiency, Brummy slid on his boots and left the tent, in search of Captain Fishburn. As Reg and Richard ran round, rousing the troop, Brummy and the Troop Leader were in deep conversation as to their plan of action. There was little time to react, the guys were told to remove the crew tents secured to the side of the vehicles and leave them. They climbed aboard their vehicles, hastily, the drivers gunning their engines. It only took ten minutes for the crews to be mounted and radios switched on; after which they awaited orders from the Troop Leader, to move out. A minute later, the vehicles headed off, in the direction of the rising sun.

The landing position was just over a kilometre to the east of their hide location. It wasn't long before the Scorpions were climbing the high ground, towards the plateau. Moving over the crest, the Troop observed, to their front, a mock-up of two helicopters, surrounded by numerous figure 11 men targets. The sound of GPMG automatic fire had already started, from a couple of the troop vehicles. Brummy turned to Richard and ordered him to load a canister round. This would be a first for Richard, as he had never fired the ammunition before. Picking up the round, he threw it into the breach, which automatically closed, as it engaged. Taking hold of the hand controls of the 76mm gun, Richard laid his sight in the centre of the amassed targets. Happy that his lay was correct, he issued the caution,

'Firing now!' as he pressed the fire button. A belch of flame erupted from the muzzle and the vehicle rocked on its platform. Through the dust, which rose in front of them, they could see splinters of wood, flying around the target area. The rest of the Troop, noting this, changed from their 7.62mm machine guns to canister. A line of orange flames danced along the ridge line, as fire was brought to bear on the position. The engagement lasted less than ten minutes. Thereafter, the Troop Leader reported back to Zero that the landing had been secured and all enemy forces destroyed. Although a hectic start to the day, it proved an enjoyable and successful one too. It was time to return to their hide, in time for breakfast and medals.

Chapter 17 – The Long March and River Crossing

The remainder of the exercise intensified, with every phase being built up, becoming more complex. Towards the end of the exercise and the final battle, Recce Troop was tasked with an important job. It was to be one of the most difficult things that Richard had undertaken. They were to move, on foot, under cover of darkness, after leaving their vehicles in a secured area. They had to move, from there, some twenty kilometres or more, to the banks of the Saskatchewan River. They would then, by boat, cross the river, with a troop of assault pioneers. Their job was to breech a major minefield, directly in the path of the Battlegroup's advance. Their orders were to travel light, with only Complete Equipment Fighting Order (CEFO). At last light, they had finalised their preparations, having arrived at the given location for the vehicles. There, they were met by the assault pioneers, who would accompany them. Each man checked another, jumping up and down to ensure their equipment did not make any sound. Satisfied everything was in order, Captain Fishburn guided them through the route they would take, and any 'Actions on', should they came into contact en route. Any questions having been answered, the assembled group set off.

In single file, the two Troops, with Recce taking the lead, headed into the darkness. The terrain was firm although undulating, and the troop covered the ground quickly. Around the half way point, Richard was alerted by Brummy, five metres in front of him. He indicated with his finger a shape, moving across their path. Suddenly, a distinctive sound could be heard, in the stillness. Richard knew at once, from the shape, that they had disturbed a rattlesnake. Around them, more of the patrol were stopped, raising their hands. To their horror, they realised that they had stumbled across an area full of the venomous creatures. Moving steadily forward and taking great care not to disturb any of the dangerous reptiles, they exited the location, as rapidly as possible. As soon as they had cleared the area, the Troop Leader called a halt, to make sure the group was still intact. He informed them that just over the ridge to their front, lay the Saskatchewan River. The patrol members nodded their acknowledgements and fell back, into line.

As they reached the top of the high ground, they were met by a group of Royal Engineers, guarding a number of steel boats, in which they would cross the river. Each boat held eight men and they dressed off both sides, preparing to lift the crafts. As they did so, Richard was surprised by how much they weighed. They needed to convey the boats, from the high ground, down to the banks of the river, on a narrow, winding track. This was easier said than done and more than one curse of 'For fuck sake!' accompanied their passage down the slope.

By the time they reached the bank, every member of the team was sweating, profusely. They gathered their breath, before setting the boats into the water. Climbing aboard, they each took a paddle and began the steady row across the river. Although not that wide at the crossing point, the current was extremely strong. Working in unison, the boat crews dug in deep, fighting against the current attempting to sweep them downriver. With a gargantuan effort and, after a lot of mutual encouragement, they eventually felt the boats touch the far bank. Hauling the craft from the water and placing the paddles inside, the troops readied themselves to continue.

It was already past 02:00 and fatigue had started to set in. Brummy made his way around the guys, to ensure everyone was ready and fit to carry on. A couple of the blokes said they had blisters, to which they got no sympathy. Securing their webbing and throwing their weapons over their shoulders, they adopted a patrol formation once more and set off. The ground levelled out and they covered the final six kilometres in just over an hour. Stopping short of the designated minefield, the recce boys took positions of defence on some high ground, overlooking the obstacle, so they could provide direct support for the assault pioneers, as they began the job of clearing a path large enough to allow a 'Giant Viper' GV to enter, at first light.

Captain Fishburn called Brummy over and asked him to split the Troop in two, with one half catching some sleep, while the other provided mutual support for the Pioneers. Richard was lucky enough to get the first hour, or so he thought, to himself. The first half hour was okay, but due to perspiration on his body beginning to dry, the cold soon made him begin to shiver. After another ten minutes, he could hardly feel his feet, so he removed his boots. His socks were soaked with sweat, so he removed them and began to massage his feet with his hands. It took some time before he registered any feeling and he was in excruciating pain. He had always, even as a child, had bad circulation and did not take well to the cold. Richard was amazed that, during the previous day, temperatures had reached 34 degrees Celsius. He was disturbed in his activities by Reg, who had been wakened to replace him.

'It's fucking freezing,' he commented, as Reg moved up beside him.

'I know, mate, I didn't get a wink of sleep. Being wrapped in a poncho doesn't exactly keep your body warm,' he said, visibly shaking with the cold. Richard nodded in agreement, knowing he, too, was going to find it difficult to get any sleep. Pointing out the direction of the Pioneers and asking if Reg was happy, he moved off the ridge and found a spot where he could wrap himself up, in his own poncho. Sleep did not come easy and before long, Richard was wakened, to be told it was his turn again, to provide over watch. This continued until first light, when the Pioneers completed their task, then made their way back, over the ridge line. They had cut the barbed wire that covered their front and had placed Bangalore torpedoes, explosive charges placed within either one or several connected tubes. Bangalores were used by combat engineers to clear obstacles they would otherwise have to approach directly, possibly under fire. They were effective in clearing a path up to 15 m (49 ft.) long and 1 m (3 ft. 3 in.) wide through wire and mines. This would be sufficient room for the GV to make its approach and extend the breech wide enough and long enough for armoured vehicles to transit through.

The whole Troop were awake now and they awaited the arrival of the Giant Viper. They had heard the heavy rumble of armour and other vehicles, to their rear. The Troop Leader informed them that the Battlegroup had formed up, in the dead ground, approximately 1500 metres behind their present location. Out of the morning mist, the unmistakable sight of the GV came into view, towing its deadly trailer behind it. In no time at all it entered the breech made for it by the assault pioneers and ground to a halt.

There was a deathly silence as the troops watched. Captain Fishburn raised his hand, to get attention and began counting down, so that all could hear. When he reached zero, the morning was split by the sound of the weapons system erupting. A 250 metre long hose snaked its way out of the trailer and into the air, projecting itself forward. Reaching its fullest extent into the minefield, there was a brief interlude, then a tumultuous explosion. It cleared a path 200 metres long and 6 metres wide. As the minefield was over 200 metres deep, the vehicle had brought another trailer. The crew jumped out, unhooked the empty one, coupled the fresh trailer and moved into the minefield, to the end of the cleared lane. Once there, they repeated the procedure, until they had cleared a path long and wide enough for the Battlegroup to move through.

Just before the 'H' hour that Captain Fishburn had given them, after receiving it over the net, Brummy noticed something on top of the high ground, on the other side of the minefield. Picking up his binoculars from his webbing, he scanned the feature and alerted the Troop Leader to a number of hard targets and infantry targets, dug in on the feature. Any vehicles moving through the bottleneck of the minefield channel would be sitting ducks for the waiting enemy. This, of course, was the reason why enemy forces deployed minefields, as a way of funnelling forces into an area, where fire could be brought to bear in a devastating manner.

'Richard, you're a bit of a dab hand with fire missions, you want to take this on?' he asked the surprised Richard.

Taking a deep breath and knowing that everyone's eyes were on him, he answered, trying not to sound nervous, 'Aye, why the fuck not?'

Brummy gave him the grid reference and Richard took the map and compass from him, to work out the bearing for the guns. Satisfied he had everything he needed, he took the radio handed to him by the Troop Leader's operator.

'Hello, Oscar 20, this is Golf 20, Fire Mission, over!' he released the pressel, waiting for the reply.

'Oscar 20, Fire Mission, send over,' came the immediate response.

'Golf 20, Fire Mission, grid 356789, direction 2100 mils, tanks and dug in infantry on top of hill, neutralise in two minutes, over.' There was a pause, then the fire order was repeated back to Richard, to confirm that they had all details correct. With no alterations to the original order coming back, the order came:

'Golf 20, this is Oscar 20, one gun adjusting, shot 20 over.'

'Golf 20, shot 20, wait out!' Richard acknowledged the time of flight and picked up the binoculars, to observe the fall of shot. It was an anxious time for him, his first live fire mission, with the whole troop watching on. A plume of white smoke appeared, three quarters of the way up the hill, accompanied, a split second later, by the sound of the explosion.

'Oscar 20, this is Golf 20, add 200, over.' Again, this was repeated back by the guns, then a time of flight given. The second round landed precisely in the centre of the amassed vehicles and infantry targets.

'Oscar 20, this is Golf 20, on target, fire for effect!' Richard shouted, excitedly. Then, after another short wait, the whole hill erupted, with a full battery of guns bringing their weapons to bear on it. After two minutes, and the smoke having cleared, the target area had been decimated. Brummy slapped Richard on the back and grinned at him.

'Outstanding work, mucker!' Brummy's sentiment was echoed by the watching troops.

Richard could hear the BG Commander giving his orders, over the air, for a full breech of the minefield. They were to exploit two kilometres plus of the minefield. Then, from intelligence gathered, they would be required to assault a major opposing force, directly to their front. This part of the exercise was known as 'El Alamein' after the Second World War action. It signalled the end of the exercise, Richard's first as a member of Recce Troop.

Chapter 18 – Vehicle Handover and R&R

They had been back in camp for two days and had begun the task of getting the vehicles ready for handover. This meant early starts and late finishes. The four weeks spent on the prairie had taken a toll on the ageing fleet of Scorpions. Although they had planned maintenance days, during the exercise phase, the mechanics from REME would always pick up faults that required rectifying. The Troops sometimes thought they just did this to justify being posted there. Everyone went along with this game and the Troop Technical Representative (Tech Rep) would take a list of parts required to get the vehicles to pass the handover inspection. This meant numerous trips to the Technical Quartermasters store (QM Tech). As BATUS was a heavily used establishment by all British forces, they stocked almost everything the vehicles needed. If they didn't have it, it was ordered and supplied, within a day or so. This was essential for the incoming Battlegroup to be fully functional, prior to them beginning their exercise.

After another long day's work, Richard and a few others decided that they would hit the town that night, for a few beers. They quickly showered and got dressed, foregoing the 'delights' of another meal in the cookhouse, deciding they would grab something in town. Some of the guys in the rear echelon and support departments had bought cars, known affectionately as 'BATUS Bangers'. These were vehicles that were handed over to incoming BGs, for a nominal price. They were used as taxis by the troops and cost half the price of a normal Canadian taxi. Richard had arranged with Len, from the QM's department, to pick them up, from the guardroom, at 7pm that night.

Arriving at the guardroom, Isaac, the RSM's driver and Richard's former roommate, was already waiting. Len was chatting to Isaac, as Richard approached and waved a hand in greeting. Richard handed over fifteen dollars, which he had collected from the lads, earlier in the day. It would have cost them twice as much, if they had ordered a regular taxi. After five minutes, they were joined by Paul Robson and Hendo. Paul was from the Holmewood area of Bradford and was a likeable character. He and Richard had not seen eye to eye on their first meeting, around a year earlier. They had since become good friends and Paul would later become Godfather to Richard's daughter, Sonia. He was married to Paula, a bubbly character from Liverpool. They had spent many drunken nights together with their respective partners. Once everyone was ready, they climbed into the battered car. Len gunned the engine and they moved off slowly but smoothly, in the direction of the camp gates. Reaching the RMP station, they halted at the white line, knowing that the RMP had fined drivers, in the past, for not doing so. Turning left out of camp, on to the 'Jenner Highway', they headed for the main road which ran to Medicine Hat. The friends chatted, as they drove towards the junction. The speed limit was 55 mph and Len was careful to observe this, as he didn't fancy getting a ticket.

At the junction, he once again indicated left and they entered the Trans-Canada Highway, which travels through all ten Provinces of the country. It was 6 pm and the temperature was still in the high twenties. The car was equipped with air conditioning but it wasn't working, so they had the windows open, to try and cool themselves down. As they continued towards their destination, they were overtaken by a train, on the track running parallel with the road, on their right. It took a full five minutes for the train to pass them. This was a normal sight, as the trains that transported goods across the country were massive, with up to three engines pulling their huge loads.

On their left was a communications tower, which could be seen at night for miles around. It was a navigation point, when the troops were on the prairie and had little else to go on.

It wasn't long before Len was pulling up, outside the Ming Tree Chinese restaurant, where they had decided to eat, before hitting the drink. As they entered, they were greeted by a very amiable waitress, who smiled at them and took them to a table. Handing over menus, she asked what they would like to drink. They decided to share a pitcher of beer, to begin with. Scanning the menu, they quickly made their choices, by which time the beer had arrived. After filling their glasses, the friends, in turn, gave the waitress their orders. Taking the menus from them, she bowed courteously and retired to pass the order to the chef.

The beers were quickly put away and, as the waitress arrived with their food, they ordered another pitcher. Each had ordered a different starter, in order that they could try something different. The first course lasted a good half hour, after which the waitress, helped by a young waiter, cleared the table. Their various main meals arrived, covering most of the table. Having confirmed that the order was complete, they bowed and wished the group an enjoyable meal. After they left, Richard laughed out loud, as he could not believe the size of the portions. Although they had visited the restaurant many times, the soldiers were always amazed at the amount of food served. The huge helpings was one of the main reasons the restaurant was frequented by so many of the Battlegroup. The owners used this policy to make their living from the men from different Regiments who passed through their doors. The meal itself was of outstanding quality and the friends spent the next hour or more, devouring their food. As the last plate was cleared, Hendo called the waitress over and asked for the bill. Looking at the piece of paper handed to him, he grinned and announced.

'Okay, guys, let's call it $20 each, which will include a tip,' they all nodded their agreement and handed over that amount.

The young girl took the money from Hendo and when he said she should keep the change, she looked as though she was going to cry with joy. As they stood to leave, the owner of the establishment appeared, from behind the bar, informing them he hoped they would return soon. He probably said that to all his customers but the lads thought it was nice to hear.

It was early evening and the blokes decided to do a bit of a pub crawl. They crossed the road, from the Ming Tree, to a well-known watering hole, the Gas Lamp. Entering the bar, the sound of a jukebox blasted out familiar sounds. The room was full of members of the Regiment and the Infantry, who formed the Battlegroup. Although it was not yet time for R&R, the troops would often pop down to the 'Hat', for a night out. There was the attraction of a strip show or the opportunity to chat up local girls. The men of the area didn't take kindly to the British soldiers stealing their women. That neither concerned nor stopped the soldiers trying and, as often as not, succeeding.

Choosing the sole vacant table, the lads sat. Paul headed to the bar, to get the drinks. In itself, this was unusual in pubs in this region. In many, drinkers needed to be seated, before ordering. In some, it wasn't permitted to walk around holding a drink. If someone wanted to join friends at another table, they would have to ask a waitress to carry their drinks for them. As this pub was mostly frequented by the British, most of whom were permanent staff on the base at Suffield, these local rules were not enforced. It ran almost like a Squadron bar, back in Germany.

As Paul ordered, he chatted to a female sitting at the bar, on her own. He returned to his friends, armed with four pitchers of beer, a stupid big grin on his face.

'Think I'm in there,' he proclaimed, quite chuffed with himself.

Hendo winked at Richard but drew a blank expression in return. Hendo placed a finger in front of his lips, indicating that he would reveal all, at the first opportune moment. That came quicker than either hoped, when Paul announced he was going to the toilet. As soon as the hopeful lover was out of sight, Hendo leaned over and informed the rest that he knew the female at the bar. She was notorious in the 'Hat' and went by the name of 'Becky Bondage'. Richard could only imagine how she had earned the nickname. The blokes burst into laughter but quickly calmed down, before Paul returned. Sitting down, Paul lifted his beer and looked over his shoulder, in the direction of the bar. 'Becky' was staring over, in his direction, with a seductive look on her face. He grinned again and took a big gulp of his beer.

'Well, you faggots can sit here telling war stories. I'm going over there,' Paul indicated towards Becky. With that, he got up and left them. It wasn't unusual for groups out on the town to lose each other, for one reason or another. They normally drifted back together, towards the end of the night though, to share a taxi ride back to base.

Pitchers of beer kept coming for another hour, until they decided to move on, to the next pub. Paul had already disappeared, in the company of Becky, so the friends moved on, thinking they would bump into him later.

The evening was gathering pace and the group's final stop was at a popular establishment called the Assiniboia Inn, more commonly known as the 'Sin Bin'. Countless troops had passed through its doors, to acknowledge it as a den of iniquity. As well as bedrooms, it comprised a restaurant, a dance floor, playing loud music and, downstairs, a strip bar. Its most popular features were that the beer was cheap and it remained open till the early hours of the morning.

Soldiers were attracted to it, like flies to shit. They would get steaming drunk, then try and pick up anything in a dress. The place was 'policed' by massive bouncers, wearing black and white hockey referee shirts. Although the backs of the shirts were adorned with the initials F.B.I., it was apparent these giants weren't on the staff of the Federal Bureau of Investigation. Most were native North American Indians and the letters colloquially stood for 'Fucking Big Indian'. They were not all male, a couple were women and there was not much different in their stature.

One infamous female bouncer worked most evenings and went by the name of Brady. Tonight was no exception and, as the friends passed through the main foyer, she was by the stairs, chatting to a friend. As they passed, to descend the stairs to the strip bar, she glanced at them, with disdain. The first time Richard had seen her, he had felt intimidated, but he grinned at her, as he walked down the stairs.

The basement room was dimly lit. The smell of nicotine and the haze of cigarette smoke drifted across the stage, in the centre of which, a young woman was gyrating, provocatively. She hadn't removed much of her outfit yet, but had the entire audience captivated.

Richard spotted one of the regulars, at the bar. Al Cooper worked in the Quartermaster's department. He had previously been a chef and had transferred to the Regiment after his first posting. Al was a loveable character, known for dressing up as his namesake Alice Cooper. In that persona, he would render a scary version of the Animals hit *The House of the Rising Sun*. He sat, transfixed, in front of the stripper, watching her every move.

Richard surveyed the room, thinking to himself, that this was the only place he had ever been, where the curtains had to be nailed on. The floor was sticking to Richard's feet, as the friends took their places, at the front of the stage. Calling a waitress, they ordered a pitcher each and settled down, for the show.

The first girl finished and was replaced by another, even more gorgeous, specimen. Al Cooper had not moved the entire time, as he would have rather have pissed himself where he sat, than leave his seat and miss anything. The floorshow blurred, one girl following another. Richard recalled being taken to his first strip joint, as a young recruit. It was the same the world over. Women fell into this career because they were single parents needing to make ends meet, drug users needing to finance their habits or, simply, that some got their kicks from seeing how they could make men react. The bottom line was that money was good and the tips even better.

The friends had seen enough of the floorshow and decided to go to the main bar, which served as a nightclub. As they arrived, Richard could sense a distinctly hostile atmosphere. As they approached the bar to order yet another round of drinks, they heard the sound of breaking glass. Brady, the female bouncer, had ripped a telephone off the wall and smashed it into the face of a female customer. These 'ladies' were affectionately known as 'Bin Bunnies' and would frequent the place, in the hope of picking up a squaddie. It was commonplace to snare an unsuspecting soldier, get pregnant and force the poor sap into marriage, thereby providing the girl with a ticket out of the 'Hat'. It had been a successful ploy on more than one occasion, with many a soldier being given the news of his being a father, having returned to barracks, in Germany. Brady made short work of the fight, forcibly dragging the girl by her hair, out of the room. No one batted an eyelid. It was just another run of the mill event in the Bin.

The evening was late, the friends had become separated, only Isaac and Richard remained, chatting at the table. They had no idea where the others had disappeared to and Paul had not re-appeared. Isaac suggested ending the night and crashing out in the Inn. They could get an early call and catch a taxi, in the morning. In his drunken state, this sounded like a good idea to Richard. They went to reception, asked if any rooms were available and were told there were. It cost them $10 each; at the same time as they paid, they booked an early call for 06:30. This would give them enough time to shower, dress and get back to camp. With that, they made their way to the lift, to get out on the third floor.

Their room was dimly lit and basic. The two friends weren't bothered, as they undressed and threw themselves into the beds. Richard looked over at the clock, which registered 03:30, a mere three hours before they were due to rise. As his head hit the pillow, he heard the rhythmic sound of Isaac snoring, then he, too, drifted off, into a deep sleep.

Chapter 19 – Consequences and R&R

In the back of his mind, Richard heard a telephone ring briefly but, as soon as it started, it ceased. He thought he heard Isaac mumble something, but it all seemed part of a dream. It wasn't until some two hours later, he woke with a start and looked at his watch. He couldn't believe his eyes, when he saw it was 08:15.

'Bollocks! What the fuck happened to our early call?' he ranted, as he threw back the covers.

'Isaac, get your arse up! We've slept in!' he called across to the next bed. Isaac stirred, seemingly not bothered that they were going to be late. He moved lethargically, getting dressed in his own time. He'd always been the same, nothing seemed to bother him. Being the RSM's driver, there wasn't much chance of his boss being at work that morning. Once they had dressed, the pair made their way, in the lift, to the ground floor. Richard was panicking, he had stayed out of the shit for so long and, after being recently married, trouble was the last thing he needed. As he made his way to the door, he looked over his shoulder, to see Isaac heading in the opposite direction.

'Isaac, where the fuck you going, you prick?' he called out, urgently.

'We are already in the shit. There's no way we'll make it for first parade. I'm having breakfast, I reckon we will need it,' he said and carried on his way.

Richard resigned himself to the fact that Isaac was probably right, turned around and followed him. The dining room was half full. Most of the clientele were members of the Battlegroup, who had already handed over and had begun their R&R. Richard and Isaac had three more days, before they officially be able to join them. They had talked excitedly, the previous evening, about their planned five days in Hawaii, not knowing what was to lie ahead. They sat and ordered a full cooked breakfast. Although it had been a rough evening, the food tasted great and they shovelled it down, in no time at all. Drinking the last of their coffee, the two friends paid the bill and left the hotel. They turned right, out of the hotel, then right again, into an alley, at the side of the 'Bin'. The taxi rank was located there, at that time of the morning it was empty. Within five minutes, a cab pulled up and they climbed inside.

The journey back to camp was not a pleasant one, as Richard pondered what their punishment would be, for being late. As they pulled up to the gates, Isaac paid the taxi driver and they began to jog towards Camp Crowfoot.

The previous night's beer and the recently consumed breakfast were swilling around in Richard's stomach and he fought valiantly not to spew. Reaching their accommodation, they rapidly got changed and headed back out the door. They ran as fast as they could across the 1500 metres, from the accommodation to the tank park.

Isaac joined his troop, who were already at work and, as he had suspected, the RSM was not in attendance. Richard carried on another 200 metres, where Recce Troop was already busy at work. As soon as he rounded the corner, he was seen by Brummy, who stood with his arms crossed, looking decidedly unimpressed.

'Where the fuck have you been, you retard?' he asked, as Richard screamed to a halt, in front of their Scorpion.

'Slept in,' Richard gasped, fighting for breath.

'Why the hell do you always fuck up when promotions are due?' Brummy bawled at him. 'You were about to be promoted when we got back! That's you fucked now,' he continued. Before Richard had a chance to offer any plea in mitigation, Brummy went on. 'You leave me with no other option. Take off your belt and beret,' he waited for Richard to comply. 'Step off to my timing, by the front, quick march!'

Richard instinctively began to move his legs and swing his arms to the rapid timing Brummy called out. He knew exactly where he was going and his heart sank. When Birgit got to hear about this, he would be in deep shit, he thought. The sun was blazing down on him and, every 50 metres, Brummy made him mark time on the spot, until he had caught up with him. After screaming abuse in his ear, he stepped Richard off again. By the time the guardroom came into view, Richard was soaking with sweat. He still had another 400 metres to go and thought his lungs were going to burst. As they reached the door of the guardroom, Brummy called out to him to mark time again. At this point Richard could barely lift his feet off the ground. It was a great relief when he was finally told to halt. He swayed from side to side, the alcohol running down his face in a river of sweat. Leaving him standing there, Brummy entered the guardroom and returned, not two minutes later, with a stern looking individual, with three tapes on his arm. There was something familiar about this miserable looking creature which struck a chord with Richard.

'Right, you horrible piece of shite. Get yourself inside now!' he screamed, in a broad Scottish accent. It was then the penny dropped. This was the same person whom Richard had met in the SQMS stores in Bovington camp, when he had attended his Control Signallers' course. He was a member of the 5th Royal Inniskilling Dragoon Guards, who were the incoming Battlegroup. He had obviously been promoted, since their last meeting and was now the Provost Sergeant. Richard doubted that he would remember him, not that that would have made any difference. He ran past the intimidating figure and came to a halt, at the counter. The Provost Sergeant followed on behind him and went to the other side of the counter.

'Your Troop Sergeant Major has said you will be spending a little time with us, till he decides what to do with you. We will now go to your accommodation. You will bring your bedding and every piece of your military equipment,' he leered, instructing one of his Corporals to take Richard away. As before, Richard was marched away at quick time, to collect his gear.

Under the burden of his suitcase and rucksack and, carrying his bedding, Richard stumbled back to the guardroom. He was met by the sight of Isaac, marking time outside the guardroom door. He smiled to himself, secretly glad that he was not the only one to be punished. Richard smiled at him, as the Provost Corporal screamed into Isaac's face, ordering him to raise his knees to the required height. Richard was marched straight past him and into the guardroom. He was instructed to go to cell number 1, to sort out his equipment. This was not the first time Richard had spent time in such salubrious surroundings and he knew the drill.

He quickly set about making a bed pack, unpacking his clothing and folding the articles to the correct dimensions. He could hear Isaac being drilled outside, knowing he would then be taken to collect his belongings. After the mid-day meal, the pair were collected by Hendo and marched back down to the tank park. Even though they had been put in jail, it did not detract from the fact that there was work to do. They were told they would be on Squadron Leaders' orders, that evening. The afternoon dragged for Richard, as he contemplated what punishment he would receive later.

After work, he was marched from the tank park by Brummy, straight to RHQ. Isaac was already there and being given the biggest bollocking of his life by his boss, the RSM. The incoming Provost Sergeant was also in attendance and sneered, as Richard approached. Headquarter Squadron Sergeant Major also threw in his comments. No sooner had Richard come to a halt, that HQ SSM called them up to attention. He marched them into the OC's office, in double quick time, halting them three paces from his desk. After being read the riot act by the OC and told how disappointed he was in them, they were asked whether they wished to be accept his award or be trialled by court martial. This sounded more serious than it was, but was normal procedure. They both agreed to accept his award, whereupon he gave them five days' detention and told the SSM to march them out.

Once outside and, after receiving another mouthful from the SSM, they were handed over to the Provost Sergeant. He fell them in outside and marched them, at lightning speed, in the direction of the guardroom. Reaching their destination, they were quickly fallen out and ordered to go to their cells.

It hit Richard that they had received five days' detention. They were due to go on R&R in three days' time. This meant their trip to Hawaii was now a non-starter. They would get two days' R&R, if they were lucky.

After being read the rules of detention, required by military law, they were each given a freshly fired 76mm brass case. The metal was tarnished and dull. Over their time in prison, they were to clean these items until they shone like mirrors. They were also issued with boot cleaning equipment, which included a brand new tin of Kiwi polish. They were informed their first job was to remove all the paint from the tins, then polish them, until they could see their own reflections. The instructions given, the Provost Sergeant left them to their own devices, stating that their first inspection would be at 22:00 hours. They spent the next three hours pressing their kit and laying it out on the bed, in compliance with the diagram given. This took Richard back to his time in training and his JNCO leadership cadre. It was not his first time in military prison, but it seemed surreal to occupy a cell while on exercise.

At 22:00, Isaac and Richard stood outside their cells, waiting for the arrival of the Orderly Officer, who would perform the inspection. They knew that as it was their first

185

night, they would get torn to pieces. Richard recalled the countless days he had spent incarcerated and was aware of the game that was played out.

The kit and cell could be immaculate, but there would always be something that would cause the staff's chastisement. A prisoner required the correct mind set, to be subservient, while laughing inside. If he let the rants and tirades of abuse get to him, then time inside would be miserable. The distinctive tip tap of shoes on the hard, highly polished floor, indicated the arrival of the Orderly Officer. The prisoners were brought to attention and waited for the young officer to approach them. As Richard was in the first cell, the officer began with him. As he stared at Richard, looking for any sign of imperfection in his dress, Richard began statement he was required to give:

'Sir, I am 24504799 Trooper Hunter. I was charged, under the Army Act of 1955, with being absent from duty. I received five days' detention from the OC. I have served one day and have four remaining. I have no complaints or requests, Sir!' he screamed the final part of his statement, causing the fresh faced officer to recoil, in shock.

The young Subaltern appeared to look down his nose at Richard, looking at him as though he were something he had stepped in. For the next fifteen minutes, the cells occupied by Isaac and Richard were torn apart, with their clothing and equipment strewn all over. This was a normal tactic and not unexpected. The inspection over, the pair were given the opportunity to have one of their two cigarettes allowed per day. Isaac didn't smoke but Richard took his, gratefully. He had to stand to attention and smoke it to the timing of the Provost staff, who increased the speed, as he smoked. Due to the lack of nicotine in his body and the rapid inhalation, Richard felt dizzy, much to the delight of the prison staff. His cigarette finished, they were ordered to get into bed and the lights were extinguished.

For the next two days, the prisoners were signed out by a member of Recce Troop and taken to the tank park. They worked there the whole day, not being allowed to go to the 'Gag and Puke' and marched to meals, in the main camp. The next day, they smoothly handed over the Troop to the incoming Recce Troop. Everyone was excited as they were now at liberty to go on R&R. Isaac and Richard were returned to the jail and carried on their cleaning duties, interspersed with long periods of drill, around Crowfoot Camp. Richard had brought his 76mm shell up to an excellent standard and was, perversely, proud of it. It was unrecognisable from the tarnished piece of brass he had received three days earlier. The Provost Sergeant had noticed how much effort Richard had put in to the shell so, on the fourth day, he called for him to present his shell, at the front of the guardroom.

'That's not a bad effort,' he sneered, sarcastically. He looked Richard in the eye, smiled, then dropped it on the floor and instructed Richard to kick it. Richard winced, as he put his boot to the shell, knowing all his hard work had been for nothing. The malicious bastard then instructed him to kick it again, then again and again. After five minutes of this abuse, Richard was ordered to pick it up and return to his cell. He did so, feeling naked hatred inside, as he stared down, at his desecrated work. He thought to himself that if he ever met this arsehole in a dark alley, he would kick the living shit out of him.

No sooner had he returned to his cell and begun to buff up the shell, he heard his own and Isaac names called, to come into the main office. They did as they were commanded and, entering the room, they were met by HQ SSM.

'The OC has decided to release you a day early, with one proviso. You may go on R&R but are to return to camp in three days' time. You are also not to leave Medicine Hat,

187

is that understood?' he made the statement in a threatening manner, making sure he was not misunderstood.

The two friends nodded their assent and were fallen out to return to their cells, to pack away their equipment and clothing. The face of the Provost Sergeant had been a picture, obviously pissed off that they were being released early. Richard chuckled to himself at the bully's disappointment. It took them ten minutes to pack away their gear and, with the release paperwork signed, they headed back to the accommodation. Entering the room, it was obvious that most had already gone on R&R, as it was only occupied by two solitary figures, who possibly didn't have the money or the inclination to waste any savings they had made on the piss. Although Richard was disappointed they had missed their Hawaii trip, he knew at least they had three days to relax, even though it was only at the 'Hat'.

In just 30 minutes, the two had showered, changed, packed bags and were heading out the door. They made their way to the guardroom to sign out and to call a taxi. Isaac greeted the Provost staff as they entered the guardroom, knowing that it would piss them off. Richard simply smiled, as he signed the book and asked them if they would call a taxi. The Corporal at the front desk did so, begrudgingly. They were told it would be twenty minutes and to wait outside. Expressing their thanks, but not really meaning it, they turned and went outside to wait.

Within the hour, they were walking into O'Reilly's bar, to be greeted with a resounding cheer from half a dozen of the Troop, who were already a good few hours into a massive drinking session. Paul Robson shouted over to them, asking what they wanted, as he was getting a round in. They replied that they would be taking it easy, so just a pitcher of beer each would be fine. Returning to the table, where Isaac and Richard had joined the rest, Paul handed over the drinks.

'You've got Brummy to thank for your early release,' he informed them. 'He went to the Troop Leader and pleaded your case. After a bit of a consultation with the RSM, they agreed to go and see the OC. I think the two of you owe him a beer or ten,' he laughed.

Richard had not yet found out what had become of Paul, on their night out, four days previously. He owned up that he had gone back with 'Becky', where it transpired she had lived up to her name. He had been tied to her bed and abused in a painful yet pleasurable manner. He was still sporting the marks on his back to prove it, which he was quite proud to display. The friends fell about laughing. It looked like this was going to be a good day and night out.

Nearly every bar in town was visited during the next ten hours, from a shit-kicking cowboy bar to a heavy rock bar called the *8 Ball*. But, as always, they ended in the 'Bin', for the much loved floor show. Isaac had been pestering Richard the whole time, saying that they should jump a bus to Regina, the main city of Saskatchewan Province. Richard had never heard of the place, but it was Isaac's theory that the local girls had probably never seen British soldiers before. Richard kept impressing on him the terms of their release and that they were not supposed to leave Medicine Hat. Isaac seemed oblivious to his remonstrations and continued the countdown to the bus's departure, hour by hour. As they drained yet another pitcher, followed by numerous shots, Richard finally succumbed to Isaac's pestering. The alcohol clouding his judgement, he reluctantly agreed to take the 02:00 Greyhound bus, from the terminal, just around the corner.

The bus journey was a blur, as the pair of drunken soldiers slept most of the way. They woke only when the bus stopped to either pick up new passengers or drop off others. They travelled through towns with strange sounding names, Swift Current, Chaplin, Moose Jaw, before finally arriving some six hours later, in Regina. It was 08:00 am and the two collected their bags, from the compartment beneath the bus. They enquired at the local information centre for hotels, which they could recommend. They decided on *The Sheraton*, a five star hotel, in the centre of the city. Taking a cab, they travelled the distance in around fifteen minutes, which was good going, as it was the height of rush hour. Paying the driver, they entered the hotel foyer. The place was a bustling with activity, with hosts of people, dressed in suits, either heading to or leaving the restaurant. Richard looked down at their jeans and T-Shirts and felt the stubble on his chin.

'I think we're a little under dressed,' he joked, to Isaac.

'Fuck 'em' came Isaac's straightforward retort.

They approached the reception desk, to be met by a prim and proper looking lady, a scarf and a string of what would most certainly be fake pearls around her neck.

'Can I help you, gentlemen?' she asked in a snooty manner, appraising them up and down, at the same time.

Their attire and their unkempt appearance was obviously not to her liking. Richard took an instant dislike to her and her attitude.

'We would like a room for two nights, please,' he smiled amiably, refusing to stoop to her level.

'I'm afraid we have a business convention in town this week. We are almost fully booked up. All we have available are Penthouse Suites.' she said, a condescending look on her face.

Richard could feel anger rising in him, but fought to control it. 'And how much are they?' he enquired, speaking through clenched teeth.

'The lowest price we have is $400 per night,' she said, driving in the blade of sarcasm, even more.

Isaac dug in his pocket, withdrew a fistful of $20 bills and answered. 'That would be fine, do you wish us to pay now?' he said with a smug grin on his face.

190

The receptionist's attitude changed immediately. Suddenly, she could not do enough for them.

'No, sir, you can settle your bill when you leave. We have full room service and mini bar available; pay on demand films and a hot tub in every apartment. We hope you enjoy your stay,' with that, she handed over the keys, giving directions to the lift.

Sniggering to themselves, the two picked up their bags and pressed the button for the lift to arrive. The doors opened and they stepped inside. They located the floor number on which they were staying and selected the button. They could feel the force of the lift as it ascended the building. Within seconds, the doors opened and they stepped out, into a broad corridor. A short walk, on plush carpeting, took them to the end of the hallway, where their suite was located. They passed only one other door, about halfway down. They intended only use the room for sleeping, but it was worth the extortionate price just to see the face of the snooty bitch, on reception. Placing their entry card in the lock, the door gave way with a click, and a green light allowed them access.

As they crossed the threshold, they were assaulted by the smell of freshly picked flowers, placed in vases, all over the room. What a waste for a couple of drunken squaddies, Richard thought to himself. The room was divided into three sections, a sleeping area, a breakfast bar and a shower and bathroom area. There was a raised area at the far end of the room, which contained a hot tub. This was so different to staying in the flea pit that was the 'Bin'. They had missed their Hawaii trip but, by God, they were determined to have a good time here. And, they had the money to do it.

Throwing themselves on two luxurious beds, the pals decided that, as they had missed breakfast, they would order room service. Scanning through the many pages of the novella that doubled as a menu, they made their selections, each accompanied by a six pack of Budweiser.

Isaac called the order in, while Richard hit the shower. After ten minutes under the steaming, hot water and, following a vigorous scrub, he felt almost human again. He delayed cleaning his teeth, knowing he would only have to do it again, once he had eaten. When he returned to the room, Isaac was lying on his bed with one hand down his boxer shorts, watching porn on the one of many pay per view channels.

'Isn't it time you had a shower, you dirty bastard?' Richard enquired. 'How long did reception say the room service will be anyway?'

'They said it would be about twenty minutes, which gives me time for a quick soak and a wank!'

Richard cringed at his reply, knowing Isaac was not joking. His mate was one of the most depraved guys Richard had met in his time in the army, but for all his faults he was endearing. As he jumped off his bed, he threw off his boxers. Richard threw a trainer at the exposed privates. Laughing like a hyena, Isaac fled from the room, into the shower. Richard flicked through the channels, until he was disturbed by the sound of knocking on the door. Before he could answer it, Isaac came tearing out of the bathroom, hastily wrapping a towel around his waist. He headed straight for the door and threw it open.

'Your room service, sir,' a timid female voice could be heard.

'That's fantastic,' Isaac replied 'could you place it on the table, over there?' he asked, pointing to the corner. The maid nervously entered the room and placed the overflowing tray on the table. Turning around to leave, she was halted by Isaac saying that he wanted to give her a tip. He went over to the chair where his jeans hung and, taking a $5 bill from his pocket, he turned to give it to her. Richard wasn't sure if what happened next was planned or not. As Isaac stepped forward, his towel slipped from his waist and he stood naked as the day he was born. The startled maid snatched the note from his hand and ran from the room, giggling as she went. Isaac followed her out, shouting apologies down the corridor. On his return, he didn't bother picking up the towel, he just grabbed a burger from the tray, opened a bottle of Bud and tucked right in. Richard couldn't contain himself, the tears were running down his cheeks as he bit his hand, to try and cease the laughter.

The food on the tray and the beer were consumed in double quick time. The pair picked a fresh set of clothing from their bags, dressed and left the room. Passing through the foyer, the formerly snooty receptionist waved her hand in greeting, which was ignored.

Leaving the hotel, they asked the doorman if he could recommend any decent bars. He said that there were plenty on the main high street, and he pointed them on the way. As they walked down the street, Richard observed that the city's inhabitants were mostly North American Indians. Alcohol and gambling was a big problem among the first nation people and they passed many of them sitting in doorways, slugging from bottles in brown paper bags. A scuffle broke out between two of them, on the opposite side of the road.

Not wanting to get involved, the pair quickened their pace. The last thing they wanted was to get lifted by the local police authorities. If this happened, it would be reported back to the Regiment and it would come to light that they had breached their release conditions. As they continued, Richard decided that he would get a gift for Birgit, before he forgot. They found a department store and went inside.

It was very quiet, with only a handful of shoppers perusing the goods displayed. Even though the customers were small in number, the one thing evident was there was not one Indian in the place. Richard stopped at a rack containing T-Shirts with slogans exalting the beauty of

Canada. He picked one out that he thought would fit Birgit and placed it in the basket he had collected. Isaac followed him like a lap dog, not in the least bit interested in shopping, when there were more important things to be doing, like drinking. Richard decided he would get one more thing for Birgit and raced fervently to the Lingerie department. As he browsed through the lacy, skimpy garments, he tried not to make eye contact with the female shoppers in his vicinity. Suddenly, out of his peripheral vision, he saw a young lady approaching him.

'Can I help you, sir?' a kind, pleasant voice sounded in his ear.

Feeling embarrassed, Richard fought to find the words before answering. 'I'm looking for some underwear, for my wife.'

The shop assistant recognised his shyness and was sympathetic towards him. 'Do you know what size she is and the type of thing you're looking for?' she lowered her voice, in order not to embarrass him further.

Richard looked the very pretty girl up and down, before replying. 'About your size and I'm looking for something in black,' he paused, before leaning closer to her and quietly asking. 'Do you have anything quite skimpy, which reveals a bit of the buttocks?' He winced as he said it, feeling like a dirty old man. He had always been one for thongs and g-strings and felt a little twinge in his groin, as he thought about Birgit wearing underwear he had bought her previously.

'We have a great range of things. I think we'll find what you're looking for,' the assistant remarked, holding up a black, lacy number, for Richard's inspection. Not wanting to draw more attention to himself than he was already receiving from the female shoppers, he nodded that that was perfect and followed the young woman back to her till. He handed over bills to cover the money she asked for and, not stopping for the change, rushed out of the store

194

with his purchases, with Isaac running behind him. They turned left out of the shop and continued up the main street. It wasn't long before they came to a bar with a big door, but no windows. They agreed they would pop in for a quick one.

The room was very dimly lit, with music playing very quietly. Walking over to the bar, they placed themselves on two stools directly in front of the bar maid. They were the only two people there, except for an old guy wearing what looked like lumberjack clothes in the corner, who looked like he was just topping up from the previous night.

'What can I get you?' the hostess asked, managing, by her tone, to mix perfect customer service and sincerity.

'What have you got?' Isaac asked, then waited, for her reply. She recited a long list, until a baffled Richard asked her to recommend a decent beer. The beers came and the friends grinned at each other when they saw their size and learned how little they cost. Not only was the place dirt cheap but the brew itself was like nectar.

Having noticed their unfamiliar accents, the girl asked where they were from. When they said they were British, she remarked that it was the first time she had met anyone from that country. The next question was one that would spoil their visit, later on that evening.

'What is it you do?' she asked, inquisitively.

Before Richard could answer, Isaac stunned him, with the most unbelievable bullshit.

'We're helicopter pilots,' he answered, straight faced.

'Wow, that's awesome,' was all the barmaid could say, staring at them, in admiration.

The conversation continued every time the girl was free from serving the many customers. They learned that she was a University student, studying law; she was single and planned to travel the world, when she had finished her studies. She was genuinely interested to know about the places they had been to. So, with the usual squaddie skill of embellishment, they proceeded to amaze her. It must have seemed to her that she had led such a sheltered life, having never left her Province, never mind her country. Richard explained that, as Canada was such a beautiful country, with its lakes and Rocky Mountains, he didn't see the need to leave.

It was almost 2 in the afternoon and the girl's relief had turned up. She quickly introduced the friends to her replacement, and began to pack her handbag to leave. Before departing, she mentioned that she would be in later, as there was a private party and they were invited, as her guests. Richard thanked her and said hopefully they would see her later.

After another two hours' drinking, Isaac's head was starting to drop. They ordered some bar food, to try and counter the effects of the alcohol. When they finished, all they felt was more tired. They settled the bill and made their way back to the hotel, for a little snooze. They promised the first one to wake would rouse the other. With that, they threw off their clothes and collapsed into their beds.

When Richard woke, he could see the sun was setting through the window. He rubbed his eyes, to wipe away the sleep. His mouth tasted rancid from the beer. Getting off his bed, he strolled over to Isaac, who was snoring like a pig. Richard slapped him on his bare arse, shouting at him to wake up. He received a grunt, in return.

Entering the bathroom, he turned on the shower, brushing his teeth, while waiting for the water to reach the desired temperature. His tongue felt furry and he attempted to clean it with the brush, almost causing him to vomit. Steam from the shower covered the mirror, letting Richard know he could get in. The force of the water felt like a thousand fingers massaging every part of his body. His routine only lasted five minutes, he was never one to linger.

He stepped from the ample cubicle and began to wipe away the excess water.

When he returned to the room, Isaac was still fast asleep. He attempted to wake him again, but was met with the same resistance. Isaac mumbled something, which Richard could not decipher. Richard shook him again, to be given the answer that he would join Richard in a short while. Richard tried to confirm with Isaac that he remembered where the bar was, to be met with a slurred reply. Selecting a shirt, jeans and a smart pair of shoes, Richard dressed and quietly left the room.

As he approached the bar, he saw the neon sign had been lit, but there was no sign of any activity, either entering or departing. He placed his hand on the door and depressed the handle. As it swung open, he was met with a cacophony of sound. Music was blaring, people were dancing and the bar was full of people having a good time. As he walked towards the bar, he noted the banner strung across the dance floor. *'Canadian Airlines Welcomes its Guests'*.

The barmaid from the daytime session was at the bar, facing the door, in conversation with two striking looking blonde girls. She raised her hand and smiled, recognising Richard and beckoned him over. When he reached the bar, she leaned over and gave him a peck on the cheek, which took him a little by surprise. She turned to the girls she had been in conversation with.

'This is Richard, the British helicopter pilot I was telling you about,' the two girls' eyes opened wide and they offered their hands, in greeting. Richard took them one by one, saying how pleased he was to meet them. He explained that Isaac was taking a little nap and would join them shortly. He then asked what the party was in aid of. One of the blonde girls, who was called Svenja, told him that it was hosted by Canadian Airlines for all the pilots and cabin crew, who were in town for the weekend. As

Richard surveyed the bar, he noticed that most of the occupants were female and one was better looking than the next. This, he guessed, was probably down to the fact that they were international air hostesses. He was like a kid in a sweet shop but, being newly married, he would need to avoid temptation. Introductions having been made, he was offered a glass of champagne.

By the time Isaac entered the bar, the party was in full swing. He staggered across the room, which puzzled Richard. Surely he had enough sleep by now for the afternoon's alcohol to have worn off? He stumbled his way towards Richard, bumping into people as he came. He fell against Richard, grasping at him to try and keep himself upright. Richard helped steady him and demanded to know why Isaac was in such a state.

'Well, I woke just after you left. I opened the mini bar and decided to have a little drink before joining you.' He slurred, his words, not forming correctly. It must have been more than a couple, Richard thought, for him to be in this state. 'Oh and by the way, I had a wank in the hot tub, you might want to empty it, if you want to use it, later,' he continued and grinned like a maniac. Richard simply shook his head, nothing Isaac did ever shocked him. 'Anyway, who are these ugly looking dogs?' he asked, loudly enough for the company to hear him.

'You will have to excuse my friend's language. He is a little worse for wear,' Richard tried, in vain, to defend him.

The next thing out of Isaac's mouth was the final nail in the coffin.

'Anyway, we only have another day left before we head back to camp, for the flight back to Germany. We need to get some serious drinking in!' he shouted above the noise of the music.

'Camp, what you mean camp? I thought you were helicopter pilots? You never mentioned anything about the military!' yelled the perplexed barmaid.

It was too late in the day to make excuses, so Richard came clean. When she heard that they were in the British Army, she didn't understand why they had lied in the first place. Hearing the explanation that squaddies very rarely admitted to their profession, due to it invariably going against them in some establishments, even causing them to be refused admittance, she understood their reasoning but was still hurt by the lies.

The conversation very quickly dried up, the two airline hostesses made their excuses and walked off, to join friends. Knowing that they had damaged any chance they might have had of having a good time, the friends decided to make it an early night.

The next 24 hours were a blur and before long they were on the Greyhound bus, en route back to camp. It had been a long way to come for a bit of shopping and two days on the piss. The final thought Richard had, as he closed his eyes on the way back, was that he was glad he hadn't use that hot tub!

Chapter 20 – Long Range Reconnaissance Patrol

It had been a week since they had arrived back in Germany. They had been given two weeks leave, to chill and catch up with their families. This was always a precious time for soldiers, whose families had to endure long periods of being without their husbands or fathers. On this particular occasion, Birgit was unable to get leave from work, so Richard was spending some time at home, learning to play the organ he had just purchased. As he was practising a few chords and trying to learn the melody to *Scarborough Fair*, he was interrupted by the sound of the doorbell. Placing the organ to one side, he got up from the sofa and ambled along the corridor, to the front door. They lived in a second floor flat, whose access was controlled by the use of an intercom. He pressed the button and asked who was there.

The unmistakable sound of a West Country accent confirmed that it was Brummy.

'It's me, marra, let me in, will you?' he blared into the speaker. Richard wondered what Brummy was doing, visiting him in his married quarter. He pressed the door release and heard the buzzer downstairs and the click of the mechanism which released the door. The sound of footsteps got louder until Brummy's face appeared at the landing. 'You got any beers in?' he asked.

'I might find one or two,' Richard replied, still wondering the reason for the visit.

'That's good, because we need to celebrate your promotion!' Brummy answered, smiling all over his face. The words didn't register, at first, with Richard. How could he be getting promoted after he had just spent time in jail? Brummy shook his hand, warmly and embraced him.

They sat in the living room, drinking bottles of beer and toasting Richard's good fortune. Brummy explained that Richard had already been on the promotion board, prior to going to Canada and, that he had been promoted away. So his little misdemeanour in BATUS was irrelevant. But he did remind him that the first stripe was the hardest to get and the easiest to lose. He also informed him that Richard would be going on his Long Range Reconnaissance Patrol (LURP) course, for which he had applied three months previously. It was something he had always wanted to do, so there was cause for a double celebration. He was to attend the course straight after leave. The two chatted for the rest of the afternoon, until Birgit returned home. Richard gave her the good news and she was delighted. Brummy made his excuses and left, saying he would see Richard before went on his course.

International Long Range Reconnaissance Patrol School (ILRRPS) was, at this time, situated in the town of Weingarten Germany. Established in 1979, its purpose was to train NATO Special Operations Forces, and similar units, advanced individual patrolling, medical, close quarter battle, sniper, survival, planning and recognition skills. Richard read through the blurb that arrived with his joining instructions. The sound of the wheels of the train, on the tracks, gave rhythm to his reading. Unusually, since it was a Sunday, the course was to start that day, at 19:00. It would initially last two weeks, although the length could vary, depending on circumstances. Many of the NATO countries supplied teachers from their various Special Forces, the UK, the USA, Germany and Denmark, among others. The patrols are small, heavily armed long-range reconnaissance teams which patrol deep in enemy-held territory, he continued to read.

One thing that did differ from any other courses previously attended was that there would be an English language test, on arrival. Any student who failed this or the fitness and navigation tests would be 'Returned to Unit' (RTU). This was one of the biggest fears of all soldiers. It was not only an embarrassment to the individual, but the knowledge that he had let down his Unit was an even bigger dread.

Richard had prepared himself as much as he could, in the short time available. His navigation skills were good enough, he felt and his fitness should see him through. If there was a problem, it was that he didn't know what these tests consisted of. Few from regular Units attended these courses, so he did not know anyone to pump for information. The only guidance he had received was from two who had attempted selection for the Special Air Service (SAS). They knew that a couple of members of 'The Regiment' had been posted to the school, as instructors. They had said it was a difficult course, but one that was well worth doing.

The train journey last six hours. When they pulled into the small station of Weingarten, in southern Germany, Richard grabbed his Bergen and heaved it onto his back. Making his way from the train, he departed the station and climbed into one of the waiting Mercedes taxis, outside. The driver greeted him in a guttural south German accent and asked him his destination. Richard read him the address on the joining instructions. The driver nodded and asked him to get in. Richard was alone with his thoughts, until the driver asked if he had been to the school before, to which Richard answered that he had not. The driver went on to explain that he had chatted with a lot of the ex-students, who had passed through the gates, all had said how difficult it was. They had given no more information. As most of the students were either Special Forces or from elite units, they were quite often very secretive.

The taxi ride only took ten minutes, as the town itself was quite small. As the taxi pulled up outside the barracks, Richard thanked the driver and paid the fare. He opened the boot and removed his rucksack, speaking a few words of farewell in German. He turned, to look at the camp. It was a dark and foreboding place, with rectangular, cold, grey-walled accommodation blocks. It had stood there as a military base for some 200 years, he had read. Showing his Identity Card (ID) to the sentry on duty, he was directed to the guardroom, to book in. He thanked the soldier and entered the guardroom.

Behind the reception desk was a man who wore the uniform and insignia of a Sergeant (Feldwebel). He stood to greet Richard, reaching at least six feet seven. Prominent was a scar, which ran the length of his right cheek, from the corner of one eye to above his lip. It reminded Richard of old pictures he had seen, of Prussian officers who duelled with sabres, in training. It was seen as a badge of honour in those particular circles. However, in these more modern times, this one had probably received his injury in active service. Having given his name to the Feldwebel, he was marked off, on the sheet on the desk. A member of the guard was instructed to take Richard to the accommodation.

Walking into the room, through a door labelled with his and other names, Richard placed his rucksack on the bed. He spent the next ten minutes unpacking, placing his clothing and equipment, neatly, in his locker. He turned at the sound of a door opening. Into the room strode a colossus of a man, a towel wrapped around his narrow waist. His shoulders and chest were broad, tapering to a well-defined six-pack stomach, with not an ounce of fat on him. He smiled at Richard, before advancing.

With an outstretched hand dwarfing Richard's, he said, in a Southern American drawl, 'Hi there, buddy, I'm Hank. I guess you're here for the LURP course?'

This, of course, was obvious. All four names on the door were on the same course. He was just breaking the ice.

'Yes, mate. I'm Richard,' he accepted the hand and felt the power of the grip, as Hank squeezed it, in greeting.

'From the way you talk, you're a Brit, right? One of the other guys in the room is one of you. He got here earlier and went down the gym, for an hour. There's just one more of us to arrive, he better be quick. We're supposed to assemble, in the lecture theatre, in an hour.'

Mercifully, he released Richard's hand and sauntered over to one of the beds, where he threw down his towel and began to don his uniform. Richard noticed the insignia on his uniform denoted Hank was a member of the American Rangers, a respected U.S. Special Forces Unit. He felt a little intimidated by this. If this was the type on the course, it definitely wasn't going to be easy. They were joined, in the room, by another, sweat running down his face. He was dressed in shorts and sweatshirt, two tone in colour, due to the perspiration covering his body seeping through the material.

'All right there, boys,' he announced, making directly for his bed space. The accent was as Cockney as Richard had ever heard. 'I'm Paul Sturgess,' he called across. 'From 4/73 Sphinx Battery, Royal Artillery.'

Richard recalled that this was a specialised unit, operating behind enemy lines, in times of conflict. He introduced himself, saying which Regiment he was from and that he was a member of Recce Troop.

When it was time for them to attend the introductory briefing, the fourth man allocated to their room had not yet arrived. They walked into the large, open lecture theatre and took some spare seats. There were only around 30 people on the course, so there was ample seating. At the front of the hall, a number of tough looking individuals faced the students.

The tall one, in the centre, wore the uniform of the German Army Special Forces, one arm of the Bundeswehr. They sat, in silence, for five minutes, until the appointed time for the introduction to begin. At that point, he instructed the calling of the register, for those loaded onto the course. This done, it was evident three had either not turned up or were late. Just as they finished the roll call, the door flew open and a breathless young man ran into the hall. He was asked his name. It was checked against the list. Confirming that he was, indeed, on the course, he was told that his presence was no longer required, as he had not paraded at the time stated on the joining instructions.

Richard drew a deep breath. Never had he been on a course, where the rules were so strictly applied. The student tried to give excuses, but was summarily discharged from the lecture theatre. The tall, distinguished man who had opened the meeting then introduced himself as the Commandant of the Training School. Each of the seated individuals were members of Special Forces and would be the instructors, for the next two weeks. They were given an outline of what the course would entail. However, before it would commence, all needed to pass an English language test, a navigation paper and, finally, a basic fitness test.

The instructors went round the room, distributing pens and test papers. The students were given one hour to complete both papers and, with that, they were asked to begin. Richard turned over the first paper and scanned the questions, the English one posed no problems and he flew through it. The navigation paper was accompanied by a map of the local area. As he had finished the first paper so quickly, he had three quarters of an hour to complete it, which he did, with five minutes to spare. Once the hour was up, the students were asked to put down their pens. The papers were collected and the men were asked to fall in outside.

From there, they were taken to the gym, where they were required to perform simple tests, including two minutes of sit-ups, press-ups and heaves. Then, they had to run one and a half miles in under ten minutes. Richard just made it, with about five seconds to spare. They were then taken back to the lecture hall and told their results of all the tests. Richard waited nervously for his name to be called. He looked around the room and saw the same look on others' faces.

Once the results had been read out, one of the instructors read out a list of names. These unfortunates were told that they had not reached the required standard and they were to report to the admin office, to arrange transport back to their units. To Richard's great relief his name was not called. His two roommates had also survived the cull, but Richard had suspected that would be the case. The three chatted, as they made their way back to the block. An early night was called for, as it looked like it would be a tough two weeks.

For the rest of the first week, the instructors went through various aspects of how to survive, if cut off behind enemy lines. Survival skills were an essential part of the course, the techniques were vital to provide basic necessities of human life. These included water, food, shelter, how to avoid consuming poisonous plants and animals and the ability to cure ailments using natural resources, skills used by ancient civilisations for hundreds, if not thousands, of years.

They were shown different first aid skills, other than the normal ones, usually taught to the 'ordinary' soldier. Normal stuff was re-covered, the treating of fractures, burns, sprains and hypothermia. Treatment of snake bites, poison and infection were an addition to these, and they were shown how to adapt items from their natural surroundings, to aid in the extraction of either themselves or a comrade.

The first lesson they received was from a member of 22 Special Air Service, who simply introduced himself as Scrapper. He was powerfully built guy, with hair protruding from his neck. His bright, blond hair and bushy eyebrows gave him the look of a Viking warrior. His voice was gruff, deep and revealed him to be from Yorkshire. Richard watched every move, in awe, as he eased through the lesson on how to build a shelter. He referred them to natural features, such a cave or fallen down tree, which were natural shelters. Then, he concentrated on, and demonstrated, the construction known as an 'A' frame. Also known as a double lean to, this comprised using branches or debris from the local area, in conjunction with a 'tarp' or poncho. Scrapper quickly lashed together a number of pieces of wood and covered them with a poncho, providing shelter from the elements. The whole process had only taken him fifteen minutes, after which he asked if the students had any questions. They were then sent off, to forage for materials and to build their own.

The time limit for the exercise was one hour and, once the time had elapsed, he commanded everyone to stop. He then proceeded to lead the course round, inspecting each shelter, in turn. He asked the students to pass comments on each one, then he gave his opinion on how each student had performed.

Everything was quite laid back, with everyone on first name terms. Richard had been told by his American Ranger roommate that was how most Special Forces operated. The first lesson had been an enjoyable one. They were then passed on to a member of the GSG9, Germany's equivalent of the SAS.

He took them through the art of fire lighting, which significantly increased the ability to survive physically and mentally. Starting a fire without lighter or matches, by using natural flint and steel with tinder.

Fire is presented as a tool meeting many survival needs. The heat provided by a fire warms the body, dries wet clothes, disinfects water, and cooks food. Not to be overlooked is the psychological boost and the sense of safety and protection it gives. In the wild, fire can provide a sensation of home, a focal point, in addition to being an essential energy source. Fire may deter wild animals from interfering with a survivor, however wild animals may be attracted to the light and heat of a fire. (Wikipedia)

The GSG9 man, who was called Frank, showed them a couple of techniques, from using a fire stick on the use of friction to create an ember to the use of a flint and tinder. As with the previous lesson, he made it look so much easier than it was, his expertise achieved through years of practice. Again, the students were instructed to build their own fires. Some, including Richard, failed miserably. He made a mental note this was one skill he would need to practise. The course itself was not a pass or fail course, the students were there to learn how to survive. In a real situation, there would not be anyone marking them on their efforts.

For the remainder of the week, they learned how to gather water. The human body could only last, on average, three to five days, without the intake of water. The need for water increases, the more the body is exerted. Also, conditions like heat and perspiration had to be factored in.

They were shown how to recognise and gather natural food. From things such as berries, fungi, edible plants and nuts to wild animals. They were given a demonstration on how to skin a rabbit. They were shown how to lay the rabbit on a heavy chopping board or block of wood and, with a meat cleaver or old knife and hammer, chop off the feet just above the knees; cut off the tail and, using the same tools and technique, remove the head. Then, they had to lift the fur at the belly and make a horizontal incision, pulling the skin away from the rabbit; insert the knife into the horizontal cut, taking care not to pierce the stomach. Next, holding the knife upside down, so the sharp edge faces upwards, slowly cut the skin, from the belly up to the neck, gradually pulling the skin away from the flesh, which, if fresh, should come away easily.

'Work your way around the body to begin with and then upward, to the front legs. The legs must be popped out, through the skin. The best way to do this, is to pull out the skin around the leg and push on the stump of the leg from the other side – a bit like taking off a jacket,' the instructor explained, as he carried out each part of the process.

'The final stage is to grip the shoulders of the rabbit and pull the skin down, over the back legs, again, like removing an item of clothing.' He completed the skinning of the rabbit and looked up at the grinning faces of the troops.

They were expecting to be given a rabbit each and have to do the same exercise. The instructors had a little surprise in store. They took the men to a pen, which contained three chickens and nominated three students to climb in the pen. They each had to catch a chicken and, once they had done so, they were to cut off the heads with axes supplied by the training staff.

Richard and the students who had not been chosen doubled up in laughter, watching the three madmen chasing the chickens, round the pen. It was like a comedy show, although the ending would not be funny at all. As soon as the prey had been captured, the panting soldiers were asked to dispatch them, one at a time. The first two completed the task without a problem. However, the third did not manage to make a clean cut and the bird escaped from his grasp, running around with blood pumping from a partially severed neck. It had been a bloody enjoyable lesson and one that Richard would remember for a long time.

The second week was spent learning interrogation techniques and the methods of how to resist them, without giving away any vital information. This was an important part of the course, as many of the troops might someday be captured, during the course of their careers.

They were taught how to be 'the grey man', not to stand out and be submissive, rather than aggressive. They should always be aware of their surroundings, always thinking of ways to escape, if possible. These lessons were put into practice on the final exercise, which was an escape and evasion phase. They were dropped off, individually, at various points and told to make their way to a final location. They were to gather information on the way, just as Richard had done on his leadership cadre. The difference this time, was that when they were captured, they would be subject to an introduction into interrogation. Every one of them was caught, at different times, and the directing staff put them through the process, including sleep deprivation, stress positions, lack of food, culminating in 'tactical questioning'. For his part, Richard was captured after two days and the 24 hours he had to endure was a mere taste of what would happen for real.

On completion of the course, the students gathered in the lecture hall. The camp commandant congratulated them on finishing the course and expressed the hope that they all had learned something. He went on to explain that various courses ran, to complement this one, one of which was a two week 'Resistance to Interrogation' course. Application forms for this were at the back of the hall, if anyone wanted to apply. With that, the instructors went round and shook the hands of every student, wishing them a safe journey back to their units. As Richard turned to leave the hall, he passed the table with the application forms. He picked one up, glanced at it and placed it in his pocket.

Chapter 21 – Cyprus

A year had passed since the LURP course. The Regiment was due to be deployed to Cyprus, as part of the United Nations Peace Keeping Force in Cyprus (UNFICYP). This was to be a six month deployment, with half the Regiment being part of the UN for three months. The other half occupied a camp in the Easter Sovereign Base (SBA) in Dhekelia. After three months, they would swap over duties.

Richard wouldn't be involved, however, as he had been chosen to form part of the Signals Troop on the 'Green Line', for the full six months.

The Troop was made up of familiar faces he had served with before, in Command Troop. Al, from his leadership cadre, Spike from his Control Signallers' course, John Mason, now a Sergeant, and Paul Goath, the new Regimental Signals Warrant Officer. Richard was looking forward to the tour, as it was supposed to be an enjoyable one, unlike some others. He would find out that it was not just sunshine, beaches and 'brandy sours' and would bring its own challenges and experiences.

UNFICYP is one of the longest-running UN Peacekeeping missions. It was set up in 1964 to prevent further fighting between the Greek Cypriot and Turkish Cypriot communities on the island and bring about a return to normal conditions.

The Mission's responsibilities expanded in 1974, following a coup d'état by elements favouring union with Greece and a subsequent military intervention by Turkey, whose troops established control over the northern part of the island.

Since a de facto ceasefire in August 1974, UNFICYP has supervised the ceasefire lines; provided humanitarian assistance; and maintained a buffer zone between the

Turkish and Turkish Cypriot forces in the north and the Greek Cypriot forces in the south. UNFICYP's Chief of Mission also serves as the Secretary-General's Special Representative in Cyprus and in that capacity leads efforts to assist the parties in reaching a comprehensive settlement.

The ceasefire lines extend over 180 kilometres across the island. In the absence of a formal ceasefire agreement, UNFICYP's 850-plus troops and 60-plus police officers deal with hundreds of incidents each year.

UNFICYP also delivers humanitarian aid to Greek Cypriots and a small Maronite community living in the northern part of the island and it assists Turkish Cypriots living in the southern part of the island.

UNFICYP supports the fullest possible resumption of normal civilian activity in the buffer zone, keeping in mind that this is still an area under permanent armed watch by military on both sides. To this end, it facilitates the resumption of farming in the buffer zone where safe, and assists both communities on matters related to the supply of electricity and water across the lines.
(http://www.unficyp.org)

As the troops descended the steps of the RAF aircraft, a wall of intense heat hit them. It was early May and summer had started with a vengeance. A short walk across the tarmac, at the military base of Akrotiri, took them to the waiting buses. Everyone was wearing their newly issued number 7 dress (Tropical) combats. These were lightweight and, as the name suggested, were designed for warmer climates. Lightweight boots did little to prevent the soldiers from perspiring profusely, though. It would take weeks for their bodies to acclimatise to the weather. They had been told they needed to drink frequently throughout the day, to help with this. Physical activity was not advised at certain times of the day, due to the danger of sunstroke, or other heat related injuries.

The troops loaded on to the bus, it set off on the journey north. Heading out of the airport gates, it headed east for approximately twenty minutes. It followed the coast road, passing through the town of Limassol. Another fifteen minutes and it joined the main arterial route of the A1, heading north towards Nicosia, the capital of southern Cyprus. The heat within the bus was stifling, even with climate control going full blast. Richard sat with Isaac, imagining the fun they could have on this deployment. He had been seconded into the Regimental Police; and would be manning the guardroom in Saint David's Camp (SDC), the Headquarters for the British forces in Sector 2, the British sector, in the buffer zone (Green Line).

As the bus approached the outskirts of Nicosia, it turned west and took a course around the city. After twenty minutes fighting through traffic, they emerged on to the main transit route, which ran east to west across the island. The Regiment's two Squadrons, A and B, would cover the whole of the British sector. A Squadron would be the western Squadron, based at Astromeritis, better known as Bravo 32, or the 'Box Factory'. B Squadron would form the eastern Squadron, at Bravo 18.

Richard would be joining Isaac, along with the HQ element of the Regiment, at SDC. They passed the old Nicosia airport on their left, which had not been in use since the 1974 invasion. To their right was what was known as 'Blue Beret Camp', the HQ for all UN forces in Cyprus.

As they continued westward, passing through the first UN checkpoint, the sentry on duty presented arms, to the bus. This was normal practice, as the sentries did not know if officers were aboard or not.

Another three kilometres up the road, they passed a Greek Cypriot checkpoint. The sentry there was somewhat less than alert, waving from his stool, with his weapons propped up against the small building. The passengers could not believe the indiscipline of the guy. It would become apparent this was normal for conscripted soldiers of the Greek Cypriot Army. Turning right on to a narrow track, the bus bumped its way into Saint David's Camp.

As the bus halted, the troops who would be living there for the next six months, left their seats and gathered outside. The sun beat down as they collected their luggage from the Bedford truck, which had followed them from the airport. The bus departed with the remaining element of A Squadron, who would be travelling to the 'Box Factory' at Bravo 32. Once everyone gathered their belongings, they were shown to their accommodation by the SQMS and his staff. Signals Troop were all in the same hut, which contained sixteen beds, eight on each side. The Troop was bolstered by four members of the Royal Signals, under command of a fresh-faced Lance Corporal. They would carry out the duties of Communication Centre (Commcen), an outdated data telegraphy system, which used a ticker tape system, to send messages throughout Sector 2.

The accommodation itself was basic, with only a couple of lockers and chest of drawers providing any privacy. Richard chose a bed space on the left, directly next to the entrance to the hut. He placed his suitcase on the bed and began unpacking. He was joined by Al, who joked:

'This is fucking luxury. You don't mind if I take this one, do you?' he said, pointing to the bed.

'Of course not, mate, fill ya boots,' Richard replied. He had spent some time sharing a tent with Al, on various exercises in Command Troop and they got on well together. In fact, the Troop as a whole was made of guys who, at one time or another, had worked together. This would provide a comfortable, harmonious working environment, or at least that was the theory. The Troop spent the next hour or so unpacking and settling into their new home. Then, after a quick lunch, they congregated at the Operation Room (Ops Room), to begin taking over from the outgoing unit, to find most of this had already been done by the RSWO and Troop Sergeant, John Mason. They were given a briefing on the use of the telephone exchange, the VHF communications, and nets that they would be monitoring. The Ops room was the central hub for all communication to and from the eastern and western Squadrons They would provide one person, in the Ops room during the day, with a Watchkeeper, who was usually a Senior Non Commissioned Officer or a Commissioned Officer. They would also provide a man for the telephone exchange, 24 hours a day. This was to prove a lucrative position, as none of the outlying satellite stations had the ability to make outgoing calls. So, if anyone wanted a taxi or takeaway food ordered, they were required to go through the exchange at SDC.

By the end of the day, the Troop had taken over all equipment and a rota drawn up. Richard didn't begin his duty until the next morning, at 08:00. The camp, although very rustic and run down, had all the amenities they needed; a shower and toilet block, a cookhouse and a small café, known lovingly as the 'choggy shop'. It was run by a Cypriot local and the Troops spent a lot of off duty time there. Another magnet for those off duty was the camp bar, basically a Nissen hut that had been fitted out with a purpose built bar, relaxing chairs and sofas, a dartboard and a pool table. The man with the enviable job of running the bar was Ian Hatfield, who had been a section commander in Recce Troop. Richard knew him well. He was in the last twelve months of his service and was due to leave a couple of months after their return, the reason for him being given such a cushy job.

Senior Ranks and Officers had their own messes, it was not seen as good form for them to be mixing with other ranks. Truthfully, it also allowed them to speak freely about people under their charge, without the fear of being overheard.

After a quick shower, in the less than hygienic settings of the washrooms, a couple of the Troop met in the bar. Stuart Messenger, who had been in the same Squadron as Richard on their return to West Germany from Berlin, came rushing in to the bar, in a flustered state.

'For fuck sake, you should have seen what was lurking in the shower room!' he exclaimed, and related that, as he rinsed the soap from his rather ample body, he reached for his towel, which he had hung on a hook provided. When he lifted it, a lizard, the length of his arm, had scurried up the wall. 'I nearly shat myself, on the spot!' he cried, falling into uncontrollable laughter. As the island had its fair share of exotic creatures, this was the sort of thing they would have to get used to.

Spike ordered three half litre bottles of Keo beer, a local beer, brewed on the island. He passed two to Richard and Al, which they took gratefully. Even at six in the evening, the temperature was still in the mid 30s centigrade. Within minutes, Alan Cooper, from the Quartermasters Department, entered the bar.

'You looking for me, flower?' he shouted his well-known catchphrase, to no one in particular. The friends grinned and offered him a chair, next to them, at the bar. He sat and ordered a bottle of Keo, from Ian.

The first evening was spent drinking, playing darts and pool. They didn't kick the arse out of it, they had been told that every morning, those not on duty would be required to go on a camp PT session. Tomorrow's session was to take the form of a run, done at an early hour, before the heat got too unbearable. Every morning, the Ops room would receive a signal from Blue Beret Camp (BBC), with the daily 'bulb test', a weather forecast for the following day. The signal informed whether physical activities were allowed and, if so, at what time. Feeling sleepy, after the six hour flight from their base in Germany and the evening's beers, most in the bar, including Richard, pottered off for a well-deserved night's sleep. This left the usual diehards, who either were on duty, had 'sick chits' or were excused the morning PT session.

Sleep came quickly, due to the long day and consumption of Keo and Brandy sours. However, Richard woke, at 03:00, sweat running down his forehead. He fumbled for the zip of the mosquito net, which covered his bed. Finding it, he drew it down and dragged his legs out of bed. Making as little noise as possible, and dressed only in boxer shorts, he slipped into his flip flops and left the hut. He had fought for over an hour to try and ignore the feeling of the urine pressing on his bladder, but had finally given up.

As he crossed the hard, stony ground towards the toilet and washrooms, something scurried across his foot. Looking down, he saw a six inch lizard run over his toes. He jumped back in shock, trying hard not to shout out, at the top of his voice. This was going to be hard, getting used to these, he thought to himself. The sound of feral dogs could be heard barking in the distance. They were almost wolf-like, their sound more howls than barks. He quickly dashed to the washrooms, out of the way of any other form of life he might encounter. As he walked into the toilets, he felt water splash over his naked feet. He hoped it lay from someone having taken a shower earlier, not from someone pissing on the floor, having not made the urinals, after leaving the bar. He emptied his bladder, before heading off, warily, back to the hut. For the next two and a half hours, he tossed and turned in his bed, not managing to get back to sleep.

Before he knew it, the room was stirring, men prompted by alarms going off, one after another. Those on day shift were greeted with a tirade of abuse. They were unceremoniously told to 'Fuck off!' by the majority, who were now slipping into shorts, vest and trainers. Mumbling to themselves, the troops sauntered over to the square, just

217

behind Regimental Headquarters. As they waited, others joined them from different directions.

The camp was made up of troops from different departments, from Quartermasters, Chefs, Motor Transport (MT) and mechanics from the Light Aid Detachment (LAD). Stuart Pearson, who had been Richard's Troop Sergeant Major in Guided Weapons, was waiting, along with the RSM. As the camp SSM, it was his duty to do the roll call. If anyone was absent, the senior member of the Troop present had to give the reason why. Some, who had stayed behind in the bar after Richard had left, were looking a little worse for wear. The roll call complete, the SSM called everyone up to attention and turned them, to the right. With the command, by the right double march, they began to jog, at a leisurely place towards the guard room.

As they departed the camp, Richard noticed Isaac, who had begun his day's shift on the gate. He grinned, with great delight, as the Troops passed him, which drew an angry comment from the RSM, who had spotted it.

'L/Corporal Brown, if you think it's funny, you can join me this evening, after you finish your shift!' he bellowed, venomously, at Isaac. This caused Isaac to redden visibly, in embarrassment and cast his eyes downward. The squad found this highly amusing and it caused an outburst of laughter, throughout the ranks.

They continued along the narrow track that led from SDC to the main road. Reaching the road, which had taken around ten minutes, one of the fitter members of the Squadron was sent forward, to carry out traffic control. He stood in the centre of the road, stopping vehicles in either direction, until the last of the squad had crossed. Then, turning, he jogged off and joined them, at the back. After another ten minutes, the sun started to take its toll on some. Richard's vest was completely soaked in sweat and he was struggling to regulate his breathing.

Their situation was made worse, when their nostrils were filled with the smell of what seemed to be rotting flesh. The origin of the stench was a building, about 500 metres to their front. As they drew level with it, they saw it was a chicken processing factory; the smell came from the abattoir attached to it. The sound of retching caused Richard to do the same. He had always had a delicate constitution and the sight and smell of someone spewing, just in front of him, prompted him to do the same.

'If you're going to be sick, do it as you run!' came the chastisement from the unsympathetic RSM, as he outwardly sneered at the prostrate soldiers.

Picking themselves up, they wiped away the vomit, from their mouths. Those who had puked were shamed by his words and jogged, to catch up with the squad. Taking a loop round chicken factory, they turned right, running parallel with the road running east to west, across the island. No one knew how long they would be out for and Richard, among others, was starting to feel the effects of the sun. His head banged with every foot placed on the ground, his mouth was dry, his tongue sticking to the roof of his mouth.

Crossing the road again, they could see the camp in the distance. The RSM asked the leading three soldiers to pick up the pace, causing a groan from most of the squad, who were feeling as if they were going to die. If this was supposed to be a slow, gentle acclimatisation run, they dreaded what future runs would be like. With 100 metres to go, they were given the order to sprint for the camp gates. The last man in would join the RSM, on a little jaunt, that evening. Richard's lungs were bursting, but he didn't want to do it all again, that night. He drew a deep breath, pumped his arms and legs and, focusing on the gate, he fought not to be the last man. Passing the guardroom, he collapsed on the floor, in a pool of sweat. Turning his head back, he saw one poor sod dejectedly crossing the line. It was at that point, he realised he would be on night shift and couldn't have gone on the punishment run, anyway. Surely this wouldn't be the way things were going to be for the full six months?

Chapter 22 – Incidents

After a shower and breakfast, Richard spent the day in the choggy shop, drinking Coke and chatting with some of the off duty blokes. He had another eight hours, before his shift started, so he decided to catch a bit of sun. Leaving the hut, he passed a portly looking guy, who looked like a local. He smiled a greeting, which was returned to him. The man then extended his hand, to introduce himself. The English version of his name was George. He would become known as 'Whisky George', as he had a liking for Scotch whisky and would often ask the troops if they would buy bottles for him. He was employed to keep the facilities running in the camp and to clean the washrooms. He lived in a small, run-down farmhouse, a couple of kilometres away. The two passed the time of day, for a couple of minutes, Richard trying to find out the best places to go to, in Nicosia. George was a font of knowledge and only too pleased to pass it on. Richard made a mental note of some of the bars he mentioned, wished him a good day and headed off, to a secluded spot, outside the hut, to bathe in the sun's rays.

For the next couple of hours, Richard relaxed, on a spare mattress, found in a room. He dragged it outside and had a towel on it, to prevent his back sticking. He only broke from his sunbathing to walk to the cookhouse, where there was a dispenser of ice cold water. They had been told that they needed to drink as much water as possible, a minimum of two litres was required in this climate. This wasn't normal, but they needed to take in as much fluid as possible. He downed a full pint of the liquid without stopping, half-filled the glass again and repeated the motion. His thirst quenched, he returned to the hut, to sit in the shade, for a while. Al had returned with Steve Rabbit, commonly known as 'Mixy', a play on the name of disease

Myxomatosis, which almost obliterated the rabbit population in the UK in the early 1950s.

Mixy had been given the task of replacing the communication lines, which ran from the Box Factory, in the west, to Bravo 18, in the east. It was a mammoth task and would take the full six months to complete. He was excused any other duties, meaning he was not required to take part in the shift pattern, like the rest. A second member of the Troop would be assigned, on a daily basis, to accompany him. It was Al's turn, that day. They had been out on a recce and had just returned, for the midday meal. They had discovered there was a junction box on the road leading up to the Box Factory. From there, anyone could tap into it to make outgoing calls. This was a perk they would surreptitiously utilise in their time there.

Getting dressed into his sandy coloured barrack dress, lightweight trousers and khaki shirt, emblazoned with the badge of the UN, Richard picked up his blue beret, placed it on his head and made his way, across camp, to the Ops room. His Troop Sergeant, John was coming off Watchkeeper duty and brought him up to speed with the events of that day. It had been a quiet one, so he had very little to be concerned with. The Ops room itself was not manned during the night, but there was an officer or Senior NCO on duty, should he be required. The net was monitored from the exchange room, during silent hours. One man from the Troop and one signaller from the Royal Signals, carried out this duty. The Signaller was only responsible for running the Commcen, however, during the course of the tour, they would split the night shift, to enable each of them to catch a couple of hours' sleep. Richard was on shift with the young Lance Corporal, who was in charge of the other three Signallers. Richard's first impression of him was that he was full of his own importance. This feeling would come to a head, later in the tour.

The evening passed quietly, with very little traffic coming over the air. The majority of the calls they received were requests to order transport by taxis or the delivery of takeaway food. They had been given the name of the owner of a taxi company by Whisky George and they would utilise this company, for the rest of the tour. In return, the owner would pick up any of the Troop for free and take them to their destination, returning at the day and time given, to drive them back to camp. This little luxury was kept to themselves, to avoid it getting back to the 'top brass'.

For the next few weeks, the troop rotated through their different shifts, alternating nights, then days. One day of every rotation was spent with Mixy, renewing the telephone cabling on the line between the various Observation Posts. By this time. they were fully acclimatised to the weather and had even taken on a bronze colouring. This had not been the case the first time they visited the outdoor swimming pool in Blue Beret Camp. A group of the guys had taken some time off, during the day, to spend a couple of hours cooling down. They strolled on to the premises, full of soldiers who had been there for months, and in some cases years. They caused quite a stir, with shouts of 'Make room for the whitey from blighty'. This was a reference to their milky white bodies, in stark contrast to the golden Adonis like bodies round the pool.

Incidents which had occurred both during day and night began to happen more frequently. On one occasion while Richard was on night shift and just tucking into the pizza just delivered, he were disturbed by the sound of a Troop from B Squadron. The Troop was occupying a location on the edge of the 'Buffer Zone' at Bravo 24, approximately four kilometres to the east of SDC.

'Hello, Zero, this is Bravo 22, we have a situation at grid 356785. One of our foot patrols has wandered into a minefield, over.' The silence was deafening, as Richard looked at the Royal Signals man, on shift with him. Richard's heart began to race, before he calmed himself down, ordering the Signaller to go and bring the duty Watchkeeper. The Signaller looked at him, with eyes open wide.

'Are you fucking stupid, you prick? Go and get the duty Watchkeeper!' he repeated, this time in an agitated fashion. This caused the youngster to jump into action. He sped out of the room, the door banging closed, behind him. Meantime, Richard got on the air and asked the B Squadron Troop if they had any further details. It transpired that the Patrol Leader had decided to give one of his younger members a bit of experience, allowing him to navigate the patrol, on their intended route. It wasn't until they were around 50 metres into the minefield, that the Patrol Leader called a halt. In the darkness, he had spotted the tell-tale triangular signs, hanging from wire, suspended between two pickets. He asked the young guy to pass his map back and, checking it, he confirmed his position. They had, indeed, strayed into a sodding minefield, which had been laid during the 1974 war.

'What's happening, do we have an update yet?' Paul Goath, the RSWO asked, over Richard's shoulder. Richard went on to explain the story, as he had been given it from the B Squadron Troop Leader. The RSWO nodded that he understood and said that he would take over the situation. Leaving the exchange, he retired to the Ops room. Richard gave an inward sigh of relief, happy the responsibility had been passed on. There would come a time in his career where the buck would stop with him but, for now, he checked his logs, to ensure he had written everything down, as it had been given. This would be be used if a subsequent enquiry transpired, if things went 'Pete Tong'.

For the next hour or so, all unnecessary radio traffic was minimised, so the air was kept free, for the developing situation. Paul frequently asked the B Squadron Troop involved for any updates. These were fed back, by their Troop Leader, who was receiving situation reports on their own Troop frequency. After two long, anxious hours, they were given the news that the patrol had been able to manage to retrace their steps and that they were clear of the minefield. The RSWO acknowledged, put down his handset and joined Richard, in the exchange room.

'You probably got that, Richard. You can record the incident as closed. Make sure you enter the time in your log. Well done on your prompt action and for staying calm. I'm off to bed, now. I'll be in my room, in the Sergeants' Mess, if you need me again.' He gave Richard his telephone number and left the building. The remainder of the night was quiet, allowing Richard and the Signaller to tuck into their cold pizza.

The following week, Richard turned up for day shift and, after getting a briefing on incidents from the previous night, moved to the back room, to make a brew. The Signals bloke manning the Commcen was called Bruce. He was an amiable type and Richard had spent a couple of days with him, repairing telephone lines in the buffer zone. There was another of the Royal Signals detachment called John, who was also easy to get along with. The young Lance Corporal and the other member, called Partridge, were the complete opposite. They were total bellends, a unanimous feeling among the Troop. They considered themselves above the rest, thinking their trade, data telephony, was superior to others. Bruce, a Linesman by trade, was more down to earth, without the airs and graces of the other two.

Richard made a brew and they settled down, for their shift. Just as they had made their way across to the Ops room, the remainder of the Squadron returned, dripping in sweat, from the morning PT session. These sessions had got increasingly hard over the past few weeks. The temperature now was regularly in the high thirties, sometimes in the forties. The troops were always keen to know what the result of the daily 'bulb' test was. Once it reached a specific temperature, no physical activity was allowed. That morning, the session had been close to being cancelled but the RSM decided to go ahead with it. Even he looked as though he was suffering, as they entered the camp gates. Richard admired the man, he had played rugby against him in inter Squadron competitions. They were also team members in the Regimental squad. Richard was thankful he had drawn a day shift, that morning.

An hour later, they were joined by John Mason and Spike, who were to man the Ops room, for the day. Richard preferred the Ops room duty to the rather mundane one of operating the telephone exchange. As with everything in the Army, they had to take the rough with the smooth. It was all part of the job, no one liked a whinger, although it was a trait that every soldier had. The saying was that a squaddie was not happy unless he was 'ticking' (complaining). Perversely, it was, at times, a source of great morale. If soldier heard a complaint, they would simply goad more, with light hearted banter.

Richard had verbal attacks such as 'never mind, mate, just think who's riding your lass, while you're stuck here!' There was no malice in such sayings, they were not meant literally, merely a way of lightening the mood, and were normally met by some witty retort.

The morning was dragging, the sun outside had reached its zenith. There was no air conditioning in the Ops room or exchange, just a couple of fans, attempting, vainly, to cool the place down. This was luxurious, compared to the Squadrons and soldiers manning the static Observation Posts. These were wooden or stone-built structures, spread all the way across the island, which were used to police the buffer zone. It was their function to see that there was no encroachment, by either side, Greek Cypriot or Turkish, north or south, respectively. Regularly, during the night and even sometimes during the day, the opposing side would attempt to move the border, even a few feet or so, in certain places. Every incident of this nature was reported by the Ops and troops were tasked to go and put things right, by arbitrating with the offending party. This was the major reason for UNFICYP in Cyprus.

Troops manning these outposts were required to 'present arms', in salute with their rifles, to any approaching or passing UN vehicles. It had become a source of fun and pleasure, for the members of the Army Air Corps, who flew missions along the buffer zone, who would approach an OP and hover, waiting for the soldier to present arms. They would then proceed to fly around the structure, so the soldier had to move in all directions, saluting as he went.

Richard had just finished a call on the exchange, when his attention was drawn to an incident unfolding on the air. One of the Ops from A Squadron had reported 'shot fired' in the area of his arc of responsibility. The net once again fell silent, giving priority to the Op who had reported the shooting incident. After around ten minutes the Op gave a full report of what had happened.

He had been observing the Turkish Op, which was his mirror, which meant that it stood directly opposite his, approximately one kilometre away, to the north, across the buffer zone. A Land Rover type vehicle had pulled up, at the foot of the Op and someone had got out. He had climbed the ladder up to the Op. This was nothing strange, and was possibly a changing of the sentry. What happened next was not normal, though. Shortly after the figure reached the Op, a shot was heard. The figure left the post and clambered back down the stairs. He opened the vehicle door, climbed inside and it sped off. Ten minutes later, another vehicle was seen approaching, from the north towards the Op. This time, three figures climbed out and ascended the ladder. After a short while, two of them were seen leaving the Op, one had what looked like a body over his shoulder. They struggled back down the ladder and threw the now discernible body into the back of the vehicle. With a roar of its engine and a cloud of dust, it raced off.

In the aftermath of the incident, after it had been reported up the chain of command, the following came to light. The first figure seen entering the Op had been the Commanding Officer of the Turkish Regiment supplying the men for the buffer zone. He was carrying out a daily check of his men. He had found the sentry asleep on duty and had summarily executed him. Richard couldn't believe this but, apparently, he had the power to serve military justice in this manner, up to three times a year. This would definitely would have been a deterrent in the British Army for falling asleep on duty. It had been many years since the First World War, where execution by firing squad was commonplace for desertion. There was nothing UNFICYP could do except lodge their concerns with their Turkish counterparts. The incident remained in Richard's thoughts for the rest of the shift and would be the main topic of conversation in the bar that night, over beer and pizzas the size of a dustbin lids.

Chapter 23 – Relaxation and R&R

Richard finished yet another night shift, this one bringing him to the end of his rotation. Thankfully, he was now going to be off for four days. Depending on the availability of the Troop, this was sometimes reduced to three. He returned to his room to shower, before catching a taxi into Nicosia. He had already called Nikos, the owner of the taxi firm they always used. He would pick him up in an hour's time, outside camp. Grabbing his towel and wash bag, he headed off to the shower block, to freshen up.

On his return, he fished around his locker, trying to find something to wear. Choosing a pair of cut down jeans, he struggled to find a t-shirt to accompany them. Remembering he still had some clean clothes in his suitcase under the bed, he lifted the lid. He was met by a series of snarls, which came from the wild cat, which frequented the room. It even used to sleep on Richard's bed some night, having taken a shine to him. The snarling, Richard discovered, was because the cat had given birth to a litter of three kittens. His nicely laundered clothing was covered in blood. He tried to move the mother gently away from her kittens but she hissed and tried to claw him. He quickly came to the conclusion that he would wait until later, before trying to remove the clothes, to wash them again.

He put on another t-shirt from his locker. It may not have been fresh, but it least it wasn't covered in afterbirth. He put the padlock on his locker, turned and left the room, in the direction of the guardroom. Reaching the guardroom, he was met by Isaac, who was on day duty. They passed the time of day while Richard waited for the taxi. Their conversation was interrupted by the sight of a battered Mercedes, travelling towards them. As it drew nearer Richard recognised Nikos, the owner, at the wheel. He screeched to a halt, inviting Richard to get in.

Turning the car around on the narrow track, Nikos floored the accelerator and sped off. They joined the main road, turning left, in the direction of the old airport and BBC. Just before the entrance road to the airport, Richard recognised Ron, who was manning the checkpoint. Ron had also been promoted and was serving the tour with B Squadron. Due to the lack of manpower, even Lance Corporals had to take their turn manning the checkpoints and Ops. Winding down the car window as they approached, Richard called out.

'Stag on, you wanker!' and waved.

Recognising Richard, a broad grin spread across Ron's face:

'Fuck you, ya prick!' he answered, chuckling and raising a hand, in greeting.

The taxi moved through the checkpoint and continued its journey, towards the Nicosia. It was a lively city and even at that early hour, was a bustle of activity. Nikos had already asked Richard where he wanted dropped off and, within five minutes, pulled up, outside a barber's shop. Richard offered him money for the fare, which was, as usual, declined. He thanked the driver and asked if he was available later that afternoon, to take him to Ayia Napa. Nikos said of course he would be available and asked that Richard call the office, when he was ready. Richard again thanked him and got out of the Mercedes.

He opened the door of the barber's shop and offered the usual Cypriot greeting.

'Kaliméra,' he said. This was returned by the barber, who invited him to take a chair.

Making himself comfortable, Richard was asked what he wanted done. It had become a bit of a habit, after coming off night shift, to have a shave at this establishment. The barber began to wrap Richard's face in steaming hot towels. He left these on for a couple of minutes, while he sharpened his cutthroat razor. Removing the towels, he applied a creamy, soapy solution to Richard's face. Once completely covered, with expert strokes, he removed any sign of facial hair. The whole process took around ten minutes, finished off with the application of fresh, hot towels. As Richard rose from the chair to pay the barber, he felt like a new man, ready to fire a few beers down range. He left the shop and headed off, to his normal starting point.

It was a local Cypriot bar, out of bounds to UN personnel. Soldiers were constantly being briefed on which pubs and clubs they were allowed to frequent, due to intelligence received by UNFICYP, of Russian KGB secret service agents who frequented the bars, trying to either gain information from drunken soldiers or to blackmail them into giving away military secrets.

Like squaddies over the globe, if told they couldn't go somewhere, it was like a red rag to a bull and they did the opposite. Richard arrived at the bar, just before eleven in the morning. Karen, the barmaid, welcomed him, as he sat himself down. She was English, from a small town in Kent and had spent the last year working in Cyprus, during the summer months. Richard recalled the first time he had been in the bar and asked for a Johnnie Walker whisky, pointing at the bottle on the shelf. She had said that he didn't want that one, to which he replied that he did. She produced a bottle from under the bar and, pointing, repeated that he didn't want that Johnnie Walker, he wanted this Johnnie Walker. Richard had been confused, as the bottles looked identical. She went on to explain that the bottles on the optics were a façade and were filled with local whisky, to be given to tourists or drunken soldiers. Karen had taken a liking to Richard, so offered him the proper job. Along the bar were bowls of fresh vegetables, covered in salt and other assorted snacks, given out for free. The heavy salt covering only caused the clientele to drink more. Richard didn't care. He liked the taste of the freebies and wanted to have a good drink, anyway. He spent a couple of hours in the bar, before deciding to go for a walk.

Walking down Regina Street, which was the main area the off duty UN soldiers used, he noticed a couple of guys from B Squadron, going through the doors of the Queen Anna Maria Bar. The place was a favourite haunt for a lot of the troops, the entertainment was legendary. A former lady of the night, whose Greek name was impossible to pronounce, was often to be found there, scrounging drinks off the young soldiers. She was a deaf and dumb mute, which earned her the title of D&D, the meaning of which was self-explanatory.

Richard decided to have a swift one in the pub, before calling the taxi office, for his lift to Ayia Napa. He was not surprised to find D&D propping up the bar, gesturing to a young lad, from A Squadron. He hadn't been in the Regiment long, but had already got himself a reputation for being a bit of a joker. D&D was, as usual, touting for drinks, which the young soldier was happy to supply. It was a favourite prank of the soldiers to pretend to put money in the jukebox, which stood in the corner. They would then pretend to dance along to it, inviting D&D to join them.

Over time she had become wise to the joke and would feel the jukebox to see if it was vibrating, before she made herself look stupid. A couple of weeks earlier, a couple of guys, from the Provost Troop, had been drinking in the bar and had gone back to her flat, for a party. As the night went on, it turned into a full blown orgy. Once all parties were satisfied, D&D collapsed on the bed and fell asleep. One of the Regimental Police took a Maglite torch, which was next to the dressing table, and placed where, a short time before, their cocks had been. Giggling away to each other, they let themselves out and headed back to camp. The story had gone round the Regiment in a matter of hours, causing great hilarity. Richard polished off his beer, and called the taxi office.

The journey from Nicosia to Ayia Napa took just over an hour. They passed the camp in Dhekelia, where the rest of the Regiment were stationed, in the eastern SBA. If not on duty, most of their time was taken up with adventure training and water sports, as the camp was located next to a beach.

Taking the coast road eastwards, Nikos steered the vehicle into the outskirts of Ayia Napa. He dropped off Richard at Nissi beach, which would be his starting point. He arranged with Nikos his pickup time, which was to be two days later, at around 8pm, in the square in Ayia Napa. Nikos nodded his agreement and confirmed he would be there.

Richard made straight for a beach bar and began on brandy sours, his drink of choice on the island. The drink consisted of two parts local brandy, one part Cypriot lemon squash, a couple of dashes of bitters, topped up with lemonade or soda and served in a tall glass, with ice. Local bars sometimes substituted Angostura bitters with the local stuff, which carried the wonderful name 'Cock Drops'.

It wasn't long before he was joined by Paul Robson, from Recce Troop, now also attached to B Squadron He had with him a number of other members of his Squadron, who were on time off. They grabbed a table and bought a round of drinks. The B Squadron blokes were only down for the day and were heading back that evening. They made the most of their down time as they could and the drinks were flowing. As they sat chatting and looking at the 'talent' strewn along the beach, one of B Squadron, who was called Mark, noticed two young ladies looking over at them, from an adjacent table. He smiled at them, the smile was returned and they then proceeded to whisper to one another. They were obviously interested in Mark he stood 6 feet 3 inches, in his flip flops and had the body of a male model. Knowing his luck was in, he rose and wandered over to the pair of girls. In the blink of an eye, he returned, with the girls in his wake. Introducing them as Agnita and Freya, he invited them to take a seat. They sat down, amidst the half pissed squaddies and began to make small talk. It transpired they were University students, who had just graduated and were now taking a year out, to explore the world. Everyone took turns in introducing themselves and the girls seemed genuinely impressed, when they heard the lads were British soldiers. As they chatted, one of the B Squadron blokes, called 'Dusty', was transfixed with Freya. He came from a rough area of Bradford and had a strong, nasal accent. Having ginger hair, he didn't take well to the sun. In comparison to the bronzed counterparts around him, he was still as white as the day he got off the plane. He leaned over towards Freya and began to sniff her neck. She was slightly startled by this and wondered what was going on. Continuing to sniff, Dusty looked up at her and asked,

'What's that perfume you've got on?'

There was a hesitant pause, while Freya thought for a moment, translating his cultural Yorkshire accent, to ensure she had heard him correctly.

'Chanel number 5,' she answered, innocently, happy that someone found her scent appealing.

'Smells bloody lovely, that,' came Dusty's blunt retort.

There was another pause, as the friends looked at each other, wondering where this was going. No one could believe he was hitting on this girl, with her outstanding, Nordic good looks and beautiful body. Dusty was around five feet eight, and weighed around ten stone, naked. He simply wasn't the sort that girls lusted after. The brief silence was broken by Freya.

'What have you got on?' she asked, politely.

Again Dusty looked her up and down, before replying,

'A fuckin' hard on, but I don't think you can fuckin' smell it.'

234

The group of friends fell about laughing, at what had been the highlight of the afternoon. Freya stared at him quizzically, not really understanding what he had said.

Mark interrupted the laughter, asking the two girls if they wanted to go for a swim. They nodded their agreement and the three stood up, to walk the short distance to the sea. They were joined by Paul, who said that he needed to cool down. They entered the water, wading out, till the Mediterranean Sea was up to their chests. The other friends paid no more attention and got more drinks from the bar. It was then Richard drew their attention to Mark and Freya.

'Do you believe that jammy twat?' he asked the others, who immediately gazed out to sea. Mark had Freya's arms around his neck, her legs wrapped round him. It was obvious to the friends that they were engaged in full blown sex, not ten feet away from children, playing in the water. A short time later, the two couples returned to the table, Mark with a smug grin on his face and Freya, with a flush on hers. Like all squaddies, the episode was treated as a normal occurrence and nothing was mentioned. The journey home was different, though, and the story would be told and retold.

Finishing off his brandy sour, Richard made his apologies and wished them a safe journey back to the Green Line. He was heading into town, where he had arranged to meet up with Mark Dumore, a member of the Royal Pay Corps, also stationed at SDC. Richard had struck up a friendship with Mark, when he had volunteered to go on exercise with Command Troop on Soltau. Mark's father had been a Colonel and he could have joined as an officer, but he decided he wanted to go through the ranks and earn his commission. The two friends got along famously, he had even tried to protect Richard, when he had bounced a cheque, two weeks earlier. Yet his efforts were in vain and Richard was charged for the offence. Even so, Richard valued his attempt.

It was about a fifteen to twenty minute walk from the beach to the square in Ayia Napa. As Richard approached the bar called Volcanoes, he saw Mark, already sitting at a table, on his own. He walked over, pulled up a chair, and said:

'Get the beers in then, ya wanker,' in the manner that only good friends could get away with. Mark laughed out loud, with his unmistakeable trade mark cackle.

'For you, mate, of course I will, ya Geordie fucker!' and set off to the bar, to bring a couple of beers.

During his temporary absence, two couples asked Richard if they could join him, at the table. From their accents, he guessed that they were of Scandinavian origin. He replied that of course they could join him. As they sat, Mark returned with the beers and was introduced by Richard. The ladies were striking in appearance, both with long blonde hair and probably in their mid-twenties. When Richard explained what they were doing on the island, they were eager to find out about life in the British Army. For once, it felt great for someone to be so welcoming, unlike many of the places that Troops visited. Some soldiers often spoilt a locality by getting drunk, upsetting the locals and fighting.

The six chatted away for the next hour, enjoying each others' company and cultures. Suddenly, one of the males spotted a tattoo of a Viking, which decorated Mark's right forearm.

'Is that a Norwegian Viking or a Swedish Viking?' he asked the loaded question. Not being stupid, having already discovering their country of birth, Mark answered that it was Swedish. This caused the two couples to stand and raise their glasses in salute.

'Skol!' they cried out, as one, and invited the two friends to empty their glasses. This done, one of the Swedes disappeared to the bar, to buy another round. While he was away, the other male discreetly whispered in Mark's ear.

Richard noticed the shocked look on Mark's face but decided to wait for an opportunity to find out what was said. The opportunity presented itself five minutes later, when Mark announced he was going to the toilet. Richard excused himself and followed, behind him. As they stood facing the urinals, relieving themselves, Richard turned his head and asked the question.

'He only asked me if I fancied his girlfriend and if I wanted to shag her!' Mark replied, incredulously.

'What did you say to that?' Richard enquired.

'I didn't commit myself one way or the other,' Mark replied, as though he wasn't really bothered.

The pair zipped themselves up, washed their hands and returned to the table. Another couple of hours passed, and a vast amount of various forms of alcohol was consumed. Without warning, the two couples announced they were moving on. As they did, they looked in Mark's direction. He, too, stood, saying to Richard that he would meet him in 'Joys', in a couple of hours. Richard smiled at Mark, knowing exactly what he had in mind, and wished him a good evening.

As they left the bar, Richard spotted JJ, who was a mechanic by trade, but was working with Al Cooper as a ration storeman in SDC, for the tour. He was from Gateshead, in the north east of England. JJ liked to party, as all people of the fair city of Newcastle do. He was in the company of two blokes from G Squadron, who were from the 15/19th The King's Royal Hussars. This unit, recruited mostly in the north east of England, was attached for the six month tour. Richard made his way over to them and JJ introduced his two drinking partners as Frenchy and Joe. They were standing outside a bar opposite Volcanoes, drinking and admiring the view. They had been on tour for nearly two months and the sight of tanned, gorgeous looking women was now commonplace. As they spoke together, a voluptuous, long-legged creature approached them. As she drew level with them, JJ halted her, with a harmless enough question.

'Do you have the time, pet?' he asked, using the Geordie term for a young woman. Looking at the watch on her left wrist, and beaming at him, seemingly glad of the attention, she answered.

'Yes, It is half past nine.'

What happened next would go to Richard's grave with him. JJ went on to address the beautiful creature, with a comment she couldn't have expected.

'Do you know what, pet? You're the ugliest bastard I've seen in Ayia Napa!' he then went on to relieve himself, where he stood. The sound of gushing urine, escaping the left leg of his colourful Hawaiian shorts, was all that was heard, in the shocked silence. With a look of complete horror and disgust, the Amazon-like woman fled from the square, trying to hold back the tears, welling up inside her. The sound of raucous laughter rang out, across the square.

It was drawing near to one in the morning. The friends decided it was time to hit Joys to continue the fun. Joys was popular with squaddies and tourists alike. Its main attraction was that, after paying six Cypriot pounds to get in, all local drinks were free. As they approached the club, just around the corner from the square, Richard observed a body in the gutter.

The wretch had his hand outstretched, his head bowed low, obviously much the worse for wear.

'Can you spare £5? I need to get into Joys.' he slurred, over and over again. It wasn't until he looked up, Richard recognised him as Dennis Law, a well know pisshead, from B Squadron.

'You fucking tramp, Dennis!' Richard said, as he pulled him up, from the gutter. 'Try and make yourself look presentable, if that's at all possible. You can come in with us.' He directed Dennis in the direction of the door, holding him up from behind, by his belt. Safely navigating him through the door, they were hit by a wall of sound, from the disco.

The place was already almost full of tourists and the odd pissed up, off duty squaddie. They got another round of drinks, but it wasn't long before Dennis disappeared in the crowd, never to be seen again. The club was open until the early hours of the morning, and Richard had been told he could crash at the flat, on the other side of the town, just off the square, shared by JJ and the two G Squadron guys. They had begun their R&R two days earlier.

When they left Joys, JJ was talking to a pretty girl in her late teens, who was somewhat unsteady on her feet. When they left the club, he escorted her back to the flat, as she had no recollection of where she lived and had lost her friends. She was Norwegian, from Oslo, and this was her first holiday abroad. Richard could understand how young girls alone could get into serious trouble. Here she was, going back to a flat with four complete strangers.

When they arrived back at the accommodation, Frenchy got some beers from the fridge and they continued to drink. The sun had risen an hour earlier, it was 06:30 am. JJ had retired, to the bedroom, half an hour earlier. The other three's attention was drawn to the sound of a bedroom door opening, where JJ stood, bollock naked.

'You got any fags?' he asked Richard, knowing the other two did not smoke.

'Sorry, mate, just had my last one. I can go and get some if you want, shops should be open by now,' he replied.

'No, it's okay, I'll go. I think I need to clear my head,' he said, and went to put some shorts and a t-shirt on. Now that he was in a respectable state, he left the flat in search of a shop. The two G Squadron guys began whispering to each other, stood up and motioned to Richard, to follow them. Opening the bedroom door, they saw that the young girl was totally sprawled across the bed. She was out for the count, which was not surprising. On the dressing table, to her left, lay a camera, which they assumed belonged to JJ. Frenchy tip-toed forward and retrieved the camera. At the same time, Joe began to take off his shorts and vest. Climbing onto the bed, he straddled the girl's head and laid his flaccid member on her face, with his testicles resting on her eyelids. Frenchy snapped away with the camera, sniggering as he did so. Richard was trying hard not to burst out laughing, he thought the prank was hilarious. He wondered what a surprise JJ would get, when he had the film developed.

It had been an interesting four days off. Nikos arrived at the appointed time and took Richard back to camp. That week was going to drag, as Birgit was flying over the following week, for Richard's R&R. Eventually, he finished his last shift and packed his bag, for leave. He had arranged the delivery of a hire car, which turned up, on time, an hour later. Freshly showered, changed and packed, he headed off to the camp gates, where the vehicle was waiting for him. He ran a quick inspection and signed the necessary paperwork. The UN guys got a special deal, so the car was his, for the full week.

He took the keys, climbed in and started the engine. He headed off, firstly in an easterly direction, then south, in the direction of the coast. It was a 75 minute drive to the airport at Paphos, where Birgit and a few other wives and girlfriends were landing. He parked the car and made his way to arrivals, checking the information board for landing times. He noticed that the flight from Germany had already landed, so he positioned himself, by the arrival doors.

One by one, the passengers emerged in the main terminal, dragging or carrying their luggage. Richard spotted Birgit right away, she was looking about, in search of his face. As she neared him, to his surprise, she walked straight past him. Turning around, he saw her still scanning the area, looking for him. It was at that point the penny dropped. With his tanned, darkened skin, he must have looked like a local.

'You not talking, then?' he shouted after her. She turned and, with a smile as wide as her face, ran towards him and threw her arms around his neck.

It had been almost three months since he had left to go on the tour. These absences were something she would have to get used to, but nothing mattered, at that moment. Richard took her luggage and they headed for the exit. Reaching the car, he threw her case and bag into the boot and they drove off, east along the coast road. En route, after passing through 'Happy Valley', in the western Sovereign Base Area of Episkopi, they drove past Aphrodite's Rock, named after the Greek goddess of love. Carrying on further, they passed Akrotiri on their right. Another half hour saw them enter the outskirts of Limassol, where 'Legs', his old commander from D Squadron, had booked their accommodation.

Legs and his sidekick Chris Souness, had the enviable job of arranging the Regiment's R&R, for the duration of the tour. They would drive around, visiting different establishments, assessing their suitability for the troops and their partners or families. The job carried a lot of perks and they were often wined and dined, by the owners of hotels, who wanted to gain their patronage. Richard had visited the hotel where they would be staying, to check it out and knew that Birgit would like it.

They pulled up outside, retrieved their luggage and took the lift, to the seventh floor. As soon as they walked in the room, they were immediately cooled by the air conditioning system, working flat out.

Birgit threw her handbag on the bed and went straight to the toilet, to inspect the hygiene. She returned quickly and smiled at Richard, giving her silent approval. Stepping out on to the balcony, they were greeted by a fabulous view, gazing south to the Mediterranean. Birgit walked back into the room, in order that that she could shower and freshen up, after her long journey.

The sun was just setting, the couple locked the hotel door and strolled the short distance on to the main strip of Limassol. They spent the evening visiting various bars and sampling all manner of cocktails. Needing to soak up the alcohol, Richard took Birgit to a restaurant he knew would serve a brilliant Mezze. This was a Cypriot speciality, consisting of different small dishes. Diners could order anything from a twelve plate to a twenty-one plate Mezze.

Richard decided they wouldn't be greedy and went for an eighteen plate Mezze. They didn't rush the food and the meal took an hour and a half to finish, washed down by Ouzo and beer. The night was getting late and the pair decided to have one nightcap, on the way back to the hotel. They stopped off at a bar not far from their destination. Taking a seat overlooking the street, they ordered what they thought would be the final drink of the evening. However, they were joined by a couple from Finland a few minutes later and, after a quick chat, they settled in to each other's company. By the time the four departed the bar, the sun was almost about to rise. This would be the first of many late nights with the couple, whose names they couldn't even pronounce.

For the next week, they toured the island, taking in the usual tourist sights. From a lace making house, in the middle of the country, up in the hills to the white, sandy beaches of Ayia Napa and the spectacular view from the Troodos mountains.

The troops had been informed, when they arrived in the country, that they weren't allowed to hire motorcycles or scooters. Yet, everyone ignored this rule. So, one day Richard hired a scooter and, with Birgit riding pillion, travelled the winding roads of the island, stopping off in small, rustic villages, eating and drinking the local produce. In these out of the way places, they paid a fraction of the price charged by the restaurants and bars in places like Limassol, Ayia Napa and Paphos.

During the day, they decided to pop to the beach in Ayia Napa. Walking onto the beach, Richard saw Spike, Al and a couple of blokes from A Squadron, sitting at the water's edge. They were armed with mini barrels, filled with their own homemade whisky and brandy sours, packed with ice. Just as Richard and Birgit approached them, Spike vomited into the sea, then again, down his front. They must have been on the sauce all day, Richard thought, so he quickly steered Birgit away, to head back to Limassol.

The week passed too quickly and the morning came when Richard had to take Birgit to the airport, for her return flight. The atmosphere was tense between them but he reminded her that he had arranged for her to come back out, in a month's time. For that visit, they had booked an empty married quarter, on Blue Beret Camp, kept for visiting relatives. Carrying her suitcases from the car into the departure lounge, they embraced, for the time they had left. She kissed him, longingly and, with a tear, turned away and walked through the check-in and on to passport control. Richard waited for a while and watched the chartered flight taxi on the runway and lift off, into the cloudless, blue sky.

Chapter 24 – Back to UN Duties

It seemed like an age, since R&R. The only distraction was the upcoming peace talks, between the Greek and Turkish Prime Ministers. When Richard returned from R&R, he had heard an amusing story, about a certain Troop, based in Dhekelia. One of the Troop Corporals, Mal Thorn, had organised a boat trip with a difference. He had given it a pirate theme, so all participants had to dress accordingly. They boarded a little fishing boat at Limassol harbour, after stowing several Norwegians of brandy sour and crates of Keo beer. The drink flowed, as it always did and, once under way, a large pirate flag, made from a bed sheet, was hoisted from the mast. The boat sailed round the island, until they anchored off a beach. Unfortunately, the beach turned out to be private, attached to a hotel, in the middle of nowhere. At this point, everybody was well intoxicated and, in keeping with the theme of the trip, decided to swim ashore and cause mayhem.

Many beers were hastily drunk but not paid for. Some of the more fearsome pirates, fuelled by drink, attempted to kidnap topless women from the beach, as 'booty', to take back to the boat. These antics didn't go down well with the locals, so they speedily set sail, again.

By this time, they had gone from intoxicated to 'screeching'. One of the younger members of the Troop was held down, over the mainbrace and a cat o' nine tails appeared. The unfortunate was summarily flogged for being a 'nig' or new pirate. A long piece of wood, its end out over the water, was hastily set up and other youngsters were made to walk the plank.

After the punishments had been administered, they set back off, until they were stopped by a Cypriot Coastguard gunboat and were promptly arrested. The poor, old, Greek fisherman, whose boat it was, looked as though he was going to collapse, but, escorted by the Coast Guard, he managed to set sail for Limassol. The beer and pirate songs continued, until their arrival in Limassol harbour, where the pirates were met by Cypriot riot police. Mal refused to surrender the ship and, following a rousing speech, they got ready to 'repel boarders'.

Following a standoff of about an hour, the RMP arrived and were allowed to board. Mal discussed the terms of surrender with them (which was to agree to be taken into their custody and be transported back to Dhekelia by bus or have the Cypriot cops take the boat by force, then lock them up in Limassol Prison).

The bus arrived and transported them back to barracks, where they were met by the Squadron Leader (OC), RSM and the camp Sergeant Major. Military summary justice was duly carried out, and that particular troop would not be seeing the outside of the camp gates, until the end of the tour.

It never ceased to amaze Richard the pranks and high jinks which the everyday soldier got up to. He smiled, as he laced up his boots and prepared himself for a day manning a cordon, to provide security for the peace talks. Those who were not on essential duty in SDC had been roped in, to bolster the numbers of those members of the Regiment securing a site, where the talks were to take place. This would last a number of weeks, therefore Richard would alternate between his own Troop duties in the Ops room and the exchange and the peace talks.

The guys from SDC had gathered in the car park, behind HQ. The Camp SSM, Stu, took the roll call, before loading everyone on to a Bedford truck. It was only a short journey from camp to the site, by the old airport. This was already a partially secured area. Access was monitored through two gates, one at the western side of Nicosia, the other just west of Blue Beret Camp. As the truck pulled up, the Troops disgorged themselves. Stu called Richard over to him, to act as his radio operator, for the day. Richard took the Clansman VRC 351 VHF manpack from the rear of Stu's Land Rover. He set it on the ground and selected the frequency for the morning and, with the use of the tuning device on the top, known as a SURF, tuned the set in. Throwing the manpack on to his shoulders, he adjusted the straps, to make them comfortable. As he walked off in the direction Stu had taken, he saw his childhood friend Pete strolling towards him. He, too, had a radio strapped to his back, and was talking into the microphone headset, as he walked. Richard paused when he reached Pete, waiting for him to finish speaking.

'All right, mate, how the devil are you?' he asked.

'I'm okay, buddy, same shit, different day. What you up to?' he enquired of Richard.

'Looks like the same as you,' was all Richard could say.

Pete had been newly promoted to full Corporal or 'full screw' as it was more popularly known. Despite his little incident in Berlin, when he and another had stolen a car, while drunk, he had still gained promotion. He had just taken over as A Squadron Signals NCO and was responsible for the communications, inspections and repairs of the same, and was the Squadron Leaders operator. It had been delegated that his Squadron Leader would be in command of the security operation over the next couple of weeks, so Pete, as his operator, was to accompany him. The two friends chatted for a while, till they were disturbed by Stu, calling out for Richard.

'Better be going, mate, we'll talk later,' and, with that, he set off, at a run, in Stu's direction.

It was only 08:30. The sun had already begun to burn through Richard's lightweight tropical combats. He felt sorry for the poor sods who had spent the last four months occupying the Ops, along the buffer zone. There was no air conditioning and the little stone or wooden structures were like pressure cookers. Stu asked him to contact the various positions that had been placed around the cordon, to confirm that they were all in readiness for the arrival of the Greek and Turkish Presidents. He did as ordered and, one by one, each confirmed that they were in position and ready.

At a little before 09:00, a call came through to Richard, alerting him that a black Mercedes, bearing the Greek flag, had begun its approach. Not two minutes later, another call was received, giving similar information of a diplomatic car, heading from the opposite direction, adorned with the Turkish flag. This was passed on to Stu, who informed A Squadron Leader.

Earlier in 1988, Georgios Vassiliou had been elected Greek Cypriot president. This was to be his first meeting with his opposite number, Rauf Denktash. The peace talks had been going on since 1985 but no end to hostilities was in sight. The two cars arrived simultaneously, drawing to a quiet halt, outside the building. The doors were open by a personal security details from both sides. The presidents shook hands, briefly, and were ushered inside.

The day was long and hot, Richard between spells monitoring the radio, drove around the cordon with the SSM, delivering water to the troops. It was the consensus of opinion that it was a futile exercise, as the leaders of both sides would never see eye to eye. However, as members of the United Nations Peacekeeping Force and, specifically because the talks were being held in their sector, they just had to get on with it.

Richard was glad to receive a call, in mid-afternoon, from one of the troops, closest to the building. He reported that the Presidents were just leaving, for their cars. The cordon was given the order to heighten security, as any attack would be likeliest as the leaders were entering or leaving the site. In the space of ten minutes, both cars had cleared the cordon and were driving away, on their own separate routes. Stu gave the order for the cordon to be collapsed and for the truck to go round and pick all the blokes up from SDC. He jumped into the Land Rover and called to Richard, to climb in the back. The vehicle roared off down the track and on to the main road, heading back, west to the comforts of Saint David's.

The next couple of weeks were much the same, boredom interspersed with minor, though no major, incidents. The only thing which broke the monotony was the celebration of a Regimental Battle Honour. It was known as Dettingen Day and was celebrated every year, as near as possible to the date of the battle.

The battle, itself, had taken place on 27th June 1743. Dettingen was fought in South West Germany, on the north bank of the River Main, some 70 miles East of Frankfurt and three miles West of Aschaffenburg. It was during this battle that Cornet Richardson (the most junior commissioned rank in a British cavalry regiment of the period) of Ligonier's Horse, later to be known as the 7th Dragoons, rescued the Standard of the Regiment and, in doing so, received 37 sabre cuts.

The morning started early, with the officers and senior ranks serving 'gunfire' to the other ranks. This was a tradition carried out in many Regiments in the British Army and was originally a cocktail made of black tea and rum. These days, it was served with coffee or tea; and whisky or rum was made available. After the gunfire, everyone went to breakfast, where they enjoyed a slap up meal, to line their stomachs for the day.

The day itself would comprise competitions, both sporting as well as drinking. Parading outside the Motor Transport hangars, the troops, who were dressed in sports kit were met with a series of obstacles and equipment. The mechanics had been hard at work, fashioning items to be used in different sporting activities. The competition itself was light hearted but, nonetheless, fiercely contested.

Alongside the races and relays, a live version of the old TV show *It's A Knockout* was fought out. The prize to the winning team was a crate of Carlsberg.

For more than an hour, the teams raced against each other, resulting in a very close contest. When the final race was due to start, there were only a couple of points between the teams. The final event would take the form of a timed 'drag' around the camp. A Land Rover trailer, weighing half a tonne, had been dragged out of the hangar. Teams of six would have to push and pull the trailer around the half a mile course. They would have to stop at various points and carry out a task. The team with the quickest time would win. The teams waited, as one by one, their opponents attempted the course. As the penultimate team pulled and pushed the trailer over the line, Richard and the members of Signal Troop readied themselves, to take their turn.

Arranging themselves around the trailer, they waited for the signal to start. On the word of command, they set off, at a lightning pace, on the first leg. The time to beat was nine minutes, achieved by MT Troop, who had crossed the line totally exhausted and covered in sweat. As the team approached the Squadron bar, they were halted by Ian, the barman, who had laid out six pints of Keo beer, on a table. They were instructed to drop the trailer and drink the beers, as quickly as they could. The team did as they were told and sank the drinks in quick time. Picking the trailer back up, they set off again. The liquid swilling about their stomachs and the blazing heat started to make Richard feel sick. His mind was distracted by Stu, who stood blocking their path, just outside the Warrant Officers' and Sergeants' Mess. He, again, told them to drop the trailer and invited them inside. As before, a table had been set out, with what looked like half pints of water. Next to each of these was a bowl, containing a solitary Weetabix. The task was to eat the cereal as quickly as possible, then wash it down with the liquid. The troops began in earnest forcing down the very dry morsel, their tongues sticking to the roofs of their mouths, as they did so. They waited until all had finished the dry cereal then, as one, they picked up their glasses and downed the refreshing, cold liquid. As the drink went down their throats, they knew it wasn't water, it was neat vodka. Forcing the bile back down, the six raced outside, to retrieve the trailer and, somehow, ran the last 200 metres, or so, to the finish line. As they ran, some, including Richard, were spewing as they went. As the trailer wheels crossed the line, they collapsed on the ground, to a man, gasping for air and emptying what little they had left in their stomachs. To their disappointment, they missed their target by some ten seconds, which drew a great cheer from the blokes in MT, who gladly accepted their crate of beer.

The rest of the day was spent in the Squadron bar. This time, the officers and senior ranks joined them. It was one of the only days where the Regiment drank together. The officers and SNCOs, cut away to their own messes, at convenient points. During the celebrations and a few pub games, Richard was approached by Isaac, who furtively pulled him to one side.

'I'm off to Syria tonight, you coming?' he asked.

The question hit Richard, like a hammer blow, out of the blue. 'Don't be stupid, you fucking dick! You know our lass is coming out again tomorrow.' was all he could say.

Isaac simply shrugged his shoulders and wandered off to the bar, to get himself another drink. For those not on duty, the drinking and fun and games continued, for the rest of the night.

In the morning, Richard had been given the day off, to collect Birgit and to move into the Married Quarter they had booked for a week in BBC. Richard had decided to go with another car rental company, who were a less expensive than the last one he had used. The downside was that they didn't deliver and he would have to get a lift into Nicosia. He had arranged the previous evening with two of the Sergeants that they would drop him off, in town. The Sergeants were the 'Humanitarian Section', dealing with any disputes between local farmers. These were regular occurrences, which required sympathetic handling, as things could often escalate from these situations. Another duty they performed was to keep the wild and feral dog population down. They would drive along the line in their sector, armed with shotguns and dispatch any animals causing a nuisance. They had the previous week, blasted the hell out of a rat's nest, which had been found under the rations store. It had been a gruesome sight to behold, as bodies, tails and entrails were blown in the air, by the force of the shotgun pellets.

Richard waited outside the guardroom, for the Land Rover to pick him up. The member of the RP staff manning the gate asked him if he had seen Isaac. He replied that he hadn't and asked why? It transpired that Isaac had been due to turn up for duty at 06:00 that morning but was nowhere to be found. Richard smiled inwardly to himself, knowing exactly where he was. The previous night was to be the last time he would set eyes on Isaac for many years to come.

The Land Rover screeched to a halt. Jim Flat and Graham Calf, the Sergeants, motioned for Richard to jump in the back. Doing so, he had to move a big, black, plastic bag out of the way, so he could get comfortable. As they travelled down the road, with a slight, warm breeze washing over them, the most evil of smells pervaded Richard's nostrils.

'What the fuck is that smell?' he asked, through gritted teeth. Jim, not driving, leaned back into the rear of the vehicle and, pulling open the black bag, revealed what was left of a wild dog.

'We shot this the day before last and haven't had time to get rid of it, yet,' he laughed, as he enlightened Richard.

Richard pushed his head over the side of the vehicle and began to vomit, uncontrollably. He felt the journey was taking an age, having to share his personal space with this corpse. Flat and Calf thought it highly amusing and directed jibes at him the whole way, until, at last, they arrived at the car rental business. Jumping out of the back of the Land Rover, Richard thanked them both for the lift and, taking deep breaths of fresh air, headed into the office, to pick up his car.

The journey to Paphos airport and back took around two and a half hours, including the half hour he had to wait, for the flight to arrive. Richard opened the door to his and Birgit's accommodation for the next week. Richard had already taken it over two days earlier, checking its cleanliness and that it contained all the furniture and cutlery listed on the inventory. Birgit had been so impressed with her last visit, she had been counting down the days, until her return. She had asked if it was possible for Richard to get a posting out to Cyprus. This was highly unlikely, as the troops stationed there were either infantry or support arms. There was no requirement for armoured soldiers, except when taking their turn as part of UNFICYP.

For the week of Birgit's visit, Richard's boss, Paul Goath, had arranged day shift for him, in order that Richard could spend as much time with his wife as possible, while she was there. They spent the evenings, relaxing in the garden of their house or eating out, at the various restaurants in Nicosia. Birgit spent the days at the BBC swimming pool, topping up her tan, from her previous visit. Before the pair knew it, it was time for her to return to Germany. The trip had been all too short, but they both took comfort in the fact that the tour would be completed in a month and he would be heading home.

Every year, displaced Greek inhabitants of the town of Morphou, which was just down the road from the western Squadron's HQ at the box factory, marched. Morphou was located in the north-western part of Cyprus, 30 miles from the capital, Nicosia. The Plain of Morphou is one of the

252

richest and most fertile areas of Cyprus, and Morphou soon grew into a significant market town. Due to the abundance of underground water, irrigation agriculture developed quickly in the area, with a variety of crops grown including apples, vegetables, legumes, grains, taro, sesame, melons and citrus.

'The name Morphou (meaning beautiful place) dates back to ancient times and is associated with the Goddess Aphrodite (the goddess of love and beauty). The Lacones or Spartans originally settled Morphou and they brought with them the worship of Aphrodite and named the town after her beauty. Near Morphou lie the ruins of the ancient city of Soloi, one of the ten ancient kingdoms of Cyprus. Numerous archaeological discoveries have been made around Morphou reinforcing the connection to the cult of Aphrodite, including the statue named the Aphrodite of Soloi.

Under British rule, in 1896, Morphou was established as a municipality. On August 16, 1974 Morphou and the adjacent area were occupied by Turkish troops and its people were forcibly expelled or fled from the town. Before the Turkish invasion, Morphou had a mainly Greek Cypriot population of about 9000 people. Since then the displaced Greek Cypriot residents have been forbidden to return to their homes and orchards.

The Morphou Town Council has since been based in Limassol on the south coast. The Turkish invasion of northern Cyprus in the summer of 1974 left 200,000 refugees, thousands dead and hundreds missing. Of the 1,618 missing persons 140 of them came from the Morphou region' (The Guardian 8th November 2006)

UNFICYP had been told that that year the numbers for the march were to be higher than normal. The event itself would try and be kept as low key as possible, to avoid upsetting the Vassiliou Denktash talks. The western Squadron would need reinforcements, to bring up their numbers, to police the march. Richard had been chosen to provide communications for the event but this time, he would be accompanying the Commanding Officer, as his personal signaller. The Squadron was also reinforced by a Troop from B Squadron, two platoons of Danes, as well as a Troop of armoured cars. On the evening before the event, the western Squadron OC called everyone together, for a briefing. He went on to lay out his plans for the next day. He ended his brief saying that they were to be prepared for anything but expected the whole thing would be something of an anti-climax.

The next day, early in the morning, Richard met up with the CO and, along with his driver, they transited the route from east to west from SDC to the box factory, at Bravo 32. The Royal Engineers had constructed a wire obstacle across the road, about half a mile inside the buffer zone. When the CO arrived, all the troops had already been deployed and it was only 08:00.

That morning, the locals held a church service, followed by a political rally, in a nearby village. They then marched, from the village to the buffer zone, to hand over a petition to the Squadron Leader. The OC of western Squadron was in charge and the CO was only there to act as an observer. The troops were deployed, out of sight, in the orange groves that stood on either side of the road. The UN Civilian Police had reported that the numbers were low, perhaps 200 to 300 demonstrators. However, in a short time, Richard, listening in on the net, heard that that figure had risen to 1500, and then again to 3500. He duly passed on this information to the CO, who seemed concerned at this change in the situation. It had become apparent that the small number of Cypriot Police would not be able to control this crowd, so the CO asked Richard to get the Australian UN police on the net. Once he had done this, the

254

CO requested that the Australians aided their civilian counterparts, which was accepted. The march had also been joined by the Greek Cypriot President and the march was led by two Greek Orthodox priests.

As the crowd strolled down the road towards the box factory, one of the Troops had been deployed across the road blocking their path. They halted the advance for a short while, but being unarmed, it proved difficult stemming this many people. Eventually, due to weight of numbers, they broke through the solitary Troop. They were then halted in their tracks by the concertina barbed wire stretching across the roads, into the orange groves on either side. Here, they were met by another Troop from A Squadron, backed up with a platoon of Danes. They were successful in stopping the majority of the crowd but the more determined managed to find a way round. In no time, they were attempting to make their way through the orange groves, on either side. They were not expecting to be met by other forces, secreted on both sides, for that purpose. Richard was one, following the CO, as he travelled among the troops, giving instructions that minimum force was to be used.

The crowds were being followed by reporters, photographers and TV cameras. As the crowd were again halted by the defensive line, they began kicking out and hurling abuse. After years of experience of such crowds in Northern Ireland, the soldiers smiled politely back at the demonstrators. This enraged them even further and a couple managed to break through the cordon. Richard spotted one, who had evaded the line, so took chase. Nearing the demonstrator, he took a well-aimed swing with his right foot, behind the knees of the runner, bringing him to the ground. Just as Richard looked around to see if there were any others who had made it through, his heart sank. A TV camera crew were focusing their lens directly at him.

Oh fuck, he thought to himself, had they captured that image? If so, how much shit was he in now? The CO had also seen the action and was making his way, at great speed, toward Richard. To Richard's surprise, the CO patted him on the shoulder and congratulated him on his quick thinking and actions. Richard breathed a sigh of relief and thanked the CO for his understanding.

The final line of defence was a platoon of Danes, not one of them less than 6ft tall. The sight of these monsters halted the marchers who had managed to get through. The chanting from the crowd became more and more subdued, as they quickly realised their attempts to gain access to their former village was futile.

It had been a successful operation, although some of the troops had sustained minor injuries. That night, back in SDC and drinking in the bar, the sight of Richard felling the Cypriot civilian, with one blow to the back of the knees, caused a great cheer to go up from all present. It had been televised on the local Cypriot TV station, much to Richard's embarrassment. Richard reddened visibly and took another swig of his brandy sour.

The final weeks of the tour were upon them and, two weeks before the end, Richard had been drinking in Limassol, on some time off. He had met up with Legs, his old commander and mentor, from his early days on tanks. He was finished with arranging flights and striking deals for accommodation from the local hoteliers. They sat in a bar on the main strip, with a good friend of Legs, a bloke call Shaun Barratt, who had also been in Richard's Troop in Berlin. The pair were inseparable and were regularly seen together. They drank and recounted stories of days gone by.

One thing Richard had never revealed was the occasion when he buried the 120mm round on the ranges, fearing he would be caught out, when he had not received enough vent tubes for their final shoot.

As he got more and more drunk, Legs came up with the idea that Richard should have two eyes tattooed on his arse, just like Legs and Shaun. It didn't take them long to persuade Richard that this was a great idea, so off they went to see it come to fruition.

The next morning Richard woke, praying it was all a dream. Pulling down his boxer shorts, he saw, to his horror, it hadn't been. He cringed at what Birgit was going to say. His next mistake was to tell the lads and show them his latest acquisition. When he phoned Birgit two days later, she asked him if he had been fighting. Bemused, he answered that he hadn't.

'Karen said Hendo told her I should ask how your eyes were,' stammered Birgit, clearly upset. Richard cackled down the phone. 'It's okay, love, I'll explain when I get home,' and, with that, he put down the phone.

Chapter 25 – Return to Tanks

Richard had been back in Germany almost a month. He had been promoted to full Corporal (Full Screw) and transferred to C Squadron. Though he had not yet taken, or passed, his Commander's course, he was given command of a tank, as the 2nd Corporal in First Troop. He wouldn't get paid for the promotion until he had passed the course, which was a month away. It seemed to Birgit that he was always away, on tour or course. He had explained to her, before they were married, that this was the hardest part of being married to a British soldier. She understood, promising she would be able to cope. The ability for a soldier to carry out his job was eased by a strong marriage.

This was something people in Civilian Street did not understand. Wives of soldiers were a unique group, each had a special bond of friendship with the other wives, within the Regiment. They would spend many hours in each others' houses, when the men were away. Children would play and grow up together. Friendships lasted long after the men had left the service and they would find it hard to attain the same closeness with others after Army life.

For the last few weeks, he had got to know his new Troop, especially his crew. The Squadron itself was commanded by an American Major, Francesco Totti. The Squadron Sergeant Major was Stu Pearson, entering into his final years in the service. He was looking at promotion, later that year, to WO1 and going on a posting, for his final two years.

Richard's Troop was led by a young Lieutenant called Charles Howarth, previously of the Parachute Regiment and was very keen on fitness. The Troop Sergeant was called Mike Cain and had served in a different Troop, in Berlin. The other Corporal was Albert, the big lad from

Cumbria, who had been Richard's Troop Corporal in Berlin. In the last five years, he had stayed stationary on the promotion ladder.

Richard's crew was a young one, his operator and loader was called Paul Hayward, from Battley, in Leeds. Although young, he seemed quite switched on and keen. His gunner was Smiler, a small guy from South Yorkshire, his accent broad and strong. Richard had to listen carefully to understand him. Finally, his driver had the dubious nickname of 'Dangerous'. Richard would find out why, on their first exercise together. That was in the future, now he needed to complete two weeks of pre-course training for his forthcoming course. Most was carried out in the Gunnery Training Simulator (GTS). This was the turret of a tank, a replica of the real thing. Partitions had been cut away, in order that people could observe, from outside, what was going on within.

There were two other members of the Regiment, who would be attending the Commander's course with Richard. One was from Huddersfield, Phil Simons, who was always cracking jokes. He, too, in his younger days, had been part of the Parachute Regiment. He and Richard got along like a house on fire, as they both had the same twisted sense of humour. The other candidate was Steve White, from B Squadron. He was already a gunnery instructor, so was helping out on the pre-course training. He would be lucky enough not to have to attend the gunnery phase because of his experience. The three would take turns in acting as Commander, gunner and loader, for the various shoots set up by the Regimental Gunnery Staff Sergeant.

His name was Judd, and he had a dry sense of humour. He controlled the simulator from a control panel on top and to the rear of the turret. Once the crews were mounted and in position, he would flick a switch, which would light a red dot on one of the tank targets, on the board in front of the simulator. The board, itself, had a picture of a countryside scene, which could be changed by means of a projector. Some of these targets could be moved, so that the crews could practise engaging targets that were not static.

Richard was first into the commander's seat, with Phil as his gunner and Steve loading. Judd presented the first target, and Richard gave the order, as soon as he spotted it.

'DST tank on!' indicating what ammunition he wanted Steve to load and, at the same time, laying the barrel on or around the target, by use of the duplex controller, which enabled him to move the turret under power. As soon as Phil had identified the target, he confirmed this by shouting:

'On!' and, from there, took over the control of the gun from his commander.

Richard ensured that Phil had laid the dot of the Tank Laser System (TLS) on the centre of the target. Out of his left eye, he was watching Steve, ensuring he was carrying out the correct loading drills, then waiting for the sound of the breech being closed and the loaders safety guard made.

'Loaded!' came the cry from Steve, as he selected the next round.

Checking that the breech was closed and all was in order, Richard gave the order to fire. This was confirmed by Phil with the words.

'Firing...now!' The gun ran back inside, under the hydraulic system to which it was connected. The breech opened and Phil threw up another projectile, in anticipation.

Within the commander's and gunner's sight, a dot appeared on the target, confirming they had destroyed it.

'Target... target, stop!' shouted Richard. He began scanning from left to right, for the next one. This went on for another twenty minutes, with Judd presenting targets, at various ranges, with some of them being 'movers'. Once the shoot had finished, the crew were asked to climb out. They were then asked how they thought it had gone. Phil said he thought it had gone well, Richard's orders and drills had been clear and concise. Richard admitted to some things he could have done better, seeing Judd nod in agreement. When it came to Steve's turn to critique, he listed a myriad of mistakes he thought Richard had made. Richard, Phil and the Instructor looked, in disbelief, at Steve.

'I think you are being a little picky there,' Judd said, sneering at Steve, who replied that it was just his opinion.

During the next two weeks, this became regular, with Steve gaining the title of the 'Smiling Assassin'. Phil and Richard decided no quarter be given, when it was Steve's turn in the commander's seat.

Before they knew it, the two weeks were over. Phil and Richard met at Regimental Headquarters, to confirm their travel arrangements for the Course. The Smiling Assassin would be joining them, after the gunnery phase. They had decided to travel by ferry from Calais to Dover. It was a long drive but they could share the driving. They purchased enough petrol coupons, which all service personnel in Germany were entitled to. This gave them a discounted rate on petrol and diesel at the local German garages. They would be taking Phil's car, a sporty, blue RS Cosworth. Once the two had received the necessary paperwork for the course, they left RHQ and travelled home, to finish off their last bits of packing.

The next morning, Phil arrived outside Richard's married quarter. Richard picked up his suitcase and hand luggage, kissed Birgit goodbye and descended the stairs of the flat. He threw his suitcase in the boot of the car, which had already been opened by Phil. The pair jumped in the vehicle and headed off, towards the Autobahn. The journey to the German border took just over two hours.

They pulled off the Autobahn at a town called 'Wankum', and drove into a petrol station well-used by all British Forces in Germany. It was the last station, before the Dutch border, where they could use their petrol coupons and, no matter what time of day it was, there were always Brits, topping up their fuel, either going to or returning from the UK. Once they had refuelled, they set off across the German/ Dutch border.

They changed over driving duty just short of Antwerp, Richard driving the final three hours, to the port of Calais. It was just before lunchtime and a ferry would be departing in the next 30 minutes, so they were waved straight on. The trip across the English Channel only took an hour and, before long, the white cliffs of Dover came into view, through the hazy sunshine. Rolling off the ferry, Phil steered the car westwards, in the direction of their final destination, the Gunnery School at Lulworth Camp, in Dorset.

On their arrival at the camp gates, all appeared deathly quiet, which was strange for a Saturday evening. Richard guessed that most of the students had gone home for the weekend or the new course would be arriving on the Sunday evening. They were in for a shock when, after reporting to the guardroom, they were told that their course had started a week earlier. They couldn't believe this monumental fuck-up by their RHQ. The guard commander said that they were welcome to stay in the transit accommodation and clear it all up on the Monday morning. They thanked him and were directed to one of the accommodation blocks. They spent the weekend drinking in a local pub, a short distance from the camp gates, eating and sleeping.

When Monday morning arrived, they reported to training offices to find out if they could join the course. They were told that, because they had missed so much, this wasn't possible and they were required to return to their Unit. Richard and Phil both tried to argue the point that they could catch up but the Warrant Officer in charge of the courses said they should return, on the next course. They would be able to come back and continue the other phases of the course, once the gunnery part was finished. Knowing that they were getting nowhere fast, the two collected their luggage, packed the car and headed back to Dover.

On the Tuesday morning, they met up at RHQ and sought out the courses clerk, who had arranged their course. It came to light that he had, indeed, sent them a week late for the course and all hell broke loose. Since it hadn't been their fault, they were allowed to re-join the course, in six weeks' time.

The last 72 hours having been wasted, they returned to their Troops, on the tank park. Mike Cain, Richard's Troop Sergeant, couldn't believe his eyes when Richard walked into the hangar. But, after hearing what had happened, he saw the funny side of it. Richard looked for his crew, who were busy working on his tank. They, too, could not believe the massive fuck-up that had befallen him.

The vehicles were due an annual REME inspection so, for the rest of the week, they spent their time carrying out servicing on the engine, running gear and gunnery systems. They made sure that anything that required a nut or bolt was seen to. The mechanics were renowned for picking these little things, known as 'A' jobs, up. It always reflected badly on a commander if the mechanics found more than a certain amount, so Richard concentrated on getting his vehicle up to the required standard. He constantly asked Dangerous if he had done this or that. Richard never checked up on any of his crew, but woe betide them if a job was noted down on the inspection that they had said had been done. Richard was tolerant and believed in giving a certain amount of freedom and responsibility to people under his charge. Trust was important in the Army and he had learned, at an early stage, the sign of a good crew was the trust they placed in one another.

The day of the REME inspection came, and they drove the vehicle down to the Light Aid Detachment (LAD), for inspection. Walking head of the vehicle, Richard reversed it into the bay allocated. As soon as they were in position and Smiler had given him the thumbs up that the gun kit had been turned off, he gave the signal to Dangerous, to cut the main engine, then the Generating Unit Engine.

From out of nowhere, a hoard of mechanics descended on them. One, on the ground, checked the running gear and the automotive side of things. Another climbed in the turret and began to check the gun and electrical side. The inspection itself took around two hours, with Richard following the REME mechanics around the vehicle, clocking carefully anything they noted on their report.

The inspection finally over, one of the REME gave Richard the report. They had picked up 5 'A' jobs, which Richard wasn't happy about. He scanned the document and very quickly saw that all were things he had asked Dangerous if he had done. Richard had a dark side to his character, which normally came out through drink. Worse yet was if he felt his trust had been betrayed, which resulted in him flying into a rage. Screaming at the top of his voice for Dangerous to appear, he waited until the driver was standing in front of him. Hurling abuse and, covering him in the spit which flew from his foaming mouth, Richard demanded to know why Dangerous hadn't done the jobs that had been picked up. Dangerous stammered, trying to find an excuse, but had none. From that point, Richard made a mental note to check Dangerous' work, as this showed he obviously couldn't work unsupervised. Although the rest of the report was outstanding, Richard was far from happy.

The weeks passed and it was time, once more, for Phil and Richard to head back to the UK and join the Commander's course. This time, they were joined by Steve, the Smiling Assassin, who had thought it hilarious when he heard, weeks before, they had turned up late at Lulworth camp.

When they arrived, they reported to the SQMS store and were allocated rooms. As they walked down the corridor of the block, they scanned names on the door cards. Just before the end of the corridor and, as they were about to give up, they saw their three names. Dropping his case, Phil dug into his pocket, to retrieve the key he had been given. He tried the door, to find it unlocked. Pushing down the handle, he swung the door open. On a bed, next to the window, the blond haired occupant looked up from the book he was reading.

'You must be the guys who missed the gunnery phase,' he said, jokingly.

'That's us!' Phil replied, walking over and introducing himself.

One by one, each of them shook his hand and made their own introductions. He was a member of the 17th/21st Lancers, better known as the 'Boneheads', from their distinctive skull and crossbones cap badge. He seemed a quiet but friendly enough guy. The three chose beds and began to unpack. As they did so, their new roommate mentioned that some of the course were meeting in the NAAFI bar later, for drinks. Richard knew from other courses he had attended, that this was one of the few releases at Bovington camp. If a soldier had a car, he could experience the high life in Wareham, or travel further to Poole or Weymouth. As these courses could be quite expensive, the guys would often leave the further away spots to weekends. So, after a quick shower, the roommates made the short walk to the NAAFI bar.

When they entered, the Lancer, who was called Andy, pointed over to a table, already occupied by some blokes. Richard assumed they must be on the same course. Andy made the introductions, as they waited for Steve to return with the drinks. One had a timetable, which he handed over for them to look at. Phil took a quick look and a broad smile crossed his lips.

265

'What've you found so funny?' Richard asked, inquisitively.

'Tomorrow, we start the Signal phase and you're down to take a lesson,' he replied, chuckling.

Richard snatched the piece of paper and, looking down the page, saw that he was earmarked to instruct the course on Infantry Tank Target voice procedure. The remainder of the table found it highly amusing, and welcomed him and the other two newcomers to the course. Richard decided he should just have a couple of beers, then disappear and prepare his lesson for the next day.

Richard rose early in the morning, showered, had breakfast and made his way to the Signal School. He had attended his Instructor's course just before Cyprus, with Spike. John Mason, who had stood in for Paul Goath as RSWO, had been expecting good things from the pair. When they returned with a 'Cavalry C' grading, he hit the roof. He called them into the office and handed them their course reports. After giving them a little time to read them, he asked what the grade said at the bottom. Richard replied, 'C', with a smirk on his face. His sole aim had been to pass the course. He had no intention passing with a grade which would enable him to be considered to teach at the school, at a later date. In hindsight, this had been very short sighted. It would have stood him in good stead for further promotion. John gave the pair a right royal bollocking, saying how disappointed he was, especially with Spike. After that, Richard never thought he would be back there, delivering a lesson.

He went through the double doors and strode confidently to the Instructors' room. Some of the Schools instructors had already arrived and were having a brew, in the tea room. Richard introduced himself and explained that he was pencilled in to take the VP lesson, in the afternoon. One of the instructors from the Life Guards, who had also been one of the instructors on his course, greeted him warmly. He passed over a folder, which contained the lesson plans for Infantry Tank Target indication, and suggested Richard read them carefully, to prepare his lesson. Richard took the folder and asked if there was a classroom available, for him to practise in. He was shown an empty room with an overhead projector, that wasn't being used for the morning. For the next three hours, Richard worked on his own.

In the afternoon, the course met in the room, where Richard was waiting for them. He had set up a whiteboard and overhead projector (OHP). It was a little daunting for Richard as, apart from Phil and Steve, the faces before him were new. It wasn't the same as his instructor's course, where they had got to know each other, prior to them giving their first lesson.

He took a deep breath. Once everyone had settled down, he began. He talked them through the preliminary introduction and fire drill, then went on to explain the layout of the lesson and what his objectives were. Satisfied that he had everyone's full attention, he turned on the OHP and began to go through the format of how to give Infantry Target Indication, from a tank.

When he finished each section, Richard paused, at a suitable point, to see if anyone had any questions. No one spoke, for which he was glad. He then began to fire questions at the class, to confirm his lesson, so far, had sunk in. He realised this was an opportunity where he could get his own back on Steve. As he posed a question, he spotted a puzzled look on Steve's face and pounced. There was a stunned silence, as the rest of the course looked in Steve's direction. With no answer forthcoming, Richard switched his attention and asked the same question to another, who replied immediately. Richard nodded that he was correct and told Steve to pay more attention, which drew a titter from the rest of the room. Steve was obviously embarrassed. Richard had achieved his primary aim.

Richard spoke for a further 40 minutes and, by the end of it, after his final confirmation, was happy that he had delivered a decent lesson. He had broken the ice with his new course mates, a couple of them even congratulated him, on an interesting lesson.

During the next two weeks, Richard delivered a couple more lessons and had to run a radio exercise, with the aid of another student on the course, who was also a Signals instructor. The rest of the time he spent in his room, reading up on tactics. This was to be the next and final phase of the course.

They assembled in a lecture theatre, for the tactics phase. Everyone had passed the signals course, although a couple just managed to scrape through. The course officer was a tall, grey-haired Major, who had come up through the ranks. He was from the Northern Ireland, a member of the 5th Royal Inniskilling Dragoon Guards. Little did Richard or the two other members of his Regiment in the room know, but they would become very well acquainted with this Regiment.

The course content was explained by the course officer and the instructors, as usual, introduced to the candidates. The School of Tactics taught not only heavy armour tactics, but also Reconnaissance Troops and Regiments. In fact there was a Recce course running, at that time, due to finish the week before the course Richard was on.

As the courses were similar, they surmised that the test papers would be the same. One lad on Richard's course approached a friend attending the Recce course and asked if he could they get a copy of the paper to him, before they left. This was agreed and it would be of great benefit to them all.

The introduction over, the blokes were asked to file outside, to get on the transport waiting for them. On the course programme, they had been told to bring with them binoculars, a compass, and a map of the local area. The first two items they brought themselves. The maps were distributed, as they left the room.

Climbing on to the truck that was waiting for them, they left camp and headed out, to an area nearby. The trip took only twenty minutes and the vehicle came to a halt, at the top of a hill. The troops left the vehicle and gathered round the Land Rover sitting there. At the vehicle was one of the instructors they had been introduced to, in the hall. He waited, patiently, for the course to assemble, before speaking.

'Good morning, gents. This morning we are going to do a little map reading test,' he began, noticing the look of dread on some faces. Richard smiled, quietly confident of his map reading skills. The instructor continued. 'I will point out various features on the map. I want you to write down the grid reference to that position. I will also give you a series of grid references and you are to give me which feature is at these points. Any questions?' he ended his opening gambit. With none forthcoming, he continued. 'If you look directly ahead down the valley, you will see a crossroads, two o'clock from that, at a distance of 200m, red top building. Give me a grid to that.'

The troops scanned the countryside immediately in front of them, found the crossroads and began to look for the red top building. They, then, compared it to the map and noted down the grid reference. Only fifteen to twenty seconds passed, when the instructor began his next point of reference.

Richard was still struggling to find the first, squinting in the morning sunlight. He hadn't noticed it before but his eyesight was deteriorating, and he was finding it difficult. Luckily, Phil was on his right and he offered his paper, so Richard could see it. He smiled in appreciation, on some courses, candidates often helped those who were struggling. This was the ethos built into the British soldier.

No-one wanted anybody else to fail. They were all in the same boat.

The test lasted half an hour, after which the instructors collected the papers in and asked the men to get back on the truck. They were conveyed back to camp, where the next lesson would be on Soviet military doctrine and tactics.

On the way into the classroom, Richard thanked Phil for his earlier help, and assured him he would have done the same, if Phil had been struggling.

Richard felt, because of the time he had been given over the past few weeks, the remainder of the course should be a breeze. He had been interested in military tactics from a young age. He would listen to his father, Tommy, talking about tanks moving 'one up' and 'two up'. Tommy would explain the reasons why, and in what situations, they moved in this way. Terms like defile drills, flank protection, overwatch and snake patrols were firmly lodged in Richard's brain.

The lecture began with a short film about nuclear warfare and went on to highlight some of the technological advances made in weaponry, on the battlefield. By the time the lecture reached its conclusion, Richard was totally enthralled.

For the next three weeks, the course was taught not only tactics but also mine warfare, a subject close to Richard's heart, having taught it, when he was in Recce Troop. Armoured vehicle and aircraft recognition was also an important theme for budding tank commanders.

These lessons were interspersed with trips into the field, on what was known as 'Tactical Exercises Without Tanks (TEWTS). Here, the students were taken to a specific area and given a scenario. They had to discuss where they would situate their tanks and any supporting arms, such as guided weapons and Milan anti-tank sections. There was no right or wrong answer, so long as the decisions and thought processes behind them could be justified and led to some lively debates, which sometimes spilled over into the bar, in the evening, over more than a few pints. As soon as the arguments or, sometimes physical altercations, were over, everything was forgotten and they were, once again, good friends.

The one person who had never quite fitted in with the rest was Steve. He was seen as a lone wolf, keeping his cards close to his chest and never seeming to want to help others, unless directly asked to do so.

All too soon, the course neared its conclusion and there were two days left until they sat the final exam. As Richard relaxed on his bed, doing a bit of revision, the door opened and Scott Richards, from the next room, stood in the doorway.

'Richard, do you have the Recce Troop Commander's exam paper?' he asked.

'No, mate, I haven't got it. In fact, we've never seen it at all.'

Scott went round the room, asking Andy the Bonehead if he had it, then Phil. They both answered as Richard had, that they didn't even know if anyone had managed to get a copy.

Pausing for a moment, Scott turned his attention to Steve, who was also laid on his bed, reading a newspaper.

'Have you seen it?' Scott asked, rather curtly.

Steve lowered the newspaper, looking over the top, pretending he had not heard the question. He asked Scott to repeat the question. Swinging his legs over the bed, he rose and opened his locker. He stretched to the rear of the top shelf and withdrew a number of sheets of A4 paper, stapled together.

'Is this what you mean?' he replied, looking at Scott, who snatched the paper from him and read the title at the top.

'Yes, it is, you fucking jack bastard!' he snarled and left the room.

Richard, Phil and Andy looked at each other, dumbfound. Richard felt an enormous sense of guilt, even though he hadn't committed any offence, Steve was a member of his Regiment and must have had the paper for days, as the Recce Commanders had left the previous week. The room fell silent and everyone got back to their revision. Steve returned to his newspaper, as if nothing had happened.

The final day of testing arrived. The course gathered in the lecture hall. The rules of the exam were set out and the papers distributed.

Phil had spent the previous evening writing down possible answers to questions, on a fag packet. He had secreted it in a pocket, to sneak a look, when he thought no one was watching. The students were instructed to turn over their papers and begin.

Richard rapidly looked through the questions. He grinned. If not the same as the paper they had received from the Recce course, they were very similar. If only they had been given more time to study it, he thought, as he glowered at Steve's back, sitting in front of him. Putting his anger behind him, he returned to the paper and set to work on the answers. The clock ticked by and, with twenty minutes left, Richard placed down his pen, happy that he had answered the questions, to the best of his ability. He was quietly confident that he had done enough to gain a pass. He looked across at Phil, scratching his head and looking in Richard's direction.

He whispered, asking if Richard knew the answers to a couple of questions. Richard nodded once and turned his paper to a position where Phil could see the answers. Phil smiled, from ear to ear and winked, as discreetly as possible.

The clock reached 12:30. They were instructed to put down their pens. As soon as everyone had done so, they were asked to come to the front and hand in their papers.

They were then permitted to go for lunch but instructed to return at 4pm, when they would receive their results.

The afternoon dragged, each of the students comparing answers to the various questions. There followed lively debate but it was too late to change anything now. Just before 4pm, the course settled, in their seats, in the lecture room, waiting for the arrival of the course officer and his instructors. The door silently opened and, in procession, they entered the room. The Major took his position behind the lectern and waited for his staff to be seated.

'I would like to congratulate you all, for the effort you have put in on this, the final part of your commander's course. I can announce that you have all passed, a couple of you just scraped through, but a pass is a pass. We hope that you put the lessons learnt here to good use, when you return to your Regiments. Remember, there could come a time when not only your life, but those of your crew and others in your Squadron will be dependent on the actions you take. Being a tank commander is a position of extreme responsibility and should not be taken lightly. We would like to wish you all a safe journey home and perhaps our paths will cross in the future.' He rose and left the room.

'That was short and sweet,' Richard whispered across to Phil, as they stood up.

'Thank fuck for that. We might be able to catch the midnight ferry, if we're quick,' Phil remarked and they left for the car, already been packed ready for their departure.

Chapter 26 – Qualifying for Command

On his return, Richard received the pleasant news that he and Phil would not now need to attend the gunnery phase at a later date. They had word from the gunnery school that, if the two of them could pass a single tank battle run on the ranges, then the qualification as a commander would stand. The caveat to this was they would have to be assessed by members of the Regimental Gunnery Wing, who had previously taught at Lulworth. The opportunity to qualify for his commander's pay came quicker than expected. The Squadron was due to commence annual firing on the ranges at Hohne, in two weeks' time.

The tank park was bustling, crews preparing their vehicles, in anticipation of the move to Hohne. The gun fire control systems and their associated electrical components were checked by the REME. The breaches were stripped and cleaned, as were the barrels. The fume extractors, which drew away any noxious fumes entering the fighting compartment, were removed, cleaned and fresh graphite grease applied. The operators were busy, ensuring all the projectile racks were fitted, as some of these had been removed, when on normal exercises. The drivers worked, making sure their hatches operated correctly and that their seats reclined to a position where they could drive 'closed down'. Having learnt his lesson from the previous PRE, Richard checked on the work carried out by Dangerous. To his pleasant surprise, he seemed to have learned his lesson, from the bollocking received from Richard.

By the time the Troops were due to move to the railhead, to begin the journey north, the Squadron vehicles had been prepared, to the highest standard. They had been checked and rechecked, by the REME's gun fitters and Electricians (ECEs). This was their bread and butter and the only real time they earned their pay. The Squadron leader would not be happy, if he didn't have a full complement of tanks, ready to fire on the first day.

Unlike the normal journeys by train, there was a distinct lack of alcohol this time. At least, that was the case for Richard. He wasn't sure if he was maturing or if he was more than a little nervous of what was to come. Some of the married guys, however, took any opportunity of 'freedom' to partake in a beer or two.

Arriving at the railhead, in the small village of Bergen, the Squadron began to remove the chocks and chains, from the tanks. One by one, they reversed off the rear of the train. Lining up on the slip road, the Squadron Leaders operator, Stuart Messenger from Signals Troop in Cyprus, gave a communications check. As soon as the last call sign had come up on the air, the Squadron left the slip road and travelled the six kilometres to the range they would be using, for the first couple of days.

As they passed the main camp of Hohne garrison, they came to a right hand bend in the road. This was familiar to Richard, he had spent his last days in secondary school at Hohne. He knew if he carried straight on, instead of following the road to the right, he would arrive at the infamous German Concentration Camp, known as Bergen-Belsen. He had visited it on more than one occasion and had been struck by the eeriness of the place. It was rumoured that no bird flew over it, nor could any sound of wildlife be heard.

He quickly put these thoughts to the back of his mind, as he directed Dangerous to take the right hand bend. Another four kilometres down the road, they were met by Stu, the SSM, and his driver, who were performing traffic control, indicating the Squadron should pull off the main road. The green control tower with its red flag on top and a big yellow 7 and letter B, indicated the name of the range.

The Squadron turned off the road as instructed and, one by one, lined themselves up on the firing point, with a suitable gap in between each vehicle. The REME were to park on the far left hand side of the range and slightly to the rear. They consisted of the Armoured Recovery Vehicle (ARV), which was a Chieftain chassis, without a turret, and equipped with winching gear; an AFV 434, with a crane for lifting the engine packs from the tanks and a AFV 432, which was the Fitter section commander, a Staff Sergeant (Tiffy).

The vehicles all in position, they turned off their gun kits and engines, one at a time. The crews dismounted and covered the hatches with sheets, to prevent any rain entering. The drivers did a quick 'halt parade', to make sure they had not suffered any leaks, on the short trip from the railhead. As this was proceeding, two white buses pulled up on to the firing point. The crews who had finished their checks were invited to climb aboard. As the bus filled up, Richard looked out, at the tanks lined up and saw Phil and his driver in the back decks, or engine compartment, of his tank. They were joined by the Tiffy and one of his mechanics. Not a good start for him, Richard thought. As the bus pulled away, he waved at Phil who, in response, gave him two fingers.

The next day was spent under the direction of the SSM, who had taken delivery of the Squadron's allocation of rounds, for the next couple of days. Any man not required to work on the vehicles, armed with pliers, hammers and the trusty Mark 1, Combat boot high, paraded at the rear of the firing point.

The projectile containers were lined up, like ancient Roman formations, in straight lines. Some people began the task of removing the lock wire, sealing the boxes, while others broke open the lids with hammers. Those that did not have hammers used the heels of their boots, to release the clamps holding the containers tight. By whatever means, the boxes were emptied and the different ammunition placed on the back of a truck, which had its sides folded down, to enable the rounds to be loaded and unloaded more easily. The bags charges, which were the combustible containers which launched the projectiles, were put on a separate truck.

The work took all morning and, after a quick lunch, the crews mounted up, ready to receive their allocation. The Truck travelled the length of the firing point, handing over the correct amount of rounds for each vehicle. These were carefully stowed inside by the loaders. The gunners would have to, at times, traverse the turrets, to enable the operator to achieve this. The loader would always ensure he had enough rounds and bag charges available, without having to traverse outside the safety markers, on each side of the range. Richard had learned this little tip, when he had loaded for 'Legs', his mentor and commander in D Squadron. There was nothing worse than a target being presented, going to the charge bins, to retrieve a bag charge, only to find them empty. Making sure that everything was packed away and ready for the next day, the Troops departed for camp at 4:30 pm, leaving an NCO and three others, to guard the range.

The evening had been spent in the usual manner, receiving the detail of firing for the first day. The rules of the range were covered, as they always were, and would be again the following morning.

The bar opened immediately after the brief and the Squadron sat, drinking beer, in their own little Troop groups. The Troop Sergeant of 3rd Troop, where Phil belonged, asked if Richard was excited about the next day. This well-built character was called Pete Tamworth and had served with Richard's father in A Squadron. He had a deep, red scar, starting behind his right ear, continuing across his face, ending at his nose, which made him look fearsome. In truth, he was gently spoken and often looked as if he was pondering something. He had acquired the facial disfigurement a number of years earlier, when Richard first joined the Regiment. A few, including Pete, had been in a bar, in the small German town, where they were stationed. A large group of Turks were present and, for some unknown reason, took a dislike to Pete. An argument had broken out. Then, out of nowhere, a meat cleaver had been produced. It was aimed at Pete's head and connected with his face, splitting it open, to the bone. His friends had managed to get him out and back to camp. Word of the assault was spread. Almost half the Regiment had gone downtown, to seek out the bastard responsible.

He had gone to ground, so they proceeded to wreck the bar where it happened. They went on a tour of other bars which Turks were known to frequent, where the same reprisal was dealt out.

Richard's memories were broken by Mike, his own Troop Sergeant.

'You ready for tomorrow, then?' he asked.

'Just about as I ever will be,' was Richard's, not so convincing, reply.

'Don't worry about a thing, we will see you right,' Mike said, as he gave him a reassuring squeeze of the shoulder.

The 'we' he referred to was the crew. Mike had volunteered to act as loader, Graham Calf, from the Humanitarian Section in Cyprus, was going to act as gunner. Graham had spent a couple of years at the gunnery school and knew his stuff, backwards. The final member of Richard's crew was Joe O'Connell, a wiry, small type from Leeds, who was to be his driver. Joe was a Driving and Maintenance Instructor (D&M). There wasn't a thing he didn't know about engines or how to get the most out of a Chieftain. Richard felt genuinely blessed, to have such good friends around him. After a couple more beers, he hit the sack and drifted into a trouble-free sleep.

The light being switched on and the sound of the SSM, telling people to get up, was the next thing he knew. Looking at his watch, it was 03:30 in the morning. It was summer, the sun had just begun to break. He never understood why, no matter what time of year it was, they would always rise and leave for the ranges at least three hours before they opened. Groans and complaints rang through the room, as some tried to go back to sleep, but were hauled out of their beds by their Troop Sergeants or Corporals. It hit Richard that he was now one of these, that he better set an example, so he made for the shower.

On his return from breakfast, he made sure all his crew were out of bed, washed, dressed and ready to go. Some would forego breakfast and grab a hot dog or burger from the SQMS, on the range. These were sold, naturally, at extortionate prices, although this was allowed since, after the SQMS and his staff had taken their cut from the profits, the rest went into the Squadron fund.

The morning began with the crews going through pre-firing checks. Generating engines and gun kits were started, twenty minutes before carrying out any checks. Richard shouted to Smiler, his gunner, to pass down a twenty litre can of oil, which they carried in one of the baskets. This wasn't to top up oil levels but as a step, to stand on, to carry out the first of his checks. He went to the left side bin and withdrew the boresight collimator, carrying it to the front of the vehicle. He took the boresight from its case, and placed it on the right wing. The method of 'bore sighting' was to adjust the sight, to align with the barrel. With the barrel at a convenient height, he stepped onto the oil can, trying hard to maintain his balance. All along the firing point, other commanders were doing the same. A white screen had been placed 1100 metres downrange, by members of the SQMS staff. Smiler had taken his seat in the gunner's position, awaiting Richard's command.

"Gunner, using your hand controls, lay the MBS mark 120mm on the centre of the observed mass, ending your lay in elevation report when on." Richard announced at the top of his voice, while looking into the boresight eyepiece. Smiler did as he was asked and reported.

'On!' confirming he had ended his lay onto the centre of the target.

Richard looked at the position of the dot in the boresight in relation to the target and asked him using his graticule adjusters to adjust, until the dot was back on the target. This done, he asked him to lock his adjusters and to break his lay and relay, once again ending it in elevation and reporting when on.

Smiler repeated the motion and reported when he was back on target. Richard looked through the eyepiece, confirming the dot was now on the centre of the target. Satisfied, he withdrew the boresight and put it away in its case. The gun fitters, at this time, were carrying out a test known as gauge plug bore. They inserted a heavy weight, the exact dimensions of a round, down the barrel. They then got the gunner to fully elevate and the weight should fall to the breach, without getting snagged. This showed that the barrel was free from any obstructions and not warped, in any way. At the same time, the loaders would be carrying out a 'vent tube alignment test'. This ensured that a ventube was inserted correctly into the flash chamber of the breach, without sticking, thus causing a vent tube stoppage. The remaining check of the computer systems lasted another half an hour. Then, there followed a communications check, from the tower to all call signs. No one would be allowed to fire, until everyone was on the net, for safety reasons.

Preparations for the day's firing done, the Squadron was ordered to assemble, at the rear of the firing point, for the safety brief. This was done on every range, as the range layout was different on each one. The man who would run the range for C Squadron, for the following two weeks, was a member the Armoured Training Advisory Team (ARMTAT), who were based at Hohne. He quickly, but comprehensively, went through the do's and don'ts of the range, pointed out any arc markers and the miscellaneous other safety points. As is common at the end of any military lesson, he rattled out the customary quick-fire questions, to confirm his talk had struck home.

Having finished his questions, he dismissed the Troops to the waiting area, a marquee next to the SQMS tent. Richard wasn't afforded this luxury. He was told to gather his crew and mount up. Rounding up his band of volunteers, they made their way to the tank and climbed into their positions, Richard being last. He breathed deeply, to steady his heart rate and calm his nerves. It was a nervous time, waiting to be told the range was open. Waiting for the order, that he had permission to go to 'red', he had the okay to load his weapons and display his red flag on his turret, to indicate he was at 'action'.

He had done this many times as a gunner and operator, but never as a commander. The next twenty minutes would determine whether he qualified for commander's pay. It meant the first major step on the career ladder.

Looking at his watch, the minute hand was drawing closer to the time the range was allowed to open. Mike was making sure there were enough ammunition and bag charges available, without having to traverse the turret out of arc. Graham was checking his sights and that the gun equipment was working, as it should. Joe was sitting, quietly, in a reclined position, having closed his driver's hatch, prior to firing.

Richard felt good. These were ultimate professionals and didn't need to be supervised. He looked down, to the right of Graham's back. Something didn't look right.

Shit! He saw he hadn't inserted the laser key into its rightful place. Unarmed, they would not be able to fire the laser. He felt his top pocket and heaved a sigh of relief, as he felt it there. He inserted it in the lock, preparing to turn it to the armed position, once given the order to go to action.

There had been occasions when commanders had forgotten the laser key, which proved highly embarrassing, with the Squadron watching on.

'Hello, Tango 13, this is Control Tower. You are cleared to go to action, load DST, watch and shoot!' The words echoed in Richard's ears, causing a split second delay, before he sprang into life.

'Action, load DST!' he shouted into his microphone, at the same time putting his head out of the turret and replacing the green flag in its holder, with a red one. Popping back down into his seat, he placed his face into his commander's sight and began to scan the ground in front, for any targets.

Suddenly, on his right side, he caught a glimpse of a target, in the shape of a tank, pop up from the ground.

'DST Tank....on!' he screamed, turning the duplex control to the right. As it neared the target, he released it. The ammunition was already loaded, as previously ordered from the control tower.

'Where's the target? I can't see it!' came Graham's reply. Richard couldn't believe this. He stopped the barrel, when it was pointing just below the tank, around 1800 metres to their front.

'There, for fuck sake! Just above the MBS mark!' Richard called down to him, in frustration. The gun moved all over the place, as Graham tried to acquire the supposed target. The reply 'Loaded' came from Mike, indicating he had carried out the remainder of his drills. Keeping his face on the sight, Richard laid the gun directly on to the centre of the target. The next words he heard were from Joe.

'Can I have a brew?'

Richard told him to fuck right off.

Finally, Graham confirmed he was on the target and reported that he was lasing. At the same time, he hit his autolay button. The gun drove up, with a neon ellipse around the target.

'Firing now!' came his second command. However, as he prepared for the shock wave of the gun firing, nothing happened. He looked across at Mike, holding the next round. Something else was wrong!

This is a fucking nightmare, Richard thought to himself. It was then that he noticed that the loader's guard hadn't been made. He pointed this out abruptly. Mike pulled the guard to the rear, completing the firing circuit. Richard gave the order to fire. The tank rocked, under the force of the projectile leaving the barrel. At this range, it was only a split second before he observed the round enter the centre of the target.

'Target, target stop!' he exclaimed, in relief.

The sound of laughter rang out, throughout the turret, as his three 'professional crewmen' fell about, in stitches.

'Did you like that?' Graham said, looking back, over his shoulder at Richard. 'We like to keep things interesting.'

It had all been a fucking joke! Richard assumed it would end, now they'd had their fun. He laughed with them, admitting they had almost given him a heart attack.

Two more targets were presented and were quickly dispatched by Graham. However, both times, Mike purposely left the breech open. Richard immediately told him to rectify, then gave the order to fire. Mike winked and smiled back at Richard, before doing what he was told. If Richard thought this was going to be an easy ride, he was mistaken.

They were given the order to advance to the next 'bound', a position around 300 metres to their front. When they were about halfway down, Joe began to veer off, to the left, as the track forked.

'Where the fuck you going?' bellowed Richard.

'I thought I would take a shortcut,' Joe retorted, glibly.

'Come on, guys, don't be twats. This is my commander's pay at stake, here,' Richard pleaded.

There was a pause and a strange silence. Then, laughing, Mike said.

'Okay, lads, enough fucking about. Let's get on with it.' With that, they got back to the job at hand.

Reaching the next bound, three more targets popped up, at varying ranges. Within seconds, each one had been hit dead centre, without Richard having to intervene. They fired a selection of ammunition, both armoured piercing (AP) and high explosive (HESH).

On the way to the final bound, Graham indicated a mover, going from left to right. Without any command from Richard, they took it out. On the final bound, another two targets appeared. One was taken out, the other missed; and their allocation of ammunition was finished. Feeling pleased with the way things had gone, Richard gave the order for Joe to take the safe lane, for the return to the firing point.

Arriving, they powered down all the equipment and turned the engines off. Climbing out, the crew sprinted across to the debriefing area, where they were met by the man from ARMTAT. As they lined up in order, commander, gunner, loader and driver, he grinned when he saw the insignia of rank on their arms, a Corporal commanding a Staff Sergeant and two Sergeants.

He leaned forward and shook Graham's hand, they both had instructed at Lulworth, at the same time. He launched into his debrief and highlighted the few mistakes observed from the tower. He was obviously unaware of what had gone on, inside the turret. He ended by congratulating Richard, on his having qualified as a tank commander.

284

A wave of relief washed over Richard, as he thanked all three of his crew, for a job well done. He also asked them never to crew for him again!

Chapter 27 – Perfumed Garden

It had been three months since Richard had qualified for his commander's pay and, once again, they were in the familiar surroundings of Reinsehlen Camp, on the edge of Soltau training area. This was to be an exercise with a difference, though. Their Squadron Leader, Major Totti, had arranged for them to take part in a Nuclear Chemical and Biological (NBC) trial, in Texas, in the USA. This had fallen through, so the Squadron had been 'volunteered' to assist on the same trial, on Soltau. It was winter, the temperature vastly different to what it would have been in Texas.

The Squadron members were housed in a number of huts on the camp. They would return every evening, the day's trials complete.

The vehicles had all been fitted with SIMFIRE/SIMFIX, a gunnery training system. It consisted of a central computer, hooked in to the IC/ radio system; detectors on the roof and around the turret; the flashing stalk (Winky Wanky); smoke, flash, noise generator above the barrel and IR/ laser unit in the end of the barrel.

It worked by either a mobility kill or a k kill (fully knocked out). A mobility kill would set off the Winky Wanky only. The soldiers were supposed to stop but could keep firing; the radios would still work. A k kill would set off the Winky Wanky and stop the use of the laser and flash/ noise unit; the radios go to receive only.

The trial, overseen by a group of scientists from the UK, involved a number of scenarios the Squadron would go through, in various stages of NBC conditions. These ranged from wearing no protective equipment to being dressed in NBC clothing with no mask, finally wearing full 'Individual Protective Equipment' (IPE), for varying timescales.

Prior to deployment to the training area, they were given mental and cognitive tests, which were recorded and would be repeated on their return, from the different scenarios.

The first day was spent making sure all the SIMFIRE equipment was in full working order. This meant the REME electricians were scurrying around, from tank to tank, as the equipment was notorious for breaking down or not functioning correctly. The Scientists had also brought with them a technical team, allocated the task of fitting the vehicles with video recording and audio devices. Cameras were fitted to the optical systems, so that the engagement could be reviewed, after the battle scenarios. This provided extra pressure, as the crews had to watch what they were saying, while in the turret. One bad word said against anyone in authority could have dire consequences for the offender.

The hours dragged by, as the REME tested and fixed faults found on the vehicles. By the end of the day, they had enough 'working' tanks to provide the enemy and friendly forces for the next day.

The Troops were not allowed to leave the camp. As always, everyone one met in the makeshift bar, set up by the SQMS and his trusty staff. Richard and his crew left the Nissen hut they were living in. Paul, his operator, was away on his Control Signaller and they had now been joined by Trev Miller, the brother of another in the Regiment. He was in the same Squadron as Pete and was a Troop Corporal. Even though he had only recently joined the Regiment, Trev had gained a reputation for being a bit of a drinker.

The Nissen hut, which housed the makeshift bar, was full of cigarette smoke, which stung their eyes, as they walked in. Richard asked the lads to sit down and he retrieved a crate of beer, from the bar. It was only just after 7pm, but a couple were already in high spirits.

287

The sound of a bell rang out throughout the camp, announcing the arrival of Wolfgang, in his blue, battle bus. This legendary character sold snacks, which were equally loved and loathed. Albert, at the next table, shot up like a Polaris missile and bolted out of the door.

'You never see him move that fast on a Basic Fitness Test,' someone remarked, which caused the whole bar to erupt.

Albert could often be seen getting into his car, which was parked outside their barracks. He would drive out of the car park, up the road, to a T junction, then turn left on to the main road which ran through camp. Travelling adjacent to the main square, he would turn left and park his car directly outside the 'Schnell Imbiss', located on camp. Sometimes, he wouldn't leave his car to make his order, instead shouting it through his open window, to the young lady, who was serving. The distance from the block to the Imbiss, as the crow flies, was no more than 200 metres; yet Albert would take his car on the 800 metre journey.

The door was thrown open after five minutes. Albert, burdened with his latest purchase, dumped it on the table. When the pink wrapping paper was torn open, the lads gaped at his snack, three chicken breasts and two portions of chips, covered in mayonnaise. Albert began tucking into the feast, the grease and 'mayo' sticking to his walrus moustache. Richard and his crew giggled behind his back, trying not to alert him to the fact they were taking the piss.

The room was becoming noisier, as the guys got more and more rowdy. One of the young lads from 3rd Troop got up and started to give a rendition of 'Zulu Warrior', a Regimental favourite. Everyone in the bar joined in, the singing getting louder and louder, as it went on. For the next half hour, song after song was started, with the rest of the Squadron joining in the choruses. As it was to be an early start in the morning, the SQMS shut up shop at around midnight and kicked everyone out.

Men staggered off, in the direction of the huts, some with their arms draped over friends, declaring their undying love. Richard quickly undressed, placed his clothes next to the bed and climbed into his sleeping bag, on the bottom bunk. He lay there for a while, listening to the banter going on in the room, quietly chuckling to himself. Before long, the alcohol took over and he was fast asleep.

At around 02:00 am, the room was startled into life by a voice shouting:

'Trev, you dirty bastard! What you doing? Get yourself to the toilet, you filthy fucker!'

Richard popped his head out of his bag, to see Smiler hurling a tirade of abuse at his new loader. Trev had climbed from the top bunk, past Smiler, who was on the bottom and had begun to relieve himself, on the floor. The piss went everywhere, some spraying a small table, on which lay an open packet of digestive biscuits, bought for the brews the next day. Trev had emptied his bladder on the chocolate covered treats and they were ruined.

'I am going to force feed you those, Miller!' Richard shouted at the incoherent soldier, who sheepishly shrugged and climbed back onto his bunk. It took Richard a while to put this out of his mind and for the room to settle back down. Then, he finally dropped off to sleep, once again.

The next morning, when questioned why he had pissed on the biscuits, Trev didn't have a clue what they were talking about. This the start of the rocky relationship between Richard and Trev. He was a hardworking, loveable character when not under the influence. Richard gave him another bollocking, this time less abrasive and he smiled at the end, indicating to Trev that he should sort himself out.

After a rushed breakfast, the Troops moved across the field, to the hard standing, where the vehicles were parked up. They removed the sheets from the turrets and the drivers began their first parades, checked oil levels, and that ensured no leaks had sprung overnight. Once the

commanders were happy, one by one, they mounted up.
They had been given the scenario they would be running
that morning. 1st Troop, along with 3rd Troop, would be
acting as friendly forces. Their opposition would be 2nd
Troop and elements from SHQ. The first serial, or exercise,
was in normal clothing, with no form of IPE. The crews
mounted, the Troop Leaders gave a radio check and, once
happy, gave the order to roll out to the training area.

The route on to the area was well known, not one
commander required his map. They transited past the
washdown on their left, under the viaduct and across the
tank bridge. Heading east between strip and finger wood,
the Troop halted, just short of their destination, a piece of
high ground, overlooking a crossing point. It was 08:15 am
and the Troop Leader decided they would have quick chat
among the commanders to decide their approach to the
scenario. He called them to his vehicle. Richard grabbed
his webbing, from behind his commander's hatch and was
handed his weapon, stowed on the operator's side of the
turret, by Trev.

Striding over to the Troop Leader's tank, he noted
Albert and Mike were already there, drinking a brew. Ted
Hutt, Lieutenant Howarth's gunner, was atop the turret,
with his brew. As soon as Howarth saw this he called out to
him.

'Is that a "jack brew", Hutt?' Richard asked,
sarcastically, indicating Hutt had made a brew for himself
but not the rest of the crew.

'Yes, sir!' came the simple, honest reply from Ted.

'Then I suggest you go 200 metres over there and drink
it with your mates!' the Troop Leader said, pointing out
into the fog.

Shrugging his shoulders and with coffee in hand, Ted
ambled off, into the distance. Once he was a suitable way
away, he stood, shrouded in the fog and drank the reminder

of his brew. The Troop Leader turned away, with a look of disdain.

For the next couple of minutes, he explained the direction they would take and how they would line up, to face the supposed enemy. He was a new Troop Leader and was trying to impress his authority on them. Mike and Albert just paid lip service to him. For the first year of a Troop Leader's stewardship, the Troop Sergeant was the real person in charge. Not until the Troop Leader had some 'steel under his ass' would he be allowed to make tactical decisions. This was normally at least one training period and took over a year, or more. It was only his second exercise, so he was still finding his feet.

They agreed on the plan and mounted back up. The engines roared and they set off, once more. Crawling up to their positions, the vehicles crept slowly, closer to the ridge line, taking care not to present the whole of their turret to the direction of the suspected enemy advance. The error of being 'track up' was seen by all as a heinous crime, which had been well illustrated on Richard's commander's course. Once they could observe the ground to their front through the commander's sight, each vehicle, in turn, turned off their main engines, leaving just the GUEs running, to power the gun equipment and, more importantly, the boiling vessel which provided their hot food and brews.

They settled down, to wait for events to unfold. They had not been given a time frame for how long this particular serial would last. They passed the time by recounting funny anecdotes from the past, always mindful that everything they said was being recorded. It wouldn't do to start slagging anybody off and dropping themselves in the crap. Richard brought up the tale of one lad in D Squadron, who had been asleep on his bed, one night. One of his Troop thought it would be a good idea to place a smoke grenade in his hand and pull out the pin. He made sure he closed his victim's hand over the lever, thereby preventing it from going off. Retiring from the room, he slammed the door shut, startled the sleeping guy, who immediately awoke. Looking down at his hand, his heart skipped a beat, when he saw the distinctive light green canister. Although panic set in, he had the presence of mind to keep his fingers firmly around the device, stopping the lever flying off and detonating it.

'Did you know that the hook on a metal coat hanger is exactly the same diameter as a smoke grenade pin hole?' Richard asked, over his microphone, revealing how that young man had extricated himself from a sticky situation. This went to show how resourceful soldiers could be, even under intense pressure.

For the next hour, the four crewmen took it in turn, to bring up their own recollections. Richard would, from time to time, press his head into his sight and scan the ground, for any sign of the advancing enemy. Just as Trev launched into another story, they were distracted, by a call in their headsets.

'Hello, Zero, this is Tango 11, contact tanks wait out!' All conversation in the turret stopped.

Richard and Smiler turned their attention to their optical sights, slowly scanning the arcs they had been given by the Troop Leader. On their far right of arc, in a tree line, was a flash of orange. Looking closer, they confirmed it was the flashing light, mounted on a Chieftain turret. Traversing the gun along the edge of the wood, they observed another three tanks, guns pointing in their direction. A full contact report was given by Mike, who had given the initial contact and could also see all four vehicles. The four tanks spilled forward, from the tree line, making straight for their position. They were approximately two and a half kilometres away, but closing fast. Putting a range into the SIMFIRE, Richard gave the order for Smiler to engage.

As he laid the MBS mark in his graticule sight picture on to the centre of one of the advancing tanks, a puff of smoke was seen coming from the turret of the vehicle to its right, indicating it had just fired. There was a pause of a second or so while Richard waited, to find out if they had been hit. Nothing came, no orange smoke, no Winky Wanky flashing light on top of their turret. However, the vehicle they were about to engage was suddenly enveloped in a cloud of orange smoke and its Winky Wanky began to flash. It ground to a halt, indicating it had been given a K Kill. Richard looked to his right, through his episcopes, which ran around his cupola. There was no sign of any of the Troop having fired a round.

It would be revealed later that one of 2nd Troop had taken out his own Troop Leader, just as they crossed the start line. This was kept under their hats and they would have to rush back to camp, at the end of the day, to make sure that part of the tape was erased, before the Troop Leader found who the culprit had been.

The battle itself lasted only fifteen minutes and the four vehicles were destroyed by the superior force of 1st and 3rd Troops. They were then given an hour to break and make themselves something to eat. Richard asked Trev to knock the crew up some bacon grill sarnies. The tin of bacon grill had been in the BV all morning, so the contents fell from the can, when Trev opened it, using the trusty compo tin opener, carried by every good operator. Slicing the cylindrical meat into equal portions, with his slightly grubby hands, Trev pressed the two pieces of bread together and handed the first one to Richard.

This reminded Richard of the time he had been in Command Troop. He had been doing exactly the same thing, making sandwiches for the crew. He had earlier been helping the driver, with some work on the engine. When Richard had offered a sandwich, the Intelligence Warrant Officer, had blankly refused to take it, as it was covered in oily prints. He was renowned in the Regiment for being fussy, when it came to matters of hygiene, always wearing gloves when on exercise; not to keep warm but to avoid his hands being contaminated by oil. Richard didn't care what the sarnie looked like. He took it, gratefully, as he was starving.

They washed their sandwiches down with a mug of coffee, topped up with a little cherry brandy, to keep out the cold.

The next scenario would begin in twenty minutes and would last around six hours. They were given the order to change into full NBC kit and close down. Some of the boffins went round the vehicles, sealing the hatches with lock wire. This was so they could tell if the Troop had cheated, by opening up the hatches. Richard and his crew settled down, to make themselves as comfortable as possible, in the cramped conditions. The feeling of being enclosed inside the confined space was not everybody's cup of tea, but was part of the job. The time ticked slowly past, with no activity to their front. Part of the experiment was to see how soldiers' senses deteriorated, after long periods of being dressed in full NBC.

The sweat was starting to run inside Richard's respirator and he could feel it collecting in the seal, below his chin. Although he tried to put the thought to the back of his mind, the feeling of wanting to rip off the mask was overwhelming. Yet he knew if he did this, it would be picked up on the microphones, recording everything inside the tanks.

The sound of a helicopter overhead alerted Richard to the fact that something was about to happen. Not only were they being recorded inside the vehicles, but also from above. They were later to find out that one of the Troop Sergeants of 4th Troop had hitched a ride on the aircraft. He wasn't interested in what was going on down below. He had asked if the pilot could drop him off at an American base, just North of Soltau, so he could do a bit of shopping, as his Troop were not required for that day.

From the treeline to their front, four tanks emerged, once again. Richard gave the order for Smiler to engage, while he sent a short contact report to Zero. Smiler laid on to the target but, due to the restriction of the respirator and the length of time they had been in NBC kit, his reactions were slower than normal. He was finding it difficult to keep the barrel pointing at the centre of the observed mass.

Just as before, as the vehicles began their assault on the two waiting Troops, an orange smoke pot erupted on top of the Troop Leader's vehicle, which had only just crossed the start line. His vehicle came to a grinding halt, once more, with his Winky Wanky light flashing.

Richard chuckled to himself, knowing full well that one of the Troop Leader's own vehicles had taken him out. The battle took slightly long than before, the effects of wearing NBC equipment was apparent. They were finally given the order to stand down and revert back their normal clothing. Richard ripped the respirator off his face and took a deep breath, wiping away the sweat from his chin and forehead. At the same time, the rest of the crew were doing likewise. The sound of someone on the outside of the turret announced that the boffins were removing the seals, from the hatches. As his hatch was thrown open, Richard blinked, adjusting his eyes to the setting sun.

As the vehicles entered camp, they lined up on the hard standing. Engines were switched off and they carried out their final parades. Once done, they made their way to one of the huts, set aside for the scientists to store their equipment. Each Commander handed in video tape from their tanks, to be analysed. The crews were then given a series of mental and dexterity tests. After this was complete, they were told that was them for the day.

For the next two weeks, the crews took it in turn to provide the enemy and 'blue forces' for the different scenarios. On one particular morning, after a heavy night in the bar, Richard's Troop deployed on to the area. Albert had consumed his usual helping of 'chicken tits' and chips from Wolfgang's van. He sat in his commander's seat, his cheek resting on the cupola. A constant stream of vomit dripped down the side of the vehicle. He blamed it on a dodgy chicken breast; strangely, no one else had suffered the same fate, having eaten the same. The crew knew Albert had swallowed almost a full bottle of Bacardi after the food and that was the more likely cause. The rest of the troop thought it hilarious and afforded not one bit of sympathy.

There was an excited conversation among some about the previous night's exploits. A couple idiots had managed to gain access to the Gazelle helicopter, parked outside the huts. They had been only a couple of switches away from starting the thing but had hastily fled the scene, as the rotors began to turn. There had been a witch hunt that morning, trying to find out who the culprits were. Of course, no one admitted to the crime.

The exercise was drawing to its conclusion. The scientists were happy with the data collected. On the final day, the Squadron was invited into a lecture hall, where the men were shown footage of the past couple of weeks. The mystery that remained was who had been responsible for taking out 2nd Troop Leader, every time he had crossed the start line. The Squadron was thanked for its participation in the trials and the men had learned some valuable lessons from them. There was no time to relax, though, as they were joining the rest of the Regiment, who were taking part in a two week 'Field Training Exercise' (FTX).

Chapter 28 – Lionheart FTX

The exercise was codenamed 'Lionheart' and was to be Britain's largest field-training exercise since 1945. Nearly 58,000 British soldiers and airmen were scheduled to take part. A total of 131,565 ground and air personnel would be involved, including British troops and airmen already in West Germany, as well as American, Dutch and West German forces, in the role of aggressor forces. The training area was just east of the frontier with East Germany, near Hanover and Hildesheim.

All normal phases of battle would be practised, including a covering force battle, a main defensive battle, river crossings, counter-penetrations and counterattacks. Lionheart would not follow a preplanned schedule. The main events of the exercise would be determined, in large part, by actions and reactions of individual unit commanders.

The Regiment deployed, to an area south of Hanover, in a wooded area and immediately went tactical. Smiler had been given compassionate leave, so Richard had been allocated a new gunner, Roger Burgess from Ripon, who fitted in from the start. Richard went with the other commanders, to be briefed, on the first phase of the exercise, by the Squadron Leader. He left the rest of the crew to finish off putting up the cam nets. On his return, he found them struggling with the simple task. Dangerous had tangled himself up and was trapped, like a fly in a spider's web. Trev and Roger were doubled up, laughing, as he hung there, incapable of disentangling himself.

'We're supposed to be tactical, you fucking clowns! Help him to get untangled!' Richard admonished them.

Still laughing, the two crewmen went to the aid of Dangerous, helping him out of the cam net. Richard went on to brief them on what was intended for the next 36 - 48 hours. They were on 30 minutes' notice to move. The whole Brigade was on radio silence, which would only be lifted when contact was made with the opposing forces. A recce screen had been deployed by one of the Division's Medium Reconnaissance Regiments, who would give timely warning of any advancing forces, allowing the Unit commanders to deploy their forces accordingly.

Mike had been busy, preparing a rota for ground sentries and radio watch. A trench had been dug, forward of their position, with communications running back to the Troop Leader's tank. They had also run a communication line from his vehicle, back to Squadron Headquarters. They would communicate through this, until radio silence was lifted.

The next 48 hours were spent observing full tactical hide drills. The vehicles were permitted to be started for an hour each day, to top up their batteries. It wasn't until the fifth day first contact was made with a force of German tanks. The Squadron's notice to move time was reduced to five minutes. They began to take down the cam nets, from their vehicles. As Richard went to make sure they didn't leave anything behind, he asked Roger to bury a black, plastic bag of rubbish they were supposed to have deposited with the SQMS, the previous night. Armed with a shovel, he walked into the light of the emerging dawn.

As Richard made the final preparations, he placed his headsets on, to await the orders that would be coming over the Squadron net. Trev was also waiting, with his BATCO wallet, a notepad and pen in his hands. Richard's thoughts were disturbed by Roger calling up to him, bashfully, from the ground.

'The Squadron Leader wants to see you.'

'What for?' Richard asked.

'Think it might be something to do with him catching me, trying to bury the rubbish bag behind his tank,' Roger said, innocently.

'When I said go and bury the bag, I meant out of sight. What possessed you to bury it in direct view of the Squadron Leader, for fuck sake?' Richard roared, as he climbed out of the turret, grabbed his webbing and weapon and trudged off, in the direction of SHQ.

He returned five minutes later, in a foul mood. He ordered Roger to get into the gunner's seat and not to speak unless spoken to, for the rest of the day.

The Squadron Leader had been less than impressed by Richard's lack of admin, pointing out to him the seriousness of dumping rubbish in the German countryside. Before Richard could dwell on the matter, the drone of aircraft overhead distracted them. The sky was full of huge transport planes, spewing out thousands upon thousands of paratroopers. The white silk canopies of their chutes filled the sky.

Richard's headset came alive, with the sound of the OC issuing orders. Trev was busy, scribbling down the message sent two letters at a time, in encrypted format. The OC paused momentarily and chose a call sign, to confirm they had received his message so far. On acknowledgement, he continued.

The first part of the orders encoded intimated a raise in the NBC State. They immediately began to put on their full NBC Individual Protective Equipment (IPE), now second nature to them, having spent the last few weeks living in it.

As Trev continued to decode the message, Richard stared out, into the distance. The paratroopers were still falling in great numbers. It was then Richard saw something which made him cringe. One of the parachutes had not deployed correctly. The parachutist was rushing to the ground at a terrible speed. Richard closed his eyes, to avert them from the inevitable. He opened them a few seconds later, to witness the poor bastard impact with the ground. Even though the troops were almost three kilometres away, Richard was sure he heard the dull thud, as the unfortunate soldier impacted with terra firma. Later statistics revealed this was only one of many accidents that occurred during the drop.

'I've decoded the order, boss. Are you ready?' Trev brought him back to reality.

'Yeah, go for it,' Richard said, putting the awful incident to the back of his mind.

As Richard began to write down the message, he realised it was an order for the Regiment to move, to block the advancing enemy force. The previous night, they had been given the positions they would occupy. As soon as he completed the orders and checked his map and the timings, the crew prepared to move out, with the rest of the Squadron. Minutes ticked by, until, at last, 'H' hour arrived. One by one, the tanks left the security of the hide area. Dangerous expertly used the ground to guide them to their defensive position, approximately two kilometres away, a piece of high ground, on one side of a valley.

The valley was the main route of advance for the opposing forces. The Regimental battlegroup had been told that they needed to hold this position, for at least 24 hours. As they ascended the feature, Dangerous automatically began to drop the gears and crawl into position, taking care not to silhouette the vehicle. Richard guided him slowly forward, until both he and Roger could observe the 'killing ground', in the valley beneath them. The vehicle slowed to a halt and Roger began to scan, from left to right. Over the sound of their own engine, they could hear the ominous roar of multiple engines. Richard again looked at his map, remembering that a pre-recorded fire plan had been set up, for the use of artillery. In the distance, a column of around 30 Leopard tanks could be seen, transiting down the road, east to west. Accompanying them were vehicles with distinguishing white crosses on them. These were umpires, who would decide the outcome of the battle.

Richard gave a quick contact report and checked his map, once more. The advancing enemy were only a short distance from a major crossroads, designated in the fire plan.

'Hello, Golf 10, this is Tango 13, fire mission over!' he said, his voice rising with excitement.

'Golf 10, fire mission, send over,' came the reply, from the artillery call sign.

'Tango 13, fire mission, fire Zulu Tango 2479, in two minutes,' Richard passed his order to the artillery Forward Observation Officer (FOO).

'Golf 10, fire Zulu Tango 2479, in two minutes, wait, out!' the FOO answered.

Two minutes passed quickly, as the waiting Squadron watched the advancing Leopards approach the crossroads.

'Hello Tango 13, this is Golf 10, shot 30, over!' the FOO informed Richard that the guns had fired and rounds would be landing in the target area, in 30 seconds.

As no live firing could take place, the rounds were simulated by umpires on the ground, using thunder flashes and smoke grenades. Staring through his commander's sight, Richard observed a number of explosions, then a cloud of orange smoke, directly in the centre on the advancing column.

'Golf 10, this is Tango 13, on target, fire for effect,' Richard confirmed the rounds had landed exactly where they needed to be and they were to fire the remaining fire mission. Within ten minutes, the advanced guard of the opposing forces had been halted in their tracks. The Squadron were then ordered to move to their secondary positions. Richard cautiously reversed the vehicle back from the crest and, using the tracks on the rear side of the slope, manoeuvred, with the rest of the Troop and Squadron, two kilometres further east, up the valley.

Sticking to the high ground, they hugged the hillside, until advancing to the crest, once more. What they saw, as they crept into position, was a host of advancing armour, on a scale Richard had never witnessed before. The floor of the valley was carpeted in German armoured vehicles, moving westwards, at great speed.

For the next four hours, the battlegroup fought a long, hard battle. Due to the opposing numbers, the CO finally gave the order for the Battlegroup to begin a fighting withdrawal. Squadron by Squadron and Infantry Company by Infantry Company pulled back, under supporting fire. The artillery laid down a blanket of smoke, to cover their retreat. As they reached the low ground of the valley, the vehicles made best speed, through the next Battlegroup called forward, to take their place. It was mid-afternoon. They had only managed to hold the advance for around ten hours. Their Battlegroup had been ordered to form a rearguard and to spread themselves, across the valley, five kilometres behind the now forward Battlegroup.

Richard's tank was travelling towards a village, when they were approached by a civilian, waving at them, to slow down. Richard told Dangerous to ease up and stop by the man, who turned out to be a local farmer. Richard climbed down and surprised the man, with his grasp of the German language. He invited Richard to take their vehicle through his field, which would take a considerable time off their journey; Richard knew the reason for this, local farmers were paid a huge amount of compensation for any damage sustained to their crops or land. Richard thanked him, a knowing smile on his face.

Climbing back up to his seat, he ordered Dangerous to take a sharp left turn and enter the field. Dangerous did as instructed, taking great delight in driving at high speed through the corn field, altering direction every twenty metres or so, inflicting maximum damage. The shortcut afforded them meant they reached their fall-back position some twenty minutes later.

Richard looked back, over his shoulder, and saw the destruction they had caused to the farmer's field. They positioned themselves next to a railway crossing and Richard asked Trev to get the crew something to eat. It hadn't dawned on him but they hadn't eaten all day. Trev had put a couple of tins of steak and kidney pudding in the BV, that morning. These were affectionately known as 'babies' heads', a favourite of the crew. They were to be accompanied by processed peas and mashed potatoes. Trev started to remove the tins from the boiling vessel. He emptied the sachet of mashed potato powder, along with some margarine, into a container, topping it up with hot water. Mixing the contents with a fork to a smooth consistency, he added a pinch of salt. Gathering the crew's plates, stowed beneath the radio sets, he divided the food equally, then passed two plates, out of the turret, to Roger and Richard. He called to Dangerous, who was fiddling about in his driver's cab, that supper was ready. Dangerous climbed from his seat and joined the rest, on the turret. Trev handed him his plate and the four sat, staring out into the distance.

The sight of their tank had drawn the attention of some of the local population, who were out taking an evening stroll. The sound of a bell ringing, hailing the arrival of a train passing through the crossing, caused the crew to look round. An elderly gentleman halted in his tracks, as the barriers barred his way. He was out taking his dog for a walk. He took the lead of his dog and tied it to the barrier, then turned around, to examine the Chieftain and its four man crew, who were happily digging into their evening meal.

'Schmecht das?' he asked, enquiring if the food tasted good. Richard gave him a big thumbs up, to indicate that it did.

What happened next would cause the four soldiers to recall the story, for years to come. So engrossed was the elderly man that he didn't hear the sound of the warning bells at the crossing point. Neither did he note that the train had passed. The sound of his dog yelping made him spin round. The poor creature was suspended from the barrier, which had been raised. This caused great hilarity among the four on-looking tankies. After they stopped laughing, Richard and Trev ran to the man's aid and helped take the weight of the petrified dog, while he undid its lead. His pet now safely on firm ground, he thanked them profusely and went, slightly embarrassed, on his way. The event brightened up what had been a rather dull lead up to the exercise and the four laughed about it, for the next hour.

The days passed with the Battlegroup defending, withdrawing, then counter attacking. They were now into the final phase of the exercise and had just returned from a shower run. These were portable showers, set up in the rear echelon area. The troops were pulled back into this administrative area, to resupply, take some much needed rest and to service and repair their vehicles. There were tanks and APCs strewn all over the area, their engine decks open and REME personnel crawling all over them. As they entered the rear echelon area, they passed another Squadron from the Regiment, busy performing track maintenance. The amount of mileage they had done had caused the tracks to stretch, which meant links having to be removed. Otherwise, the tracks would bang against the suspension, making the vehicle difficult to steer. It was a job every armoured soldier detested, except for the perverts who were Driving & Maintenance instructors. Richard waved, when he recognised Pete, now Signals NCO of the other Squadron. Pete was busy talking into his microphone and didn't notice Richard, as their paths crossed.

They were directed to an area, where they could park up. Another Troop, from the Squadron, had already arrived and the men were dismounting.

They were to carry out any essential maintenance, before showering. Mike smiled, as he told them they had been given twelve hours rest, in the rear echelon area, until first light, the next day. As they were in a secure area, there was no need for ground sentries, as it was guarded by members of the echelon. They would, however, still have one person on radio watch, in case the situation changed. Roger and Dangerous smiled at this news, it wasn't often the drivers and gunners got a bit of a break.

Moving the vehicles to firm level ground, the crews began their last parades on the tanks. They powered down their engines. Oil levels were checked, tracks tightened and, if needed, links removed. The tracks on Richard's tank had been changed prior to the previous exercise, so they just needed tightened. As they finished, the SQMS arrived, with his fuel pod, ration truck and water bowser. The Troop filled the vehicles to the brim, knowing this would probably be the last chance they would get. The water cannisters were refilled and enough rations grabbed, to last them another three days.

Once this had been done, the Troop moved into a wood, just off the road. Although the area was secure, they still had to maintain hide discipline. Cam nets were erected and the normal hide routine began.

Richard's Troop grabbed their washing kit from their bags stowed in the baskets and a change of clothing. At that point, Richard remembered that he had not changed his socks or boxer shorts for the past five days.

He could actually smell the stench emanating through the leather of his boots. As they entered the mobile shower unit, the smell of sweat from unwashed bodies hit them like a sledgehammer. They found spare places on the benches and began to undress. Now fully unclothed, Richard grabbed his towel and shower gel from his bag and made for the communal shower area.

He took a vacant spot, next to one of 3rd Troop, greeting him as he did so. As the water hit his head and he massaged the shower gel into his scalp, dark brown water ran down his chest. As he looked down, dark streams were running from every shower space, into a number of drainage holes. He was not the only one to be so dirty.

As he looked down, he heard a yell from a few yards away. A giant from 3rd Troop was pissing down the leg of a N.I.G. from his Troop. Recoiling in disgust, the boy let out a tirade of abuse at the offender.

'You fuckin' dirty bastard!' he screamed. Everyone else in the shower area was howling with laughter. Richard felt for the lad, remembering when he had been the victim of a similar prank, back in training.

It took a full twenty minutes for Richard to remove the built up grime from his body. Just as he was finishing off, the water suddenly went cold and he leapt back, in shock. He shouldn't have been surprised, as the shower unit had been so heavily used. He left the shower room and returned to the bench, where he had dumped his dirty clothes. He tossed them into a black bag, which he then placed them in his bag. He removed a nice, clean pair of coveralls, socks and boxer shorts. Drying himself off, he slipped into his fresh clothes.

Exiting the shower unit, he could hear curses from the next intake, who had just begun to shower, to find the water was freezing cold. Chuckling to himself, he wandered back to his tank, to await the arrival of the rest of his crew, who were still getting changed. He stowed his bag in its place, in the commander's bin. As he did so, he was re-joined by the rest of the lads, who put their bags back on to the vehicle.

After a massive 'all-in stew', Richard cracked open the beers. It wasn't long before everyone was feeling tired after the past ten days. Snoring filled the woods, as the Troop took a well-deserved, uninterrupted sleep; apart from the commanders and operators, who each took an hour on radio watch.

The sound of the dawn chorus greeted Richard and he unzipped his sleeping bag. Although it was the height of summer, at that early hour, there was still a chill in the air. He rapidly dressed and opened the flap of the tent, tied to the side of the vehicle. He lit the petrol cooker, set up outside the tent. The metal Dixie pot on it contained a tin of baked beans, one of sausages and some bacon grill. Happy that the cooker had enough pressure, he opened one of the stowage bins and removed a washing bowl and frying pan.

Returning to the tent, he wakened his crew, who moaned but slowly began to emerge from their sleeping bags, each like a moth from a chrysalis. Trev was first out of the tent, it was his duty to make breakfast. He had slept well, having drawn the first radio stag. He began by lighting a second cooker they had brought with them and placed a frying pan, with a little oil in it, on the stove. The previous evening, when they had collected their rations from the SQMS, they had been given eggs. As the pan started to sizzle, he cracked open four, into the frying pan. By the time the others had emerged, Richard had already washed and shaved. They all ate together, then took it in turns to get washed, the remainder packing away the sleeping bags and tent, then putting away the cooking equipment.

Looking at his watch, Richard asked Dangerous to start up the GUE and for Trev to turn on the BV. As they moved to the vehicle, Richard thought back to the days of his first exercise, some ten years previously. He had been the newest member of the Troop and had found that a steep learning curve. Here he was now, with a crew who, although not entirely experienced, did everything that was asked of them, often without being told.

Everything had been stowed back on the tank. The friends sat on top of the turret, drinking a brew that Trev had provided. Richard sat, wearing the headset, listening for any sign of activity on the net. He was disturbed by the Troop Leader, signalling his attention and calling him over. Mike and Albert arrived at the same time. Troop Leader informed them he had received orders from Battlegroup, over the echelon frequency. They were to move from the echelon area, back into a forward blocking position, five kilometres to the east. He indicated on a map where he wished them to position themselves. He knew, of course, that the individual commanders would assess the area when they got there and situate themselves accordingly. Satisfied that everyone knew what was expected, he told them to mount up and be ready to move in ten minutes.

The commanders returned to their tanks and quickly briefed the crews. Once everyone was mounted and the call came for the Troop to move, they rumbled forward, out of the wood and turned left on the track, where they had carried out their maintenance. The journey to their forward positions took only 40 minutes; they moved from single file into line abreast. They moved forward slowly, over the open ground, scanning with their barrels as they did. Richard had already noticed, from the lack of contours on the map, that it would prove difficult to find any form of cover, in this terrain. The Troop halted in the best position they could find, Richard placing his tank on the edge of a field, with his gun pointing down the valley. They had spaced themselves well apart, to limit the chance of them being taken out, in the event of an artillery barrage. Now came the waiting game. They were to cover the withdrawal of the Regiment which was currently in contact with the enemy.

The hours passed slowly, as the Regiment, who were now spread out across the valley, waited for news of the ongoing battle. Richard and his crew watched as the farmer whose field they were on, drove up and down it, with a tractor and trailer. He was harvesting sugar beet, a plant from the same family as beetroot and chard. As he went back and forth, with the trailer overloaded with cargo, some sugar beet fell off, on to the road, which led to the farm building complex, to their front. Just before lunchtime, the farmer walked the length of the road, kicking the fallen sugar beets, back into the field. Halfway through the task, he trudged back along the road, in the direction of the farmhouse. It seemed he had decided this was lunchtime.

Trev removed his headset and began to climb out of his hatch.

'Where you going?' Richard asked.

'Just had a great idea, watch this,' he said, leaping from the turret onto the ground. Moving to the driver's bin, he removed a machete, from its sheath. Richard was curious as to why he needed the weapon.

Looking round, Trev casually set off, down the road, in the direction of the farm. He stopped at a point where some of the sugar beet were still strewn across the road. Picking one up, he turned and made his way back to the vehicle. When he got there, he split the vegetable in two, with the machete. For the next couple of minutes, he began to scoop out most of the insides. Richard could not believe what Trev did next. Dropping his coveralls, he placed the hollowed out sugar beet to his bare arse. Straining visibly, he proceeded to defecate into it. Once finished, he placed the top back on. Smiling up at his mates, watching from the top of the turret, he walked back down the road. Placing the 'loaded' vegetable where he found it, he ambled back, whistling out loud.

'This should be fun,' he remarked, as he slid back into the operator's hatch. Richard just looked at him and shook his head.

They sat and waited for the farmer to return from his lunch. Roger and Richard were watching through their optical sights. Trev had borrowed Richard's binoculars, to observe what was about to unfold. Half an hour later, the farmer returned and resumed clearing the road of sugar beets, once again kicking them back into the field. As he approached the contaminated article, the entire crew began to snigger, in anticipation. He kicked the sugar beet, the top dislodged and its contents spilled on to his boot. He was so engrossed in his work, he didn't noticed it. Raucous laughter rang out within the tank, until it was cut short.

'Hello Zero, this is Bravo 21, contact tanks wait, out!'

Richard immediately ordered Roger to start scanning. The 1st Troop Sergeant who had made contact was only one kilometre to their right. It wasn't long before Roger confirmed he could also see the contact. Richard peered through his commander's sight and could also observe six Leopard tanks, advancing across the open ground. Then, in his own arc of fire, another eight appeared. The net was going wild, with contact reports from all Troops within the Squadron.

This was obviously a major assault. The umpires had situated themselves 200 metres behind the engaging Squadron. Richard quickly realised he would not have time to call in artillery support. The battle raged for an hour or more, the umpires driving along the Squadron positions, informing each vehicle in turn they had been knocked out.

There were only three call signs left, including Richard's. With the Squadron Headquarters taken out, each commander needed to think for himself. Just as Richard was about to reverse, to fall back to another position, the sound of aircraft could be heard. Three Jaguar planes screamed from behind them, their undercarriage lights flashing, to show they were engaging the advancing Leopards. Before Richard had the chance to make his move, he was informed by an umpire that he had been taken out. Richard ordered Roger to elevate their barrel, to comply with the umpire's decision. As he did so, the most welcome announcement broke the airwaves.

'Endex! Endex! Endex!' came over the Battlegroup net, confirming the exercise was over.

This exercise had been the most realistic Richard had been involved in, although no live ammunition was used, which wouldn't be the case when the Regiment deployed, once again, to Canada in six months' time. There, Richard would be tested under live fire conditions.

Chapter 29 – Canada Medicine Man 7

Richard dozed, as the RAF Tri-Star aircraft began its descent into Calgary Airport. A lot had changed within the Squadron, in the last six months. The Squadron Leader, Major Totti had been replaced by Major Clairmont. He was tall and slim, elegant, almost aristocratic looking. He had known Richard's father well, having served with him as a young Subaltern Troop Leader. Also, to Richard's great delight, his former mentor and commander, 'Legs', had taken over as Squadron Sergeant Major.

The month before, his gunner, Smiler, had been involved in a serious accident, while guiding a Reconnaissance vehicle (CVRT) in the Light Aid Detachment (LAD) hangar. As he had directed the 9 tonne vehicle into position, he had, stupidly, placed himself directly in front of it. The CVRT, driven by an inexperienced driver, had leapt forward, crushing Smiler between it and a Bedford truck. He had been rushed to hospital and was still there, to that day. His injuries were to prove so serious, he was later invalided out of the Army. So Richard had maintained the same crew as he had on the last FTX.

As he snoozed, he remembered a tale his father, Tommy, had told him of a time commanding in Canada in the 1970s.

They had been taking part in an attack on a position, when the smell of smoke had drawn their attention to the engine decks. Looking over his shoulder, Tommy had seen bright, orange flames erupting from the main engine grills. At that time, they had been fully 'bombed up'. If the fire had spread into the fighting compartment, things could have gone very badly wrong. Leaping from his seat, his father had climbed on to the top of the turret, which had allowed the gunner to exit his position. At the same time, he had ordered the driver and operator to vacate the vehicle and run a safe distance away. They had done as they were told and, along with the loader, had sprinted across the prairie. Tommy had jumped from the turret and had pulled the fixed fire extinguisher handle, located near the driver's bin, causing its contents, situated in the engine compartment, to smother the flames. He had turned to run and had followed his crew, into the distance. Richard smiled to himself, hoping that this exercise wasn't going to be so eventful.

The sound of the pilot informing them they were descending into Calgary woke Richard from his slumber. The Troops who were lucky enough to have them, began to gather their heavy parkas. 'Medicine Man 7' was notorious for being an extremely cold exercise. It ran from late November for a month. Everyone had dressed accordingly and were wrapped in three layers. As the wheels touched down and the engines increased in pitch, the aircraft slowed to a steady speed and taxied towards the arrivals terminal. Once stationary and the seat belt lights extinguished, they were invited to disembark.

The doors were opened, front and rear. The soldiers filed out, into blazing sunshine. The temperature was in the high twenties centigrade, not at all what they were expecting. By the time they made the short journey into the arrivals terminal, Richard was beginning to perspire.

'What the fuck is this all about?' he muttered to Mike, who was walking beside him.

'Fucking typical, mate, I bet it doesn't stay like this,' Mike quipped.

Travelling through the terminal building, they were not required to pass through passport control. There was a separate exit for them, leading them to the main building, where they mingled with other passengers arriving. As they walked, one smart arse from SHQ Troop began muttering something about bombs. He knew airport security staff were listening out for certain keywords. He wouldn't have found it so funny if he had been lifted by them.

Climbing on board the bus which, strangely for that time of year, had its air conditioning blasting out cool air, they took their seats, for the final leg of the journey.

The two hours passed quickly and, before long, they were exiting the Trans-Canada Highway and hung a left, up the familiar Jenner Highway. Five minutes from the junction, they passed the small village of Ralston, where some permanent staff were housed. Finally, the bus turned right, into the entrance of Crowfoot Camp, with its luxurious accommodation. It was a well-trodden path for a lot of soldiers, who practised there almost every year.

Leaving the bus, the heat hit them again, it had not relented over the journey. It was only 10:00 and the weary soldiers made their way to the Movement Control Check Point (MCCP). Here, their baggage had been unloaded by a party at the airport, awaiting their arrival. Made up of people who had dropped a bollock, in some shape or form, this was a form of punishment. Finding their luggage, they turned, to find the SQMS standing there, waiting to allocate rooms. He was a big, powerfully-built bloke, who always had a cigarette hanging out of his mouth. In his younger days, he had been a member of the Royal Armoured Corps Parachute Squadron. Due to his heavy smoking and having had a pacemaker fitted, he was no longer as fit as he used to be. When he spoke, his voice was raspy from the years of nicotine intake.

'Right, you lot, listen in and I will give you your block number!' He began to read out which Troops were assigned to which huts.

The information having been disseminated and directions given, Richard began a slow walk towards his new home for the next week, while vehicles were prepared, to deploy on to the prairie. They had been given 30 minutes, to drop off their baggage, then assemble in the

NAAFI, for the customary RMP brief. Richard opened the door to the hut and was relieved to find the air conditioning was functioning. Selecting the first bed on the left, he placed his luggage on it, then, hastily, unpacked his civilian clothing and put it in the locker. Noticing he only had ten minutes until the brief, he put on a padlock the locker and stuffed the key in his pocket. Finally, he took off his pullover and removed the vest from under his shirt. Having adjusted his clothing, he headed out the door, in the direction of the NAAFI bar.

The bar was already full of new arrivals who were waiting for the RMP to start his brief. Once they had all settled down, he began with the usual ground rules. Then, he enforced a warning, with a two stories from previous exercises.

The first was about a young cavalry Trooper, who had been on R&R in Calgary. On his first day, he had got extremely drunk in a local bar, then had decided to visit the zoo. As he wandered round, he stopped, to admire the polar bears. As he looked down into the enclosure at the magnificent creatures, his cigarette packet fell from his shirt pocket, into the pit. The watching crowd gasped in horror, as he proceeded to climb over the rail and lower himself into the enclosure. In his drunken state, he had only one thing on his mind and that was to get his packet of cigarettes back. Picking it up, he turned, to climb back out again, only to find it wasn't going to be easy. The next thing he knew was being thumped by a force like a steam train, as the polar bear threw him to the ground, with one strike from its massive paw. For the next two minutes, the creature played with him, as though he was a football. The crowd were screaming for someone to help. Eventually, one of the keepers managed to distract the bear, while a couple of others hauled the seriously injured soldier out of the pit. He then spent two months in hospital, before being flown back to his Unit in Germany.

His next cautionary tale was of an Infantry soldier who, while on an evening out in the 'Hat', struck up a conversation with a couple of local girls. They were students at the local university and asked the guy if he wanted to come back to their apartment, to party. Not believing his luck at the chance of bedding both girls, he agreed, in a heartbeat. They called a taxi, which they insisted on paying for and took the short trip to where the apartment was located. When they got there, the soldier saw the party was in full swing. In the room were half a dozen pretty girls and only a couple of young lads. Drinks flowed and the party games commenced. The two girls were all over the infantryman and he, of course, reciprocated. The next thing he remembered was waking up, in the alley outside the 'Sin Bin', his trousers round his ankles, his arse bleeding and his ID card wedged between his bum cheeks. To top it all off, his wallet was completely empty. The RMP left it to his audience's imagination as to what had happened. It was a sobering thought to end on.

Next morning, Richard and the rest of the Squadron paraded on the tank park, to begin the process of taking over the vehicles from the previous Battlegroup. They had finished their exercise four days beforehand and the vehicles were looking in decent nick. The tools for each vehicle had been laid out, ready for the handover to begin. Mike took the 'Complete Equipment Schedule' (CES) from the outgoing Troop Sergeant and called out each item, in turn. As he proceeded down the list, each item, as it was called, was held up and placed either back on the vehicle or in a tool bag.

By the time they had finished, an hour had passed and the temperature was rising. A couple of items were missing off each tank, but this was a minor matter and the Squadron Technical NCO would be given the list later, to make up the deficiencies. The REME had joined them by that point and the tanks were inspected for roadworthiness. Any fault, major or minor, had to be rectified by the outgoing Troop. Richard was happy with his vehicle, as it only got picked up for a couple of minor issues. The crew handing over rushed around and fixed everything, on the sport.

By lunch time, Richard's crew had finished and, as they were not deploying for a couple of days, he asked Mike if it would be okay to knock them off, till the next day. Mike, whose vehicle was not in such a good state, was envious of Richard's position but agreed to his request. Thanking him, Richard returned to his tank and let his crew know they could chill till the next day. Richard understood the concept of rewarding Troops, which could work in his favour.

Legs, as a commander, had been a hard task master. They would often work late or, even sometimes on a weekend, back in camp. However, when they were finished, Legs had always made sure they had time off, while the rest of the Squadron were flapping, trying to get ready for an inspection or exercise. He did it in such a way that the men had wanted to work for him. He had instilled pride and comradeship in all whom he had commanded.

Two more days were spent finishing, getting the tanks ready to deploy. When done, they gathered on the dust bowl, once again, in blazing sunshine. The Squadron mounted up and the order came for them to move out. They followed the 'Rattlesnake Road', past the exercise control at BRUTUS and headed to their first area. The sheer size of the area never ceased to amaze Richard. It was approximately the size of Wales and it took them almost two hours to reach their first location. As they arrived, they pulled up, line abreast, with their barrels facing in the same direction. Before any exercise, the tanks needed to go through a process called 'Confirmation of Accuracy by Firing' (CABF). This was much the same as the bore sighting they had carried out on the ranges at Hohne. No vehicle would be allowed to proceed, until they had passed this phase.

As they were not yet 'tactical', there was no need to put up cam nets, but they were required to provide a ground sentry and a radio watch. The latter was essential, as they were required to listen in on the safety net. All vehicle movement was strictly controlled by the safety staff. If anyone wanted to move from one place to another, they would have to be escorted by a safety vehicle, or be given a safe route. This ensured no-one entered any 'live firing template'.

Richard had drawn one of the first radio watches. The temperature had dropped dramatically. Richard shivered for the first time since they had landed a week before. He needed to put on his parka and sat, for the next hour, until it was time to climb into his sleeping bag, after his 'stag'.

They were woken by a crunching noise, as their tent flap was thrown open.

'Good morning, chaps. It's a nice, clean, crisp start to the day,' the Troop Leader stood in the doorway grinning. 'Hands off cocks and on with socks!' he joked and retired.

Pulling down the zip of his doss bag, Richard immediately felt the cold in the air. His breath was clearly visible, as the warm air met the cold. He pulled on his woolly pullover and coveralls, over the thermal mountaineering underwear, purchased especially for the trip. Lacing up his boots, he opened the tent flap, to be met with a sea of white, as far as the eye could see. During the night, the temperature had plummeted and there were almost two feet of snow on the ground.

The sound of some of the tanks GUEs could be heard starting up. This was not just to get them to operating temperature, prior to firing, but also to heat water for brews and washing. Trev began to start the cooker and prepare breakfast, while the rest started to pack away the tent and sleeping bags. The SSM, Legs, was already out and about, going round the Squadron, making sure everyone was up and getting washed and shaved. As a former instructor of gunnery, at the Gunnery School in Lulworth, he got a hard on about live firing. He was firm but fair, but woe betide anyone who fell foul of him. When he had taken over from the previous SSM, Stu Pearson, he had created a fictitious Troop. He called this Troop 'Penile Troop' and anyone who fucked up or crossed his path was placed in this Troop. The period of the sentence depended on the level of the misdemeanour. Anyone who had the misfortune to swell its ranks was given all the shitty jobs that came up. Trev had been late for a number of parades, after several heavy nights on the drink and he was currently serving a period under Legs' authority.

The administration of the day over, the Squadron began preparations for firing. As usual, the commanders and gunners went through their checks, while the REME performed any repairs required. No firing was allowed until safety vehicles arrived, at around 08:00. The Troops had already mounted up and were waiting for the okay to commence firing.

'Hello, all stations, this is Safety 2 Bravo. You're clear to go to red, your left of arc is your left hand track guard, your right of arc is your right hand track guard, watch your forty fives. Out!' came the order, from their safety call sign for the morning.

For the CABF, the vehicles were expected to hit within or break the line of a black circle on a white target at 1100 metres. As Richard's crew sprang into action, he watched them, with pride, not having to step in at any point. This was a marked difference from when he qualified on Hohne ranges, a year earlier. The sound of the breech closing, the loaders guard being pulled back and the reply of 'Loaded' indicated to him that all was in order for them to carry on. He did a quick visual check of the gun, to see that all appeared in order, then put his head back into his sight. Making sure that Roger had laid his MBS mark on the centre of the target and ended his lay in elevation, he waited for him to give the order 'Lasing'. As the range came up in his range readout, he confirmed it was correct, the gun drove up with an ellipse centrally around the target.

'Fire!' he shouted. The return was 'Firing now!' The tank lurched, the breech drew back inside the vehicle, breaking the loader's guard and opening the breech. In a split second, it ran back in and Trev began to load another round. However, there was no need, as Richard observed the round pass directly through the centre of the painted black circle.

'Target!' he screamed, excitedly, 'Target stop!' He brought his left hand down on Roger's shoulder, in a congratulatory manner. Their prep that morning had paid dividends and they could sit out the rest of the morning, watching the others, who had not achieved 'perfection'. An hour later, Richard observed Phil Simons, the 3rd Troop Corporal who had attended the same commander's course. He was shouting at his crew to dismount and line up, at the side of the tank. Richard's call sign was located directly next to Phil's and, even over the sound of the engine, Richard could tell he was not happy. The crew were all still wearing their vehicle helmets.

'One of you three fuckers is going to feel something in a second! If you don't and you hear a sound then you're free to go,' he ranted at them. With that, he raised a shovel, from behind his back, striking one of them squarely on the helmet, felling him instantly. The other two scarpered behind the vehicle as he had ordered them to. Richard almost wet himself, watching the poor, unfortunate crewman trying to regain his feet. The lad was met by further tirade of abuse from Phil, who kicked his arse hard.

For the remainder of the day, the Squadron continued with qualifying on CABF. By the time the sun was starting to set, every vehicle had qualified and the crews were relaxing. The temperature had dropped steadily through the day and it was now around -8 degrees centigrade. It was

320

cold but bearable, not unlike the weather they had experienced in Germany in winter. The Squadron routine continued for the rest of the evening, with ground sentries and a radio watch posted. Richard and his crew retired to the tent early and climbed inside their sleeping bags, to try and keep warm. They chatted amongst themselves, in the background the sound of a wild dog howled. Burying himself deep inside his doss bag, Richard finally dropped off to sleep. He woke in the early hours, his teeth chattering, his body shaking. He eventually got back to sleep, only to be woken by the ground sentry, throwing back the tent flap.

'Reveille, guys,' he said, as his breath turned to vapour, indicating how cold it was.

Not wanting to leave the relative warmth of his sleeping bag, Richard turned over. He waited a moment, to see if any of the crew were stirring. After a couple of minutes, he decided he would have to make the first move and unzipped his bag. At the same time, he called out to Roger and Dangerous to get their lazy arses up. Trev was on radio stag and hopefully would have a hot brew waiting for them. Richard could hear the sound of the GUE, heating up the water in the BV. As he dressed, he could hardly feel his fingers. He struggled to roll up his sleeping bag, blowing on his numb fingers, in an attempt to warm them up. The other two were in the same predicament. The inside of the tent had frozen ice crystals from the exhalation of their breath during the night.

Exiting the tent, the three began the task of packing everything away, apart from the cooking and washing kit. Trev sat on top of the turret, with his headset on. He was busy frying sausages and beans. By the time the others had joined him, he had dished out the piping hot food. All four ate quickly, before it got cold. Richard looked at the thermometer he had brought, which hung inside the turret.

The temperature had dropped ten degrees. 'Surely this can't get any worse,' he thought to himself.

That morning, the Squadron took it in turns to carry out a machine gun battle run. They were called forward, one tank at a time, and directed down a single lane, under instructions from the safety vehicle. As they travelled down the lane, a series of transport and infantry targets were visible, at varying ranges. Richard's run went without a hitch and he was pleased with the crew's efforts. The only incident was when they had a stoppage on the co-axially mounted GPMG, which was secured to the side of the main gun and moved up and down, in line with the barrel.

Trev was leaning over the gun, attempting to clear the stoppage. They had been moving and the gun was rising and falling, due to the terrain. As he leaned over, the gun came up, trapping his head against the turret roof. Seeing the danger, Richard immediately elevated the gun. Luckily, Trev had been wearing his helmet or his head would have been squashed, like a piece of fruit.

A more light-hearted incident occurred when the Troop Leader's tank had been driving, to take up his position in the lane, to commence his run. The SSM, Legs, needed to take a dump, just before the beginning of the battle run. Seeing him, the startled Troop Leader drew attention to him, amazed that someone could answer the call of nature, in the middle of a live firing range. Turning round, Legs grabbed hold what that had just exited his bowels. Mimicking a Test cricketer, he bowled the turd at the passing tank. It arced high in the air and struck the tank cupola and the young Troop Leader, splattering his glasses, what was left embedded itself in the cam net, wound around the turret. As the air was so cold, it froze solid. The Troop Leader had to discard his glasses and scrape away the excrement, later.

The exercise continued into the next week, building up in intensity. The temperature continued to fall and plummeted to a ridiculous -30 degrees, without the wind chill factor. It was so cold, one of the tanks from A Squadron got itself stuck and had to be blown out, with explosives. The Royal Engineers who performed the task, were a little overzealous with the amount of plastic explosive (PE) they had used. It ripped off one side of the tank's bins and a couple of road wheels.

Richard felt sorry for the infantry who, although they were slightly better equipped than themselves, were living in shell scrapes, not tents like the tank crews. They resembled members of Captain Scott's ill-fated Antarctic expedition. The day before, the Squadron had been involved in a Squadron Company attack on a large force. They had assembled in the Forming up Point, waiting for H hour. As they sat, the silhouette of a Chieftain tank could be seen, to their front, wandering aimlessly, from right to left, obviously 'geographically embarrassed' and searching for the FUP. Looking through his binoculars, Richard identified the call sign on the back. It was Charles Templeton-Savage, the young Troop Leader of 2nd Troop. He had joined the Squadron that year and this was his first Canada tour. His Troop Sergeant was Joe O'Connell, who had driven Richard, on his qualifying for his commander's pay, on the ranges. Joe was a fiery character, from Leeds. The air was blue, with him sarcastically giving directions to the young Troop Leader. The rest of the Squadron thought this was hilarious, although the attack was delayed until the young Troop Leader found the FUP and joined his Troop.

Richard's Troop had been assigned as 'Close Support' for the infantry, who were to take the objective. As H hour arrived, the Troop, along with the Company of infantry, rolled out of the FUP. The chieftains were laying down high explosive and machine gun fire, on the enemy position. The reminder of the Squadron were doing the same, from the high ground. A Fire Mission had also been called and was co-ordinated to cease, when they were around a kilometre from the objective. The scene was enveloped in smoke, from the falling artillery. Richard fought hard to see the targets, to their front. The artillery finally ceased and the smoke, slowly, began to clear.

The infantry armoured personnel carriers were following up, close behind the tanks. They were also firing their GPMGs, supressing the enemy to the front. Suddenly, Richard heard a pinging sound. All of a sudden, the episcopes, to the rear of his cupola, shattered. The instruction from the safety vehicle commanding the infantry to 'Check Fire' broke the airwaves. This had been no accident, the infantry had shot up the tank, for the fun of it. The platoon responsible were later given a right royal bollocking. Richard later discovered his sleeping bag, in the commander's bin, had taken at least three rounds. The attack itself had been successful and the Squadron regrouped about 500 metres past the objective.

They had been on the prairie for just over two weeks. The cold was taking its toll. One of 3rd Troop's operators had slipped on a frozen-over turret. He had sustained a serious break of his lower leg. A member of the Officers' Mess staff, back in Crowfoot, was brought out to replace him. Although serving Officers and administration were his primary roles, he was a trained tank soldier, like all who worked in that and the Warrant Officers' and Sergeants' Messes. It had been some time since he had worked on tanks, which was obvious, as he lasted only two days, before he was injured, too.

They had been travelling cross-country, at speed. He had been inside the turret, making a brew. At the precise moment he hauled himself up, though the hatch, the vehicle hit a bump. He had obviously forgotten to secure the split operator's hatch. It closed swiftly, trapping his fingers, he fell, inside the turret. The force had broken all four fingers on both hands and he had to be returned to Crowfoot.

Another incident involved the Troop Leader's tank. It had suffered a major coolant leak and was travelling around, with a massive plume of white smoke billowing from the engine decks. They had been given a location to go to, where they were met by the REME. As they prepared the vehicle for a pack lift, they narrowly escaped having an artillery bombardment brought down on them. This was due to RHQ not informing exercise control, that they were in a template which had gone live. Due to the diligence of the safety call sign responsible for the template, a disaster was averted.

One a particular morning, three weeks into the exercise, Richard checked his crew's feet, for any sign of frost bite or frost nip. Happy that, although they were cold, their colouration was as it should be, he proceeded to take his own boots off and inspect his own feet. For the last couple of days, they had felt like blocks of ice and he had trouble getting his circulation going. He had run on the spot, in a vain attempt to get the blood flowing. His feet were cold to the touch but their colour was normal, if a little pale. They were having to survive extremely low temperatures, this was not just a training exercise.

On the last attack the Squadron were involved in, it was down to just six tanks. The infantry had suffered more and could only muster a platoon of men, to assault the position. Many of the Battlegroup had succumbed to cold related injuries. They had long since burned the wooden poles issued to erect their cam nets. The nets themselves were frozen solid and unusable.

The Commanding Officer had visited the Squadron, two nights ago. He had asked Roger, who was on ground sentry duty if he was cold. Roger had openly replied that he was 'fucking freezing'. Unflustered, the CO had told him to put on another shirt, which would do the trick. Within seconds, he jumped back into his warm Land Rover and was driven away, leaving the dejected Trooper, shivering in the cold.

Late the following afternoon, the Squadron received an order from Battlegroup HQ, to move to a different location. When they arrived, they saw the whole Battlegroup assembling there. They formed up, in a massive 'box league', the tanks on the outside with their barrels facing outwards.

The snow was driving hard across the prairie. Richard had found it almost impossible to navigate. Once in position, the SSM went round the vehicles and informed them they were leaving a skeleton guard force of two per Squadron. The remainder would move back to Crowfoot, to see if the weather had broken. The unlucky ones, remaining behind would be replaced the following day. They would later find out the BATUS Commander had called a halt to the exercise, not their CO.

The journey back across the area, then through the gate on to the Jenner Highway was a torturous one. The troops huddled together, to create warmth. The floor of the truck was cold and slippery, like an ice rink. Seats had been removed, to allow more bodies in. Around 30 soldiers were crammed together.

Richard, by this time, was almost in tears with the pain from his extremities. He felt physically sick and fought to keep the bile in his stomach from erupting over his neighbours.

The lights of the camp penetrated the darkness in the back of the vehicle, as the truck came to a halt and the tailgate dropped. Richard followed the rest to the rear of the truck and gingerly lowered himself to the ground. He feared that, if he jumped off, his feet would shatter, so intense was the pain. As he hobbled towards the accommodation, he could feel a little life returning to his feet. As he opened the door to the hut, he walked into a wall of heat. Removing his parka, he slowly lowered himself down, until he was sitting on his bed. He was beginning to feel light-headed and perspiration was forming on his forehead. The body heat that had withdrawn into his core was now returning, slowly, to the outside. It took him around fifteen minutes to remove his clothing and untie the laces on his boots. His fingers were tingling, as the blood returned to them, causing discomfort. As he removed his socks, he was astounded at the change in the colour of his feet, from that morning. They were a crimson, almost purple, colour, as opposed to the lily-white of some twelve hours earlier.

'You seen these?' he asked Albert, who occupied the next bed.

'Yorrrrt,' was Albert's reaction, seeing Richard's feet. 'That's not good, marra,' he said, in his deep Cumbrian accent.

'They'll be okay, once they warm up,' Richard replied, unconvinced. Grabbing his wash kit and towel, he hobbled off, for a hot shower.

The piping hot water was a welcome luxury. Richard stood, his hands against a wall, supporting his body, as the water restarted his circulation. He tipped shower gel onto his hands and massaged it through his hair. Working his way down, from head to toe, he saw his feet changing colour. His left seemed particularly bad, as it turned from lilac to a very dark purple.

'Fucking hell! You seen this?' he shouted to the figure next to him.

'Bloody hell, mate! I would get that checked out, if I was you,' came the shocked reply from the bloke, who turned out to be Phil from 3rd Troop.

'Should be okay, once the circulation gets pumping again,' Richard replied, shrugging off the concern.

Returning to his bed space, he dried himself and inspected his toes again. He wasn't sure if it was his imagination but they seemed to have worsened. He pulled

327

on a pair of jogging bottoms and sweatshirt. Squeezing into a pair of trainers, he winced, as he tried to lace them up. He called across to Phil, who had just come from the shower and asked him if he fancied going for a beer.

'Aye, I do but not before I drop you off at the Medical Centre, mate!' he retorted, deadpan. Phil wasn't going to take no for an answer and, asking Steve, the Squadron Tech Rep, if he would run them there, he bullied Richard to the Land Rover, outside. It was only a two minute drive to the Med Centre, on the other side of the road from Camp Crowfoot. Inside the building, Richard took a place, at the end of a very long queue. He recognised most, from the Argyle and Sutherland Highlanders, who had comprised the infantry on the exercise. Many had their boots off and seemed to be suffering from the same problem as Richard. Yet, when he removed his boots, it caused a murmur to ripple down the length of the queue.

'I think you better go tae the front, pal,' the bloke next to him said, sympathetically, indicating the state of Richard's ever darkening left foot. Taking up his invitation, Richard began to shuffle his way to the front. Seeing his condition, the waiting soldiers made way for him.

Richard presented himself to one of the medics for examination.

The next thing he knew, he was waking up, in bed. He rubbed his throbbing right arm. The discomfort made him recall a medic ramming a hypodermic needle into it, whereupon Richard had blacked out.

Feeling no sensation in his left foot, he precariously lifted the sheets, to make sure it was still there. To his great relief, although it was very swollen and looked like it had been charred in a fire, it was still there. They must have given him ultra-strong pain killers, as he couldn't feel a thing.

He was aware of someone on his right, on the other side of the room, in his peripheral vision. This person appeared to be staring intensely at Richard, making him feel uncomfortable. Trying not to let it prey on his mind, he turned to watch the TV in the corner of the room. After ten minutes, he could still feel the stranger's eyes staring at him.

'You got a problem with me, pal?' Richard called over, unable to ignore the situation any longer.

'What?' grunted the guy, almost Neanderthal-like.

'You've been staring at me for the last ten minutes,' Richard said, trying not to sound aggressive.

The stranger went on to explain why he was sitting there. He was an infantryman, who had been instructed to drive an AFV432 APC back down the Rattlesnake Road, that evening. Foolishly, he had not bothered to wear his driving goggles. The snow storm and wind had been so strong and the temperature so low, the snow had formed crystals on his open eyes. The crystals had frozen solid, building up the further he drove. When Richard had woken, the poor bugger had just been put into the bed opposite. The medical staff had put drops in his eyes, in an attempt to dissolve the ice which had frozen his eyes open. Richard apologised profusely and the pair saw the funny side.

Over the next few days, with the analgesics being reduced, Richard felt a great deal of pain. The doctors treating him said that was a good sign, indicating the nerve endings may not be too badly damaged. They took roll upon roll of photographs, which would be used in future, to show soldiers how to identify frostbite. Someone from the Squadron visited Richard every day, smuggling in a few cans of beer and fast food from the 'gag and puke'. In typical squaddie fashion, no compassion was shown and the visiting time was spent taking the piss out of him. They told him of the fantastic night they had enjoyed in the Sin Bin. The exercise had been ended, The weather didn't break until three days after they left the area.

They were busy now, preparing to get the vehicles ready, to hand back to the permanent staff. The next Battlegroup wouldn't be out until early spring. No one knew at that point was that it would turn out to be the last ever Medicine Man 7.

Due to his injuries, Richard had been told he would be flying back, on an earlier flight. He had been in hospital for a week and suddenly realised he had not contacted his wife! He arranged to make a public call, from the telephone by his bed. He waited as it rang out. Looking at his watch, he knew that, allowing for the time difference, Birgit would be at home, not yet at work. On the fourth ring, she picked it up. When she heard Richard's voice, she seemed excited.

'Where are you ringing from?' she asked, knowing when they had last spoken, that the exercise should not yet be over.

'I'm in hospital,' he said, confused.

'Hospital? What are you doing there?' she fired the question at him. Richard realised the rear party, back in Germany, must have omitted to tell her what had happened. There followed ten minutes where Birgit slagged off the Regiment, furious that no-one had informed her of her husband's situation. Knowing her, Richard cringed at what she might do next, so tried to calm her down. He could tell he was fighting a losing battle. Someone was going to get both barrels from her, sometime in the near future. When she had been given the full story about what had happened and that he was okay, she began to calm down. They talked for another five minutes, during which Richard told her he would be flying back the next day. This changed her mood from anger to happiness and he ended the call, saying he would see her the next evening.

The journey to Calgary Airport was, this time, by ambulance, accompanied by a medic. Richard was helped out of the vehicle and taken, by wheelchair, to the aircraft. He was assisted up the steps of the plane by the medic and guided into his seat. The medic told Richard he would be met, at the other end, by medical staff, who would take him directly home from the airport. Richard was happy he was returning early but was slightly pissed off that he had missed out on the R&R. As he settled down, to try and get some rest, he imagined the shenanigans the lads in his Squadron would be getting up to, in the next three days. As the aircraft climbed to its cruising altitude, his left foot began to throb, reminding him of his injury. This would be a feeling he would have for the rest of his life, when the temperature dropped below freezing point.

Chapter 30 – Site Guards

It took almost three months, until the proper colour returned to Richard's left foot. His little toe, however, was still discoloured and not out of danger. He was walking with a slight limp but the warm, summer weather meant that he wasn't in any pain.

The Squadron was due to begin a site guard, a regular duty, performed by Regiments in Germany. He thought back to when he was a Lance Corporal and had been given the responsibility of transporting ammunition, to a small Site Guard, just south of Hameln.

There had only been himself and a driver from Motor Transport Troop (MT), an excitable character from Newcastle. Since both came from the North East, he had reckoned they would have plenty to talk about, on the trip.

It had been a cold, foggy, winter's morning. Richard had met Trooper Michaels outside the Quartermaster's department. The ammunition storeman had been waiting for them and had placed the ammunition, to one side. Richard had signed the necessary documentation, after counting and making sure it was all there. Between them, they had placed the rounds in the back of the Land Rover, parked outside the block. Checking his map and the route they were going to take, they had driven out of camp, turning right and heading north.

The visibility had been down to less than 50 metres and they had needed to slow down, so Richard could confirm they were still on the correct road. As they had passed through a small village, he checked the name on the map and was pleased to see they were still on track. It was only 05:30 am and the windscreen had started to freeze over. Although the heater was working, he had still felt the cold, coming in from the rear of the Land Rover. They had continued north, towards the town of Hameln. Richard had continuously checked his map and, as he had looked up, he had noticed they were in a residential area.

'Have you turned off the main road?' he had asked the young, Geordie Trooper.

'Nah,' had come back the obstinate reply.

They had continued through a maze of streets. Richard had known at this point that they had, somehow, become lost. He had directed the driver to take a number of turns, trying to get his bearings. As he had checked his map once again, he had felt the vehicle change direction. Looking up, he had seen the shape of an archway, as they passed through it. He had caught a glimpse of a yellow sign with the word 'Fähre'. It had taken a few seconds for his brain to translate the word, then it had clicked.

'Stop!' he had screamed at the driver, who looked at him with a startled expression on his face. He had immediately slammed his foot down on the brake pedal.

They had begun to descend a 30 degree slipway, towards the ferry crossing point. Due to the freezing conditions and the surface of the road, the vehicle's wheels had locked and the Land Rover had continued forward. Richard had just been able to make out the murky blackness of the river Weser, in front of them. The vehicle had lurched to the left, as a click was heard. He had been propelled forward, as the vehicle dropped off the side of the slipway. His head had hit the windscreen and, as he had looked up, all he could see was water.

The driver's seat to his left was empty and water had begun to fill the compartment. He had quickly undone his seatbelt and had clambered over the rack, directly behind him. Having climbed over the ammunition boxes, he had managed to reach the rear of the Land Rover, which was now at an angle of around 45 degrees. Its nose had been in the river, its rear end sticking up. His legs had been soaking, with the icy water, which had entered the forward compartment. He had jumped from the back of the vehicle

333

on to the slipway, where the embarrassed Trooper stood, looking dumbfounded.

'Are you okay, Richard?' he had said, sheepishly.

'You fucking twat! What possessed you to put us in the Weser, you prick?' Richard had yelled, as he stood, shivering with cold. Things were not good and he had needed to find a telephone box, to call for a recovery vehicle. He had needed to act fast, before the effects of the water and freezing cold weather took hold.

He had had the foresight to write down emergency numbers in his notebook. Like all decent soldiers, he knew the number of the guardroom back in camp, so had decided he would call them, to arrange the recovery. First of all, he had needed to find a phone box and confirm exactly where he was. The map had been left in the vehicle, with their weapons.

'Right, you fucktard! Wade into that water and get our weapons and my map!' he had bellowed at the driver, who was completely bone dry. Shaking, the young lad had nodded his head and had entered the water, coming back with the weapons and map, totally soaked from his feet to his waist. Richard had smiled at him, glad that he now must be as cold as he was. Having taken the map from him, he had looked to find the ferry crossing point, somewhere near their intended route. Finally having found it, he had stormed off, into the built up area, to hunt down a public telephone box.

It had taken a full ten minutes for him to find one. He had left the Geordie fuckwit to guard the ammunition. With frozen fingers, he had dialled the number of the guardroom. It had been answered immediately and he had explained the situation. The guard commander, at the time, had been someone Richard knew well and he had burst into laughter, when he heard what had happened. After the tears had stopped rolling down his cheeks, he had said he would get on to duty recovery and let them know. Richard

334

had been told to ring back in twenty minutes, to find out the score.

Richard had thanked him for his 'compassion' and had asked him to be quick about it, as he was freezing his balls off. This had drawn another burst of laughter from down the telephone. The minutes had ticked by. Richard had decided to call back and the guard commander, with no humour in his voice, had told him it was going to take an hour and a half for the recovery vehicle to reach them.

Dejected, Richard had made his way back to the hapless young Trooper, who was now walking round, stamping his feet, trying to warm up. Although the sight had been amusing, Richard had known they were in danger of developing hypothermia. Then, he had remembered he had stowed his day sack in the back of the vehicle, with the ammunition and had climbed inside, to retrieve it. The vehicle had been wedged in position, so there was no danger of it shifting and falling into the water. He had climbed back out, opened the bag and had taken out a thermos flask. Having poured a cup, he had offered it to the lad, who had taken it, wrapping his fingers around it, to try to gain some heat. It had only taken a few minutes to drain the contents and the hot drink had probably saved them from hypothermia.

When the recovery vehicle had arrived, the driver and his commander had jumped down and had approached the two sorry individuals. They, like the guard commander, had spent the initial minutes asking what had happened, then taking the piss. Having hooked up a tow rope to the rear of the Land Rover, they had winched it out of the river. Like all good REME recovery, they had charged Richard a crate of beer or 'yellow handbag' for the trouble. Richard, this time, had been all too eager to oblige and had promised he would get it to them, by the end of the day. They had climbed inside the recovery vehicle and had made their

way back towards camp, the Land Rover behind them,
unable to be driven.

The memory faded and Richard was brought back to the present.

There were a number of Site Guards throughout their area in Germany. They were rumoured to be the locations where the Americans held their nuclear warheads. No one ever knew if that was true or not. The story was that they moved them around from site to site, to make it difficult to know which site they were on, at any particular time. It made little difference to those guarding them. It was just seen as a fuck about factor, like much in the British Army.

The SSM had put together the Operation Order (OP Order) and managed to scrounge members of other Squadrons, to make up the numbers of his own Squadron, who were away on courses. He also had to check that everyone had an up to date and undamaged ID card. The Americans, who ran the inner compound of the site, were really anal about things like that. He then had to prepare a list of personnel, which was sent to the CO, for his signature. This was then forwarded to the US Commander of the site, a number of weeks before they were due to commence. Only originals, not photocopies, were acceptable, and God help anyone who went sick, prior to the guard commencing. All the paperwork and preparation work had been completed and the day had arrived for them to set off, for the two week stint.

The site to be guarded was a short 45 minutes truck ride from their camp. It was situated on the other side of the road from Athlone Barracks in Sennelager, a camp which housed another tank regiment and had been home to Richard's dad, Tommy, many moons before. Sennelager, unlike the Carlsberg commercial, had the reputation of probably being the worst lager in the world. The site was directly east of Athlone Barracks, on a single entry road, running off the main range road, which ran from south to north. The outer perimeter and access into the site were the responsibility of the guard force, while the Americans controlled the inner compound.

The Squadron had been split into two groups, one to guard the site, the other on standby, at a nearby barracks. The standby group were known as the Backup Augmentation Force (BAF). They, as the name suggested, were to reinforce the troops deployed at the site, in the event of an incident. They were on 30 minutes' notice to move and had to carry their webbing and weapons everywhere they went. They couldn't leave the barracks where they were situated but were free to relax, as much as possible.

Initially, Richard was to be part of the site guard force and would be there for the first week. As a Corporal, he would either be in charge of eight soldiers or the Security Alert Team (SAT), comprising one NCO, a GPMG gunner and another to load the GPMG. They were on immediate notice to move and were expected to exit into the compound, within 30 seconds of getting the call. They were the Immediate Reaction Force to an imminent threat to compound security. They occupied three chairs in the main relaxation area, with easy access to the internal door, direct into the compound.

They spent eight hours in this role, then would be relieved by a different trio. During that time, they would endure endless hours of pornography, played on the video machine and TV, the main form of entertainment, while on site.

There was also a Quick Reaction Force (QRF), made up of four men, including an NCO. They were responsible for any immediate threat to the outside of the compound and would crash out, to deal with it. If unable to contain any problem, they would be reinforced by the BAF, a decision made by the QRF commander, on the ground. The remainder of the Site Guard Force provided four men for

337

each of the guard towers at the corner of the perimeter; a
one man foot patrol, who would walk between the towers.
A second was stationed in what was known as the 'bubble',
a room made mostly of glass, with a door leading to the
compound, which was next to the American control room.
A third was assigned to the Intruder Detection System
(IDS) tower, which housed the alarms for the various
detectors, which ran around the site. These were very
sensitive pieces of equipment, often set off by rabbits,
which were abundant in the area or other small wildlife.
Whoever was on duty manning the tower would assess if an
alarm was genuine, by using binoculars, to scan the area of
the alarm. If he knew the cause of the alarm was innocuous
enough, he would inform the control room, downstairs to
stand down from crashing out the SAT.

The Squadron entered the site. Their ID cards were
taken from them, to be checked for serviceability and that
they were on the list of personnel forwarded by the SSM.
Happy that everything was in order, the cards were returned
and redistributed. The SSM organised issuing ammunition
to the Troops, belts of 200 rounds for the SAT GPMG
gunner, members of the QRF and the other GPMGs, within
the Troops. The rest were given 9mm rounds for their
Sterling submachine guns.

A rota had been drawn up for the week. Richard saw
that he was first to be on SAT. The GPMG gunner would
be Ted Hutt and his 2ic, Sean Spouse, the Troop Leader's
gunner and loader respectively. They put on their webbing
and ensured the magazines were secured in their pouches.
Sean put a belt of 200 rounds across one shoulder, making
him look like a Mexican bandit. Taking three seats next to
the door, they settled down to watch three naked girls
employ large rubber objects on a video.

The ones who were to man the towers and patrol
between them were got ready by the posting NCO. He
made sure they had all their equipment with them and took

338

them through the security air lock, into the compound. He marched them to each tower, loaded them up and watched them each climb into a tower. There, they would be briefed by the person being relieved, who would then join the posting NCO, at the bottom of the tower.

As they approached each tower, they stopped at a white line, painted on the paving slabs. They were then challenged by the sentry, in the tower, with the words 'Who goes there?' The posting NCO identified himself and the men with him. The sentry replied 'I recognise you as members of the on-site guard advance'. The NCO lowered his hands and continued forward, with his charges in tow. The ground sentry paced round the perimeter of the compound; when he came to the white line before each tower he was again challenged. This routine continued until it was the sentry's turn to occupy one of the towers.

Inside the accommodation, the troops either slept, watched videos or brewed up. After only one day, they settled into this mundane routine.

Richard's stint on SAT was almost seven hours in. Rising from his chair, he asked if Ted and Sean wanted a brew and got the obvious reply. Richard made his way towards the small kitchen, next to the TV room. As he entered, he was disturbed by an alarm. Knowing instantly that it was a crash out, he rushed back to the TV room, where the Squadron Leader was standing.

'We've got persons inside the wire, by bunker 4!' he directed the information at Richard.

'Okay, lads, lets go!' he shouted.

Taking their positions by the door, they waited for the Squadron Leader to throw it open. As he did so, the glare from the compound floodlights blinded them. Bursting through the door, Richard led the other two into the compound, retrieving a magazine from his pouch and cocking his weapon, as he did so. He knew, looking at the map, that bunker 4 was at the far north eastern end of the compound. Ted was close at his heels, transporting the 13kg GPMG by its carrying handle. Sean was lagging slightly behind, as he wasn't built for running, nor did he have a love of it, at the best of times. Nearing the bunker, Richard indicated that Ted should take up a position, on the ground, approximately 100 metres from it, facing the doors. Ted threw himself down. Finally, Sean caught up and began loading the belt of 7.62mm ammunition, from around his shoulder. Richard got on the radio he carried and informed the Ops room that they were in position. Two minutes later, the door into the compound flew open and eight others joined them. They moved forward, two at a time, covering each other as they went. Just as everyone had taken up their positions, the familiar voice of the Squadron Leader shouted:

'Gas! Gas! Gas!'

Instinctively, the troops went to the respirator sacks, attached to their webbing and ripped open the top, withdrawing their respirators. They had nine seconds to get the masks on before they were susceptible to the gas attack. For the next ten minutes, the Squadron Leader issued different locations for the supposed attack, moving them from bunker to bunker. The guys were breathing heavily under the effort. Finally:

'Endex! Endex! Endex!' rang out, across the compound.

They got up, from their positions on the ground and made their way towards the exit. For security, the door they had come through wasn't accessible. They needed to pass through the American control room air lock. As they did so, each man had to show his ID card, which was inspected and checked against the list. Richard's team were the last three men to go through. Before them, one unfortunate from 3rd Troop was desperately patting his pockets. Richard knew exactly what he was looking for, from the look of panic on the lad's face. The American in the control room was getting agitated by this point and called the Squadron Leader over. He asked the hapless bloke if he had his ID card, to which he replied that he must have left it in the accommodation.

The OC called over the 3rd Troop Sergeant, the fearsome looking Pete Tamworth, his scar clearly visible in the floodlights. He was not a man to piss off and he tore into the unfortunate Trooper. The Americans were amused and satisfied by this and happy to let the guy through, after he was vouched for by Pete and the OC. The poor sod was going to be in for some shit jobs, Richard thought to himself. They all finally got through the air lock and back their own accommodation. It had been a hectic end to the first day and Richard was glad to hand over to the oncoming SAT Commander. This done, the three of them vacated their chairs and trudged off to one of the back rooms to get their heads down.

The next few days were much the same, with continual crash outs almost every day. Sometimes, it was the OC, and other times, the Americans. The Squadron's drills became really slick and the Americans were impressed; so the drills became fewer and fewer.

Two days earlier, the American base commander had tried to gain entry to the compound. He had shown his ID card to the sentry on duty. Inspecting it, the alert young Trooper had noticed it didn't show the commander's face but that of a gorilla. Smiling at him, politely, he had respectfully declined entry. Nodding approval, the American Colonel had then produced his real ID and the Trooper had let him in. When this news reached his Troop Sergeant and the OC, the beaming lad was congratulated on his vigilance.

The days were not without incident. On their second day, a shot rang out, from inside the compound. It transpired that one of the tower guards had challenged the ground sentry, patrolling between the towers. As he had done so, he had poked his SMG through the gun port. The cocking handle of the weapon had caught on the side of the opening and had been pushed back sufficiently to feed a round into the chamber. As the working parts had gone forward, it had fired off a round, in the direction of the startled sentry. The tower guard had been given the bollocking of his life, and was later charged for having a 'Negligent Discharge'.

The same week, a new lad, having just joined the Squadron, had been posted in tower three. He had only been on duty for half an hour, when a call had come through to the Ops room from him, requesting a comfort break. The posting NCO had ignored it, assuming that, if a piss was needed, it should be done out the tower's door. It hadn't been a piss that was needed, however. In desperation, the newbie had removed one of his NBC gloves, from his webbing pouch and had defecated into it. In a futile attempt not to get caught, he had tried to dispose of the evidence, by throwing it over the perimeter fence. To his dismay, the black, rubber glove had caught on the razor wire and had hung there, suspended, for all to see.

The offending article had been spotted by the Americans, monitoring the CCTV. A patrol had been sent out to investigate. Having discovered it was an NBC glove with an unusual content, the young bloke was, quite literally, in the shit!

Two days before they had been due to take over the duties of BAF, back in the barracks in Sennelager, one of Richard's Troop had been taking a brew to the bloke manning the IDS tower. He had, carefully, negotiated the steep, winding staircase to the top. As his head had emerged through the opening in the floor, the sight which had met his eyes had left him speechless and motionless. One of 2nd Troop's Lance Corporals, Paul Seaward, had been spinning on a swivel chair. This wasn't unusual, but Paul had inserted a right angled torch into the webbing straps, on the front of his helmet. Spinning in a constant motion, he had been making whooping sounds, calling:

'I'm a lighthouse! I'm a lighthouse!'

The mug with the tea had almost fallen from his hand, as he stood, open mouthed, staring at the Lance Corporal. He had first wondered if the poor sod had started to go stir crazy. Paul had turned and had taken the brew off him, and had asked if he get a couple of painkillers for a headache. Paul had been told to sit tight, that the painkillers would be brought to him.

Twenty minutes from this encounter, Richard had been carrying out the duties of posting NCO. After dropping off the sentries at the towers, he had thought he should check how things were, in the IDS tower. Stealthily, he had ascended the stairs, trying not to make any noise, which would have alerted the soldier on duty. As he had entered the space, he saw a head, lowered on the central console. The figure had had a finger pressed against one nostril, inhaling a line of white powder from the surface, with the other. Richard had flown into a rage, thinking that this moron was snorting cocaine.

The perpetrator's excuse was that the powder was aspirin, chopped up into a fine powder. Heaving a sigh of relief, Richard had realised that he would not have to lock the clown up. He had felt relieved at escaping the mountain of paperwork involved. Lastly, and most importantly, he had known disciplinary action would have had them down one man. The incident had still been serious enough for Richard to tear into the Lance Corporal.

His fury had been interrupted by the sound of an alarm. The intercom had burst into life. From one of the towers, a sentry had stated he had spotted two figures in the treeline, to the north of the site. The QRF had immediately been crashed out and had entered the woods, in only three minutes. After an anxious spell, the call had come for everyone to stand down. When the QRF had returned, they were pissing themselves, laughing. The two mysterious figures had turned out to be a local German couple. It had been difficult to work out who had received the bigger fright, the young lovers, who had been caught shagging in the grass or the four soldiers, whose torches shone on a teenage girl's bare arse, as she rode her boyfriend.

This had been an amusing end to Richard's stint on the site, as they were to hand over to the BAF, the following day.

The barracks where the BAF were located was less than a ten minute drive from the site. It was old and run-down, primarily used as an ordnance depot, for the storage of equipment. The half of the Squadron comprising the BAF was housed in a couple of damp smelling transit rooms. The showers worked, after a fashion, but the water ran mostly cold. Having being cooped up in the claustrophobic confines of the compound, it was a welcome change of surroundings. The troops were especially pleased to possess a new batch of videos to view. Richard loved the John Landis masterpiece, The Blues Brothers with John Belushi and Dan Aykroyd but he knew the script off by heart, having seen it around 50 times, over the last week.

The week spent on BAF seemed to drag. There had only been one call out, on the second day, even that was a practice. The site guard was due to finish on Sunday morning and it was now Saturday. Things were starting to get more relaxed. Richard noticed one of his Troop, wandering down the corridor, having been outside to the mobile YMCA van, which visited twice a day. He questioned him as to why his webbing and weapon were not being worn and carried. When he got the nonchalant reply from the trooper that they were on his bed, Richard exploded:

'You're supposed to be wearing it or to have it hand, you fucking jelly-head!' he screamed. Before he could go any further, he was halted by the sight of his Troop Leader, popping his head out of the Ops room door.

'Crash out! Protesters outside the site! Get the lads together, we're moving out in five minutes.' He disappeared back into the Ops room.

Richard ran to the room, to let everyone know the situation. Without hesitation, they began putting on their webbing and grabbing their weapons. Rushing down the stairs, they mounted up, on the back of the Bedford truck outside. Within a couple of minutes, they were joined by the Troop Sergeant and Troop Leaders. The Sergeants jumped in the back of the truck with the men, while the Troop Leaders leapt into one of two Land Rovers, parked outside.

Pete Tamworth, 3rd Troop Sergeant, took the lead and briefed the BAF on the situation. A number from the 'Campaign for Nuclear Disarmament' (CND) had attempted to gain access to the site but had been halted by the QRF. Due to the size of the crowd, around twenty strong, the BAF had been asked to be deploy.

The truck made its way towards the site and within five minutes, the BAF were deploying, to reinforce the QRF. They formed a line across the access road to the site. After a brief discussion with one of the Troop Leaders, who had a basic grasp of German, the protesters agreed to continue their demonstration some 200 metres back, just off the main road. The BAF walked them back to the junction with the main road, remaining in a defensive line, to prevent them moving forward again.

The control room had, by this time, reported the incident to the German Civil Police (GCP). When they arrived, the 'Tree Huggers' soon lost interest and the demonstration fizzled out. The GCP thanked the troops for the way they had sensitively handled the situation. The experience of handling this type of situation was born out of the many days, weeks and months spent on the streets of

Northern Ireland. The days of the 'Cold War' were unstable and the world was a volatile place to live in, especially in Germany. The BAF were stood down and climbed aboard the truck, for the short journey back to barracks. They were handing over the following day and Richard was relieved. He knew, though, it would not be the last time they would be performing this same duty.

Chapter 31 – Troop Trip

The Site Guard was a couple of months behind them. They had returned to camp, to some upsetting news. It had been confirmed that they were to amalgamate with another Regiment, the following year. This wasn't a surprise, as the army was reducing in size, as a result of the perceived lessened threat from the Warsaw Pact. The news was resented by many within the Regiment, who did not want to see 300 years of history wiped out. Richard's opinion was that the name of the Regiment would never be lost, as it was written in the blood of those who had filled its ranks, over the Regiment's history. The Squadron Leader arranged a photograph of all ranks to be taken. This was organised for the tank park, with a backdrop of two Chieftains, their barrels facing inwards, forming an arch.

The Squadron paraded early one morning and the SSM, Legs, had organised seating for the officers, SNCOs, NCOs and Troopers. The group also included their REME fitter section who, unlike their standing elsewhere, were treated and accepted as part of the 'Regimental Family'.

In his usual efficient, humorous manner, he seated the officers, SNCOs and commanders on the front row. Then, in order of size, the tallest on the outside, the other three rows were arranged, to make a uniformed ensemble. Happy that everything was in order and that the photographer was ready, Legs took his place, next to the OC. The front row placed their clenched fists on their knees and crossed their legs. The photographer asked everyone to give a big smile, which was difficult for some, as they knew this would be the last time they would be photographed together. Richard tried to put this to the back of his mind and looked around, at the faces surrounding him. He felt a pride to have served with such outstanding gentlemen. He had come so far, since leaving that garden in Germany, some ten years earlier. The click, click, click of the camera continued for a couple of minutes, until the photographer was satisfied he had taken the best possible shot. This photograph, framed and with a plaque underneath it, bearing the words 'The Last C Squadron' and the date, would adorn a wall in the homes of many in the Squadron.

As the new Regiment could only comprise a certain number of soldiers, some in the Regiment were offered the chance of redundancy. To Richard's surprise, Legs chose to take this option. He would be a sad loss, not only to his current Regiment but also to the new one.

Others had been given the unfortunate offer of receiving a 'brown envelope', the chance to serve in other Regiments, which were low in numbers. Some took up the offer, those who did not were given compulsory redundancy. Many of the SNCOs and JNCOs were offered postings in other establishments. Mike, their Troop Sergeant returned to the U.K., to work with the Territorials. Albert, the Troop Corporal from Richard's time in Berlin, began a two year posting to BATUS, where he would see out the remainder of his career.

In an attempt to uplift the Troop's spirits, Mike, with the Troop Leader, had organised a trip to Berlin. They were to leave the following Friday and it was keenly anticipated.

Friday came and the Troop was taken by minibus to Hanover. From there, they caught the train to Helmstedt, a small town, on the East German border, where they grabbed the British Military Train (BMT) to Berlin. There were only three ways into the city for military personnel, by train, by road along the corridor or to fly into the military airport at RAF Gatow. As the minibus dropped them off at the station, the driver assigned to take their luggage down the corridor to Berlin, waved them goodbye. They were early and had three hours to fill before their train was due. Mike decided to take them for a stroll around town. Making their way along the cobbled streets, they found a bar that was open. It was 10:30 in the morning but their motto was that it was never too early for a beer. They piled in and Mike ordered the first round.

The beer flowed for 45 minutes. Someone came up with the brilliant idea that they should take a walk around the red light area, just over the road from the bar. One bright spark came up with the plan that everyone contributed 10 Deutsche Marks into a kitty. They would then write their names on bits of paper and, after agreeing on a suitable girl, one name would be pulled from a hat. Mike got paper and a pen from the barmaid and distributed the pieces of paper among the guys. They took it in turn to hastily scribble their names and place the papers in their pockets. Once this was done, they polished off their beers, left the bar and crossed the road.

The prostitutes' place of work was a multi-story block of flats, the first four floors dedicated to their working environment. The floors above were where they lived, when not at work. The Troop toured, inspecting the girls standing outside their doors or sitting on beds, their doors open. A full twenty minutes was spent deliberating, until they finally agreed on one particular girl. Everyone produced their bits of paper, which were placed in Albert's flat cap, which he always wore off duty. This done, the cap was offered to the girl. She understood what was required and smiled, as she dipped her delicate, well-practised fingers into it. Having withdrawn one paper, she opened it up, smiled again and, with a dramatic pause, read out the name.

'Roger?' she beamed, looking around at the eager faces.

'Eee, that's me, that is!' Roger shouted, turning a bright crimson at the same time.

The lads burst into laughter and patted him on the back, telling him to enjoy himself and that they would be in the same bar, over the road, when he was finished. The prostitute took him by the hand, led him into her room and closed the door.

The losers turned around and made their way back down the stairs, crossed the road and re-entered the bar. Sipping their beers, Mike congratulated them on a job well done. Richard recalled when, as a raw, young soldier, it had been organised so he "won" his hole from a hooker. It had all been a preconceived plan, an old Regiment trick, arranged prior to them leaving camp. They had planned to do it in Berlin but, as the opportunity had arisen early, they had jumped at it. Everyone had written Roger's name on their own bits of paper, so the outcome had been inevitable. As they laughed and joked, Ted Hutt saw Roger, emerging from the block of flats and glanced at his watch. It had only been fifteen minutes since they left him. As Roger crossed the road, he was fiddling with his groin, arranging his privates into a more comfortable position. When he entered the room, a great cheer went up and he was offered a beer. When he found out that it had been a setup, he was initially livid, but saw the funny side and thanked them. It had been his first time with a lady of the night but wouldn't be his last.

The train journey to Helmstedt took them around an hour. Before long, they were boarding the BMT, for their onward leg, to the city of Berlin. As they crossed the border, the train was halted by Russian and East German guards, who gave the train a thorough inspection. They were ensuring that no one except legitimate travellers were trying to cross into the East. This was bizarre. Who the hell would have wanted to leave the West for the East? Richard thought to himself. As the guards circled the train, they surreptitiously showed items for sale, cupped in the palms of their hands. This was normal practice. Many of the soldiers on board exchanged money or cigarettes for stuff unavailable in the West, sold by the guards. Richard had once been fortunate enough to purchase a genuine Russian sable fur winter hat.

The Troops were served a three course gourmet meal during the trip. It was like being on the Orient Express and they savoured every moment, including the free Champagne.

By the time the train pulled into Charlottenburg station, they were well and truly oiled. They were met by the minibus and the Troop Leader, who had taken his own car. Seeing the state of them, he pulled Mike to one side, clearly unimpressed. Mike defended his corner, explaining that it was the last time they would be together, before the amalgamation. Although still not happy, the Troop Leader let it slide. All climbed into the minibus, now void of their luggage, as it had been dropped off earlier at their accommodation. The bright lights of the city were a familiar sight to Richard. As they passed the bar Mon Cheri, Richard smiled to himself, recalling many a happy Friday night there, during his two year posting.

Transiting north, they hit the roundabout at Theodore Heuss Platz, which led on to Heer Strasse. Twenty minutes later, they turned left, on to the road which led to his old camp in Smuts Barracks. The sentry, on the gate, opened the barrier, after inspecting the driver's ID. The minibus dropped them outside the transit accommodation they had been allocated.

The troops climbed out and made their way, up the stairs, to their rooms. Mike and the Corporals had been given single rooms, while the rest shared two rooms, with six men in each. They quickly showered and changed and congregated at the camp gates 30 minutes later. They sauntered back down the road, under directions from Mike and Richard. Taking the number 194 bus from Heer Strasse, they changed to the tube, for the final leg into the city centre. Leaving the tube at the Zoological Garden station, they exited into the bustling centre.

It was only 7pm and they had a long night of drinking ahead of them. The two old hands took the Troop around their old local haunts on the Kurfürstendamm. Inevitably, it wasn't long before they fragmented into smaller groups, some wanting to visit the more exotic sights of the city. Richard, having experienced all this before, decided to call it an early night at around midnight. He and Mike took the last tube home.

Morning broke. Richard rose early and had breakfast. On his return, he went to one of the rooms, where the lads were just stirring. Asking them how the night had gone, Ted answered that they had almost not made it back. They had missed the last bus and tube back to Spandau, the area where the barracks was located. Four of them had jumped in a taxi and when the driver had asked where they wished to be taken, they simply answered, 'The barracks'. When he asked which barracks, they quickly realised that none of them knew the name. Sean had recalled that it was in a place called Spandau, so the taxi driver had taken them on a tour, in search of it. After visiting every barracks in the area and almost giving up hope, they recognised the road that they had walked along earlier and gave a sigh of relief, as the taxi pulled up, outside the gate.

Richard found this hilarious, remembering when he was new to the city and had got lost, on more than one occasion. Leaving the boys, he entered the other room, where he was met by Roger. He put his finger to his lips, indicating that Richard should be quiet. He pointed to a bed in the far corner, where Gary Sutton, Mike's gunner, was sucking on the massive breast of a voluptuous blonde haired girl. Giggling to himself, he whispered to Roger that, once he was finished with his morning frolics, Gary was to get rid of the girl, as soon as possible. More seriously, he told him that they needed to be in Service Dress by 10:00, as they were taking a trip into East Berlin.

352

Assembled, at the appointed time, by the minibus, Mike ensured everyone was there. The Troop Leader again decided to do his own thing, so Mike had been left in charge. Taking a quick head count and confirming everyone had their ID cards, they boarded the minibus. It took just over an hour for them to reach Checkpoint Charlie, in the Kreuzberg area of the city. This was the only crossing point for military personnel in the city. They had previously submitted their names to the British Brigade HQ, for their planned trip over the Berlin Wall. On their arrival, they were required to show their ID cards. The names were ticked off, against the paperwork Mike had brought. Everything in order, they crossed over, into the East. The mood of those who had never been inside an Eastern Bloc country changed. Gone were the smiling faces of the local inhabitants, replaced by scowls and an air of suspicion, as they walked along the streets. Richard noticed as soon as they had crossed over, that they had picked up the usual tail, one of the Stasi, the State secret police. He followed them the whole morning and positioned himself outside every establishment they entered.

One bar was full of Russian soldiers, also in their service dress uniforms. Spotting the British soldiers, one motioned for them to sit down and have a drink with them. Trying to be sociable and, in an attempt to keep up East/West relations, the blokes obliged. One of the Russian called for more glasses and passed them around the Troop. He went on to pour a liberal amount of vodka, from the bottle he was holding. Once all the glasses were charged, he raised his own and saluted the Brits.

'Na Zdorovie!' he toasted in a gravelly voice.

The Troop returned their various salutes, "Cheers", "Slainte" and "Up Yours, mate", then downed the contents of their glasses, which were quickly refilled. For the next half hour, they went glass for glass, with their Russian counterparts. Regretfully, the lads had to make their excuses, as they had a table booked for a meal.

Richard had organised the Stadt Hotel, one he had visited many times, during his two years there. The group staggered from the bar, bidding their new found friends farewell.

The Stasi policeman outside closed the newspaper he hid behind and tagged on along, behind them. As they made their way inside, he positioned himself outside the entrance. Taking the lift, they ascended to the top floor, where the restaurant was situated. They were met by the Maitre d', resplendent in pin striped trousers and tailcoat. The lads sniggered, he reminded them of the Penguin in Batman, with only the top hat and monocle missing.

He showed the group to their table and waited for them to be seated. Asking them their choice of drink, they asked for Champagne. The exchange rate, at that time, was eight East German Marks to one Deutsch Mark, so their preference was not going to be expensive. The head waiter smiled and handed them a menu each, then left to get their drinks. He returned with a line of waiters in tow, handing a bottle of champagne and a glass, to each of his guests. He took their order, delighted at the money they spending, the troops started with caviar and quails' eggs, then each chose an expensive main course and dessert.

For the next two hours they ate and drank like kings. When asked if they wanted anything more to drink, Ted asked for a Black Russian, which drew some very strange looks from the up market clientele, sitting around them. Most were high ranking Party officials or senior officers, in the army or police. The look of disdain on their faces made it obvious they did not take kindly to interlopers from the West. The troops paid them little or no heed, revelling in the five star treatment.

At the end of the meal, they each tipped the waitress 5 DM, which equated to almost six months' salary for her.

She was beside herself with happiness and thanked them, profusely. Ted remarked to the lads that if he got his knob out, she would have sucked him off, there and then. They got up from the table and staggered out the room, thanking the Maitre d' for his help, slipping him a decent tip, for his attention.

Mike looked at his watch. They had just under an hour to be at Checkpoint Charlie or be in the shit. They staggered along the road, laughing and joking, as they went. It had been an enjoyable night and, as they stepped back into the West, they turned, as one, to wave goodbye to their personal chaperone.

Catching the tube and bus back to Smuts Barracks, the friends talked about what they were to do in the days to come. Mike suggested that they did something which, for once, didn't involve drinking, for which he received a tirade of abuse. He would have to write a post exercise report or PXR. He couldn't just write that they visited every pub and most of the restaurants on the Kurfürstendamm, as that would not go down well. So, for the next few days, they would take in the sights of the city, taking photographs to prove it.

They visited the zoo, Brandenburg Gate, Charlottenburg Palace and the Berlin Wall itself, taking photos, looking over into the East. It turned out to be a great time, except, perhaps, for Mark Johnson, from Albert's tank, who was chatted up by a homosexual, with a dog on a pink lead, while ordering a burger, from a van. The sight was surreal but funny, nonetheless.

After an afternoon drinking, they returned to the accommodation, to get changed. Gary Sutton had managed to get laid the night before, having pick up a girl in a bar. No one else had got lucky. For a joke or out of envy, the guys decided to hold him down, strip him and stick a broom handle up his 'chutney chute', as Ted so eloquently described it.

The week passed all too quickly. Richard, with Sean, Ted and Roger, decided to go for a drink, in a local pub in Spandau. As they walked through the streets, they found very few pubs open. At last, they found one with its lights on and decided to check it out. As they opened the door, they saw that it was empty but took their places at the bar, anyway. The proprietor was a stern-faced individual and not the friendliest of hosts. He grunted something, as he passed the beers over to them. Richard glared at him, unhappy at their treatment. The others told him to calm down and just ignore the prick. Richard heeded their advice and began a conversation with the barman, to try and break the ice. It was hard going but the barman reluctantly engaged with him. Seeing his attempt not really going anywhere, Richard turned his attention back to his friends. They chatted about the events of the past week and what a successful and enjoyable trip it had been. They toasted each other and the Troop, which would be parting forever, in the coming months.

After a couple of rounds of beer and schnapps, Richard tried to order another. For no apparent reason, the barman seemed reluctant to serve him. Richard began a heated exchange, when, out of nowhere, the barman produced a pistol. With the gun aimed it directly at Richard's head, his pulse began to race. Surely this fucking idiot wasn't going to put a round in his napper, purely because he'd taken a dislike to them? The others urged Richard to leave the bar, as it was a shithole anyway. Not taking his eyes off the barman, Richard, cautiously, nodded his agreement and eased off his stool. They left the bar, to search for a friendlier establishment. As they were walking out, Richard turned and flicked the lit cigarette he had in his hand in the direction of the barman. With that, he left, their former host hurling a string of abuse in their wake.

The following day, the minibus was waiting outside, to take them to the station to meet the BMT and commence the journey back to the West. As they waited on the platform, Mike checked that everyone had their ID cards. As he did, one of the party was rummaging through his pockets, a concerned look on his face.

'Don't tell me you've not got it?' Mike asked.

'It's in my bag, in the minibus,' the panicking Trooper admitted.

Luckily, the Troop Leader was on the platform, to see them off. He told the unfortunate bloke to get in his car and that he would take him to Checkpoint Bravo, to meet up with the minibus there. He found a public phone box and made a call to the Checkpoint, asking that they hold the minibus for them. They sped off, making their way to the only exit from the city for military personnel. It had been the perfect end to what had been an eventful week and everyone laughed and joked all the way back to Hanover.

Chapter 32 – "Fare Thee Well"

Three weeks had passed since the Berlin trip and the Regiment was busy with preparations for handing back their camp and equipment, prior to the amalgamation.

The first job in hand was to strip down the vehicles completely and clean them inside and out. Every road wheel was removed, one by one and behind them cleaned. One of the biggest jobs was changing the spring packs, gigantic springs which provided the suspension for the 60 tonne beasts. It was a complex and physical job, as the springs needed to be compressed and then levered out of their housings. Richard and his crew had two to change on their tanks and the first was proving troublesome. They had manged to compress it but were finding it hard to get it out of its position. Albert watched them struggle for a few moments, before ambling over. Barging Roger and Dangerous out of the way, he took hold of the spring, with his massive hands. With one deft movement, he pulled it free and rested it on his thighs. Straightening his back, he heaved the huge spring clear and threw it on the ground, in triumph.

'Fucking wimps,' he muttered, as he walked back to his own vehicle.

Richard stared in disbelief at the gigantic Cumbrian, as he continued work on his own vehicle. Men were active everywhere on the tank park. Tracks were being changed, sprockets, road wheels and turrets stripped, cleaned and reassembled. They had been hard at it since the Troop's return from Berlin. They started early in the morning and worked late into the night. As the weeks passed, more and more were picked for other tasks, required throughout the camp.

Before they left, the living accommodation had to be spotless. Richard's old gunner, Smiler, who had been

358

crushed between vehicles some months earlier, had been released from hospital. Due to the extensive nature of his injuries, he had been medically discharged. He had avoided all the bullshit which went with getting ready for a handover, small compensation for the cutting short of his career.

Two from each Troop were assigned, on a daily rotation, to work with the SQMS. Beginning at the top of the block, they were on their hands and knees, scraping the corridors with sharp instruments, removing any traces of boot polish and scuff marks. It was a gargantuan task and it seemed they would never be ready in time for the handover.

In the evenings, those who lived in had to paint their rooms. Nearing the end of the redecoration, they were fast running out of the magnolia paint, standard for living accommodation. One enterprising lot thought it would be a good idea to paint their room eau-de-nil, which they had found on the tank park. Eau-de-nil was the colour of the smoke rounds, which the Chieftains carried. When the SQMS inspected that room, he went off his head, as he entered and was blinded by the pale yellowish green walls. He scrounged some tins of magnolia from the QMs and ordered the jokers to repaint their room. One advantage to this cleaning regime was that the bar was always open, providing sustenance to the working Troops. Richard visited his Troop one evening after work, to find them absolutely rat-arsed, having a corridor party, as they scrubbed, cleaned and painted everything that didn't move.

The vehicles were gradually being handed over, as they were made ready. Each of their tool kits was carefully checked and bills issued for anything that was missing. This caused quite a bit of friction as tools were found, thrown into one of the many skips situated on the tank park for scrap metal. One particular morning, a couple of the Squadron tanks were leaving, to be sent for 'back loading'.

On the way to the exit, one descended the slope which led to the rear camp gates. After doing his checks that morning, the driver had forgotten to close the valve for the brake accumulator. As a consequence, the braking system didn't have sufficient pressure. As the driver applied his foot to the brake pedal, in preparation for turning out of camp, nothing happened. The vehicle was heading directly for the RMP van, which was there to escort them. The driver managed to steer the vehicle away from the van, only to end up driving it into the hangar building.

The massive beasts were also used to crush fridges and other white goods, no longer needed. This was a task which every tank driver wanted, as it was immense fun.

All the bars and messes had to run their stocks down. Second Troop Leader Charles Templeton-Savage held the title 'Regimental Bar Officer' and was known for partaking in a drink or two.

Regimental items were also sold off in the President of the Regimental Institute (PRI) shop. These shops are run by the Regiment and governed by the Queen's Regulations. Any stock left was let go at bargain prices and was much sought after, as the Regiment would shortly be consigned to the history books.

One day, Richard was assigned to escort a prisoner, from the Regimental jail to the airport, where he would continue his onward journey to Military Corrective Training Centre (MCTC), Colchester. The principal function of the MCTC is to detain personnel, male and female, from the three Services, as well as civilians subject to the Armed Forces Act. The MCTC took servicemen and women, sentenced to periods of detention from 14 days to 2 years. Although Richard never had the dubious pleasure of staying at this most infamous of establishments, he had served enough time in the Regimental jail to feel an affinity with the poor guy. He met a driver and a Lance Corporal at the jail and the prisoner was handed over to his custody. He handcuffed the young soldier to the Lance Corporal and they climbed into the rear of the Land Rover. He took his place, in the front with the driver and they headed out of camp. Once out of sight of the guard room, Richard dipped into his bag and produced a container of Herforder beer, which he handed to the prisoner. It would be the last time the lad would be afforded such a luxury and he took it gratefully. The beer was consumed and by the time they turned into the gates, only one bottle remained. As he was helped out of the back of the vehicle, it was obvious he was unsteady on his feet. The lad, foolishly, concealed the last bottle down his sock. He was handed over to the RMP, for his onward journey. Knowing he would have to go through customs, so made an excuse to go to the toilet. He tried to retrieve the bottle from its hiding place but was caught in the act. On Richard's return to camp, he was met by the RSM, who gave him a right royal bollocking. The RMP had wasted no time in grassing Richard up.

More and more tanks left camp, for their journey back to the UK. As the equipment got less and less, the Troops were freed up, to partake in other tasks, for example weeding the tank park and other areas around the Regimental lines. Armed with knives, they formed a line and, on hands and knees, scraping out the moss which had accumulated over the years, between the cobblestones. These cobblestones covered vast areas of the camp and it was a Herculean job. Most could not see the point of it, as it would be back to its former state, within a year. The camp was not going to be occupied by another Regiment and it was regarded as just a way to keep the Troops busy.

Personnel, as well as equipment, were leaving. People who had put in for voluntary redundancy or had chosen to transfer to other Regiments gradually left. It was a sad day when Legs held his final parade, outside the Squadron accommodation block. Richard felt a lump in his throat, as the SSM thanked them for all their hard work and the experiences they had shared, during his time as SSM. Richard was standing in as Troop Sergeant, as Mike had left for his final two years at a Territorial Army unit in York. As he fell out his Troop, he wandered over to Legs and shook his hand warmly, wishing him all the best for the future. He had been his mentor in his early days and had learned so much from him. The respect and regard he held for Legs would stay with Richard forever.

That afternoon, Richard completed the handover of his and Albert's tanks. They had spent the last six weeks working day and night, for them to be at this stage. Every single nut and bolt, if missing, had been replaced. Any defective parts had been ordered, received and fitted. Any new crew could eat their dinner off the turret floor, so high was the standard of cleanliness. As the vehicle rolled out of the hangar, on its journey to the railhead, to be returned to the UK depot, where it would sit idle, Richard's mind stored the number plate. Many years later, he would see this registration again, on the plains of Alberta and wonder why the hell they had spent so much time and effort cleaning it.

Two weeks later, with most of the camp handed over, what was left of the Regiment paraded on the Regimental square. The advanced parties and key personalities had already left for their new barracks, 40 minutes away, where they were beginning the process of taking over their new roles. This left approximately half of the Regiment on parade, that particular morning. There was no fanfare or formal parade, it seemed a very sombre occasion. The RSM marched on to the square for the last time, after the parade he would be leaving the Army.

His successor in the new Regiment had already been chosen. It had all been or at least tried to be as fair as possible, with the Commanding Officer coming from one Regiment and the RSM from the other. He called the assembled Troops up to attention and awaited the arrival of the CO. The CO marched on to the square, with his Adjutant close behind him. He halted directly in front of the RSM, who took one pace forward, saluted and handed the Regiment over to him. The CO returned the salute and waited until the RSM had taken his place, at his right.

Raising his voice so that the Troops could hear his address, he began what was an emotional ten minutes oration. Even the most seasoned and hardened soldiers, hanging on his every word, found it difficult to dispel feelings of emotion, welling up inside. Richard ran his eyes over some of the faces, not just of his own Squadron but others, too. He had served and shared many happy times and some not so happy times with many of them, over the past ten years. As the CO began to wind down his final address, he wished them all well in their future careers in the new Regiment and handed over to the RSM. The RSM marched forward, halting, once again, directly in front of the CO. He asked his permission to march the Regiment off the square for the last time. The CO gave his assent, saluted and took a pace backwards, to let the RSM take over.

'Parade, parade 'shun!' he bellowed across the square, his voice reverberating off the accommodation building which surrounded the parade square. 'The Regiment will march off. Parade, by the right, quick march!'

The band struck up the Regimental quick march St. Patrick's Day and the soldiers stepped off, as one, on their left feet. The sound of boots striking the ground echoed around the parade ground. As they drew level with the CO, they were given an 'eyes right' and the Squadron Leaders saluted him, in turn, as they passed. As they departed from the square Richard, called to mind the Motto of the Regiment they were joining "Fare Thee Well"; it could not have been more apt, on such a day. He spared a moment's thought for all those who had recently left, for one reason or another, and others who had paid the ultimate sacrifice, over the years in service to Queen and Country.

He also looked forward to new challenges, meeting new friends and more ups and downs, of the kind that he experienced over his military life, so far.

About the Author – Ian S Varty

I was born in the North East of England, before moving overseas with my parents, my father was a member of the British Army.

After leaving school at 16, I followed my father into the military. I spent my first three months at the Royal Engineers, Junior Apprentices College at Cheptstow. In a short period of time I realised this was not the right career path. It was at this point I transferred to the Royal Armoured Corps, and was badged to the same Regiment as my father.

During my 22 years service, of what could be described as a 'colourful career', I spent most of it overseas. Like everything in life you never appreciate things until they are gone.

After leaving the Forces in March 2003, I began work in the Information Technology Industry. I served my first 2 years at a Secondary School in Durham, as an IT Technician.

I have always been one for striving to better myself, I think this was my military upbringing. With no opportunities for advancement, I left the Education system and moved into the Healthcare arena.

For the next 8 years I worked for a Foundation Trust within the NHS in the North East of England. For the first few years it was all exciting and new. It wasn't long before I realised, due to funding of the NHS, things were beginning to become strained. Resources were short, and staff both medical and administrative, were under intense pressure.

With the death of my father in April 2010, I began to question why are we here? He had been a big influence on my life, and I wanted to recount the memories I had of him.

This led me into the world of publishing, as a vehicle to not only honour my father, but to try and show some of the hardships that faces the modern soldier. The bond of friendship and brotherhood that binds these modern day knights, cannot be underestimated. It was this very point that was my beginning to my journey into authorship.

The story of 'From Denim to Khaki' started as a one off book. I quickly found out that it would lend itself to a Trilogy. It is fiction, but based on facts that I have experienced, or indeed others who I have served with. It details the life of a young man, from joining the army straight from school at 16. It follows his career from the 'Cold War' of the 1980's, up until the Afghanistan conflict.

"Soldiers are required to close with the enemy, possibly in

the midst of innocent bystanders, and fight; and to continue operating in the face of mortal danger. This is a group activity, at all scales of effort and intensities. Soldiers are part of a team, and the effectiveness of that team depends on each individual playing his or her part to the full. Success depends above all else on good morale, which is the spirit that enables soldiers to triumph over adversity: morale linked to, and reinforced by, discipline."

General Sir Richard Dannatt
Chief of the General Staff

Other books by the Author

"Denim to Khaki"
"Quis Separabit" to be released in 2016

Acknowledgements

Thanks to Richard J. Galloway for his help and encouragement into the world of publishing. Also, to the many colleagues I have worked with over my years in the military, for their support in this venture. I would also like to thank Jim and Margaret Gardiner, for translating my spoken word into some legible form of English.

Printed in Great Britain
by Amazon